Love

or Something
Like It

Love

or Something
Like It

A NOVEL

DEIRDRE SHAW

Random House
New York

Published in the United States by Random House,
an imprint of The Random House Publishing Group,
a division of Random House, Inc., New York.

RANDOM HOUSE and colophon are registered trademarks
of Random House, Inc.

Grateful acknowledgment is made to Hal Leonard Corporation for permission to reprint an excerpt from "California," words and music by Tom Petty, copyright © 1994 by Gone Gator Music. Reprinted by permission of Hal Leonard Corporation.

Library of Congress Cataloging-in-Publication Data
Shaw, Deirdre.
Love or something like it: a novel / Deirdre Shaw.
p. cm.
ISBN 978-1-4000-6770-1
1. Young women—Fiction.   2. Self-actualization (Psychology)—Fiction.   I. Title.
PS3619.H3925L68 2009
813'.6—dc22   2008023469

Printed in the United States of America on acid-free paper

www.atrandom.com

2 4 6 8 9 7 5 3 1

First Edition

Book design by Kathryn Shaw

For my family

For Jay

California's been good to me
Hope it don't fall into the sea
Sometimes you got to save yourself
It ain't like anywhere else

—Tom Petty

CONTENTS

Part One

The Summertime Party   3

The Best of All Possible Worlds   18

Jimmy James   48

Sick   72

Attila   87

The Magic Castle   100

Part Two

Baby   127

Out of Body   146

Love or Something Like It   156

Postcard from Nebraska   166

The Perfect Stranger   179

Do You Know Who I Am   208

ACKNOWLEDGMENTS   241

Part One

The Summertime Party

THE FIRST TIME we got lost on the way, winding up into the hills, crawling by mailboxes, peering at house numbers, finally spotting the gates by complete accident, the valet practically hiding in the bushes for godssakes. Inside, the host greeted us. He was Toby's boss and the host of a late-night TV show, and after shaking my hand, he immediately spirited Toby away to an alcove and spoke to him in earnest tones about the day before's diminished ratings. I moved away and stood awkwardly alone by the bar, trying not to look in the direction of any celebrities, who, it seemed to me, considered it an affront if a layperson so much as glanced at them.

This, I suspected, was why they had gathered in celebrity-only clumps around the house, though I had the sense that their behavior wasn't particular to this party. There was one such clump on the patio by the pool, just outside the open French doors, where they were all huddled together on several chaise longues: the retired but still beautiful 1970s model, the former *Saturday Night Live* cast member, a young movie actor whose cachet, like that of a wealthy fraternity boy, was somehow increased by his being known as an asshole. I made these identifications only after several furtive glances and soon felt I couldn't risk another, so I spent the rest of the time reading the labels on the bottles of wine sitting on the bar.

Finally Toby reappeared, along with the host, who stuck his hand out to shake mine. "Nice to meet you," he said slickly, barely looking at me, and when I said out of reflex, "Oh, but we've already—" he stopped me and said without a smile, "I'm *just kidding*."

I was twenty-nine and had only just moved to Hollywood, having met and fallen in love with Toby eight months earlier while he was visiting New York—I'd been in the audience at a comedy club where he was doing stand-up; he'd heckled me from the stage, then come up to me afterward to apologize. This was my first celebrity party. So though it annoyed me that if people spoke to me at all they did it while constantly scanning the room for someone of higher stature to talk to, being annoyed by it was a cliché; it was what *everyone* had complained about when I'd asked them what Hollywood was like. And so I moved past it and instead took in the room with a sense of gratitude. This was the kind of party that I had previously only managed to spy on via the pages of *InStyle* magazine. I was lucky just to be here, I told myself, and being here was enough.

Toby and I kept mainly to ourselves that night. We spoke only with a few other lowly talk-show writers; Toby was a TV writer, and outside of Hollywood his job monopolized conversations; I was a newspaper reporter with the education beat, an occupation that guaranteed my status here as a nobody. We ate alone at a candlelit table out by the pool, and then we smoked cigarettes on the front patio, eyeing the celebrities as they came and went along the steep front steps.

We left early that night, thanking the host and skittering down the granite steps, bursting with a strange feeling of relief that we were young and undiscovered.

But it was Toby's boss's party, and this man, possessing an astonishingly mistaken sense of his own permanence in the town, had made it clear that he had a vision—his parties would become Hollywood legends, the town's hottest tickets. A few months later, another invitation appeared in the mail. And so we went.

"Nice to meet you," said the host again, but this time it wasn't a joke, and I just shook his hand and smiled. I drank too much early in the evening so I could get up the nerve to look at the celebrities, and I hid in a corner, talking about elementary schools with the unfamous wife of a famous movie actor.

Later Toby came to get me to smoke a cigarette and we stood with a few other writers on the small front patio, listening to the chatter of the guests inside the house. Again I felt the silent rules: the unspectacular people should gather here, should speak only when spoken to. Three months had passed since I'd moved to Hollywood, and I had spent them mainly covering school board meetings for a tiny neighborhood paper in Pacific Palisades. Toby and I had been nesting at home; at night we cooked and watched movies and cuddled on the couch. Now I wondered how Toby fared in this town of secrets that lay so close to the surface. "A four-three seven on a Wednesday night, and the demo's a three," I'd heard earlier as I'd passed through the living room. What could it mean? I imagined Hollywood as a brick castle; outsiders circled it looking for a door. Once you knew the password, a trapdoor opened, a magical world revealed. Now I looked at Toby; in his preppy white shirt and khakis, he was so sweet and fresh. The men at this party wore black shirts with black ties. They knew something that Toby didn't, I thought, but I didn't know what.

Just then the door to the patio swung open and we looked up, and there was Merv Griffin. He wore a green sport coat and he had a thin brown cigarillo in his hand.

He approached us and Toby offered him a light.

"Thank you," said Merv, and then he was quiet.

"Did you come to the last one?" I asked him, because no one else said anything.

He looked at me. "I did, my dear, and it was just as awful as this one."

I let out a barking laugh, and he laughed, too.

Then the patio door opened again, and a man stepped out and then a woman. I recognized them immediately. They were a young couple, both pop singers, eccentric, very cool. They were known, but not by the masses; their fans were people who listened to more than Top 40. They had been popular when I was in college. The girl wore a pin-striped ochre suit with an ochre tie, her purposely stringy black hair and nerdy glasses still not able to obscure her beauty; his retro gray suit was reminiscent of flapper days. They were *dressed* by Hollywood standards. But they were awkward and self-conscious; they lit their cigarettes and looked at the ground.

Their evident insecurity coupled with my confident afterglow from talking with Merv made me turn and say stupidly, "I guess there's no chance of getting you guys to sing for us tonight, huh?"

The guy looked at me coolly. "You're kidding, right?"

I turned away. I was humiliated, my cheeks burned. But then I thought, Well, who the hell are they, really? Washed-up singers. I'll never see them again anyway.

But later in the evening, when Toby and I took our plates from the buffet and walked up a few steps onto the patio by the pool, looking for a table, there they were, the only ones sitting at a table set for ten.

"Should we?" I whispered to Toby, staring straight ahead.

"Why not," he said with a shrug.

So we went and sat down with them, leaving a seat between her and me. We introduced ourselves, using first names only, and they did the same: Charlotte and Jack. We somehow began chatting about the high divorce rate among the party guests, which led me to ask if they were married, though of course I knew very well from reading *People* that they were—they had married in Hollywood a few years earlier in a suite at the Chateau Marmont; she had worn a blood-red dress. And they began to tell us about their wedding, how his brother (also a famous musician) had brought his horrible children and they had tipped over the cake, and how they therefore strongly advised us— were we to ever marry—*not* to invite children to our wedding, at which we all laughed, and Toby said, "At least not your brother's children," and then some-how, suddenly, we began to hit it off.

They admitted their suspicion that they were being used—invited to this party just to lend the host a little edge—and they didn't know why they continued to come, because they didn't know how to handle themselves with all these mainstream celebrities, and we laughed and Toby said, "Eh, it ain't that hard," and I watched with pride how at ease Toby seemed in the conversation—*with celebrities!*—and then later, when Merv came up the stairs, looking for a seat, for some reason he took the one in between Charlotte and me, and then he gave Toby and me advice on where to go on an upcoming vacation—*The French Riviera will bore you to tears,* he announced; *try Italy or Ibiza instead*—and then more celebrities came over and sat down, until the very host himself came with his plate and sat, having decreed ours the best table in the house.

"This ain't so bad, huh?" Toby leaned over and said to Charlotte and Jack at one point, and winked. And they laughed and I could tell they agreed; they were having fun now, thanks to us.

Later the four of us went inside to the great room, by the grand piano, and we all sat on a couch together, and I was drunk. "How come you don't have children?" I asked, realizing at once how inappropriate it was but pushing on anyway. They talked about how hard it was being on the road, away from each other, and I admitted that never in my life had I imagined I would be at a party like this.

Then Merv appeared and walked down into the sunken room. He winked at Charlotte and me and then took a seat at the piano. The room quieted.

That was the first time Merv played the piano at one of these parties—as he did afterward for several years—and back then, in the early part of 2002, at the beginning of a new century, Merv was so unhip he was hip, and it was seen as a sort of a kitschy coup to have an outdated celebrity perform. It made the night seem special, a treat of a lifetime, something you might tell your grand-kids about. It conjured up old Hollywood, everyone pressed into the over-flowing and dramatic great room, with its huge dark wood beams and bookshelves, and of old-fashioned, innocent pleasure; he even played "Piano Man" and we all sang along—including Charlotte and Jack. You could look openly around the room at everyone; no one was in the bathroom doing coke or slinking around dark corners talking up starlets.

That was also the night that "Summertime" became a tradition at the party. It all started with Merv at the piano, enjoying his comeback, the room quiet just for him, when an Irish girl—she was almost middle-aged by Hollywood standards, probably in her early thirties, and dowdy, a little heavy, wearing an ill-fitting green taffeta dress—stood up and said, "Merv? Merv? May I sing one?"

No one knew what to do then; there was a feeling that something very dis-tasteful had just occurred, and Merv said, a little rudely, "Darling, do you know who I am?" but that didn't faze her at all; she stared back at him full on and said, "Come on, love, just one." And we all stared at him, waiting for his reaction, and then someone booed, and then there came a chorus of boos, and Merv, apparently feeling he had somehow egged the crowd on into this impolite territory and now needed to make up for it, shushed the room and held his hand out gallantly to the girl. "What shall I play?" he asked.

" 'Summertime,' " she said, and he began to play.

The young asshole movie actor immediately stood up and left the room, making a great show of it. A couple of starlets followed him out. But everyone else stayed.

"Summertiiiiiime, and the livin' is eaaaaaaaaaaaasy," the girl bellowed.

She had a very decent voice, deep and strong, but I was embarrassed for her. My cheeks burned as if I were the one singing; I could barely look at her. And when she finished Merv shook her hand and kissed her cheek and then stepped away from the piano, saying he'd had enough, and then we all blamed the end of Merv's singing on her.

The four of us headed outside for a cigarette, Charlotte critiquing the girl's range, and about ten minutes later Merv stepped out, too, and stood with us, smoking his little cigarillo. Charlotte and Jack began to clap for him, their cigarettes dangling from their mouths, and Toby said, "Bravo! You were very gentlemanly."

"Yes, well done in there, Merv," I added.

And Merv Griffin looked down at me, as if trying to recall where he had seen me before. "My Genevieve is here," he said out of nowhere.

And then he looked over his shoulder, down onto the street. .

There was a golden Rolls-Royce there, its back window open halfway, and a little white dog had its head out, panting heavily and looking sprightly around.

"Genevieve!" Merv called. "Come here, girl!"

She looked up at him and started to bark, and then a driver stepped out of the front door and opened the back door, and the little dog jumped down from the seat and ran through the open gate and up the steps, breaking two of the little glass candleholders that lined the darkened stairway on the way up. She found Merv and jumped at him, up on his legs. He reached down, picked her up, and said, "Ah, my little Genny."

That moment to me felt magical, and I suspended the scene in my mind so I could go back and play it again and again like an old movie—Merv's glance down at the Rolls, the driver slowly stepping out of the car in a crisp white shirt, the little dog bravely jumping up the steep steps, and the reunion shot of little Genevieve jumping into Merv's arms. In the slow-motion background Charlotte and Jack were laughing at something Toby had just said, and Toby was petting the dog in Merv's arms, and they were all smiling.

And suddenly the evening inspired a glossy déjà vu, like a lovely and familiar drug, and though I almost refused to acknowledge it, I could feel a nostalgia for the evening already setting in, a longing just for the existence of this night building before my eyes.

But after a while I sensed that Toby was growing tired, and I knew that even though the party was still in full swing—it was perhaps only midnight—soon he would say he wanted to go home. I knew that Toby was not as impressed by celebrity as I was. He worked for a celebrity, after all, wrote his jokes, met the stars who came on his show. "They're people just like you and me," he said. He had promised me that I would get used to it, the way he had. And in fact, his confident sense of belonging to this world was part of what had attracted me to him in the first place. But though his shrugging off of fame was appealing, I had a hard time imagining ever doing it myself.

And so now when, after a few minutes, Toby yawned and said he wanted to go home, I couldn't stop myself from feeling resentful. We told Charlotte and Jack we were leaving, and she said we should all get together sometime, and I said by all means we should, and they walked us to the door and we said good-bye.

In the car I didn't look at Toby as I said softly, "Why would you drag me out of a party like that? When will I ever get to be with people like that again?"

Toby looked at me for a while. "Smooch," he said, using our shared nickname, "she gave me their number."

"What?"

He took a small piece of paper from the inside pocket of his jacket. *Charlotte and Jack,* it said, and their phone number. "I gave her ours, too," he said.

"Jesus," I said. "Well, we can't call them."

"Why not?" he said. "Of course we can."

"What would we talk about? What would we invite them to?"

But three days later the phone rang and it was Charlotte, inviting us to dinner.

"What?" I said when Toby told me.

"On Thursday night. Pane e Vino, eight P.M."

"First of all," I said, "who ever actually goes through with calling other couples when they meet them at parties, even if they do ask for their number?"

"So? We liked them and they liked us."

"They're celebrities, for godsakes. Don't they have enough friends? What do they want with us?"

WE WENT. It was awkward. I was terribly nervous; my mouth was paralyzed, I was too afraid even to get drunk, and they were big talkers, analyzed everything, didn't want to talk about anything unless it was something they could tear apart. Religion, U.S. imperialism, Toby's boss and whether he was gay—that one for about forty-five minutes. If I said anything, they seized upon it and questioned me. Why was I a Democrat? Did I really even know what the word *Democrat* meant? (They were independents, of course.) I felt scrutinized, studied, paid attention to. I started to feel like I just wanted to get out of there before I said anything stupid. When the check came I smiled for the first time all night.

"That was awful," I said to Toby in the car on the way home. "Awful. We'll never hear from them again. I don't even want to hang out with them again anyway. Jesus Christ, I felt like I was at some shrink session or something."

"Well, to be honest," Toby said, "I'm kind of relieved. At least they weren't trying to recruit us for some weird sex thing, or drug thing."

I laughed, and agreed. But in the back of my mind, I knew why I was being disdainful. I'd blown it. My anxiety at dinner had been palpable. I'd been too quiet, too timid, not interesting enough.

But then, a few days later, the phone rang. It was Charlotte. Would we like to get together again? Toby and I looked at each other with wonder and exhilaration. We went for dinner at their huge home in Silverlake, a hip area of town, which seemed to fit their image as chic outsiders.

And then, somehow, we became friends. I started to like them. They invited us to hear them sing at a small bar, even put us on the guest list, and we had dinners at our place and theirs, museums, movies, art parties, and weird stupid benefit parties that they liked to go to just to make fun of the crowd.

Toby started to drop their names sometimes—"Our friends Charlotte James and Jack Sheet," he would say with an anticipatory smile, eating up the look people gave us—but I felt this betrayed them, that they wouldn't like it, that we were friends with them despite their celebrity.

Charlotte paid particular attention to me, almost as if she was trying to show me that it was okay that I wasn't a celebrity, that she was above all that, that she liked me for who I was. She went out of her way to tell me things she knew I would be interested in. "Lacey, I went to New York and met Dave Eggers," she said one night from the backseat of our car, on the way to a silent movie, one of their penchants that fit their eccentric image. When she spoke directly to me, used my name, I felt a warm light on me; she had singled me out, I was special. She had a lovely, lilting voice with a slight southern accent that was even more pronounced when she sang. I listened to her albums constantly.

They were both cynical yet terribly earnest, and they would drone on for far too long about uninteresting esoteric topics. He in particular had done a lot of reading and could talk in depth about completely random topics, like Asian cults and unknown circus performers. When I brought up Scientology one night, for instance, they got so excited it was hard for them to stay in their seats. The history of it, the evil of it, the attempts to silence any criticism, its leaders, the celebrities who believed and why they did—it all came tumbling out, and they spoke on top of each other, stopping only to hear our questions, on and on until at one point my mind actually drifted, and then I suddenly snapped back into myself, wondering madly if I had missed anything important, if my nods had been convincing.

I wondered if this was why they needed friends. Perhaps it was a deep, deep flaw—perhaps they were sort of crazy, and everyone in Hollywood knew it except us. But there was, too, something so appealing and disarming about their enthusiasm. It was real; they spoke to us as if we were their friends, as if *of course* it was worth it for them to expend all this energy in order to change *our* minds about satanic cults.

They were famous and so they had famous friends. In their living room, late at night, at their intimate parties, we were regularly stunned to walk in and shake hands with our favorite musicians, our teen idols. Everybody in the music world seemed to roll into town and end up at Charlotte and Jack's, where they mainly sat around and played guitar and ate Chinese food and talked about gigs and shows and told stories from the road. No one questioned our presence; Charlotte and Jack had accepted us, so we were automatically cool. There were several nights when we sat on their couch, our mouths practically open in shock—even jaded Toby was finally starstruck—as the candles burned low and some of the biggest rock stars in the world sat across from us and harmonized, tried out new chords, came up with new lyrics, asked for our opinions.

Charlotte was the queen; she ruled the scene and managed the comings and goings of an ever-changing group—and she preferred change, I noticed. She liked diversity, a new face, the mystique of a stranger in the room. As a result, she regularly tried people on for a while but then quickly let them go. They would be around for a couple weeks or so and then vanish. At first I felt threatened by these new presences—funky young singers, sophisticated actresses, the hot new couple on the scene—but eventually and unfailingly they would not be invited back. "Too much of a show-off," she would confide to me at the end of the night, or "I didn't like how she said good-bye, lingering at the door for fifteen minutes. Shoo." They all disappeared. Everyone except for Toby and me. For a while I lived in perpetual fear, waiting for the ax to fall, but it never did.

After a time Toby came to accept their friendship with us, but I continued to question it. What could they possibly want with us? We were plebeians, mortals, nobodies. I had no answer. And Toby became impatient with my questioning—*They like us, okay? Get over it. They're not gods.*

And then slowly I began to admit something to myself, something vain and secret, something I never would have spoken aloud: maybe *I* was the attraction. Maybe *I* was the reason Charlotte and Jack liked us. I had always suspected, deep down, that I had a special glow about me, a charm that made men fall in love with me and women want to be my friends. Charlotte and Jack's friendship with us was a natural consequence. I thought of my little life back in New York, working in a windowless cubicle for a small weekly paper, falling in and out of short-lived relationships, occasionally having a nice dinner with my dad whenever he was in town. I had just been waiting for someone to notice me, for my real life to begin—and now it had. Toby had plucked me from my own obscurity and brought me out here into the sun. Now I told myself that it was only a matter of time until I, too, would become a star, surrounded by interesting people, adorned with beautiful things, enriched by creative work, bathed in a spotlight that illuminated my most fascinating and heretofore hidden qualities. I sat in Charlotte's living room late at night, my eyes glassy from pot or the late hour, and I looked around at the stars and thought smugly, I have as much right to be here as anyone else.

And then, without warning, just as quickly and as headily as it had all begun, it ended.

It was about three months after we'd become friends with Charlotte and Jack. Toby's thirtieth birthday was approaching, and I had planned a big party for him. I sent out invitations a couple of weeks before, and as the date neared I was busy ordering the food and confirming numbers with the bar. Then, two days before the party, I realized that Charlotte and Jack hadn't RSVPed.

"Have you heard from them?" I asked Toby.

"Not in the past few days," he said.

"I don't understand," I said. "Does this mean they're not coming?"

Toby said they would be there; he reminded me that they weren't exactly etiquette-conscious: they were rock stars, after all. But they were coming, he assured me—why wouldn't they?

I decided to call them anyway. Perhaps they hadn't received the invitation; perhaps they had forgotten. They didn't answer; I left a message. They didn't call back.

"I don't know what to do," I said to Toby. "What should we do?"

He shrugged. "Either they'll show or they won't."

His cool enraged me. Why did I have to carry this weight of anxiety while he could just let things go? *Stop letting everything roll off your back,* I thought. *Feel something! Care!* Yet at the same time I coveted his casual attitude, wished I could feel nothing, too.

The night of Toby's birthday arrived. The party was held at a chic bar in West Hollywood, and I was distracted all night, keeping my eye on the door, waiting for Charlotte and Jack to arrive. But they never showed.

I sent them an e-mail the following week, a cheery one, as if nothing had happened: *We missed you at Toby's thirtieth! The late-night antics definitely beat out charades!* (We had all played a horribly reluctant game of charades at our place one night, at Toby's and my drunken insistence.) I heard nothing back. I called and left a message. Nothing. I checked their websites—they weren't on tour.

Weeks and then months went by, and we never heard from them, and after a while, it became clear that Charlotte and Jack had dropped us. I didn't know why. Our last contact with them had been innocuous enough—we'd seen them for dinner, had discussed her upcoming album. I didn't understand it, and I was devastated. "Why do you think they're mad at us?" I asked Toby at least once a day. "What could we have done?"

I went back in my mind. Maybe Jack was annoyed that we had forced them to play charades that night—Charlotte had done very poorly, had stood there for long silent moments thinking and had finally thrown up her hands, saying, "I can't do this"—and maybe he resented us for putting her through that; she was delicate, an artist. Or maybe someone had told them that Toby had gone around dropping their names. And, slowly, quietly, secretly, I became angry at Toby. I blamed him. This was his fault. They had sensed his nonchalance and it had pushed them away. Sometimes when I looked at him lounging on the couch, I almost hated him. When he leaned over to kiss me, I had to will myself not to pull away.

Toby felt this and became frustrated. "What's the matter with you?" he said.

I grasped for a way to explain my unhappiness. "She listened to me" was all I could come up with. "I told her Neil Young was my favorite singer and she gave me that CD of her playing with him."

"You have plenty of other friends who listen to you, Smooch."

"But I liked Charlotte and Jack."

Toby looked at me and sighed. "It's not about Charlotte and Jack," he said. "It's about the fact that she knew Neil Young. It's about the fact that they were celebrities."

"I can't believe you would say something like that," I said, pretending to be hurt, but I knew he was right. Then I defended myself. I couldn't help it if they had succeeded in wooing me, I told him. They were stars after all—they had charisma, that special something that makes people famous. The whole world had fallen in love with them—how was I to help falling for them too? Why had they done it? Why had they made me fall in love with them and then left? Was it some kind of game to them? Was it all a game out here and I just didn't know the rules?

Driving by clubs on Sunset Boulevard, I was taunted by their names in lights. *Once you had VIP access here,* the signs said. *Once you were a somebody. Not anymore.* I had been elevated and then lowered back down. I began to fear that I had already reached my peak in this town, that my whole life from now on would be anticlimactic, one big letdown. I had unknowingly squandered my fifteen minutes of fame; I had had my chance at being forever inside the velvet rope, and lost it.

I thought then of leaving L.A., of moving back east, to my little apartment and my nothing job. What was I doing here, after all? This was all a farce. I didn't belong. It wasn't my town. I was an interloper, sneaking in on Toby's coattails.

Yet I could not go. I felt I had started something I hadn't finished, or hadn't mastered something I was supposed to learn. And it was too late for leaving anyway: Toby and I were in love. I stayed. I focused on work, Toby made me laugh, I moved on.

Then one bright summer day, several months later, I went innocently to check the mail and there it was: a white envelope with familiar black script. An invitation. Another Summertime Party. I clutched the envelope to my chest. I breathed a sigh of relief. And I began to lay awake nights, imagining seeing them again.

Toby said we shouldn't go. "I don't want to see you get hurt," he said, looking at me with concern.

"Are you crazy?" I snapped. "We have to go."

The night of the party, while dressing, I felt ill from anticipation. I had a glass of wine at home and smoked a cigarette. "God, I'm being absurd," I said, and laughed nervously, but when I tried to stand, I couldn't get out of the chair, and had to endure a half hour of Toby's attempts to convince me that it was no big deal, they were just flaky, that was all. If they were there, it would be great to see them; there was nothing to be nervous about.

In the car I smoked more cigarettes, and I made us stop at the gas station so I could buy more. "I don't want to run out," I said.

"Well, I don't think there's a chance of that," Toby said when I came out, clutching two packs.

For a moment I hoped fervently that they wouldn't be there, that I wouldn't have to avoid them. I couldn't bear the thought of having to face them and their lame excuses, and then I nearly prayed that they would be there, that maybe there was some explanation; maybe one of them had had an accident or been sick; maybe they had been on some kind of last-minute tour and cut off from their phone, mail, and e-mail; or maybe they had had an awful fight and nearly divorced and hadn't wanted to see anyone they knew for a while but now they were all mended and ready to resume their social lives—and in fact they wanted to see us immediately, in fact they had so *hoped* to see us at the party so they could apologize in person for not coming to Toby's birthday party—because they were, they really were, so terribly, terribly sorry!

Inside, the host greeted us. I told him how nice it was to meet him, then moved into the great room, sweeping it quickly with eyes down. I didn't see them. We went to the bar, where I had a full view of the celebrity clump out by the pool. Not there.

I saw Merv and he said hello and promised that his dog, Genevieve, would make an appearance later.

I started to relax.

Then Toby's voice, friendly, a greeting: "Hey!"

And there was Jack. I watched them hug, shyly looked at Jack's face; he seemed genuinely pleased to see us.

"So sorry we haven't seen you!" he began. "We've both been in the studio and we haven't seen anyone, really. We've been like cave dwellers."

"It's okay," I said happily, flooded with relief. My smile came back for the first time in what felt like months. My heart released. I soared. "Is Charlotte here?" I asked.

And suddenly there she was.

"Hello, Lacey," she sang, and her golden glow surrounded me, bathing me in the warm night, and I smiled in slow motion and she hugged me and I was happy, insanely happy, strangely, giddily happy.

But then she touched Jack's arm, and he looked down at her and then back at us.

"Oh, excuse us for one sec," he said, and then, "We'll catch up with you later?" They turned to go.

I watched them, and then I couldn't help myself. "Wait," I called. "Charlotte."

I thought she wasn't going to turn back, but finally she did, and when she did she looked at me coolly, a quick glance up and down, the way I'd seen her do with the people she inevitably cut the next day. I was out. And there was nothing to be done about it. She stared at me for a moment more, then turned again. They walked off.

I looked at Toby; I knew my mouth was open. He shrugged.

I moved through the rest of the party like a heartbroken lover. I stood in corners, smoking, and drained glass after glass of wine. I wanted to leave; I couldn't bring myself to leave.

Finally, mercifully, it was time for Merv to sing, and Toby began to steer me toward the great room. But I saw them sitting in there, on the same couch we had sat on those months ago, and I turned away. "You go ahead," I told Toby. "I'll be in the bathroom."

Instead, I hung back and listened to Merv. And I watched them down there, but they didn't look at me; I was just a blip. I saw Toby, sweetly standing across the room, near the patio doors.

It was time for "Summertime," and a nobody starlet was going to sing it. There was a buzz in the room, and suddenly I wanted to go stand next to Toby, my sweet, good, innocent Toby, the Toby I knew, the Toby who knew me.

I felt myself moving forward, into the great room, and then I felt a white heat on me. I was blinded by the spotlight, I couldn't see a thing, couldn't see Toby anymore; my heart was pounding and I was frozen. Everyone began to clap, they thought I was the singer, and I looked blankly out at where I knew the crowd was, out at the great sea of everything, the world of possibility, and I waved my hands, *no, no,* and then I took one small step backward, out of the light.

The Best of All Possible Worlds

WHENEVER I COMPLAINED of troubles as a young adult—the typical troubles one has in one's twenties, those of the "What will I do with my life and when will I meet someone?" variety—my father would counsel me to slow down and enjoy being naïve and fallible because, as he liked to say, you don't know anything until you're thirty, and you don't *really* know anything until you're thirty-five. I held on to those words throughout my twenties as I made mistake after mistake with boys and careers and friends. *When I get to my thirties,* I told myself, *I'll know what I'm doing. Just wait it out.*

I celebrated my thirtieth birthday at a small restaurant in SoHo in New York. It was also a good-bye party of sorts. I had moved out to Los Angeles a year earlier, unsure of whether I would stay, but now Toby and I were engaged. Toby's career was in Hollywood. We would make a life for ourselves there, raise a family there. I would not be moving home to New York again.

MY FATHER HAD PREDICTED that Toby would propose to me on my thirtieth birthday, and earlier that day, getting down on one knee outside the comedy club in Times Square where we'd met, he had, the two of us hugging for dear life as the crowds streamed by. After he'd asked and I'd said yes, I had the strange feeling that I had been waiting for this, this quintessential moment in a girl's life, this next step that I had wanted to take with Toby—but now that the moment was here, I didn't know what to do with it, or how to move forward from it.

"What are we going to do now, Smooch?" I said strangely, joyfully, into Toby's neck as we hugged. "What are we going to do now?"

But later that night, at the party, as my friends gathered around to appraise my ring, I looked across the room at my father and he winked at me. He was pleased, I could tell, that his engagement prophecy had come true. And I thought then about what he had always said about turning thirty, and I felt again the security of those words, another of his prophecies coming true. I was settling down in Los Angeles and I was getting married. I was thirty and I finally knew what I was doing.

My father had questioned my decision to stay in L.A., but only in his Socratic style. He rarely came out and said what I should do with my life, preferring instead to ask me questions until I figured it out. He had never been a father in the traditional, prohibitive sense, a father who told me what I could and couldn't do, even when I was a child.

In junior high he let me have parties in the basement playroom every Saturday night, and he never came downstairs or asked what my friends and I were doing down there, which was drinking his liquor and playing strip poker. When I told him I wanted to go to boarding school the following year, he helped me research schools and then let me pick the one I liked best. He was more like a consigliere, an advisor, a co-muller-over, someone to sit with at dinner and talk to, and he preferred to think of himself as a father in this way.

The only time he'd ever made a decision for me was when I was seven years old, after he'd torched my mother's life in a bright blaze of embarrassment by sleeping with her best friend and country-club tennis partner in Larchmont, a suburb of New York, where we had lived since my twin brother, Sam, and I were born.

Ostensibly my parents were trying to work things out; back then Sam and I had only the vaguest of sensations that anything was awry. That changed the

night my mother announced at the dinner table that she was marrying someone named Richard, moving to Palm Beach to live with him, and taking Sam
and me with her.

"Who the hell is Richard?" my father said.

I knew who he was. His name had always hovered faintly above our lives.
When she announced that she was marrying him, I hadn't yet met him, but
felt I already knew him. Even at age seven, I had been privy to my mother's
daydreams. Long before my father had cheated on her, my mother had dug
photos out of the attic to show me what her prom date looked like. At eighteen, Richard Walker had slicked-back dark hair and a little bit of a James
Dean thing going. He wore a white dinner jacket, bow tie, and boutonniere
and reminded me of Frankie Avalon in *Grease,* in the dreamy scene where he
sings "Beauty School Dropout" to Frenchy in the diner.

My mother's high school years in Palm Beach sounded pretty dreamy, too.
She told me about them in a voice that even sounded dreamy as she nursed a
glass of wine at the kitchen table while I finished my ice cream and hung on to
every word, imagining my own grown-up life. She was from a wealthy, socially
prominent family—they knew the Kennedys—and she had been beautiful, of
course. I could see that from the prom photo: dark hair waved in that soft
1950s style, high cheekbones, flashing dark eyes. Given her wealth and
beauty, my mother's high school years had passed in a happy blur. There were
dances at the country club, a red convertible from her parents on her sixteenth birthday, the phone ringing off the hook for dates, and finally her first
taste of true love, at seventeen, with Richard, who was from a similarly
wealthy family in her neighborhood (his father played golf with hers; both fathers bought their wives jewelry at the same exclusive shop; they belonged to
the same country club). Richard took my mother parking but did not push
things, and he brought her a pink wrist corsage every Saturday night. Then he
went off to Stanford, where he wrote her every day and sent her flowers every
week—that is, until my mother went north to Smith and, one Saturday night,
to a mixer at Yale. There she met my father, who had no family and no past,
and who wooed her with nothing more than his charm. They married six
months after they met, at age twenty-one.

Yet in all these years, Richard had never married.

"Why?" I asked when my mother told me this tidbit one night. I could
sense that she was bursting to reveal a secret, and I could sense her pride in

the answer, too, her anticipation in sharing it with me. And so, on some level, I already knew what she was going to say.

"I think he's waiting for me," she whispered with a smile. I pictured Richard, still in his white prom tuxedo, waiting patiently in Palm Beach with a wrist corsage. "Isn't that romantic?" she said with a sigh, and I couldn't disagree. It seemed like something someone might do in a movie—wait for his true love forever—but not in real life.

Yet to me, the story of Richard was always just that: a daydream, a fairy tale, a reminiscence of a time before my mother had settled down with my father. I never imagined him as a real person, a grown-up, a man—that is, until my mother announced she was marrying him and he would become our stepfather.

A week later the photo arrived in the mail.

Richard, who had grown up to be a successful Palm Beach businessman, now lived in a large white mansion—at least that was the word that came straight to my seven-year-old mind when I saw the photo he'd sent to acquaint us with our new life. The house, which had a fountain spurting off to one side (the photo had actually caught the water midspurt), was like something out of *Fantasy Island*, with the sea stretching out behind it, a manicured lawn in front, and palm trees waving all around it. On top of all that, Richard had gone out and bought a replica of the red sports car my mother had received for her sixteenth birthday, and it sat jauntily in the circular driveway, perfectly angled to set off the house and its white columns. I felt nervous about living in such a place, about what kind of manners and clothes Sam and I might be expected to have, but I was ready to go. My mother would be there, after all, to take care of us.

MY FATHER CONFRONTED US one Saturday morning while my mother was in Palm Beach, scouting churches for her wedding. Sam and I were lying on the shag rug in the den, eating cereal and watching cartoons. My father came in, snapped off the TV, and sat down on the couch. He looked at us for a moment or two, took a deep breath, and began.

"What would you like to do?" he said. "Go to Florida with Mom or stay here with me?"

We looked up, our spoons dripping milk. We didn't say anything, and after a moment my father said quietly, "It's okay. I can handle it."

"I want to go with Mom," I said quickly—I was six minutes older than Sam and usually the one to speak first—and then Sam said: "Me, too."

My father nodded and swallowed hard. "I understand," he said.

Suddenly my heart started beating fast. I had been asked to choose one parent over the other, and I had done it. I burst into tears and fled the room; my brother soon followed.

My FATHER, for his part, considered our answer—for several days, he says now—then made the decision to disregard it. He warned my mother she was in for a fight, drew up the papers himself, and sued her for custody of us.

It was my MOTHER who broke the news to Sam and me—my tall, stunning mother whom I loved to hide behind, who smelled of Jean Naté and wore her long dark hair tucked behind her ears—on our green velvet couch in our silent, elegant living room. The only time I ever went in there was during my parents' cocktail parties, when I was allowed to pass the hors d'oeuvres, a small figure in a smocked party dress wandering the crowd. Now Sam and I sat on the couch, our feet dangling off the edge.

My mother knelt before us and took our hands.

"The judge gave me a choice," she said. "I can stay in New York and have joint custody with your father, or I can move to Palm Beach and have nothing."

If that was her only choice, she said, she would take nothing.

"Nothing?" I said. No one would take *nothing*. If you had a choice between something and nothing, you would take something, of course.

Yet my mother was not smiling. I did not understand. I had expected this to be easy. The gray-haired, stern-faced judge had called Sam and me into his chambers and asked us what we wanted, and we had told him, right to his face. Sam had been too scared to talk, and I, too, had been aware of danger in those judge's chambers, lined with dark wood and thick books, and of the old man's power, his sole ability to decide our future, and so I had said it simply and firmly, so there would be no misunderstanding. "We want to live with our mother," I had said, loud and clear. If there was one thing I could be sure of, it was that I wanted to be with my mother. Sam and I would move to Florida with her and start a new life.

But now our living room was very still. Dust motes swirled in a sunbeam on the rug, and I had the sense that everything was about to change.

"I don't . . ." I said. "We can't come live with you?"

"The judge said it's not fair to move children so far away from their father," my mother said. "Your father wants to be close to you."

"So we're staying here?" I said. "We're not moving to Florida?"

My mother wept into my lap, clutching me, then dried her tears and announced, her voice firm, her eyes suddenly cold, that she was sorry, but Richard's business was in Florida and he could not move to New York. And so she could not stay—not if it meant losing him again.

"Can you understand?" she said, softening a bit, searching my face as if I actually might. "Your father, he can't, he doesn't know how . . ." She trailed off, then looked up at me again. "You see, I've been with the wrong man all this time. Richard asked me to marry him when we were eighteen, and I turned him down. I can't make the same mistake again."

She married him a week later. They went on a two-month round-the-world honeymoon cruise, then settled into his huge house in Palm Beach. She would be pregnant within the year. She was thirty-five years old, and she was finally living the life she was meant to lead. And so Sam and I began our own new life with our father.

AFTER MY MOTHER LEFT, I was angry at my father for wanting us. I did not want him. He had asked me what I wanted, I had told him, and then he had prevented me from having it. I had been very attached to my mother. I was the type of child who had trouble spending the night away from home. When I spent the night at friends' houses, I often woke the parents up in the middle of the night and made them drive me home. (Perhaps I was afraid my mother would leave even before she left.)

Now the realization that she was gone was too much for a seven-year-old girl to handle; the grief, the longing, the heartbreak, most of all the sense that she was alive yet unattainable, that she was existing in another space without me, where I could not get to her, was overwhelming. For months afterward I cried myself to sleep.

But right from the beginning, my father tried. He did what he could to be both father and mother to us. Yet he was a lawyer in New York with his own thriving practice, and juggling parenthood and work was not always successful. We were often, for instance, left waiting with our teachers when the latest sitter failed to pick us up after school; there were many mornings when there was no milk for our cereal—and there were often ants in the cereal anyway, probably because no one had cleaned the kitchen recently, or the bathroom, or our clothes, and so I learned how.

Yet, eventually, and more quickly than I had imagined, I did what children do: I adapted, I moved on, I was resilient, as children are. I got used to the shuttle of live-in housekeepers who came and went (Joanna, with her hippie skirts, who gave me my first drag of a cigarette; Helena, a harsh German with short white hair who locked the cat in the basement at night and forced Sam and me out of the car if we squabbled in the backseat; Maggie, a jolly Irishwoman in a white nurse's uniform who pressed us to her huge breasts and loved us as if we were her own). I looked forward to the nights when it felt like we were a family: when my father made it home in time for dinner and settled into the den with a drink—Sam and I playing cards on the rug in front of the fire, John Denver on the stereo—and asked us about our days and told us his own stories as well. And I spent a lot of time in my room reading. I read everything I could find for my age group, and then I read everything on the living room shelves. Eventually my father began to take me to the library every Saturday, and I would pile my arms high with books. For me, books were, as they are for so many children, an escape from a reality I might not have wanted to look at too closely. I did well in school, probably because of all the books, and that helped me as the years went on.

Sam, however, did not do well—not with grades and not with sports and not with friends. He was angry. He picked fights with other boys and with his teachers. He spent a lot of time by himself in the woods, watching the older kids ride their motorbikes through the river wash, graffitiing the rocks and throwing their cigarettes on the ground.

But at night, after my father went to bed, Sam would become small and scared again. Especially in those early days after my mother left, he would often come into my room in the middle of the night and sleep on my floor. I would usually wake up.

"Are you okay, Sammy?" I would ask.

And he would always say, "Yeah, it's just the light from the moon is bothering me in my room."

But we both knew why he was there, and the truth was I felt better having him close by. We were both scared of things now, like the dark, or the empty house at night when my father forgot to hire a sitter, or the taxi drivers who sometimes picked us up from school, who we knew were plotting to kidnap us.

Back then, if my brother fell down or if we fought and I hit him, he would cry, and then wail, his chest heaving, "I waaaaant my mommy!" It was the most heartbreaking sound in the world, the most painful thing to witness—a little boy wanting something as simple and clear as his mother, crying out to anyone who could hear him, and no one doing anything. *What a travesty,* I heard the other mothers say when the nannies came to pick us up, and it was. Even as a child I sensed it. I felt like crying out myself, pulling at someone's sleeve to get attention for my brother. I was managing to stay alive, but my brother was drowning, or falling, or imploding, and no one said a word or did a thing. He was like a house burning down before our eyes.

MY PARENTS, for whatever reason, had a lot of Edith Wharton on their shelves (my mother had left all the books behind, saying they now belonged to me), and so I read *The Age of Innocence* at quite an innocent age, perhaps nine or ten, taking in the descriptions of the New York upper class with a sense of familiarity. In it I recognized snippets of my life, or of my father's life anyway, and so I grew up thinking that we were WASPs, and special. We weren't WASPs, as I found out—we were Irish Catholic—but to some degree, in the sense that my father knew how to celebrate a good time, how to mark an occasion and make it memorable, we were special.

We went to the theater and to '21' for dinner every Saturday night; he took us to see *Annie* on Broadway every Christmas; he threw a black-tie dinner every other year at Mory's in New Haven to celebrate the Harvard-Yale game, or Yale-Harvard, as my father liked to call it, being a Yalie himself. His friends had full-floor apartments on Park Avenue, and memberships at private clubs in the city where portraits of Astors stared down at us.

He liked to go everywhere, to be at the center of every party, and he didn't want to trade that for fatherhood, yet he didn't want to leave us alone more than he already had, so he simply took Sam and me with him. Wherever he went, to cocktail parties, on business trips, even occasionally on dates at restaurants, there Sam and I were. His friends and girlfriends got used to our presence; we were quiet and amenable, two twins playing Uno in the corner, sipping Shirley Temples at a table nearby, watching TV in a den off a strange kitchen. We learned to fall asleep in coat closets and under tables; my father would carry us to waiting taxis.

My father knew all the right people and all the right places in New York, but he wasn't a snob. He was an only child, and both his parents had died before he was eighteen; this had given him an openness to life that people with parents, who try to protect their children from strangers and bad manners, do not have. He had gone to Yale, yes, but he had put himself through Yale running poker games, then made his success as a lawyer without help from anyone, and so he still had a taste for the down-to-earth; he appreciated a rowdy piano bar, for instance, or a taxi driver who could talk Yankees with him.

Despite his career success, deep down my father remained a gambler, and eventually he could not resist moving from the staid security of his successful law practice on Madison Avenue into entrepreneurial schemes that promised him big money for little work. He was special, he believed, above an ordinary life, and so we believed it, too.

IN THE MEANTIME, Sam and I traveled once a month to Palm Beach to visit my mother and Richard and their infant son (and, later, their daughter). Frequent fliers by age nine, we became versed in the protocol for unaccompanied minors on airplanes: we preferred Delta because they gave us coloring books and wings to pin on our shirts; if we sat next to adults, we dutifully answered their questions as they tried brightly to muster the encouragement to chat with us before folding into their books, our twinness at least adding some novelty to the conversation. ("So, what's it like being a twin?" was the leading icebreaker; Sam, in response, while jerking a thumb at me: "It stinks"; followed by "Do you feel pain if the other twin is hurt?"; Sam, while pinching me: "Let me see. Um, no.") We remained patiently seated after the plane landed until the stewardess led us to the gate, where my mother would be waiting. No matter how, over the years, I thought I might have gotten used to the separation, every time I saw her familiar outline standing there waiting for us—*My mother! At last!*—her dark hair framing her face, her big smile, my throat closed up with the pain of missing her, and then my heart flew out of my chest to her, and I smiled and ran into her arms, happy and safe for one moment, enveloped by her Jean Naté smell.

Richard and the children would be waiting for us at the big white house, where Sam and I even had our own room and connecting bathroom, quite a grown-up room, I thought proudly, with flowered wallpaper, raw-silk curtains, and towels monogrammed with our initials. (It was a few years until I realized the room was not entirely ours: I found more towels under the sink in our bathroom; they were monogrammed, just like ours, but with the word GUEST.) The house had its own lingering smell, the way some houses do, and to me it was always the smell of *baby*; even after their two children (Richard junior, called Ricky, and Georgina, both perfectly nice, sweet children) grew out of diapers, the house always smelled, to me, just faintly, of baby powder, baby oil, soft baby skin.

But we never spent much time with our half-siblings. As soon as we arrived, even as they stood waiting for us at the threshold of the huge white house, Ricky and Georgina would be handed off to the nanny, relegated to the background, almost as if my mother wanted us to see her physically disassociate herself from them. During the transition, as my mother pulled away from them and trained herself on us, she literally seemed to grow in stature, becoming, for us alone, a giant, the übermother, trying to imprint us with the experience of having a mother in the short time we had, homing in on us with a laserlike intuition for what we needed, then swinging instantly into action, providing us with anything and everything on the spot: a new bathing suit would be waiting on my bed; copies of our textbooks would appear on our bookshelves so we wouldn't have to lug them back and forth; the refrigerator would be stocked with our current favorite foods.

"If your mother doesn't do it for you," she would say as she bought me a new toothbrush or told me which clothes I should wear for school photos, "who will?" It was a valid question. My father, everyone acknowledged, had always been more about the big picture; he failed to grasp such parenting details as the necessity of new underwear or the advance purchase of Halloween costumes; we regularly ended up, for instance, rushing out to Rite Aid at five o'clock on Halloween to buy the lone plastic superhero costumes left on the rack, invariably two sizes too small for us.

In Palm Beach we therefore spent much of what little time we had with our mother running errands, eating three square meals a day, and generally cramming ourselves full of health and learning. We went shopping for school clothes and got measured for new shoes; we had swimming lessons at the country club and piano lessons in the living room; we ate fruits and vegetables; we had cavities filled and braces tightened and annual checkups with a Palm Beach pediatrician. While we were there I had a taste again of a normal life, one in which there was always milk in the refrigerator and grilled cheese and tomato soup waiting at lunch. There were rules about how much television we could watch, and every morning my mother brushed my long dark hair and twisted it into French braids if I asked her to.

I knew, without anyone having to tell me, that these chores made my mother happy, sensed that in fact she was at her happiest when we were with her, when she could witness us gorging on mothering for the weekend. Her happiness stemmed not from being with us per se but from the fact that being with us gave her a chance, once each month, to try to make up for what she had done.

At the close of a weekend, as our departure approached, I would cry and cling to her, and my despondence would make her desperate to get out from under her own blame. My father was an easy target. "This is so unfair," she would whisper to me fervently as Sunday evening approached, stroking my hair as we sat together in a lounge chair out by the pool. "He doesn't deserve you. He only wanted you to get back at me for leaving him."

It wasn't surprising, then, that when I left my mother it always took me a little while to orient back toward my father. Back in New York, for several days after a visit, I looked at him suspiciously, wondering if what my mother had said was true. I stayed in my room reading, ignoring him. I spoke to him only when he spoke to me. Over time, especially as my mother's resentment grew and my parents began to communicate solely through my father's secretary or Sam and me (usually via notes we ferried in our backpacks), my father began to see what was happening, and he grew used to my coolness after a visit to Palm Beach. Picking us up at the airport, he would take my sullen hand, drive us home, and tuck us into bed, waiting patiently for my distrust of him to blow over. "I love you, Lacey," he'd say as he kissed me good night, somehow understanding what he was up against. "That's why I fought so hard to keep you."

I didn't care. I wanted my mother. Besides the one weekend a month, we spent every other Thanksgiving, Christmas, and spring break with my mother and Richard, and at the end of every trip, when it came time to leave her, it was like going through it for the first time all over again: the pain washed over me anew, and my heart, rooted deeply into my mother's soil once again, felt like it had been ripped out. On the plane ride home I cried and cried, Sam silently holding my hand, the only time he ever had to take care of me.

THE PHONE RANG on my thirteenth birthday. It was a bright fall afternoon, and I was standing in the kitchen with my boyfriend. My father was not home, Sam was up in his room, and we had just emerged from the darkness of the basement playroom after an hours-long make-out session. Up in the kitchen we were pouring bowls of cereal and adjusting to daylight. I answered the phone.

"Happy birthday, baby," my mother cried. "Now you can come live with me."

Ever since my mother had left, she had been telling Sam and me that when we turned thirteen, we could legally come to Palm Beach and live with her. At that age, she said, the judge would let us decide for ourselves, no matter what my father wanted. I do not know whether this was true under the law, or whether that old judge might have made a different decision had we gone to see him then, but I do know that at that moment I realized I had changed: at age thirteen, I did not want to go and live with my mother.

"Thanks," I said into the phone. "But I'm going to boarding school next year."

"You are?" my boyfriend said, the Lucky Charms box frozen in his hand.

I nodded at him. I had just come up with the idea in the moment, but I was already sure. Some of my friends' older siblings had gone to boarding school, and they came home for vacations light-years cooler than their former class-mates, listening to CSNY, knowing how to smoke pot out of Coke cans, wearing flowy Indian-print skirts. As if it were a revelation, I realized boarding school was the solution to everything.

I don't remember consciously not choosing my mother on my thirteenth birthday, though of course this must have played into my decision. Certainly, in the back of my mind, I must have felt something akin to *Well, you left me when I was a child, when I needed you most; I'm not coming back to you now.* But perhaps it was simply that I did not want to have to choose between my parents again. More than anything, I just wanted to get away from the two of them, from the back-and-forth and the tug-of-war, from never knowing where I truly belonged.

I researched and applied to boarding schools, my father weighing in when I asked for his advice. I was accepted by a few, then chose the one I liked best, a small school in Massachusetts. The following September I said good-bye to Sam, feeling a mixture of guilt at leaving him behind and relief that I would no longer be responsible for him, and my father drove me up to the school and moved me into my dorm. The school had a friendly, warm vibe: the competition was low, the teachers were gentle, and the students were from small towns and stable families. There I met girls who would become life-long friends, I dated nice boys, I did well academically, and I finally felt I belonged. High school was, as it had been for my mother, the happiest time of my life.

That autumn day months earlier, my thirteenth birthday, was of course also Sam's birthday. After I told my mother I was going to boarding school, she asked to speak with Sam. I yelled to him to pick up, and then I stayed on the line in the kitchen while she wished him a happy birthday and repeated her invitation to a new life in Palm Beach. My brother said no, too, but he did not offer an explanation.

"Thanks," he said simply, "but no thanks."

AFTER I WENT AWAY to school, Sam grew angrier. He wasn't interested in school and his teachers were even less interested in him. He had pissed off all his friends, and girls were nonexistent. My dad didn't understand him; he urged Sam to take up a sport when he preferred to hide in the basement and play video games, or to study harder when he found everything in school pointless. When Sam was sixteen he took a swing at my father, who, taken by surprise, reflexively swung back and knocked out one of Sam's front teeth.

I got the call that night in my dorm at 2 A.M., my bleary-eyed housemaster who was also my English teacher shaking me in my bed. I remember the strange intimacy of her appearing in my room in her white eyelet nightgown; even in the dark I felt I should look away. Her voice was raspy. "Your brother says it's an emergency," she said, then disappeared. Fumbling in the darkness,

I went downstairs to the common room, curled into the alcove where we kept the dorm phone, groped for the receiver.

"Hey, Lace," said Sam, trying to make his voice sound gruff. He told me what had happened. My father had promised him weeks earlier that he could use the car to drive his friends to a concert. My father, not so surprisingly, had forgotten his promise, staying in the city for dinner until midnight, along with the car. My brother and his friends had tried instead to take the train to the concert and had been left stranded when the train stopped running at 11 P.M. After my brother and father both arrived home around 1 A.M. they'd fought, and afterward, when they saw that Sam was bleeding and his tooth was missing, my father had tried to force him into the car so he could take him to the emergency room, but Sam had fled. Now he was calling me from a phone booth outside the commuter train station in our town.

"What are you doing there?" I said.

"Can I come stay with you?" he said. I almost thought I could hear a lisp from where his tooth was missing. "In the morning I could take a train into the city and then get one to Boston."

Sitting there in my warm dorm, the silence pulsing in the night, my friends tucked away and sleeping in tiny rooms all around me, I imagined what taking in my brother would entail: sneaking him into my room, explaining his presence to my roommate, smuggling him food from the dining hall three times a day, making a bed of pillows for him every night on the floor. I would probably be suspended if anyone found out.

"Sure," I said faintly, trying hard to sound so.

He was silent for a moment. Could he hear the tentativeness in my voice?

"Sam?" I said. "Come. We'll figure it out."

"I could go to Mom's," he said.

"Have you called her?"

"No," he said, and I knew why: he was scared of her answer. She had asked us to come to Palm Beach, and we had said no. Since then she had turned icy.

"Do you have any money?" I said.

"I took five hundred dollars from Dad's cash drawer," he said defiantly.

"Come up here then," I said, feeling more sure somehow, perhaps because he had money. "Take the train to Boston. Call me in the morning and tell me what train. I'll meet you at the station." Already I didn't know how I would enact even that much of the plan. Leave school during a weekday?

I couldn't; it wasn't allowed. Sneak off without asking permission? That was a serious offense; I would risk being suspended. Hire a taxi to take me to the T? That was fifty dollars—my entire allowance for the month. "Come," I said anyway.

"I will," he said.

"It's all going to be okay," I said. "Really. It seems bad now because it's nighttime."

"Thanks," he said.

He hung up, and I pictured him slipping the receiver back into its cradle and then looking around. I imagined how he would feel after he had lost the connection with me, alone in the cold, spotlit under a street lamp outside the deserted train station—the same place where a year before a delinquent-type kid from our high school had been killed walking on the train tracks late at night, accidentally stepping on the third rail in the darkness, the same tracks Sam and I had crossed one afternoon afterward on a double dare, scared out of our minds that we'd make contact and fry, elated once we'd made it to the other side, immortal and untouchable. Picturing him now, I thought irrationally of my brother as homeless—irrational because he had a roof and a place to sleep not two miles from the train station—but then I realized with a jolt that he wasn't far from it.

My dad called me at school the next day.

"Sam left," he said. "Do you know where he is?"

"No," I said.

My mom called the day after.

"Your brother's run away," she said. "Do you know where he's gone off to?"

"No," I said.

I didn't hear from Sam the next day, or the next, and then I called my parents, and they were both angry with me for lying to them, and still we didn't hear from him, and I was on the verge of leaving school to go search the Boston train station when Sam called, a week after we'd last spoken. He was in Breckenridge, Colorado. A friend's older brother had been planning to drive cross-country, and Sam had hitched a ride with him at the last minute, the day after we'd spoken.

"Sorry I didn't call you back," he said. "The guy was trying to make it across the country in four days, and he wouldn't let me out to piss, never mind use the phone." When they'd finally stopped to spend the night in Breckenridge, Sam had decided to stay. Everyone there was young and rootless and trying to lose themselves on the ski slopes. There was a bar in town where Rolling Stones cover bands played and people came to dance and flirt and find someone to sleep next to for a night.

"I got a job there as a barback," Sam said, adding proudly, "I'm making $4.50 an hour."

"Okay," I said. "Okay." Sitting in the dorm phone booth again, late at night again, I could tell I was trying to remain calm, not for Sam but for myself. I could feel my heart beating, my chest constricting in panic. I knew where my brother was now, but instead of feeling relieved, I felt scared. He had somehow landed out there, in a limbo land of ski bums and atrophied ambition, and it seemed he was going to stay. This wasn't how Sam's story was supposed to go. This wasn't how any sixteen-year-old's story was supposed to go. He was supposed to be in school, coming home at night to a family. But my mom had left, and my dad had been gone most of the time, and then, I realized with a shock of horror, I had left, too. It had barely even occurred to me. I'd acted to take care of myself, because no one else was going to do it—but in the process I'd abandoned my brother. I clawed at a way to get him back on track.

"Do you want to come out here?" Sam was saying now. "You could live with us"—he'd moved in with some of the bartenders and was sleeping on their couch—"and get a job as a waitress."

If I did that, I thought, would I be able to stop him, get him to come home and go back to school? I pictured it, living with my brother and his friends, waitressing at this bar every night, working a ski lift during the day, coming to know a whole town full of people who'd decided to check out for a while. I would become an expert skier, meet new people, start a new life. It could be fun. I imagined the reactions at school: "Did you hear about Lacey? She's taking a year off to go out west and ski."

There was a girl who'd dropped out of school the year before to follow the Grateful Dead. Other students would run into her at concerts from time to time, and their reports would filter back to us: she was making money selling burritos and braided bracelets in the parking lot, wearing the ritual Birkenstocks and Indian-print shirts, bracelets covering one arm, her hair twisted into a knot of long blond dreadlocks. She was spoken of in reverential tones.

So young, and she already knew what she wanted, was already willing to take a risk and leave the security of school, of a clear path. None of us, we agreed, would be bold enough to do something like that.

Now, as my brother waited on the line, I thought: Am *I*?

I thought of what I'd be giving up in order to try to save my brother: my friends, teachers who actually cared about me, my cozy room with my books and my flannel sheets and my Georgia O'Keeffe posters, the high-ceilinged dining hall with its vats of milk and honey, the warm library, always over-heated in winter, where I often fell asleep stretched out on a couch reading. And what about my future? What would happen if I left all this, even for a year, even for six months? Would I still get into a good college? Would I even be able to go to college?

I sighed. "I can't right now, Sam," I said finally.

He was silent.

"Maybe I'll come out this winter."

"Uh-huh," he said.

"Maybe I'll come out over Christmas," I said.

"Uh-huh."

"Or maybe you'll come home for Christmas."

"Maybe," he said and already his voice was icy, too, like my mother's when we'd told her no. "I gotta go," he said. " I have to get to work."

He didn't call me again. The next day I tried to find him. I called a few bars in town, but no one had heard of him. I told my parents where he was, and my dad said he'd try to get in touch with him, but I knew he wouldn't be able to track him down on the phone. They'd have to go out there and talk some sense into him. I kept waiting for either of my parents to tell me they were going to fly out there and get him, but they never did. *Huh,* I thought. *So this is how little it would take for me to disappear.*

IT WAS AROUND THIS TIME, just after Sam left home, in the middle of my years away at school, that my father lost all his money. After that he became less spe-cial, in the sense that the bank foreclosed on our house, he could no longer go to the places that money affords one access to, and many of his more socially acceptable friends stopped calling (that old cliché is true, he discovered). My father fell upon evil times, as he put it (although his fall had not so much to do with the morality of the times as with his decision to invest heavily in speculative real estate in Texas just as the market blew up), when I was sixteen and a sophomore in high school, and at the time I did not understand why he could no longer pay my school tuition, or buy me new fall clothes, or dole out my monthly allowance. My mother reluctantly stepped in to do these things instead.

Two years later, when my father fled the country to avoid going to prison for tax evasion, my mother stepped in then, too, sending me checks from Palm Beach and advising me to cut my father out of my life, as she had. She paid the bills when I went to Yale as a legacy, and then I supported myself after graduation as a temp at an ad agency, renting a studio apartment in Alphabet City.

By the time my father had returned from his exile in the Turks and Caicos—tan, magically flush with cash again, and clutching a deal from the prosecutor's office that allowed him to avoid prison time by paying a hefty fine—I was twenty-two and I had learned how to fend for myself. My father knew he would never be able to tell me what to do again. Yet—and this is, I believe, the most accurate way to describe it—we remained friends.

THE NIGHT AFTER our engagement and my thirtieth birthday party, Toby went off with friends to do stand-up at one of his old haunts and I had dinner alone with my father. I met him at Carmine's on Forty-fourth Street, where he'd already befriended a middle-aged touristy-looking group sitting at the end of the bar.

"This, my friends," he said when I arrived, sweeping me into a sideways hug, "is my daughter."

"Oh!" they cried. "Congratulations! We've heard all about you. Let us see the ring!"

My father had recently turned sixty-four, though he has never looked his age. He is very attractive and has been since he was a teen (I've seen his prom pictures, too). He is six foot three and broad, with salt-and-pepper hair, and his style is multicolor preppy, Brooks Brothers on acid. On this night, for instance, he was wearing pink linen pants with a green sport coat. At the party the night before, he'd had on a bright purple Hermès shirt and an orange tie with matching socks. At Christmas his green corduroys have red candy canes embroidered on them. He's got a big smile and a great sense of humor, and he can charm anyone into anything.

"I'll be in touch, Margaret, darling," he said then to one of the women he'd been talking to at the bar—she was blond, mid-forties, attractive. I saw that her eyes were shining back at him, and I felt a twinge of sympathy for her. Perhaps he would call her, perhaps they would go on several dates, perhaps they would even take a romantic trip somewhere exotic if he happened to be particularly flush at the moment, but either way, it would not last. There were, unfortunately for Margaret, so many other women to meet, and in so many ways.

I don't know what happened, what went awry so that my father cannot stay with one woman who loves him or one job that pays his bills. He seeks other things: the late-night drink, the party in the back room, what's around the next corner. These things often get him into trouble. Since returning from his exile in the islands, he has lost all his money again, won it back, then lost it all again, and again and again and again; there have been drunk-driving episodes, calls from the SEC, repossessed cars, and periods when he did not have a phone number. I have shared strange meals in strange places with people who seem terrifyingly close to characters from *The Sopranos*.

Yet one would never know it to look at him. He once belonged to country clubs, after all, and he still looks the part, so everyone—women, the police, the innocents he gets to invest in his schemes—all of them think, "This guy? Well, this guy looks like he has a house in Nantucket and a Park Avenue apartment. Of course I can trust this guy."

And, to be fair, it isn't that they cannot trust him. My father truly believes in his own ventures. He is not trying to take money from anyone; in fact, if he has it, you're welcome to it. He just wants to make more of it quickly, and so he will listen to anyone who claims to be able to help him do that.

THE NIGHT AFTER the engagement, for instance, when we sat down at our table and I asked him what he'd been up to lately, he said, "Well, let me tell you, Lace, I have a big deal that's closing on Tuesday. Very big. By this time next Tuesday, your father will be a millionaire. In fact, I'm leaving for the islands tomorrow to scout out my dream house."

His deals are always supposed to close on Tuesday, but they never do.

Something always goes awry, yet he remains faithful. "Well, the money is there," he will say on Wednesday, "but there was some problem in Mumbai at the wire center, so now it's looking like Friday."

Still, on this night I could instantly see that he had some money. Whenever he had it—and I preferred not to know how or where he got it—he spent it. The newfound cash might all be gone by morning, but at least he'd had the spending rush. There was nothing to be done about this. I had talked to him time and time again about the virtues of a savings account, health insurance, security. He pretended to listen, then ordered caviar. In the end the only thing to do was hold on and enjoy the ride while there was still gas in the car.

This night was a pretty typical evening if my father had just received an influx: a hotel room at the Plaza, a car and driver, a front-row-center seat at the theater, a late dinner afterward at Carmine's. We almost always ate at Carmine's when my father had money, just the two of us, even though it was a family-style restaurant; by the end of the night we'd be surrounded by platters of too much pasta and spinach and chicken parmigiana.

We enjoyed eating together; I'd tell him about my love life, he'd tell me about his. My father rarely dated one person for very long, so more often than not he was between women, and alone. In fact, I sometimes wondered if people thought I was not his daughter, but his date; he looked like the kind of man who dated women half his age. Yet they rarely thought it for long, because he loved to introduce me to people, and when he did, I sometimes saw them smile with relief as they got it—*Oh, she's his daughter!*

For instance, now he said to the waitress, "This, madam, is my daughter. She just got engaged. I think champagne is in order, don't you?"

When she brought it, my father raised his glass. "To Toby," he said. "A lucky man."

"Thanks, Dad."

"Tell me how you knew he was the one," he said. "People say they just know. I wish I would know. I've never experienced it. It's a feeling that's always eluded me."

"Didn't you feel it with Mom?" I asked.

"Well, then it's a feeling that's eluded me since your mother." He took a sip of his drink and waited for me to talk about Toby.

My father did not know Toby that well yet. I had moved to Los Angeles to live with Toby somewhat impulsively. We'd hit it off instantly that night we met at the comedy club, staying up all night in the back of an Irish pub on Forty-second Street, giggling quietly and holding hands. He dropped me off at my apartment in a cab as dawn broke over the city. He was leaving to go home to L.A. that day, but before the cab pulled away he asked what I was doing the next weekend, saying he wanted to fly back to New York to see me.

We spent that whole next weekend in his hotel bed, going out only late at night, famished, to dark bars downtown, eating ravenously and talking until 3 A.M. "Where do you want to go on our honeymoon?" he asked me late one night in bed, and in that moment I fell in love. We quickly began a routine of flying across the country every few weeks to visit each other. If Toby's life in Hollywood intrigued me, then my familiar East Coast roots—he'd grown up in Philadelphia—probably reassured him and made him believe I might be someone of substance, especially compared with the models and actresses he was meeting. At times I wondered what would become of us, whether it was wise to be somewhat casually dating someone long-distance when all my friends were getting engaged and settling down with their longtime boyfriends in New York. At times I wondered what Toby and I were doing. We didn't have all the time in the world anymore, after all; it was time to take life seriously; we were twenty-nine, or as Toby put it, "on the cusp of our thirties." Yet I felt reluctant to commit to him, perhaps because, despite his questions about our honeymoon, I wasn't sure if he wanted to commit to me.

On September 11, 2001, I was in New York, at my newsroom in midtown, and Toby was home in L.A. We couldn't get through to each other on our cell phones, but I e-mailed him to tell him I was okay. The downtown block where my apartment was had been cordoned off, I wrote, and the area was being evacuated. My father was in the islands, and I hadn't been able to get through to any of my friends in the city. I was going to start walking uptown and then knock on some of their doors.

Toby took control. *What shoes are you wearing?* he typed. *Heels,* I wrote back, confused. *Go buy yourself some sneakers,* he wrote, *because you can't walk all that way in heels. And if you can't get in touch with your friends, then you can go to my friend Adam's apartment uptown. He's home and he'll know who you are.*

I did as he said. I found a store that was open and bought the first pair of sneakers I saw—gray and red and made for running—and then I walked, alongside people covered in dust, thirty blocks to Adam's apartment. I met Adam, who like Toby was a comic. He was on this day not funny at all: he was tall and dark and silent. We hugged, and he had some people over—all New Yorkers our age, all friends of Toby's—and we all hugged, even though we'd never met before. That night I fell asleep on the floor alongside people who had been strangers but now were not, my red and gray sneakers still on, the towers falling over and over again on the glowing television.

Four days later, as soon as the airports opened up, I flew to L.A. There had been bomb threats at the L.A. airport, so they wouldn't let cars pick people up at the terminal, and I had to take a shuttle bus to a parking lot a few miles away that they'd turned into a makeshift receiving area. It was raining. As the bus approached I could see a large group waiting. Everyone stood under a big white tent except for Toby. He was out in the rain, standing in the middle of the street, looking for me. When I stepped off the bus he snatched me and lifted me off the ground, burying his head in my chest, hugging me so tightly that I burst into tears. Finally he pulled back to look at me. He was crying, too, now. "Don't ever leave me again," he said—and I didn't. We flew back to New York two weeks later, put most of the furniture from my tiny studio out on the street, and packed up my clothes. I quit my job and sold my bicycle. I felt like a traitor for leaving the city, but I couldn't help it. I was waking up drenched with sweat from nightmares, crying in my sleep. He was the only place where I felt safe.

Now I thought about Toby and why I had done that, why I had fallen in love with him so quickly. It was a visceral feeling, had mainly to do with how he smelled and how he smiled and how he said my name when he curled into me at night, the way he made it sound like I was the last decent thing alive in this world. His dark hair, flecked with premature gray, was on the longer side, curling over his ears, and when it went a few days unwashed, which it often did, I loved to breathe in his smell. When I climbed on top of him on the couch and hugged his whole body—at home in front of the TV he was often cocooned, all bundled up in flannel pajamas and a sweatshirt—his own smell mingled with the cigarettes and pot he smoked, and it was a smell so familiar to me, so much like the boys I had known in boarding school, that I felt comforted, as though I were back at the school I had loved, where I had felt so at home, once again.

But now, at Carmine's, I didn't know how to tell my father all this, and he was waiting. I struggled to boil Toby's appeal down to a few talking points.

"Well, he makes me laugh, first of all."

"Yes, you've certainly got number two down," my father said.

My father had a theory for what makes love work. There are certain things one needs for a relationship to succeed, he believed. Whenever I asked him what made him such an expert, seeing as he hadn't remarried after my mother, he said that all these things were very hard to find in one person. But he vowed that once he found all those things in one perfect woman, he'd get married again. Until then he preferred to hone his theory of love.

According to my father, the number one thing a couple had to have was loyalty and trust. Number two was a shared sense of humor. Number three was that you had to enjoy spending time alone together. After that it was up for debate, so we often debated it. I often said number four was respect for each other, while he often said it was appreciation for one another but it changed, and that was the fun of it. He'd say, for instance, after a good date, "Have I got a new number four for you, Lace: *similar goals*. What do you think about that?" But before any of these things, before even loyalty, at the very base of things, like the number zero, was chemistry. "If you don't have that," my father would say, "forget it."

"Toby and I have good chemistry," I said, "and I respect him. He made his way on his own from doing stand-up comedy in no-name New York bars to writing for a network TV show in Hollywood."

"And what about number one?"

"I trust him," I said, "of course. I have no reason not to."

"So you would say that all the major factors are in place," my father said.

"I would."

"Well, then, my job is done," he said, smiling. "I've finally married you off."

Then we spoke of our wedding plans—Toby and I would marry the following summer in Vermont, where Toby's mother had a summer house—and of my father's latest deal; he was confident this one would come through.

Eventually the food arrived, and we sat surrounded, as usual, by platters of too much food. I heaped chicken and pasta onto a plate and passed it to my father.

"Have you talked to Sam lately?" I said.

My brother had not attended my thirtieth-birthday party the night before; I had not expected him to. Last I'd heard, he was running a heli-skiing tour in Zermatt. He got helicopters to drop him and his clients on the tops of mountains so they could be the first to ski down fresh snow.

My father shook his head.

"Well, if you speak to him, will you ask him to come home for the wedding?" I said. "I know it's a long way, but I really want him to be there."

My father shifted uncomfortably in his chair. In adulthood, my father and Sam had an on-again, off-again relationship. I was never sure whether the lines of communication between them were open or closed. Sam and I, too, had not spoken in several months. Last time I called it was just to check in and make sure he was still alive; we spoke for a few minutes over a crackly connection—I pictured him at the top of a ski slope on his cell phone, the wind blowing. "Tell Mom I'll call her soon," he'd yelled, then said good-bye.

"Well," I said now, "if you and Sam aren't talking, don't worry about it. I'm going to call him anyway."

"No, it's not that," my father said. "I have something to tell you. I was waiting until after the party."

"What?"

"Sam is . . . missing."

My heart started to beat fast. "Missing on the mountain?"

"No, no. We just don't know where he is. He seems to have just taken off."

I exhaled. "But that's not unusual. He's always off doing his own thing."

"Yes, well, apparently now he has a girlfriend."

I raised my eyebrows. Sam had never been one for dating, even as an adult.

"This girl called your mother from Switzerland. She hasn't heard from Sam in over a month."

"Well, he'll turn up. This is just the way he is. She'll have to get used to that if she wants to date him." I took a sip of my drink.

My father looked at me. "She's pregnant," he said. "And she's keeping it."

My heart surged. In many ways, despite our being twinned, I felt so separate from Sam, but in this instant it almost felt like I was going to have a child, too. I looked at my dad. "Does Sam know he's going to be a father?" I said. "If she can find him, and tell him—"

My father nodded grimly. "He knows. He ran off a week after she told him."

THE LAST TIME I'd seen Sam was two years earlier, in Deer Valley, Utah, where he'd gone to train ski instructors. That's how good a skier he'd become over the years: resorts hired him to teach their instructors how to teach. "Stupid fucks," Sam had said, laughing. I flew out and met him when he was done with his gig at one of the resorts, and we skied for a couple of days on our own. He showed off for me, leaping wildly off high jumps and leading me at top speed down winding paths through the trees. We ate well, skied well, and went to bed early, sharing a room with twin beds. Before we fell asleep we'd talk in the darkness, the moon shining into the room.

The last night we were together it began to snow. As we lay in our beds and watched the snow coming down in the moonlight, I began to feel melancholy about heading back to New York. In the dark I confessed to my brother that I was anxious about how my life was unfolding. I'd recently, and somewhat abruptly, left my job as an English teacher at a prestigious high school on the Upper East Side with no prospects for another job. Out of financial desperation as well as a growing voyeuristic interest in lives that were not my own, I'd taken an entry-level job as a reporter at a small weekly newspaper—a questionable career move this late in my twenties, as I was now making twenty-three thousand dollars a year, barely enough to cover my rent, and I didn't see how I was going to start making more any time soon. A few nights earlier, I'd picked a fight for no reason with a guy I'd been dating for a few months, and the next morning he'd left my apartment without saying good-bye, and now he wasn't returning my calls. And all my friends, it seemed to me, were paired up and doing couples things all the time, dinner parties and weekends away at B and Bs. I was lonely, I told my brother.

"Join the club," said Sam. "This weekend with you is the first real connection I've had with anyone in months."

I was taken aback. I'd imagined Sam's life in Colorado as carefree and light, full of good times and good friends. I'd never imagined him as lonely. But before I could process this, he made another confession: he was partying a lot, drinking too much, staying up late, and doing drugs—mainly coke and speed—to stay awake on the slopes during the day.

I sat up in bed. "How long have you been doing drugs?" I said.

"A few months, I guess."

"Well, you have to stop."

He shrugged. "It's all I have," he said. "That and skiing. And the coke makes the skiing better."

I pictured his life in a flash, skiing all day, every day, his nights spent in that same bar for the past ten years. Maybe he *was* lonely.

"What about girls?" I said. "Dating?"

"What's the point?"

"What do you mean?"

"You date so you can get married and have kids," he said. "And I am never getting married."

"Come on," I said. "You're twenty-seven years old. You can't decide that now."

"I've seen enough. Even when they were supposedly happily married, Dad was cheating on Mom and Mom was pining for her old prom date."

"Yeah, well, that was them."

He snorted. "Don't kid yourself," he said. "That's *us*."

"What about kids?" I said. "You're going to have kids, aren't you?"

"Are you serious, Lace?" he said. "You better think long and hard about that decision. We are too fucked up to be parents."

That quieted me. Sam eventually drifted off, but I couldn't sleep, thinking about his words. Yes, life was less than perfect right now, but I didn't feel *fucked up*. Then again, perhaps all my problems were simply lying dormant; perhaps they would explode to the surface like lava when I tried to make a happy life for myself down the line. I lay awake for a long time watching the snow fall. It kept on coming down all night, and finally the softness of the world outside lulled me to sleep.

When we awoke everything was white. We were supposed to fly out that morning, but Sam shook me from sleep at 6 A.M.—"Bam!" he shouted giddily, pulling back the curtain to reveal several feet of snow—and we smiled and jumped out of bed. At Sam's gleeful urging we called the airlines and pushed back our flights, and Sam convinced the lift operator, by now a friend, to let us get on before it opened. We rode the lift, just the two of us, up over the white hills, to the very top of the mountain, and we stood there, our skis pointing down. The mountain sparkled below us. We were alone together at the beginning of everything, with fresh snow for new tracks. I felt a lump rising in my throat; how gorgeous the world was, and how much potential we still had. We could still be happy; we could still have good lives. I turned to tell my brother this, but just then he lifted his poles in a salute to the mountain, clapped them together above his head, and jumped. I watched him zigzag across the mountain's face, and then I did the same, following his tracks all the way down.

Near the bottom I could see him smiling as he waited for me, and I skied down to him. "You know what," I said in a rush of exhilaration. "Maybe I'll move out to Colorado. I'm ready to leave New York. We could have some fun together. And you could stop all that stuff, go to NA or something. I could even go with you. You're going to be okay, Sam. I promise."

His smile faded and he looked at me with a flash of anger, then pity. "You know what," he said. "I wouldn't worry so much about me, Lacey. I'm doing fine. If I were you, I'd worry about yourself. Driving your boyfriend away, quitting your job, losing your friends? The way I see it, you're the one who's going to need saving."

He skied away. I stood there, shaken. I wasn't sure where his anger had come from, and he was twisting my words: I hadn't driven my boyfriend away (had I?), and I did so have friends, good friends—but then I stopped. That wasn't why I was shaken. It was because I felt like he knew something about me that I didn't, like I had a curse on me, like he was seeing into my future. I skied away from the lift and went inside to the hotel room, and I didn't ski for the rest of the day. Sam and I said good-bye with false hugs, and I didn't look back when I boarded my plane.

After that weekend we didn't talk as much. It was my fault. I was scared of what his words could do to me.

Now I looked at my father. I didn't want to tell him what Sam had told me two years earlier—that he had never wanted kids, never wanted a wife. There was nothing we could do about it now. Sam was gone, again. We had lost him, again. This time I would not try to save him.

"He'll come around," my father said, and I nodded.

The evening was almost over. Dessert had arrived, and we sipped our decaf. We spoke about when my dad might come to L.A. for a visit, or when I might come home again to see him.

"How long do you think you're going to stay out there?" my father said.

"You mean, in L.A.?" I said. "Well, forever. I mean, that's where Toby's work is. He's a TV writer."

"Right," he said, and then we were quiet for a moment. "Look here," he said abruptly, and his face turned serious. "Are you sure about this, Lacey?"

I looked up. "What do you mean? About Toby? We're getting married, Dad. Yes, I'm sure." I could hear the instant anger in my voice, feel it surging, the way it did whenever my parents questioned my choices: *Don't tell me what to do. Don't offer me advice. I did fine without you growing up; I'm doing fine now.*

"I'm not trying to upset you," he said.

"Okay," I said.

He sat back heavily in his chair. "I understand wanting to leave home," he said. "I was very glad to leave home and go to college. Very glad."

I knew this story. After his father died when he was eight, his mother grew dependent on him, wanting him home every night for dinner, asking his advice on matters romantic and financial, even wanting him to come with her on her dates. "She idolized me," he said now. "She leaned on me. Too much really. It wasn't fair."

"But then you went away to Yale," I said. "And you got a little freedom."

He waved his hand. "She came up and visited all the time. It was absurd. My friends commented on it. *Does your mother want to enroll?* Finally, when I saw the chance to get away from her, I took it."

I had heard snippets of this story, too. He went to Rome for the fall semester junior year. His mother wanted him to come home for Thanksgiving, but he said no; he would be home in a few weeks for Christmas. They argued on the phone. It ended up being the last time they spoke. A day before Thanksgiving, he got a telegram: CALL HOME. When he did, his aunt answered his mother's phone, and he knew before she told him that his mother was dead. A brain hemorrhage. She'd been unconscious in her apartment for two days before anyone found her.

"I'll never forget it," he said to me now. "The guilt."

"You didn't know," I said. "You'd have come home for Thanksgiving if you'd known. You wouldn't have gone to Rome at all."

My father shook his head. "Not about that. Not about any of that. I was guilty because, on the plane ride home from Italy to my mother's funeral, I felt sad, yes, that my mother was gone—but underneath that was this feeling of

I'm finally free. I'm finally alone. I was nineteen years old. I didn't want my mother to die. But I had felt trapped for so long. And now I felt free. Maybe it was a subconscious feeling, but I remember having it."

He sipped his drink. We were quiet. I felt slightly stunned by his honesty. He had just told me that part of him was glad that his mother had died. How would I feel if my parents died? Not free. Lonelier, I thought. Emptier. Yet I could understand wanting independence as a teenager. I had broken free from my parents at that age by going to boarding school. But what about now? Was I going to L.A. partly to escape my parents? Maybe I was.

"It was only later in life that I felt guilty for leaving my mother," my father said. "After I became a father. You won't understand it until you're a parent. And now, you and Sam, well, you're off doing your own thing just like I did."

I thought of my father, an orphan at age nineteen, no siblings, no parents, having to make his way in the world alone. He'd wanted his own family so badly, and he'd created it, and then—what had happened? I didn't know why he had cheated on my mother and screwed up their marriage. This was one thing, among many, I had never asked either of them. But he had managed to lose my mother, and in that moment I realized why he had fought so hard to keep from losing Sam and me. We were all he had.

"Sam's going to turn up, Dad," I said. "He just needs some time to clear his head. And your deal's going to come through on Tuesday, and you're going to be a millionaire." I stopped. He appeared unconvinced. "I don't want to leave you," I said then. "But I have to, because I love Toby, and we're going to be happy together for the rest of our lives."

"I know," he said.

"Toby's going to take good care of me," I said.

"He better."

"I know."

We were both resigned to what would be, and so we were silent for a moment. Then my father tried to brighten. "To Toby," he said one more time, with forced cheer, "a lucky man." And we raised our champagne glasses, but there was nothing left in them, not even a drop.

"More champagne, madam," my father called to the waitress, and she came to the table with the bottle. "My daughter is going to be happy for the rest of her life," he announced, "and by this time next Tuesday, I will be a millionaire."

We had another glass of champagne, chatting about his most recent date, a woman who'd bounced back from a recent divorce (number four, he felt sure now, was a positive attitude), and then we got our second wind and moved to the bar, where a small crowd of diehards still stood, chasing a good time. My father joined right in, of course—*This, my friends, is my daughter*—and by the end of the night, he'd bought a round of drinks for everyone in the place.

The next morning Toby and I flew back to L.A. to begin our life together, and my father flew to the islands to scout out his dream house. When I spoke to him the following Wednesday, his deal had not yet closed.

Jimmy James

TOBY'S NEW AGENT, Jimmy James O'Brien, had recently arrived in L.A. from Brooklyn, and he had so much confidence that he wore white linen suits, exaggerated his New York accent instead of hiding it, called everyone in town "that friggin' asshole," and, in an industry where people traded up their spouses faster than their homes, was devoted to his wife, a blond model who'd clearly been sold on Jimmy by Jimmy.

I had a hard time determining whether Jimmy was fooling everyone or really knew what he was doing, but even I had to admit that Jimmy could sell anything. He'd sold fake Rolexes on Fourteenth Street as a kid, TVs at Crazy Eddie's as a teenager, and engagement rings in New York's diamond district for ten years before finally moving to L.A. to become an agent.

His habits apparently died hard. "Sure, that's nice if you like 'em old," he observed when he glanced at my engagement ring, which had belonged to Toby's great-grandmother, circa 1860. "You ever want to trade that in for a shiny new one, you let me know."

Toby and I had met Jimmy James at a recent Summertime Party. Charlotte and Jack had stopped coming by then (apparently they had dumped Toby's boss, too, which secretly pleased me) and Toby and I were standing out on the patio smoking, having just finished a lengthy dinner with Merv and the same asshole movie star as before, who, after several drinks, had confided to me that Keira Knightley had broken his heart ("completely and utterly shattered it, man") and it had taken him almost a year to get over it. "Now, of course," he added proudly, "I'm dating Velika"—a Bulgarian supermodel whose breasts had recently starred, to great acclaim, in a layout in *Maxim*—"and I don't think Little Miss Flat Chest can compete with that, do you?"

I was breathlessly relating this conversation to Toby when Jimmy James approached and introduced himself. He was surprisingly subtle in his white linen suit, and he seemed at ease in the room. I'd seen him arrive earlier with a phalanx of other agents, all dressed in black, most of whom now stood in a pack by the bar, eyeing the celebrities in the room with obvious hunger. A few had actually ventured over to the celebrity clump and had been taken in; the others watched enviously. None of them appeared to be envious of Jimmy for talking with us.

We chatted for a moment about the party, and then Jimmy James said casually to Toby, "So, your boss is quitting late night to pursue a movie career, huh?" He was referring to the host of the party, whose career change was news to me and, from the looks of it, Toby. "Not the wisest of moves given his acting abilities," Jimmy James continued, "but what can you do with an ego like that? Anyway, tough break for you." He clucked his tongue and shook his head.

"What do you mean?" Toby said.

"New guy's bringing in a whole new writing staff, is what I heard. Poached a bunch of people from *The Onion*."

"Are you saying I'm about to be out of a job?" Toby said, stunned.

Jimmy James looked at his watch. "In about, oh, three weeks," he said. He looked up at us. "Your agent didn't tell you?"

"Well, no," Toby said.

"Well then, since he didn't even know about it, I'm assuming he also hasn't made any effort to find you a new job," Jimmy James said. "What a friggin' asshole."

Toby looked at me and then off into the distance. "Fuck," he said softly.

"Yep," Jimmy James said, as if there was nothing more to say, and there wasn't. He handed Toby his business card, and on the way home that night we discussed it.

Toby's current agent was a middling guy at a middling agency who exhibited very little awareness of Toby's existence: he rarely returned Toby's calls, and when he did, he inevitably bungled his last name, pronouncing it *Fried*man (instead of *Freed*man), as if Toby were an egg. Jimmy James not only seemed like a go-getter but, perhaps more importantly, was with one of the biggest agencies in town. If Toby signed with Jimmy, he would actually be able to say his agent was at Endeavor, a heady prospect that made us giggle with giddiness. And so the decision was easy: in the morning Toby fired his agent and hired Jimmy.

As it turned out, Jimmy had just been promoted from assistant to agent last month. In fact, he announced proudly, Toby would be his first client.

"It's you and me against the world now, kid," Jimmy James said.

"Are you serious?" Toby said. "I'm your first client? Do you even know how to do this?"

"You kidding?" said Jimmy James. "I could beat this town in my sleep. Hollywood, get ready to rumble."

It all played out exactly as Jimmy James had said it would: one week later Toby's boss announced on air that he was leaving his show to pursue an acting career; two weeks later the new guy announced he was bringing in his own writing staff, and precisely three weeks after Jimmy had predicted it, to the day, Toby was out of a job. His boss gave him two weeks severance, and Jimmy immediately took that up as the deadline for finding Toby a new job.

"Two weeks," he promised, and his urgency unsettled me. I had a hard time believing anyone could get a job in Hollywood in two weeks; it seemed impossible. But Jimmy was sure. "You'll be on a new show in fourteen days," he vowed to Toby, "or I swear to freakin' God I will leave this town forever and go back to selling fuck-me rings on Forty-seventh Street."

BY THIS TIME I had settled into L.A. Everyone says it takes at least a year to feel comfortable living in L.A. after you move from New York, and I had found this to be true. If you looked past the fact that people rarely talked about the latest Middle East peace summit or French presidential election—or, for that matter, were even aware that these events had occurred—and talked instead about movies and deals and the entertainment business, you could come to like a lot of things about L.A.

In L.A., for instance, the people our age were friendlier and more open than they were in New York. There weren't the impenetrable cliques that you found in New York, where people came to parties with certain friends and stayed with those same friends all night. In L.A., everyone was happy to meet you. Of course, that was mainly because they hoped you might be the next success story and would be able to do something for their careers, but in the end, who really cared?

"They say people are fake here," observed my friend Henry. "But they don't make you stand in the corner and feel like an asshole either."

Henry was married to my oldest and most beautiful friend, Catherine, whom I'd met back in Larchmont in nursery school. Our twenty-six-year friendship had withstood junior high cliques, a separation when I went to boarding school, even a summer backpacking trip around Europe together. (Cath was so beautiful that all summer long, men came up to her and asked her to marry them. "Go away," she was always saying in Italian or German or whatever language was appropriate, holding my hand and pulling me next to her, all to no avail. And once the alpha dog had won her attention for the night, his sidekick would inevitably drop back to settle for me, the consolation prize. It was a long summer.)

Cath had moved out to L.A. right after college to try to become an actress. She had persevered for all of six months until she realized that she saw no end to driving all over the city to walk into a room for two minutes only to get rejected. She had promptly gone back to school to get her master's in social work, and she now worked mainly with Hispanic families in East L.A. She was a very L.A. social worker. She was into things like raw food and kinetic energy, and she was constantly trying to get her families to eat organic vegetables and do yoga. But she was down to earth about it, and at times she couldn't hide her East Coast attitude. "Jesus, Juliano," she'd joke to the chef at her favorite raw-food restaurant, "can't you make this taste a little less like cardboard?"

Cath had met Henry in an acting class when she'd first moved out here six years earlier. Henry was a screenwriter and had taken the class to try to understand actors. He had almost mythic status in our eyes because six years later he was still writing the same screenplay: a semiautobiographical feel-good drama about a young man who grows up hating his chess-champion father for always beating him at chess, and then goes on an obsessive quest to become a chess champion himself so that he can one day beat his father. In the final climactic moments, during their highly anticipated match in front of thousands of people, the young man discovers his father has Alzheimer's and can no longer remember how to play. The screenplay was called *Beating Dad,* and Henry was forever asking people to read it and give him notes so he could improve it; he had done a major rewrite on it probably seventy-five times, first revamping the characters, then the plot, then the themes, then the characters again.

Henry's day job was as an assistant to a literary agent whom he despised because no matter how many times he asked, the agent wouldn't read the script and give him notes. "Not my thing," the guy said every time, and every time Henry came home pissed. "How does he know it's not his thing unless he reads it?" He woke up at 5 A.M. every day to write before going into work, and he was a huge fan of Robert McKee, the screenwriting guru, attending all of McKee's L.A. seminars and endlessly studying his books. Every time Henry came back from one of McKee's lectures he would launch into another rewrite: "Story is supreme, man," he would say, shaking his head, "McKee is so right. That's my whole problem. The story. I've got to go back to the story." He was a bit of a downer, serious and intense, too much so for Hollywood, I often thought after spending an evening with him. "Be effervescent!" advised a campy book I had read on how to succeed in Hollywood. "The town is filled with people who like to entertain, and they want to be entertained back. You must be bold, loud, and fun. If you're not, take lessons on how to be." Where did one go to get such lessons? I wondered. Was this what they learned in acting class?

Catherine and Henry were the only friends I had in L.A. when I moved, but Toby had more than made up for that. His friends were all aspiring actors and writers and musicians, funny and crazy and dark, and they made room for me in their little social circle right away. Everyone loved it when someone else from the East Coast moved to Hollywood to try to make it; it made them feel less alone at the edge of the earth, and less crazy for trying to make it themselves.

Every weekend there was a performance to attend; one of Toby's friends was always doing a new comedy act at the Laugh Factory, or playing with a band at the Viper Room, or putting on a one-act play at a tiny playhouse on Hollywood Boulevard. They were always calling Toby and me at the last minute, afraid no one would show up, begging us to come and help fill the house, and so we always went and clapped and congratulated, and then afterward we'd go to the bars that everyone goes to when they first come to L.A.: Jones and the Cat & Fiddle and the Dresden and Lola's, all packed to the gills with the transplants, the late-twenty- and early-thirty-somethings who had recently arrived.

Late night, everyone inevitably ended up back at our place for drinks or a late supper. Since we'd become engaged, Toby and I had rented a cute red cottage in the lower regions of Laurel Canyon, in the hills just above West Hollywood, and the comfort of the house, combined with the fact that I was the only girlfriend (now fiancée) in a group made up mostly of young single guys, meant we played host most of the time.

I'd cook, and Toby and his friends, many of whom were comedy writers, would entertain. They'd stand around in the kitchen telling stories, making jokes, keeping the night alive. In the living room another group would be telling another story, and as I approached, even before I knew what they were talking about, I'd begin to smile. Just the tones of their voices, edgy with anticipation for the laugh, carried me along and made me look forward to laughing. The important thing was to keep the jokes going and the laughs coming, as if they were a crowd at a concert keeping a beach ball flying high.

There was, inevitably, an element of competition around this effort, and though it kept everyone entertained, it could occasionally get tiring. There were times when I felt that Toby and his friends didn't notice me or the other women in the room as much as they did our *attention*. They intuited whether or not we were really listening without even looking at us, sensing, like dogs, whether we were anticipating the punch line. There were times when I felt I was not me, not Toby's fiancée, but a member of an audience, my house a theater.

Yet most of the time the joy I felt at our parties corresponded with the joy I felt at being with Toby, a feeling of such straight and pure delight, a rush of such love and pride, that I sometimes felt as though I was levitating to the ceiling. I felt like Charlie and his grandfather in *Charlie and the Chocolate Factory* when they float up to the top of the cage, almost too close to the razor-edged fan. The fact is that when it is good with someone who is funny, it is very, very good. It was the way I had heard my brother describe cocaine. Our nights were a lot like being on drugs. When Toby made me laugh, when he shined the bright light of his humor on me, when he laughed with me, nothing was better. I felt invincible, that we were invincible. It was hard to imagine that we weren't the happiest, luckiest couple in the world.

We were in love, and everything was before us, and during that first year that I spent in Los Angeles, our brimming happiness spilled over into the wee hours. Our parties on the patio started late and ended late, the candles burning down and everyone talking at once, someone passing around a joint, Norah Jones's timeless yet just-discovered voice the ever-present soundtrack to the night.

WE HAD A DINNER PARTY soon after Toby lost his job, and the talk around the table that night was meant to be encouraging, to cheer Toby up; everyone told funny stories of getting fired, and someone told, again, the well-worn story of a forty-something friend of a friend, a struggling screenwriter living for the past twenty years in a basement apartment in the West Hollywood flats, who had recently sold a screenplay for a million dollars. The studio had bought it "in the room," meaning the guy had walked into the meeting, pitched it, and the execs had taken it, right then and there. This was the kind of story people in L.A. loved to hear—it was proof that overnight success did happen in this town, that anything could change for the better in an instant.

"Getting fired is a blessing in Hollywood," said Cath. "It forces you into the next new thing."

"Yeah, like the unemployment line," Toby said, but he smiled.

"No," Cath said, "this will give you a chance to come up with some brilliant new idea. You'll come up with a show or write a script and Jimmy James will sell it and you'll be off on a new adventure." She looked around the table. "You know the difference between New York and L.A.?" she said for the hundredth time since I'd arrived. She hated the way everyone back east ragged on her adopted town for being plastic, and she was endlessly comparing New York to L.A., in L.A.'s favor.

"If we come up with an idea tonight," Cath announced, her eyes flashing, "we could make it happen. The wheels could be set in motion at this very table. No one would think you were crazy for pitching it, and tomorrow the idea could be a reality. In New York that would never happen."

Watching her, I believed that, too, though I wasn't sure why. There were just as many opportunities for success in Manhattan, after all. But then I thought I saw the difference. In New York people were always asking about your past: where you were from, what schools you'd gone to, who your family was. And there was security in that; your background gave you something to hold on to, something to rely on. But L.A.'s culture and economy were based not on solid ground but on thin air, not on where you had come from but on where you were going—on potential, possibility, on ideas not yet even spoken aloud. And somehow in that moment, despite Toby's career setback, or perhaps even because of it, the future rushed up close to meet me and smiled. *Anything can happen here. Anything.*

"We have news," Cath announced now, smiling, waiting a moment for effect, then turning to Henry.

"I quit my job at the agency," he said.

There came a chorus of congratulations from the table. We all hated the agent, vicariously, on Henry's behalf. "It's about time!" we cried.

"I couldn't take it another day, you know?" Henry said, half smiling, proud.

"What are you going to do now?" someone asked.

"He's going to write," Cath said proudly. "We've saved up enough so he won't have to work for six months, which is more than enough time to finish the screenplay, right, babe?"

Henry nodded. "More than enough," he said emphatically.

"And then he's going to sell it," Cath said, "and I'm going to star in it, and we're all going to be rich and famous!" Then she leaned in close to me and whispered, "Unless we have a baby first."

"Are you *trying*?" I said, surprised.

"No," she said, smiling. "But we're not *not* trying either."

I knew that Cath had been on the fence about having children because her mother was an alcoholic and her parents had dragged her through an ugly divorce, and she was worried she would damage her own kids, as she herself had been damaged. But when I asked her about this later, she shrugged and smiled a happy, guilt-free smile. "This is California," she said. "Out here everyone gets a second chance."

I LAY AWAKE THAT NIGHT after everyone left, Toby sleeping fitfully beside me, thinking about Cath's words. Toby had lost his job, yet this was the way of the world in Hollywood. Soon enough, I knew, something would happen to change everything. Everyone got, as Cath had said, a second chance. Perhaps Henry was naïve for quitting his job, but then again he could always find another job doing something else. One kept going, no matter how foolish everyone back east thought you were for forgoing security to pursue your dream, no matter how many times people repeated the statistics: it's easier to get struck by lightning than to make it in Hollywood. The people who said those things were not the dreamers; they lived their ordinary lives, their nine-to-five jobs, plodding up the ladder, with no chance for a big break. Everyone who came to L.A. believed in the possibility, perhaps even the inevitability, of their own success. They would get the audition, write the script, pitch the idea that would send them shooting to the top. We had all just turned thirty. No one entertained the concept of becoming a failed artist. This was not part of the dream.

I, OF COURSE, was only an observer of this world. I was still a reporter covering education for the same small community paper in Pacific Palisades, a wealthy neighborhood on the west side of town overlooking the ocean. My beat was the elite private schools, including charity benefits thronged with intimidating celebs, and PTA meetings packed with overinvolved moms whose husbands worked as agents and executives, most of whom were at the pinnacle of their Hollywood careers.

This small segment of the population that I followed was the established side of Hollywood, where no one was sleazy and everyone worked hard; these were the people who had made it long ago, the pillars of the community. These were not the people who left their wives for younger models or went to trendy restaurants or were photographed lounging on yachts in the south of France. These were the people behind the scenes whose ancestors had built this city, whose grandparents had donated wings to the city's major museums, whose parents had been beloved heads of studios; they were not even just Hollywood royalty, they were the bedrock of Los Angeles's elite society, the people who were here to stay. Perhaps they glanced at the newcomers, the starlets, the rising agents and the reality-show producers, but those people were so far outside their blue-blood world they might as well be living in Iowa or Mississippi or wherever it was they had come from to seek their fortune here.

The editor of my newspaper, Bob, a skinny, birdlike man with pale blond hair, thick glasses, and carpal-tunnel wrist protectors, was slightly in thrall to this ladies-who-lunch crowd. "So, who was there?" he'd ask as soon as I returned from a charity event, and I'd put my feet up on my desk and tell him what they were wearing and how they had looked and what they had said.

From Bob's point of view, the biggest story of the season was ShoeFest, a fund-raiser for an elite private school called Crosslake, where many celebs and members of the old guard sent their children. ShoeFest was essentially an outdoor shoe-sale/cocktail party, held on the school's front lawn. Prominent shoe designers such as Jimmy Choo and Manolo Blahnik, among many others, donated their shoes to the school, and then the wealthy moms came and bought them at substantially lowered prices, and the money went to Crosslake for whatever projects they were working on that year. This year, for instance, it was a new science building.

I had covered the event last year, and while I had initially been enthralled by the whole scene (it epitomized the fantasy world of L.A. to me) and by all the celebs—Michelle Pfeiffer, Brooke Shields, Felicity Huffman—I had also been slightly put off by it. All these wealthy women schmoozing, competitively grabbing shoes out from under one another at absurdly reduced prices, as if they were at Filene's Basement, all to benefit a school that already had the best of everything: an Olympic-sized pool, a gym that rivaled Equinox, including yoga and spinning classes (for high schoolers!), a computer lab filled with 250 of the latest model Macs, teachers who had graduate degrees from Ivy League schools. The students drove themselves to school in BMWs, SUVs, and Lexuses; one even arrived daily in a candy-red Porsche (the kid's father had bought himself a new one and had somehow believed it appropriate to pass the old one on to his eighteen-year-old son). This was one of the richest schools in the country; why didn't they simply raise the $30,000-a-year tuition to $35,000, which all the parents could easily pay, and hold ShoeFest for an underprivileged school district or a children's shelter? It just bugged me. It seemed like such a charade, where everyone congratulated one another for doing such good by—what?—shopping? Giving themselves a deal on expensive shoes? Sometimes, oddly, and perhaps dorkily, I made myself feel better by thinking about the 8.25 percent sales tax on each pair of shoes that at least was going to the government, perhaps, I thought optimistically, to help needier public schools.

Now ShoeFest was approaching again, and so I geared myself up for it, buying a trendy new dress and trying to remember the names of the women who were members of the PTA. Lately I had been growing restless with my beat, with all these fluffy, lightweight, nothing stories about how great the elite Pacific Palisades schools were, especially when I compared my job with those of Henry and Toby and his friends. What they were doing—risking everything to have a creative life—seemed the opposite of my steady, boring, straight-and-narrow job. And so, in a meager attempt to excite myself, to feel I was making a difference, I decided to try to give the story a different angle, one that broke down the financials of the benefit, and what the money was used for, including the taxes it raised for the state.

I called Minnie Jones, the president of the PTA and the head of ShoeFest, a blond wife of a studio head, and asked her if I could come in and look at the financials surrounding the event. She was always overly cheerful, agreeable, and solicitous around me, and why wouldn't she be? I had never written anything critical of the school. In fact we had a very cozy, friendly relationship. When I sometimes confided to her that I was envious of Toby and his friends and their creative work in Hollywood, she encouraged me to try TV writing, giving me advice on how to break in, and promising to help me if I ever wanted to try it. She often called Bob to compliment me on my stories about the school; it felt at times as if there was an unspoken understanding: the *Palisades Pal*—yes, that was actually its name—was a *nice* paper; we were all friends; we did not stoop to cover controversy.

"Of course, Lacey," she said when I asked her for the financials, "anything you need." And she handed the files over to me the next day.

A WEEK AFTER THE "everyone gets a second chance" dinner party, when Jimmy James's deadline was six days away, and I honestly felt I might murder Toby if he did not get up off the couch, Cath called to tell me she was pregnant.

I met her at the flea market on Melrose. I hugged her and congratulated her. She looked terrified. She was shaking and holding an unlit cigarette in her mouth.

"I just took the pregnancy test this morning. I never thought it would happen this fast. Look at this"—she removed the cigarette and stuck out her belly, which, obviously, did not yet look any different. "I'm already fat. Plus, I can't drink, and I can't smoke. I'm going to be huge. I've already eaten four bags of sunflower seeds, and it's only eleven A.M."

"You need to quit smoking anyway," I told her. It was her secret vice when she was stressed. Her lame efforts to hide it were endearing; even Henry pretended not to notice when she came in from "watering the plants" smelling of smoke.

"You need to quit, too," she said.

"Yes, but I'm not pregnant," I said, at which she threw up her hands and moaned.

"This is a horrible time for this to happen," she said. "Henry just left his job, and I just got assigned a new family from El Salvador and their youngest has like eight different kinds of learning disabilities. He'll never survive without me."

"You have nine whole months to take care of them, Cath, and besides," I added sagely, as if I knew what I was talking about, "there's never a right time to get pregnant. You have to take that leap of faith."

"But I was just doing it as a sort of *dare* to myself," she said, "to see how I felt about having kids. I never thought it would happen so soon. I've been smoking and drinking. While I was pregnant. I'm a bad mother already."

"Come on, the baby's like two minutes old. This is wonderful news. We should celebrate."

"I can't," she said, popping the unlit cigarette back into her mouth. "Not until I'm sure I'm going to have it."

I told her what an amazing friend and wife she was, and I told her Henry would help her. "You're both going to be wonderful parents."

"But Henry's still a big child himself," she said. "He still smokes a joint every night."

"Toby smokes a lot of pot, too." I shrugged. "He says he needs it for the jokes. I think a lot of comedy writers do. I don't really mind." Although, I realized with a bit of unease, he had been smoking quite a bit of it since he'd lost his job.

"I think the jokes are just their excuse for getting stoned out of their gourds every night," Cath said.

"I like it that Toby makes me laugh," I said, a little defensively.

"Yeah, well, just remember, 'if they make you laugh, they'll make you cry.' That's what they used to say in acting class about comedy writers. What the hell are you doing with one, by the way? I mean, being married to a writer is bad enough. Henry and I were basically forced to get married. We'd put so much time into getting to know each other, it would have seemed like a huge waste to give up and start over with someone else. But you have a chance to be with someone normal. A comedy writer? Really? Don't you want to marry a nice agent or something?"

I laughed, and finally so did she.

"Come on, my love," I said. "You're just freaking out. It's normal. Let's celebrate. Let me buy you a nursing bra or something."

"Seriously, Lace," she said, and she stopped and took my hand. Her voice dropped to a whisper, and she really looked scared. "Henry and I barely even have sex anymore. We did it one time the other day to celebrate him leaving the job. Honestly, I don't even know how I got pregnant."

I walked home feeling shaken. My sex life with Toby hadn't been that great lately either. It had faded more quickly than either of us had anticipated. There were many nights—most nights, now that I thought about it—when we got into bed, wished each other sweet dreams, and fell asleep in our huge California king bed without even touching. We had become affectionate without being passionate.

When I got home, Toby was lying on the couch, watching a football game on TV. I could see that he was stoned, glassy-eyed and mellow.

I motioned for him to move over, and I lay down next to him on the couch. "How long has it been since we've had sex?" I said to the ceiling.

"Three weeks," Toby said.

"Really?" I said. "That long?" It startled me that he had been keeping track.

"Yep," he said.

"I think we should do something about that," I said.

"I agree," he said with a smile, and hugged me close. I breathed in his Toby smell. But he kept his eyes on the game and made a joke, and I got up to do some work, and within a few minutes we had forgotten our agreement.

THAT AFTERNOON, at home, I sat down and pored over the ShoeFest financials. I could see right away that there was a problem. In the three years they had held the event, they had never filed tax reports with the IRS, had never given any money to the government. Last year it had all—$345,678—

gone to a new athletic center. The year before, $306,789 had gone to new computers.

"Holy shit," I said.

"What?" Toby said, and I told him.

"Wow," he said. "That's a good story you've got there, Smooch. I'm proud of you."

It was. I smiled. I felt proud, too.

It was Saturday, and Jimmy James had called for a "family conference" that night; it took me a moment to realize that by family, he meant Toby and me. Our familial event was, incongruously, to take place at the trendiest place in town, a supper club owned partly by Ashton Kutcher. It was a hot spot; paparazzi stood outside, snapping mostly the B-list as they came and went. As we approached, Bill Maher entered the club ahead of us and the photographers clicked away, then lowered their cameras as we passed by.

Inside, however, as we met Jimmy and followed the maître d' to our table, I was surprised to spot a hugely famous actress in a large corner booth, encircled by a group of women. This was at the height of the media's fascination with her, scrutiny that had only increased after she had, the day before, announced her broken engagement to a hugely famous actor. I could not stop staring as we walked by her table; she was laughing and she looked casual yet radiant. At that moment a photographer walked over and began snapping away, the flash blinding us in the dark club. I'd noticed her bodyguard standing a few feet away, and now I expected him to demand that the paparazzo leave or, at the very least, to block him from taking her picture, but he did not. The photographer kept on snapping, and she kept on smiling, her friends chatting excitedly to her. We passed in a rush as the maître d' led us by, and then the moment was over.

We sat, Jimmy ordered champagne, and then he looked at us intently. He had determined, he announced, after careful analysis and consideration, that Toby should leave the late-night talk-show world—"It's a total dead end, hack writing, crap money, friggin' bottom-of-the-barrel job in this town, really"—and go write for sitcoms instead, where he would be promoted steadily over the years until he became a story editor, then a producer, and finally an executive producer. Eventually, Jimmy predicted, Toby would get a studio deal and create his own hit show, and *that,* Jimmy announced, was when we would hit the big time. "A few years in that racket and they back the money truck up and dump it in your front yard. How's that sound to you, Lace?"

"As long as Toby's happy," I said, and I really meant it. In many ways I felt I was just along for the ride when it came to Toby's career. Yes, I tried to listen and advise if he asked me, but he had made it this far without me, and now I just marveled at the fact that here he was, living his dream.

"Happy?" Jimmy cried, as if I were crazy for not jumping out of my chair and hugging him. "Jesus Christ, he's gonna be ecstatic. And what about you, the luckiest girl in the world? Getting married to this guy? You're a real lucky duck, you know that? Lucky Lacey Duck. Luck. Eee. This guy is what's known as a real comedic talent. He's gonna go places, you mark my words. You're gonna have that big house in the hills in no time. Yep, real lucky is what you are, Lucky."

I could see that Jimmy James was waiting for me to display some enthusiasm for the whole situation, but the truth was I was having trouble listening to him because I was slightly starstruck by the actress in the corner.

I felt distracted by the bizarre thought that I might go over and tell her I was sorry about her breakup, that I hoped she was okay. Of course I wouldn't do that, and yet it was dawning on me that it was possible that I could, more so here than anywhere else. I realized that what I was experiencing now—the anticipation that someone important might walk into a room at any moment, and the additional anticipation that one might engage with that person in some meaningful way—was a metaphor for the culture here; it illustrated the heightened tension in the air, the sense that something huge and unexpected could happen any day, that one could meet the right person with the right project, that life could change in an instant.

"So, listen," Jimmy James said to both of us, "if you're both into the whole sitcom deal, then I got Toby a job yesterday."

Now I whirled my head back to the table. "Really?" I said. "Wow."

"Wow is right, Lucky," Jimmy said, smiling and shaking the hand that Toby thrust toward him in gratitude. "I know, I know, how did I do it? It's easy. I do what I say I'm going to do. That's the secret in life, did you know that?" And here he pronounced each word slowly: "Do what you say you're going to do. You know how many hacks in this town make promises they don't keep?" Here he simpered: "I'm writing a screenplay, I'll call you, we'll set up a meeting." Then he straightened up, pointing at Toby and me: "Bullshit. Friggin' assholes. No. Say you're gonna write a screenplay, write it. Say we're gonna have a fun time tonight, have it. Say you're gonna get my friend Toby here a job, get it."

I could feel my whole body relax. Stress about money had been lurking in my bones. Our wedding was in a couple of months, and though our parents had each given us some money for the wedding—excluding my father, who was in a downturn at the moment and couldn't spare anything—we had already spent over fifteen thousand dollars of our own money, and there were still more bills to be paid. I hadn't been sure how long we could survive with Toby out of work, especially in the cute little red cottage that we'd rented, which was costing us more than we could really afford.

"What's the show?" Toby said.

"It's a new show, launching in the fall, called Better Luck Next Time, and it's about a family with really bad luck. All these terrible, outrageous, fantastical things are always happening to them, like their dog learns to talk and starts spreading gossip about them, the daughter gets the chicken pox at the prom, that kind of thing."

It sounded silly, like a typical sitcom.

"When do I start?" Toby said.

"On Monday," said Jimmy James. "And don't worry, Lucky, I told them he has to take two weeks off for the wedding and honeymoon, and they were down with that."

Toby raised his glass. "To Jimmy," he said, and Jimmy said, "To the newest sitcom writer in town," and we all clinked and drank. We had a happy night, eating and drinking and celebrating.

Toward the end of dinner, I noticed that the famous actress's group was standing. I expected them to head out toward the front, in the opposite direction of us, but apparently they were going to go out through the kitchen. I realized that they were headed toward us, that she was going to walk right by our table. If I wanted to say anything supportive to her, this was my chance.

"I'm going to say something to her," I said aloud, to try to convince myself.

"Go for it, Lucky," said Jimmy, nodding. "That's the spirit. Do what you say you're going to do."

The actress approached, smiling, for all in the crowded restaurant to see. Our table was the last table she would walk past before reaching the kitchen, and I was quickly preparing myself to say something, my heart pounding. But by the time she got to us, I could see that her smile was fading and her eyes glimmered with what looked like tears. It was as if she had been struggling to hold her smile frozen in place and now could finally release it. It was a private moment, one I was almost ashamed of having seen, and as she passed us, I tried not to look at her, and I didn't say anything.

"Ah, Lucky!" Jimmy exclaimed. "You totally dropped the ball there! I'll get her; let me go after her for you." He rose, and I knew he would have gone had I not prevented it.

"No, no," I said. "It was a bad idea. Forget it."

TWO DAYS LATER, the photos of the actress and her friends smiling and laughing at the club appeared in *People* magazine. When I saw them I felt a strange sense of being part of the story, though of course I was not. The article described how well she was doing post-breakup (it was now five days after they had called off their engagement), and it dawned on me then, of course, that the photos had been staged, that the whole evening had simply been a PR event, a photo op so that she could look like she was fine, and over him. Some of my friends later said how callous that made her seem, as though she was trying to send a message to the world that she had been the one to end it, and not him, but I disagreed. When I thought back to the night, I remembered the sad glimmer in her eyes as she had passed me, and the wilting of her smile, and all I could think was how naïve and young she seemed to try to convince anyone, herself especially, that she was over anything.

ON MONDAY MORNING I called Minnie Jones.

"I'd love to talk to you about the finances of ShoeFest," I said.

"Sure," she said. "Shoot."

"Well," I said, and I realized I was not sure how to begin. In New York I had also covered education for a weekly paper, but there it had been hard news, public schools that were failing, city councilors constantly infighting and looking for me to quote them on how terrible their opponents were. I was used to questioning people ruthlessly, arguing with them, even raising my voice if I had to. But now I felt tentative. The rules felt different here, as if more decorum was required, as if one mustn't upset the happiness. "It's great how much money you all have made for the school—"

"Isn't it?" Minnie said. "We're really proud of it."

"Right, right. I just have one small question," I said, literally squirming in my seat, dying not to have to ask it. "Have you ever filed and paid taxes on the shoes sold?" I finally blurted.

There was a silence.

"Let me get back to you on that," she said, rather coldly I thought, and hung up.

Half an hour later she called me back.

"Why don't you come up to my house and we'll talk?" she said. I agreed, and she made room in her schedule for me to come have lunch with her the following week.

AT HOME I was relieved to have Toby off the couch, although of course the trade-off of his having a new job was that I rarely saw him. Sitcom hours are notoriously bad, so Toby was now either working or sleeping, all the time. He had been at *Better Luck Next Time* for one week, and already, before the show had even aired, the word on the street was that it was doomed for cancellation. The studio wasn't behind it, the actors didn't like the scripts, and the writers, a group of nine mostly unmarried men, were goofing off in the writers' room instead of writing, telling raunchy stories that had nothing to do with the show, passing around a bong, and playing "Who in Hollywood would you sleep with if you had the chance?" until the wee hours, when they finally got down to work and patched together crappy scripts in the middle of the night. Toby was sometimes "at work," pitching jokes, smoking pot, and eating pizza, until 4 A.M.

MINNIE JONES'S HOUSE was the kind I had imagined when I had dreamed of living in L.A. It was white, modern, made of glass, and overlooking the ocean, with sleek white furniture lining the living room before a blazing gas fireplace. The room seemed packed with more big-name modern art than MoMA: a huge colorful Calder mobile hung in the huge foyer, a Picasso on the wall behind it, a Chagall on another wall. Minnie wore a purple Chanel suit, which set off her blond hair. *Is she trying to intimidate me?* I wondered.

We ate outside by the pool. A butler served us Waldorf salads.

After we chatted for a few minutes and I complimented her on the house and the grounds, she said, "So, listen, Lacey, I spoke with the tax board today, and you are absolutely right—we are required to pay taxes on those darn shoes. It seems like the concept of taxes just slipped all of our minds. None of us has worked at a nonprofit before this one. And let me tell you"—she laughed—"my husband's studio is definitely not a nonprofit."

I put my fork down, fiddled in my purse, and brought out my notebook.

Minnie stared at it. "Are you going to take *notes* on this?"

"Well, yes."

"Is this a *story*?" she said.

"Well, yes, it's just a simple story that you haven't filed the taxes and now you're going to. So I assume you're going to pay the back taxes, too? Did the tax board tell you how much it will come to?"

"Why is this relevant to anyone besides the school's board and administration?"

"I guess because other schools and charities could learn from it. And also, that's a lot of money you'll be putting into the state coffers. It will be nice for the community to know you're doing that."

"It makes us look like fools and you know it. And it makes me look like the head fool."

"Oh, Minnie, with your reputation, no one could think—"

"That's the point: with my reputation, I'm not supposed to make mistakes of this size. Do you realize that with this error, I lost about ninety thousand dollars for the school?"

"Or, you could look at it as, over three years, you helped the school *earn* over eight hundred thousand," I said.

There was a long silence.

"Listen, Lacey," she finally said, "a little bird told me you've been sending out résumés, looking for a new job."

I was startled. I did not know how she would know this. It was true: I had been looking for a writers' assistant position on a TV drama, as a way to get my foot in the door in Hollywood. I had grown tired of feeling like an outsider in this town, left out of all the excitement and gambling on the future, but I was afraid I would have no success breaking in, so I hadn't told anyone that I was trying, not even Toby. If I did have luck getting a job, I'd planned to surprise him. But now someone at one of the shows I'd sent my résumé to must have recognized my name from the newspaper, put two and two to-gether, and told Minnie. *That* was how small this goddamn town was.

"Oh, well, I've been sending out résumés," I said. "No luck so far, but I'm trying—"

"Look," she said, "when we talked about it in theory a while ago, I said I'd love to help you, and I meant it. My husband, as you may know, runs one of the studios, and of course he knows everyone, and I know he'd love to help you get a job as a full-fledged staff writer. None of this starting-at-the-bottom assistant stuff. You're certainly qualified to be a staff writer, so it would just be a matter of making a few well-placed calls."

I was stunned. She was willing to help me, just to stop me from writing the story. A tiny little "Oops we made a mistake" story that no one would give a shit about. Offering me a job as a staff writer? Under normal circumstances, as a total outsider with no TV writing experience, I'd have to work my way up as an assistant for at least a year, probably two, before I could even think about getting a job as a writer. I was prepared to do that, of course, but the idea of skipping over all that low-level drudgery, especially at my age, was lovely. And yet—

"Thanks, Minnie," I said, "but no thanks."

BOB ACCOSTED ME when I got back to the office that afternoon.

"What were you thinking?" he said.

"About?"

"Going up to Minnie Jones's house in the name of this newspaper and ac-cusing her of using ShoeFest—*ShoeFest,* for godssakes!—to cheat the govern-ment?"

"That's not exactly how it went," I said, "but how did you even know I was up there?"

"She just called me in hysterics."

"I was following a story."

"What story?" he demanded. "A sweet little fund-raiser for Crosslake?"

"You mean sweet little Crosslake that hasn't paid taxes on the event in three years? They raised $345,678 for their school last year. That means roughly $30,000 didn't go to the state. Over three years that's almost $90,000."

"So?" Bob said. "It's a private thing. Why does the government have to get involved?"

"*Bob,*" I said, as if he was an idiot. "You're a newspaper editor. This is news."

"*Lacey,*" he said. "This is a community newspaper. We are *proud* of our community. We *celebrate* our community. This is not a newspaper of exposés. And besides, this was an honest mistake."

"How honest do you think it was? Minnie Jones's husband runs a studio. She probably racks up a three-hundred-thousand-dollar bill at Barneys every year. You think the concept of taxes just escaped her mind? And all the minds of every board member?"

"Are you accusing them of deliberately cheating the government?"

"No, but I think it's pretty shoddy accounting on the part of people who I'm pretty sure understand how sales tax works."

"I really don't care, Lacey," he said. "Now that you've brought it to their attention, they have agreed to collect taxes going forward, and to pay the back taxes."

"All because of my reporting," I said.

"Good for you then. And good for the government. Now let's move on."

"Are you saying you don't think I should write the story?"

"I'm saying you're not *going* to write the story. And if you persist in this line of reporting, if you ask any more questions of Minnie or anyone else on that board, I'm going to have to ask you to look for a new job—which, by the way, I heard you've been doing anyway."

I stood there, dumbfounded. Was he a crazy person? This was totally out of line with the ethics of journalism. I felt like someone else was having this conversation. It felt like a soap opera; I could not actually be speaking these words, living them, but then I heard myself say: "You won't have to ask me, because if I can't write this story, I quit."

"Fine," he said, continuing the cliché. "Have your resignation on my desk by the end of the day."

He walked away. Despite myself, tears came to my eyes. Though I had nominally been the one to quit, it was the first time in my life that I had ever been fired.

"YOU QUIT YOUR JOB?" Toby said at home that night.

"I had to."

"What, they put a gun to your head?"

"What's your problem? I'll get a new job."

"My show is shit, Lacey. It's going to get canceled as soon as it airs, I guarantee it. And now you're out of a job, too. And we're about to get married. And since the bride's parents—the people who are usually responsible for paying for a wedding—haven't exactly stepped up to the plate here, we're going to owe a lot of money when this is all over."

"I know," I said.

"Then why did you quit?"

"Jesus, Toby. I didn't mean to."

"Then why did you?"

I burst into tears, ran into our bedroom, and shut the door.

A few minutes later he came into the room and lay down on the bed next to me.

"I'm sorry, Smooch," he said.

"I know," I said. "I'm scared, too."

We held each other for a while, and then we took off all our clothes, and afterward, we went to sleep until it was a new day.

CATH DECIDED to keep the baby. "I'm ready," she said, holding my hand, and we both cried. A week later she had a miscarriage. She sobbed and could not get out of bed. I brought some chicken soup, but a red-eyed Henry stopped me at the front door.

"She doesn't want to see anyone," he said. "We're going to hunker down for a while."

It occurred to me then for the first time that we were getting older, that our pain and misfortune might not always be erasable, that our lives going forward might hold some major disappointment, the adult kind, the kind that mattered.

TWO DAYS LATER I got a call from a show that had received my résumé and needed a writers' assistant. It meant I'd be starting from the bottom, doing menial tasks, making twenty-eight thousand dollars a year, probably for the next two years.

"It starts July 6," they said, which meant I'd be able to attend my wedding and go on my honeymoon before starting work. "You're overqualified," they said, "but if you want the job, you've got it."

"I want it."

When I told Toby, he broke into a huge grin. "Welcome to the family business," he said, hugging me.

BETTER LUCK NEXT TIME lasted for only six weeks, after airing twice. It was canceled the week before our wedding, and Toby was out of a job once again. "Those friggin' assholes," said Jimmy James, shaking his head.

Toby started lying on the couch all day again, stoned, and I felt myself getting angry.

"Why don't you start writing a screenplay?" I suggested. "Just until Jimmy gets you your next TV job."

Toby glared at me. "I just got fired two days ago. Can't I have two days to recover? Two days? Jesus."

Later Cath and Henry called, to invite us to a party in Laurel Canyon. "It'll cheer him up," Cath said.

Toby declined. "You go if you want. My stomach's been acting up. I'd rather stay home."

This was his standard reply these days. He seemed to prefer staying in to going out. This wasn't necessarily new; Toby's domesticity was something I'd liked about him at the beginning. Yet now I felt like we never left our house, like all we did was sit at home and watch TV, like my life was shrinking. Before dinner, he'd light a joint and I'd pour a glass of wine and we'd eat, hunched over the coffee table, in front of the TV. I realized that I had essentially started drinking alone.

A FEW NIGHTS LATER, the night before Toby and I were to fly back east for our wedding, Jimmy James came over for dinner. We had a nice time, sitting out on the patio, the three of us trying to be positive about Toby's future. At the end of the night we walked Jimmy to the front door; Toby and I stood at the threshold with our arms linked. I had looked at our finances that afternoon: we had spent $24,987 of our own money on the wedding; we had $3,869 left in our checking account and a credit card bill that had not yet come in. I wondered how anxious I should be about all this. As I stood at the door, I began to worry a little, then stopped. We were flying to Vermont the next morning to get married, I reminded myself. We had our whole lives before us.

Jimmy had barely mentioned our wedding all night; he'd seemed to have his mind on work. I knew that he'd been working hard to get Toby some meetings, but nothing had panned out. Now I could see that he wanted to send us off with a little reassurance.

"There are lots of other shows out there," he said as he turned to leave, but there was false cheer in his voice, and underneath, a weariness I'd never heard from him before. Behind him, the sky was light and the moon was full, and it was a night for celebration. I thought back to a few months earlier, when Jimmy had called me the luckiest girl in the world and vowed to find Toby a job in two weeks. This time around, I noticed, he did not promise us anything, and he was no longer calling me lucky.

Sick

I AWOKE THE MORNING after our wedding to the sound of my feet hitting the floor, then ran to the bathroom to throw up. If it occurred to me that this reaction did not bode well for our marriage, it did so only as a faintly comic thought. If I considered being sick as a clear and physical sign that I had made a mistake, then it was only in a fleeting and dismissive way, the same way in which I scoffed at friends who visited astrologers or believed in God.

I was not pregnant, I was simply sick to my stomach, and in the wee hours of our marriage I was too ill to consume anything—even water forced its way back up—and so I missed the brunch downstairs at the old Vermont inn where we'd married. Toby stood in for me, shaking hands with our 150 guests and explaining that I was under the weather, everyone probably assuming the bride was actually just very hungover. Upstairs, Cath packed for me, and my new mother-in-law and my five bridesmaids came awkwardly to the door of my room, waving at me as I lay pale and spent on my bed.

My mother went downstairs sporadically to survey the buffet, for which she had paid. "Those Friedmans really know how to eat," she told me, sotto voce, after one voyage downstairs. "They're going back three and four times, piling up their plates."

Eventually, everyone left. My mother went back to Palm Beach and my father to New York (but not before slipping me an envelope thick with cash; when Toby and I opened it later we found five thousand dollars in hundred-dollar bills; I was too grateful to worry about where he'd gotten it), our East Coast friends headed back down I-95, our friends from L.A. took their rental cars to Logan Airport. Even Toby's mother finally drove back over to her ancestral summer house a few miles down the road, the reason we'd married in this little Vermont town.

From my upstairs window I watched the cars round the inn's circular driveway one final time, kicking up dirt as they turned onto the main road. I couldn't help but feel abandoned. Our family and friends had gathered from across the country to watch us marry; they had pledged to support our union. But now we had to go it alone. Down in the grassy field next to the inn, workers were already starting to take down our big white reception tent: inside it, the ghosts of our guests danced and drank and laughed.

My brother had never even shown up. I had thought he would, up until the last minute. Everyone assumed my tears at the altar were tears of joy, but midway through the ceremony I realized that Sam hadn't come yet—and he wasn't going to. My parents vowed to cut him out of their lives for not showing, which almost made me smile over how much they missed the point. He had disappeared. No one had heard from him, and now his girlfriend, Olivia, had gone incommunicado, too. My mother had not heard from her since she had called that one time to say she was pregnant. But soon—Olivia was due any day now—Sam would be a father, and I would be an aunt, and my parents would be grandparents. Sam's child would be born somewhere out in the world, but none of us—perhaps not even Sam—would be there, or know anything about the child. I wondered if I would ever be able to forgive Sam for missing my wedding, but I knew for certain that I would not be able to forgive him if he walked out on his own child.

Now Toby came upstairs and helped me finish packing. "Aw, Smooch," he said, stroking my hair as I lay in bed. "Everyone missed you down there." I took a woozy shower and stopped drinking even water, hoping to handle the drive to Boston without getting sick again.

But as we drove down that afternoon to spend the night at the Ritz-Carlton, it was Toby who began to complain of nausea. And so we sat rigidly in the car, Toby behind the wheel, both of us girding against the prospect of his having to throw up on the side of the road, stuck as we were in traffic on Storrow Drive.

From my cell phone, I asked reception at the hotel to expedite our check-in. "My husband isn't feeling well," I said. And in this manner I referred to Toby as my husband for the first time.

Up in the room, which was swathed in yellow muslin and perfumed by a bouquet of pale pink peonies, sent by all four of our divorced parents, Toby claimed he continued to feel nauseous. For one second I eyed him suspiciously—the illness I'd been experiencing had me running to the bathroom every five minutes, but Toby hadn't gotten sick once. Moreover, he had a notoriously weak stomach and was often waylaid by it, canceling our dinner dates in favor of tea and broth at home, calling people at the last minute to say we couldn't make it to their parties, habits that frustrated me to no end because I couldn't tell when he was actually sick and when he was just using his stomach as an excuse for not wanting to get off the couch. But then I chided myself for being unsympathetic. I definitely had a bug; he probably had it, too, just on a smaller scale.

And so we lay in bed all evening watching pay-per-view movies amid the fluffy Ritz pillows, wrapped up in the duvet, forgoing the room-service menu as well as the Veuve Clicquot sent by the best man.

But by morning we felt well enough to consummate our marriage, and afterward we agreed that we were therefore probably well enough to follow through with our honeymoon plans.

On our economy flight to Paris that night, we refused to eat, neither of us risking the Brie and cheap chardonnay they offered in little baskets, the void in our stomachs gnawing at us, then subsiding, and soon we lapsed into listlessness, reminiscing lazily about the wedding, about how wonderful and happy it had been, even with the light rain that followed the ceremony, about how well our East Coast boarding school and Hollywood comedian crowds had mixed, about the mishaps and the ceremony and the toasts, about who had gotten drunk, and who had made asses of themselves, and who had hooked up with whom. We were quiet for a moment, and then Toby tentatively spoke.

"I have to tell you something, Smooch," he said. "About the wedding."

"Okay," I said.

"I didn't want to tell you, but I feel like I should."

"What is it?" At this point I was imagining some mistake that had seemed important at the time, something everyone had shielded the bride from: the rings had been misplaced, or the marriage license wasn't valid, or the caterers nearly hadn't arrived, something like that.

"I came to your room the night before the wedding, at like three A.M."

We'd slept in separate rooms that night at the old inn, in keeping with the tradition of not seeing each other until the ceremony; we had kissed and said good night around midnight and gone to our separate rooms.

"What do you mean?" I said, confused. "I didn't hear you come in, and you weren't there in the morning . . . ?"

"No," he said, "because I couldn't get in. Your door was locked, and the front desk was closed so I couldn't get a key."

"Why didn't you just knock and wake me up?"

"I *did*, but you didn't hear me—"

"Oh Jesus," I said, immediately picturing the scene; my room had a small living area, and the door from the living area to the bedroom had been closed, and the air conditioner had been on, and on top of that I'd had several glasses of wine over the course of the evening, so I had been sleeping very soundly. There was no way I'd have heard him.

"And then I kept knocking, for like half an hour, but I guess you were just dead to the world. And there were no phones in the stupid rooms, and our cell phones didn't get service up there, so—"

"Oh Smooch, I am so sorry," I said, knowing him so well, picturing him on the other side of the wall, a little boy again, anxious and nervous about the next day, suffering from the loneliest of insomnias, looking for help and comfort from the only person who could have given it to him, and me so close by, unable to help.

"So I just sat outside the door for a while," he continued, "hoping you might finally wake up, and then I knocked one more time, and then finally I gave up and went back to my room. I probably fell asleep at like five A.M."

My face fell and I truly despaired for a moment—what a stupid, stupid mistake! If I'd only left my door unlocked, or given him a key! I felt an uneasy sense of wanting to go back and do the weekend over again in order to repair that moment, as if the wedding had been irreparably marred by it. Now all I could do was clutch Toby's hand and tell him over and over again that I was sorry, that I wished I had been there for him that night, and then after a while we were quiet again.

It was a red-eye flight, and soon they dimmed the lights. Then Toby, who did not like to fly, took a Xanax, slipped on an eye mask that I had managed to finagle from a stewardess in first class, and turned away from me. He slept soundly, breathing regularly, but I sat wide-eyed and erect in my seat, trapped and claustrophobic, unwilling to turn on my reading light for fear of waking Toby and the other passengers around me. Toby had the aisle seat, and the view outside my window was only darkness. As the hours passed, I felt suspended in a barren hell where I couldn't move or read or think about anything other than the fact that I needed to stretch my legs. My back stiffened, my knees ached. Time ceased and the night went on forever, the stewardesses gliding by silently, an occasional passenger snoring or turning in his sleep. I felt sure I was the sole person awake on that entire plane; only the slow, numbing drone of the engines kept me company. Later Toby grumbled and turned in his sleep to face me. The gloomy trail of floor lights along the aisle illuminated his face, his dark hair falling over his eye mask, his stubble just starting to come in, his lips open in sleep, exposing his teeth, so unruly in childhood photos, now white and perfect after being constrained for years in braces. As I watched him sleep, I thought, *This boy is my husband.*

OUR HOTEL—L'Hôtel was its name—was charming and small, located in the Sixth Arrondissement. It had a dark velvet-trimmed bar in the lobby and a cavelike chamber in the basement where they served breakfast by candlelight. We arrived in the morning, fell into bed, and slept until that evening. We woke, the sun still shining at 6 P.M., feeling stronger, grounded. Toby came at me hungrily as I emerged from the bathroom in my negligee, an ivory silk one from the trousseau my mother had insisted on assembling for me, as if I were an heiress.

My father had booked us into the famed restaurant Taillevent for dinner that evening as a wedding gift; I was excited about going. "Do we have to?" Toby said, lying in bed, looking at French TV without the sound, and I glared at him. Finally he roused himself and we called a cab.

At the restaurant, Monsieur Vrinat himself greeted us and took our coats. The dining room was paneled in light-colored wood, with modern paintings that were spotlit, and fresh flowers of all colors towered in every corner. We had come early in terms of the Parisian dinner hour; only one other table besides ours was engaged, by a group of slim, suited businessmen who were smoking cigars. We sat a comfortable distance from them, and the waiter brought white wine for me and a Coke for Toby. We ordered our dinner—we hadn't eaten in more than forty-eight hours and I was famished—and then Toby's nausea began to rise again.

He disappeared to the bathroom.

As I waited for him, I watched the white-coated waiters perform their calibrated ballet. Their work, though seemingly effortless, was not so, I realized. The focus was visible in their upturned faces, their precise timing, their anticipation of a party's needs—the curving slide of plate onto table, the silent pour of a glass of wine, the dramatic strike of a match to light a cigarette—all were done as if by second nature, though the strain was there to be seen if one sought it out.

After Toby had been gone for quite some time, I was able to discern that the waiters were trying to stop themselves from glancing at our table. Their looks bounced away before I could be sure of them. I knew that our food was ready, and they couldn't bring it to us until Toby returned to the table. Slowly, I felt my irritation growing.

Finally Toby returned. He couldn't eat anything, he announced.

"Did you throw up?" I said, unsmiling.

"No," he said. "I just don't feel well."

When they brought our foie gras—two waiters dramatically removing the domed silver covers at the same time and then bowing—Toby left his untouched. Presently Monsieur Vrinat approached.

"Is everything all right?" he asked.

When I explained, he offered a special French concoction, meant to settle stomachs.

"No," Toby said. "I'll be fine, thank you."

I ate my dinner, and we left without dessert, without coffee. We declined the maître d's offer to call a cab, stepped out into the gloomy twilight, and stood for a moment on the corner of the Champs-Élysées.

I looked at my husband. He appeared healthy enough to me. "Are you okay?" I asked.

"I don't know," he said.

"Are you sick?"

"Why are you asking me that?"

"Because sometimes you say you're sick when you're not."

"What does that mean?"

"Like when you don't want to go out at night you say your stomach's upset so we have to stay home, and if I force you to go out, then afterward you're always saying you think the oysters were bad, or the crab cakes might have given you food poisoning."

"Well, this could be food-related," he said. "I don't know why I don't feel well now."

"You know," I said after a moment, "*I* was actually the one who was sick, the day after our wedding. And I actually *got sick.* I actually threw up."

"So—what?—throwing up proves something?"

"Well, maybe," I said, "but the point is, can't I have a turn at being sick? I never get sick. Never. Do you have to go around saying you're sick, too?"

"What are you saying? That I'm faking it?"

"Well, you know, Smooch, sometimes, as a child, you *did* fake it. Your mother let you stay home from school all the time if you told her you were sick. You told me that once. She never questioned you, so that was your excuse. And I don't want to be your mother. I'm your wife now, and I need you to be my husband and be strong."

"You know what, Lacey?" he said. "There is absolutely no danger of me confusing you with my mother, let me tell you that right now. My mother would never treat me like a criminal for not feeling well. My mother would be taking care of me right now."

"All I'm *saying*, Toby, is, just once, just *one time*, *I'd* like to be the person who gets taken care of, instead of being the one to take care of you."

Toby looked at me for a second, and his eyes turned empty. Then he bent over, slowly, stuck his finger down his throat, and retched his Coke over the sidewalk. With nothing else in his stomach to purge, he could only continue dry heaving, over and over. The awful aborted effort of his gagging, the outline of him doubled over, the jerking of his upper body as it convulsed—it was all horrible, but I couldn't look away. I felt my watching sustain him, and yet I could not move myself to comfort him either. Finally he looked up, tears swimming in his eyes. "Is that good enough?" he said. "Now do you believe me?"

I was stunned. My mouth hung open. I didn't know whether to cry or run away. I saw then that his tears weren't only from throwing up; he was crying. He was the saddest thing I had ever seen, and I wanted to take him in my arms, surround him with comfort and care. I wanted to love him, to be the supportive wife he needed me to be, to tell him he never needed to do anything like that again. And then I wanted to smack him, again and again, for being so weak; I wanted to run away from him forever, for proving his weakness to me, for making me stand there and watch, for being the only husband I had, for being the only thing in the world I had to hold on to.

We walked back to our hotel in silence and he went to sleep. I needed some air, but I didn't feel like walking around Paris alone, so I went down to the bar and had a glass of wine and smoked a cigarette. The only other people there were a French couple. They were a bit younger than Toby and me, probably in their mid-twenties, attractive and chic. They sat a few stools down from me at the tiny bar. I made no effort to talk to them, nor they to me. The bartender disappeared. After a while, the couple began to argue. I don't speak French, so I couldn't understand what they were saying, and somehow they figured this out, because though they tried to keep their voices down initially, after a while they began to speak at full volume. Finally the boy stood and left, and the girl continued to sit there, crying, wiping her eyes, then lighting a cigarette and looking at herself in the mirror above the bar, then crying a little more. I thought about trying to console her, but I had heard that the French get offended if you speak to them in English. I remained silent, but after a while my silence felt rude, so I stood and went back to the room and got into bed, where again I watched my husband sleep.

I felt sorry for him then, and for me, and for our baby of a marriage. I wanted to wake him, to tell him I was sorry, to tell him I would take care of him whenever he needed me to, no matter what. Could we start over, pretend the scene on the street had never happened? He had needed me and I hadn't been there for him, had yelled at him instead, and I felt guilty about it now, and yet—what about what I needed? Would he ever be an adult, or would I have to take care of him, and myself too, for the rest of my life? I was so used to taking care of myself—I had been doing it my whole life—and I was so tired of it. Would my life be curtailed from now on? Would every dinner, every event that he did not want to go to, be cut short? My life ruled by his sensitive stomach forever? My husband was from weak stock, I thought. Our children—my children—would be from weak stock.

I did not understand what was happening to us. Why was there this sudden resentment now that we were married? We had lived together for a year and a half; I was used to his stomach problems, thought I had come to accept them. What was the difference now—marriage was just a piece of paper, right? Or, if not, then wasn't marriage supposed to make one feel more secure, and not less, cocooned in the safety of a relationship instead of left out on a ledge alone?

The next morning, and over the next several days, Toby continued to claim that he felt sick. After a while, he was able to walk around Paris with me a bit, and he'd sit with me at the cafés and have tea and toast while I had wine and pâté, but we didn't talk about what had happened, and if we did sleep together, it was only one or two more times, neither of them healing us the way I had hoped.

Stress, people said when we returned, was the reason for our illnesses, whether real or imagined. Or perhaps a bug had been going around at the wedding. A bridesmaid had felt ill, in fact, someone reported, but had been loath to tell me and tarnish our wedding; perhaps we had caught something from her. Others had heard that my husband's aunt and her children had gone home sick, too. *No matter. The wedding was lovely and that's what's important. Just imagine if you'd been sick the day of the wedding! How would you have gone through with it?*

ABOUT A MONTH after we returned to L.A. from Paris, we flew back to the East Coast for a bar mitzvah for Toby's cousin. We were to stay with Toby's mother, who lived in a suburb outside Philadelphia. She picked us up from the airport, ecstatic, as always, at seeing her son. I liked Toby's mother very much—she was tiny and slim and brunette, lively and sweet and generous, always giving me thoughtful gifts in my favorite colors, referring to me as her daughter—but when Toby was around, it was hard to feel that I ever had her full attention. When he walked into a room I might as well have been the coat-check girl. Her eyes lit up, she took his hand, and she didn't look away the entire time she was with him.

I understood their closeness to a degree; in fact Toby's story mirrored my father's in some ways. When Toby was ten years old his father divorced his mother and moved to Israel to open an import business. They kept in touch only sporadically, and Toby didn't like to talk about him. He had come to the wedding, but they weren't close. "I never missed my father growing up," Toby would say, "because my mother was both mother and father to me."

Now we drove out to her house, a very pretty white Colonial, an all-American home, the flag flying over the front door. I had always liked driving up to it. But once we brought our luggage inside, I began to notice for the first time that the whole place was a museum of Toby's childhood. The décor hadn't been updated since the 1970s. Chocolate-brown shag carpeting covered every inch of floor. Huge brown flowers smothered the wallpaper. Swirly glass marbles, I LOVE MOM mugs, and dusty Disney figurines lined the kitchen windowsill. Twenty-five-year-old photographs of my husband clogged every surface. Toby's room still had *Star Wars* wallpaper and twin beds with *E.T.* sheets. A bottle of baby aspirin under the bathroom sink had an expiration date of 07/80.

Toby, I realized now, had encouraged his mother in the maintenance of this time warp. He whined if she changed anything at all about the place. Last year, when she replaced the kitchen garbage can with a new one—a modern white plastic number with a swinging lid—he mourned the old silver steel can as if she'd had the family dog put down.

Accordingly, my husband reverted to eighth-grade behavior at his mother's house. When we arrived that evening, he immediately plunked himself down at the kitchen table, as if the school bus had just dropped him off, and, glassy-eyed, began to watch his mother's hulking old-school TV—a TV for which, by the way, she continued to pay a cable bill, including the premium channels, despite the fact that the only person who watched cable at her house was my husband, who lived three thousand miles away in Los Angeles, and had for the past five years. He then began force-feeding himself from the stock of nostalgic junk food in the pantry that she had apparently reinforced for his arrival: Ring Dings and Twinkies, Slim Jims and Apricot Fruit Roll-Ups. His mother, upon entering the room and finding him unwrapping an array of junior high snacks, laughingly scolded him about ruining his appetite before dinner.

Watching them, I seethed. What mother encouraged her child to behave this way, at any age? No wonder he didn't want to do anything at home except sit on the couch. Looking at him, I wanted to choke my husband until he spit up his Twinkie.

Instead, I poured myself a glass of wine. Toby was not a big drinker, and his mother didn't drink at all, but she kept wine in the house for me, which I appreciated, especially now.

During dinner his mother asked us all about the honeymoon, and when we told her about Toby being sick she said, "Oh, I'm not surprised, not at all. I used to leave bottles of Pepto-Bismol in strategic positions around the house. He has a very nervous stomach, you know. Especially when he's anxious."

Really? Toby had grown up on Pepto-Bismol? Why did it suddenly seem like I was finding out things about my husband that I should have known before we got married? Suddenly I felt panicked, trapped. This wasn't what I'd signed on for, not at all. Yet her words stuck in the back of my mind. *Especially when he's anxious.* We had been on our honeymoon at a beautiful hotel in Paris. We were newlyweds, young and in love. Why had he been anxious?

After a moment, perhaps seeing me look a bit unsettled, she cleared her throat and said, "You know that can be a Jewish thing, right, dear?"

I was taken aback. Mrs. Friedman, or, rather, Judy—I had a hard time calling her Mom, as she had asked me to—and I rarely acknowledged that Toby was Jewish and I was Catholic. I was certainly aware, through Toby, that she'd wanted him to marry someone Jewish, but she had never once mentioned it to me or made me feel unwelcome or unloved because of it.

The only other time I felt uncomfortable with Toby's mother regarding religion was when I was reminded in her presence that I had not taken Toby's last name. I knew, via Toby, that his mother believed it was because I did not want a Jewish-sounding last name, but this was not the case. I had always planned on keeping my name, even when I had thought about marrying my last boyfriend, Edmund, a stuffy British investment banker whose last name was Eaton. I wanted to keep my name because I liked the sound of it. Lacey Brennan: to me it sounded like the name of a friendly Irish barkeep, a woman with a big family and a loud laugh, someone who was strong and rooted and sure. Lacey Friedman—or Lacey Eaton, for that matter—simply did not have the same down-home ring. And besides that, I didn't want marriage to erase my identity. I was Lacey Brennan before we got married, Irish and Catholic, my father's daughter, and I wanted to stay that way. Yet it was occurring to me now that perhaps there was something else at work under the surface. Perhaps I was scared to be married, scared to merge my identity with another person's, afraid I myself might disappear.

"I'm sorry," I said now to Toby's mother. "Excuse me?"

"A nervous stomach," she said. "You know that can be a Jewish thing, don't you?"

"Well, actually, no," I said. "I didn't know that."

"Oh, yes," she said merrily. "It's actually sometimes even called 'Jewish stomach.' Haven't you ever read Philip Roth? It's just our way of releasing anxiety. Sort of the way your people do with too much drinking." She nodded at the wineglass in my hand.

"Oh," I said, setting the glass down.

"Oh, come on, Smooch, you knew this stuff, didn't you?" Toby said, preparing to lighten the mood with some humor, I could see, yet also clearly irritated at me for having somehow neglected this area of my cultural education. "The stomach thing is all part of being anxious and neurotic. Haven't you seen a Woody Allen movie? *Seinfeld*? *Curb Your Enthusiasm*? Jews have sensitive stomachs, they don't use public toilets, they don't go camping, and they don't fix things like cars and appliances. They make money specifically so that they can stay in nice hotels with nice bathrooms, and hire people to fix those things."

"And they have overbearing mothers who love them too much," added Toby's mother, who patted her son's knee and laughed, and so I did, too.

I felt that this was a natural and pleasant end to the conversation, and so I began to yawn, complaining of tiredness. I wanted to be alone with my thoughts, and I also knew that Toby's mother would appreciate some time alone with her son, so I said good night.

I got a glass of water, went down the hall to the bathroom, and took a long look at my face in the mirror. I washed it and brushed my teeth, then went into my husband's childhood bedroom and climbed into one of the twin beds with the *E.T.* sheets. I tossed and turned for a while on the thin, sagging mattress; it likely hadn't been replaced since my husband had slept on it as a child.

I felt around the bed until I found Toby's childhood security blanket, Pibby. It was beige and ratty, a knitted yarn thing, string hanging off all the corners. It couldn't have been washed in years. Still, I folded it up like a pillow, then flopped over and lay on my stomach, my face buried in it. I breathed in. The blanket smelled like Toby, like his hair when he hasn't washed it, his favorite sweatshirt after he'd worn it all weekend. Suddenly a rush of affection for Toby filled me, and it seemed sweet rather than negligent that his mother likely hadn't washed the blanket all these years.

I lay in bed for several moments before I became aware of my husband and his mother talking in the next room, which shared a wall with his bedroom. I couldn't hear what they were saying, just the low rumble of Toby's voice. But there was something about the way they were talking that made me strain to listen. The conversation sounded serious.

It was mostly Toby talking—he was trying to whisper, it seemed—but his mother replied occasionally. I could hear what sounded like the word *she* a lot—it was beginning a lot of Toby's sentences, but that was all I could make out. It sounded like another language, a Martiany, Muppety language, and muffled at that. I felt as frustrated as I had trying to understand the fighting French couple at that bar in Paris.

I sat up, my elbow on my pillow, and pressed my ear against the wall. Nothing. My glass of water was sitting on the bedside table. I picked it up, drained it, pressed it to the wall, and rested my ear against the other end. Still nothing, even when I flipped the glass and tried again, and again.

Finally I gave up and began to drift to sleep, when I heard Toby right outside our door, saying good night to his mother. Then he slipped into the darkened room.

"Hello, Smooch," I whispered.

"Hello, Smooch," he whispered back.

He went to the window and opened it, the breeze fluttering the white curtains. He took off his clothes and got into his own twin bed, which was pushed up next to mine, a makeshift couple's bed. He noticed Pibby on my pillow, pulled the raggedy thing away from me, and tucked it under his arm. I wondered if this was simply an ingrained habit, the way he'd slept when he was a child.

We talked for a little while—about the night, about his mother and the dinner. Then Toby said he wasn't feeling so hot and wanted to get some sleep. He kissed me good night and turned away in his little twin bed, his back to me.

I lay there.

"What were you and your mother talking about in the other room?" I said.

"What do you mean?" Toby said.

"What were you two talking about?"

"Nothing, just the honeymoon, my career, that kind of thing," he said.

A long silence.

"I heard you," I said.

I felt the slightest shift on his side of the bed.

"What do you mean?" he said.

"I heard you. I heard what you said."

Another long silence.

"I'm sorry," he said, and he turned on his pillow to face me.

"Why did you say that about me?"

There was a pause. I could hear myself breathing.

"You mean, about that night?" he said.

I nodded, afraid to speak, afraid he would know I was lying, that I knew nothing.

"I didn't really mean it," he said. "I wasn't really having doubts."

My mind raced to make sense of this. *Did he mean the night before the wedding?*

"Then why did you come to my door that night?" I said, playing along, my heart beating fast. I felt I was bluffing in a game of poker, that my life hung in the turn of each next card. "Did you want to tell me something?"

"I don't know," Toby said. "I couldn't sleep. It was the middle of the night. We were about to get married, but I felt so alone." He paused. "It wasn't doubts. It was just cold feet."

"What's the difference?" I said.

"Well, when I woke up in the morning, the feeling was gone."

We were silent for a moment, letting that sink in. "What about now?" I said, though as soon as I said it, I wished I could take it back.

Toby didn't answer.

"I needed to vent to someone," he said finally. "I don't know what else you heard."

"I heard everything," I said.

A long silence.

"I'm sorry," he said.

"Why did you say those things about me?" I said. "That you think I drink too much, that I don't know how to take care of you like a wife should."

Again there was a silence for a moment.

"Because they're true," he said softly, and then he sighed, as if he was relieved. His relief, his sense that finally the things that could not be said were being said, scared me.

We were quiet for a time, and the room shifted; a cloud must have moved in the sky, and the moon shone through the window. I could see my husband's face, his eyes. It was the same sweet face I had fallen in love with two years ago in New York, the same face I thought I couldn't live without.

I began to cry. "Is something happening to us?" I said.

"You've had too much wine, Smooch," he said. "You're just emotional."

"Okay," I said.

"My stomach is really upset," Toby whispered. "I think I'm sick."

"You're just anxious," I said, through tears. "Don't be anxious."

"Okay," he said.

"Do you want to talk about it?" I said. "About us?"

"We can't right now," he said. "I'm sick and you're drunk." Then he clutched his blanket and turned away from me again.

Attila

IT WAS SUMMER IN L.A. and I had just gotten married and there was a pit bull roaming the halls at my office. Hollywood was hazy and slow and Toby was out of work, and the pit bull had a white coat splotched with deviant brown shapes that made me think of heart disease.

The TV show where I worked was lawless; people did what they wanted and said what they wanted. Toby was lying on the couch all day in our apartment with the windows open and the fire trucks roaring past and the noise and the heat and the pot he was smoking making him never want to get up. The pit bull was unleashed and strong, and it slinked by my door several times a day as I proofed scripts in my tiny office. When it came too close, I leaned across my desk, shut the door, and locked it.

The dog, whose name was Attila, had a muscular body, a square face and jaw, and empty, flat, button eyes like a doll's. It belonged to our show's executive producer, RJ, who had rescued it from a shelter. "I went to this place in the Valley," he told a group of us in the hallway one day, "and there was Attila— and I said, 'What the fuck is that thing?' And they said, 'This dog has been abused by humans, and this dog needs to get trust back in its life.' And I said, 'Okay, man,' and that was it. It just felt right and I'm so sick of second-guessing myself."

RJ, my new boss, was tall and thickly, darkly handsome. He wore a gold chain and a baseball cap and sunglasses, even inside. He had come up with the idea for the show and written and directed the pilot, and so he was, in the straightforward shorthand of Hollywood, the "showrunner," meaning, as it sounds, that he ran the show. He was fortyish and never married, and he gave off a serious vibe of cocky Hollywood asshole. I tried to stay out of his way.

RJ's assistant, Misty, was twenty-two and wore beach clothes to the office. She was constantly trying to recover from him yelling at her. You could walk into her office at almost any time of day and she would be crying, another assistant bent over her, murmuring sympathy and counsel.

"I just want to make this dog trust someone again," RJ said to us in the hallway. "If I do that, I think I'll feel good about myself."

ABSOLUTELY NO ONE was nice to me at my office, and when sometimes Misty and the other assistants threw Attila its big stuffed bone down toward my end of the hall, it would come racing down the rug, ravenous and reckless. I would close my door and lock it, and they would yell "Sorry," because they knew I was afraid, but when I opened the door afterward they would be standing there giggling, their hands pressed over their mouths.

Soon the dog started to stalk me. It sought me out, leaving the stuffed bone untouched, glowering at me as it passed my door, threatening me with its unseeing eyes.

It was male, I felt sure, though I never got close enough to look between its legs. No one ever called it "he" or "she." They always said Attila: "Aww, Attila, how're ya doing?" or "Attila needs a new toy, doesn't Attila need a new toy?" RJ had asked us to call the dog Attila to its face as often as possible because a dog psychologist had told him that a new name would help the dog settle into its new life and take on a new personality. Attila had had another name when it had lived on the streets and belonged to a gang, before it was rescued by RJ. The dog had once been known as Dee'andre, and it had been a fighter in the backyards of South Central. It had scars and wounds that would never go away. It had even fought and killed a dog that had turned out to be its own father, was what people said.

Despite this, no one else in the office seemed to be afraid of Attila. If nothing else, it seemed they could love a dog that might one day end up ripping out their throats. They went right up to it and petted it, and when their children visited the set, they let them pet it, too. But I was afraid.

I never did anything about it, though. I didn't want to complain. I was only the writers' assistant, one step up from intern, and I had only been working there since Toby and I had returned from our honeymoon in Paris. It was my first job in Hollywood and I didn't want to mess it up. I was thirty years old and from a good family back east. I had gone to boarding school and backpacked around Europe and started and ended two perfectly decent careers in New York. I was giving myself one last chance at starting over. My job now was to swallow my pride and get coffee and take notes and do whatever the writers said.

"Can you bring this pen to my office?" one of them asked me on my second day. She was lounging in the writers' room, reading the newspaper, and she handed the pen to me without looking up. I didn't know what she meant, but I did it, I carried it to her office several doors down and I laid it on her desk, and I felt I had passed a kind of test.

The writers were insecure egomaniacs, and when I moved in and out of the shark den of their meeting room on the fourth floor—Hollywood's ivory tower—I tried to shrink into myself, to become pale and flat, a cardboard ghost. Many of them had started as assistants when they were in their twenties, and they seemed to feel they had earned the right to treat me poorly. I was older than the other assistants, and so apparently I was a threat. The writers seemed to fear that I might actually have some good ideas, that I might sit down at the table and pitch a season's worth of stories if given the chance. They relegated me to a little desk in a corner of the room, where I took notes and listened to their chatter. I tried to hide my irritation, but the writers were on the lookout for attitude and encroachment, and inevitably one of them would see something in me I couldn't hide: *Lacey doesn't look exactly eager to fetch our coffee today,* or *Look at Lacey, pretending to be all quiet, but ready to take our jobs as soon as we turn our backs.*

But the truth was I didn't want their jobs, their languorous, stultifying hours spent in a gray-walled room picking at piles of pretzels and M&M's, talking about anything but the scripts they needed to write, their children and spouses waiting at home while they opined on blow jobs and the war and last night's episode of *ER*, dismissing one another's story lines before they could even spit them out—*Oh God, no, that will never work, the characters would never do that, we need something less boring*—their brains gelling into a paste that could be smeared on any bright idea, suffocating it with focus and purpose until it no longer held any potential for doing any kind of good.

These were the kinds of beneath-the-surface truths that I had come to know since beginning my job. I took notes for the writers and ordered them lunch; I washed their silverware and listened to them waste their time discussing which agent had said what about whom. I watched what went on in that room, and I rearranged my face minute by minute in an attempt to hide what I knew showed there: disdain, boredom, disappointment.

No, I didn't want to be them. But I had wanted something from L.A.: love, a career, friends, money—what?

I HATED THE JOB, but it was Attila who made me want to stay in bed in the mornings. I was beginning to feel terrorized in my own workplace. When I told Toby this, he said I was being dramatic. I had never thought of myself that way.

Then he began to tell me that I was cold.

"You can't even love a dog?" he said. In Toby's dreams he was still a baby, warm and held and bottle-fed. I wasn't totally oblivious; I understood what he was pleading for underneath the criticism, but that didn't mean I could give it to him. His needs! They ran so deep. At parties he was jealous, he wanted to stay home and cuddle instead; sometimes when he smoked too much pot, he would come into bed and wrap his arms around me, hugging me with such desperate force that I believed he would never let go.

ONE NIGHT, Toby asked me if I was going to make trouble at work.

"Make trouble?" I said.

"About the dog."

"You mean the one that wants to maul my face off?" I said.

"Are you going to?" he pressed. "Because you know we need the money right now. You can't quit like you did last time."

"Wow, thanks for being such a supportive husband," I said.

Then I felt guilty. We really did need the money. With Toby still out of work, we had already faced the fact that we couldn't afford to stay in our little red cottage in the hills. We had moved from the wooded seclusion of Laurel Canyon down into the concrete Hollywood flats, where we rented a small second-floor apartment for $1,150 a month and used our credit cards to cover everything else. Jimmy James had promised us that he would get Toby another job eventually, but the sitcom market was tough right now, apparently getting battered by reality-TV programming, so I needed to support us until he did. I didn't mind that, not really, and yet Toby was now home all day on the couch, and no matter how many times I asked, he wouldn't get a temporary job just doing something—anything—for a little while. "I get paid to write for TV, so I need to watch a lot of it," he said.

When I left in the mornings he was already lying on the couch in his flannel pajamas, watching TV, and when I returned at night he was in the same position. The TV shows he watched were cartoons for adults, and I didn't feel like cooking unless it was something he didn't like, and so he toaster-ovened frozen pizza and I made chicken curry and we ate separate meals in front of the television. I tried to read a novel on the couch while *Family Guy* blared so I could feel like we were spending time together, and then I took my bath and went to bed.

"I have to tell you the truth," whispered Toby one night when he got into bed, when I could tell he wasn't sure if I was awake. "I'm not sure if I love you anymore. Did we make a mistake?" I kept my breathing even and slow. I don't think he saw my eyes, wide in the dark, nor did he suspect that the frame of the room was shifting back and forth, as if I'd been hit over the head. His words huddled in my brain like a hematoma, a sinister truth now pulsing with life.

I TRIED TO ESCAPE to work, but the writers still ignored me with a passive-aggressive vengeance, and Attila continued to stalk me. Up on the fourth floor, in the writers' room, it would come up and sniff me while I tried to take notes.

The dog also liked to strut around the studio lot, which was huge and without boundaries, with fake streets and fake homes and fake bars and restaurants where they filmed crime shows. It liked to nose around, sticking its head into seedy back doors and wandering down fake alleyways that probably reminded it of its old life on the streets. Sometimes it would pick forlornly at fake trash—fake plastic banana peels and fake rubbery chicken parts—and then Misty would pull it away by its collar and say, "Don't do that, Attila. That's disgusting."

Our show was a nostalgic family drama set in the 1950s, and among the characters were a little boy with a bum leg and a mother with a blond bouffant who was home every day after school, and a strict dad who owned a neighborhood five-and-dime, and the possibilities were endless because America hadn't yet put a man on the moon.

When Attila deigned to wander over to our show's set, which was a clean suburban house with window boxes and a white fence, not unlike the house I had grown up in, it would range around like it owned the place, and its presence was so unclean, so not of the show's fifties naïveté, that its very ugliness, its very evilness made me grateful to be alive and in the world now, where evil could be seen and marked as such. It would sit on its scarred back legs, disdainful and restless, impatiently watching the actors move about the house, and I imagined that it sensed, as I did, that everything it watched was false, a lie, a superficial gloss thrown over an era that already had a superficial gloss—it was a time before pit bulls, when reality was hidden away. But now the pit bull was out in the open; it was the dog of its time, and it knew it.

WHEN I HAD BEEN WORKING on the show for two months, I tried to talk to Misty one day, hoping we might bond over mutual fear—hers of her boss, and mine, by extension, of his dog. I stopped by her desk, which was in a little room adjoining RJ's palatial office.

"He's a tough one, huh?" I said, nodding toward his office.

"Not really," she said quickly. "We get along fine." Then she looked up. "You have to get along with people in Hollywood, you know." It sounded like a warning directed at me.

"Yeah," I said. "Um, I guess I need to make more of an effort here. I think I've gotten off on the wrong foot."

But she went on, as if I hadn't spoken. "I've worked for tougher people than him," she said. "My last boss asked me out every day until I said yes, and after I slept with him he dumped me and started sleeping with his other assistant. But if you want to make it in this business, you have to really want it, you have to have that obsession . . ."

She trailed off. I sensed she thought she'd said too much.

"You don't have to put up with that," I said, a little stunned by her revelation. "I mean, I know RJ's mean to you, and that dog—"

"It's fine," she said. "I love dogs. Most people do, you know."

THE NEXT DAY Misty poked her head into my office. As she did, Attila poked its head in, too. When I looked alarmed, Misty narrowed the door's opening to a crack, forcing Attila away. It was clear that she continued to find my fear mildly humorous.

"I think RJ is looking for you," she said.

"Why?" I said, concerned. I rarely had reason to speak to him, and I doubted very much that he even knew my name. As the showrunner, and the boss of all 150 people on the show, RJ was like a celebrity in the office. When he walked into a room everyone stopped talking to hear what he had to say. We all laughed at his jokes and did whatever he asked, ASAP. He was constantly on the phone, or in a meeting with the studio, or down in the editing bay; when we passed in the halls I kept my head down and surreptitiously eyed him as he rushed by, pecking at his BlackBerry. I was slightly thrilled by the idea that he wanted to talk to me—yet terrified at the same time. "What does he want with me?" I said.

"I don't know," Misty said, "but he said to tell him if I saw you. Figured I'd give you the heads-up."

"Thanks," I said, and I meant it.

I went down the hall. Attila was pretending to sleep on its Neiman Marcus dog bed outside RJ's door. I steeled myself and walked past. The dog opened its eyes and glared at me, but I just stared straight ahead. I peered into RJ's office and there he was, working on a gleaming laptop at a huge mahogany desk parked several yards from the door. A royal-blue carpet covered the expanse between the door and his desk. His sunglasses sat on top of his head, across the bill of his baseball cap.

"Hey," I said quietly.

He looked up, then went back to his computer. He didn't say anything. I stood there for a moment, waiting for—what?

"I heard you were looking for me," I tried.

"Did you," he said, staring at the computer.

At that point I was still not sure he knew who I was. Maybe he'd been looking for someone else and had confused my name with that person's. Maybe

Misty had misunderstood him. I considered backing away from the office. I looked over my shoulder, toward Misty's office, and then:

"Are you afraid of my dog?" RJ said.

I turned back to him; he was still looking at his computer. "No," I insisted.

"Then why don't you want Attila around?" he said. Still not looking up.

"Who said that?" I said.

"The grapevine," he said. "Although that's not really any of your business. Anyway, word is, you're afraid of Attila."

"I just don't think—"

"There's no reason to be afraid," he said, suddenly looking up. He stared at me, then glanced out at Attila, who lay sprawled in the hallway. "Attila wouldn't hurt a fly. Isn't that right, Attila?"

At that, Attila strode in, its body taut and alert.

"Okay, good, good," I soothed, nodding and staring at RJ but keeping Attila in my peripheral view.

"So," RJ said. "You're married?"

I looked down at my huge diamond engagement ring and the eternity band that circled my finger. I nodded.

"What's your husband do?"

"Nothing," I said. "He's unemployed." Instantly I felt bad. I could have said he was a comedy writer and left it at that. "He'll get a job soon," I said.

"What a guy," RJ said. And then: "You want to be a writer, right? On the show?"

"I know I'll have to work for it," I said. "But if you give me a chance, I promise you I can write."

He ignored me. Instead he came around his desk and squatted down and petted Attila's head, smoothing its skin back so its upper lip lifted, revealing its teeth. "See," he said, gazing at Attila. "What a sweet dog."

"Yes, you're right," I said.

"Why don't you pet Attila?" he said. "Right now."

"Okay," I said. But I didn't move. Then I put my hand out. I stroked the dog's head lightly, with the tips of my fingers.

"That's it," RJ said. "Doesn't that feel good?"

I nodded, too scared to talk. I felt RJ looking at me, watching me. "See," he murmured, moving closer to me. "It's not so bad." Then he put his hand on top of mine, covering it.

Reflexively, I snatched my hand away. "Don't," I said.

RJ eyed me. He stood. "This is just a poor defenseless dog who's been abused," he said. "What's your problem?" Before I could answer, he said, "You know what your problem is?" As I shook my head, he said, "You think you're better than everyone else."

"I don't."

"Yeah, you do," he said. "You're so quiet all the time, hiding in your office, judging everyone, like you're above everything. You think I don't see it?"

"I'm not judging," I said. "I just don't have anything to say."

"You don't have anything to say? And you want to be a writer? On this show? Good luck." He sat down behind his desk. "Misty!" he shouted. "Get in here!"

I turned and left, running into Misty just outside the door. I stopped her. "Don't go in there," I said.

"Right," she said. "Good decision."

She pushed past me, went into his office, and closed the door.

It was around this time that I began to admit that things were not quite right, that although a plan was in action—I would work as an assistant and rise, rise, rise—I could see already that it was never going to take shape. RJ couldn't stand me, I would never get a chance to write a script, to prove that I could do it, and the writers were already seeing in me derision and disobedience. There were other plans, too—a marriage, a home life, a life of the mind—yet I could not connect with anyone I met at parties, the books I read were not the books other people were reading, and no one seemed to think I was anything special anymore.

It was a time when smoking a cigarette alone by our window made me as sad as I'd ever been and I wished for friends, but when we went to friends' homes and they talked about agents and deals and how to get them, I wished I was by my window again. A single palm tree against the Sunset Strip and my lone steps resounding on a sidewalk at night could make me anguish for people who lived by themselves, but when I got home to our cramped apartment I yearned for my own private space. And I wished often then for the summer twilights when I was a child, when my mother would put me to bed early, just as the sun was setting, the cars driving by slowly in suburbia, their headlights making windowpane shadows against my little walls. When I got into bed with Toby he was often already asleep, or if not, he was stoned, red-eyed and glazed, a ham awaiting dressing and a pan and a knife.

When my mother questioned me about Toby—"Are things still very romantic between you two?" she'd ask, in her old-fashioned way—I would say that we were fine, and that we were happy. I wished at times that I could turn to her for counsel, but I could not. In junior high, when Adam Logan broke up with me and I called my mother crying, she soothed me and told me he wasn't good enough for me, but a few weeks later, after he'd gotten back together with me in the cafeteria, and I, elated, told my mother, she stood at the top of the stairs looking down at me, her eyes empty with disappointment, and she's never shaken that look since. I knew that if I were to go to her and collapse in her lap and say, "This isn't working, this life, I made a mistake," she would look down at her lap and say regretfully, like she had kept quiet all this time for my sake, "I know."

I TOLD TOBY I thought we should begin marriage counseling.

"It's something we should start now," I said, "before things get out of control."

"Where'd you come up with that idea?" he said. "From the writers at your office? You always say they're the ones who are fucked up."

"We've only been married six months, and, well, I just think we shouldn't let things get too far gone, you know?"

He paused for a long moment. "Don't you think they already are? We snap at each other too much. You're pissed off at me all the time for sitting on the couch."

"I think you're just depressed. You need a job and you'll feel better."

"My getting a job isn't going to change the fact that we never have sex."

"The first year of marriage can be hard," I said. "Everyone says it. We just need a little help."

He shook his head. "It all feels wrong," he said. "Maybe I was too young to get married."

The room started shaking again, and I spoke through a haze of terror. "But you were thirty when we got married," I said.

"I don't feel thirty," he said. "I feel old." He looked up at me. "Maybe we're not going to make it."

"You can't say that," I said. "We took a vow to stay together."

"You can say that I can't say it," he said. "But I just did."

SOMETIMES, after work, rather than going home right away, I would drive around for a while instead, smoking cigarettes and listening to music, and then I would inevitably get lost and end up in one of those nondescript neighborhoods, one of those absolutely nothing and nowhere sections of L.A., in that vast expanse of concrete between Culver City and the Westside, in the shadow of the 405, the parts of town that freaked me out more than anything, haunting me with the feeling that I might end up there someday. Just passing through those neighborhoods I would become convinced that I was seeing into the future, that one day I would be forced to stop and pull over and set up shop there, in some crappy efficiency apartment above some crappy no-name bar, in a part of town no one had ever been to or heard of, the fringes of the city—all of it reminding me again and again that out here in L.A. all bets were off, that most people failed at their dreams, that anything could happen, and that meant anything in the worst sense, in the quietest, most dismal sense. I could grow old here never having reached my dreams, not even one, without ever knowing any sense of success; I could die out here or disappear here, sink into drink and despair here, and no one would notice.

ONE DAY AT WORK, I ran into Attila in the hallway. We were alone. I didn't want to hurry by, because I didn't want to goad the dog into chasing me. I thought about turning around and heading back toward my office, but Attila was heading in that direction anyway. Suddenly terrified, I stopped. The dog stopped, too. It stared at me and there was something there, like a dare—*Come on, what are you going to do about it?* And I felt irrationally that the dog was challenging me, that it could see into me and knew that, both here in the hall and in my larger life, I would do nothing but keep walking toward whatever end was coming. I wouldn't try to change my life for the better, the way it had. Ashamed, I began to edge by the dog, clinging to the wall with both hands as I did. It watched me go.

"Attila!" RJ bellowed then, from down the hall, his voice fast and huge.

The dog instantly turned its head and bolted toward RJ. There in a flash, it lay down at RJ's feet, and the two of them stared at me. After a moment I turned my back on them and walked away. As I did, I felt in every bone of my body, in every muscle, Attila's disgust for me, its disdain for my fear, its urge to run down the hall and jump me, to tear me to shreds, to expose my nerves and organs and leave me to bleed to death.

"I MIGHT GO STAY at Rob's for a few nights," Toby said that night.

I noticed then the duffel bag on the bed. "We can fix this," I said.

"I need you to know that that may not be true," he said.

THE NEXT MORNING at work, no one was around.

Misty came to the door of my office. "Did you hear?" she asked.

"What?" I said.

"It's Attila," Misty said. "He had to be put down."

"What?"

"Yeah, last night." She nodded down the hall, toward RJ's office. "RJ's brother and sister-in-law and baby niece are visiting from New York? And the baby started crying? And Attila suddenly barked at the baby. Really barked, RJ said. Like, ferociously."

"Oh my God," I said. "And then what?"

"I know," Misty said. "Who would have thought?" But then she looked at me. "Well, of course you—"

"Did Attila actually touch the baby at all? Was the baby hurt?"

"No, but he came really close to her, I guess, when he barked."

A pause. "So, wait," I said. "Attila is a he?"

She just looked at me. I felt a little dazed.

"You know what?" I said, snapping out of it. "Maybe Attila just can't be around babies. Maybe there was a crying baby in Attila's old life and the reminder of it set him off. "

"Lacey, it's done," Misty said irritably. "RJ had him put down last night. He like rushed him to the vet and had it done." She looked at me with curious annoyance. "Why do you care anyway? You hated that dog."

"I didn't hate him," I said.

Just then RJ walked by my office, apparently having overheard. "You," he said, staring at me. "You're probably happy about this."

"He barked at a baby?" I said.

"That's right," he said. "I can't take any chances."

"Maybe the baby antagonized him, you know, made a sudden movement or something," I said.

RJ shook his head. "You're always right, huh? You've wanted my dog gone the whole time you've been here, and now he's dead and you're questioning me?" Then he said slowly, "He barked at a baby." He looked me up and down. "Do you really think you're a good fit here? I don't know how well you're getting on with the writers anyway. I hear things."

I backed away from him, then shut my door and locked it.

I went to the window. The day was already coming in clear—the haze was gone and I could see the studio lot and the fake trees and the fake streets, looking so real from here. Beyond, just outside the studio gates, I could see the surrounding neighborhood, and rows and rows of low-slung tenement apartments, a place where Attila might have grown up in his past life. The people who lived there were poor and Hispanic, and their children played in the streets, and the women sat on stoops and traded secrets with their neighbors.

But looking down on them, I imagined something different, somewhere in the future. When their children grew up, I imagined, they would make money, lots of it, and they would move away from here, to the suburbs, where they would build fences around their homes and sit inside on summer nights, televisions glowing. Only in fleeting moments of nostalgia, and from a place of shelter and safety, would they think back on the hardship of their youth.

And then I imagined Attila, sitting beside me on his dog bed, still alive, but sweet and friendly, having lived a different life—a life of security and care. I imagined Toby, my damaged husband, repaired and healthy, his arm around me, protecting me. I imagined myself, warm and loving, unafraid and confident, my life full of all I'd ever dreamed.

But down on the streets below, the world swirled. There was no going back. There was only the pressing onward of inevitable bad times and good, the future marching over us like a tank, flattening our pasts and our goals, leaving us insubstantial as paper, so thin you couldn't see us when we turned sideways.

The Magic Castle

"SO WHEN DID THINGS start to go badly?" asked Ira, our marriage counselor, a fatherly man with a gray beard, during our first session.

My husband looked at me. I looked back at him. My mind searched. There were so many possibilities. The morning after our wedding, when I threw up? The honeymoon in Paris, when we fought the whole time? Right then, trapped in a dim office, answering to a stranger about my marriage?

I did not say anything. I did not know when or how things had gotten so bad.

"The lime thing?" Toby offered. "At the reception?"

Wow. That early? The wedding reception? We'd been married for six hours.

Then Toby suggested it might have been even earlier. Perhaps it was during the toasts, or in the middle of the wedding ceremony. He cast his mind back even further, grasping for the first inkling of disappointment in our married life.

"Well, if you really want to go there," he said reluctantly to Ira, then turned to me: "Why did you wear your hair up at the wedding when you know I like it down?"

So things had started heading downhill from the moment he saw me walking down the aisle?

"No," Toby decided. "It was the lime. That lime was a sign of things to come." He was suddenly certain. "That lime," he said, "was the beginning of the end."

THE NIGHT of our wedding, when the dancing was over, as Toby and I stood waving in the green of a Vermont field to our guests under a billowing white tent that glowed with candlelight, someone threw a lime wedge at me. It hit me smack in the chin, and it hurt. Stunned, I put a hand to my chin. Outraged, my husband looked first at me, then out into the crowd, trying to find the culprit. A group in the back looked guilty, but no one stepped forward to claim responsibility.

"It was just a joke," I said, turning to Toby, trying not to cry in front of our guests, most of whom hadn't seen it happen. "Someone trying to have fun."

"I don't care," Toby seethed. "They hit you in the face."

"Who do you think threw it?" I said.

"I bet it was that drunken idiot Jason who you used to work with and that horrible date he brought who wore a cowboy hat to the rehearsal dinner," Toby said bitterly. "I knew we shouldn't have invited them."

"Maybe I should say something to them," I said. "Throwing a lime at the bride?"

"They probably meant to hit *me,*" Toby said, and I knew he was trying to make me feel better, but it came out sounding like I was inconsequential, not even worth pelting with a lime on my own wedding night.

I DO NOT KNOW why I did it. I was angry, yes, but I like to believe there was more to it than that. Perhaps, for instance, a proactive desire to commandeer Toby's chosen symbol of our marriage's implosion, as if I could drain it of power and expose it for what it really was: a piece of fruit, meaningless.

It happened a week after our first session with Ira. Toby had come over to the apartment for dinner. He had been staying at his best friend Rob's for the past several weeks as we tried to work things out, and now we were trying, at

Ira's quixotic suggestion, to have dinner at home together once a week, as if we were on a date.

I was making guacamole in the kitchen while Toby sat on the couch watching TV. When I saw a lime wedge sitting there on the cutting board, somehow I could not help myself. I picked it up, stepped out into the living room, and whizzed it at Toby's head.

Surprised, he looked up at me.

I stared back at him, guilty. "I'm sorry," I said.

Toby looked back at me warily. "It's okay," he said.

But later that night, as we were doing the dishes, he threw a wedge at me across the kitchen, catching me square in the chest. At first I was shocked, as he had been earlier, but after a moment it was so absurd I almost smiled.

After that night we began to throw limes at each other on a regular basis. Each week we resumed the match, as if it were an ongoing game of tag: first I would get him, then he would get me, and it just kept going. I collected the limes from a tree out in front of our apartment each week, hoarding an ample supply in the bottom drawer of the fridge (a chilled lime made more of an impact than one at room temperature); I left a knife alongside a lime on a wooden cutting board on the kitchen counter. Mostly we just tossed them at each other, a light chuck, but occasionally there was a faster throw, a beaning. The limes became a language all their own. We used them to say different things at different times: *Lighten up, I'm pissed, I might still love you, I hate you, You were right and I was wrong,* and *Fuck off.*

I enjoyed the levity the limes provided, yet I sensed that Toby was using them for exactly that, to create a false sense of security within me, a misguided belief that things were not as bad as they really were. The limes were merely a cheap diversion, a clown juggling balls off to the side while in the main ring the lion bit off the tamer's head.

When I told him my suspicions, Toby sighed. "You're just being negative," he said, "the way you always are."

And when I questioned it in therapy, Ira was exuberantly dismissive of my fears. "This all sounds so healthy!" he exclaimed. "It's a great way for you to communicate your feelings nonverbally."

Isn't that what sex is for? I thought. But I didn't say anything. I was trying to be more positive.

"Just be careful," Ira added, regarding us both sternly. "It's all in good fun until someone gets poked in the eye."

AT WORK there was also a strange sense of being on the edge of something, of reality combusting silently under the surface. There was, for instance, a palpable undercurrent of sex at the office. Everyone was sleeping with everyone. There were dirty, dirty things happening everywhere you looked, over in the actors' trailers, up in the writers' offices, down on set in the characters' bedrooms. Even the two stars of the show—a forty-something blond bombshell and a beefy ex-wrestler turned actor—had started angrily fucking. They played a happily married couple on-screen but offscreen their relationship veered all over the place; they were either overly lovey-dovey, making the crew nauseous, or pissed off and jealous, coveting each other's close-ups, snickering openly when the other blew lines or missed a mark.

Meanwhile, up on the fourth floor, the mid-forties snakewoman of a head writer was having a lecherous affair with a hot twenty-two-year-old production assistant. The PA's job was to deliver scripts to the writers' homes after hours, and apparently one night the snakewoman had met him at her door in a see-through negligee. I found their relationship highly entertaining, but the other writers barely mustered the energy to mock them about it. They were irritable and tired and spent, even more so than usual.

Over the past two seasons the ratings had been declining, and the show had just barely been spared from cancellation. The network had granted us a third season because their pilots had sucked this season and they had nothing else to fill the slot. Now the word had come down from on high: the network president had seen a rough cut of the season premiere and hated it, but, more importantly, the TV testers, the regular Joes who had walked in off the Las Vegas streets to rate the show, had *despised* it, rating it a 1 out of 9 on the interest scale. There was nothing to be done, the network president had declared, except kill the premiere, come up with all new story arcs, and shoot a new one, a decision that would cost the studio at least a million dollars. Now they expected the writers to come up with a new premiere ASAP, and it had better be exciting—chock-full of sex, violence, and "promotable moments," a tall order for a family drama set in the fifties—or the network would fill our slot with *Will & Grace* reruns faster than we could say *canceled after episode two*.

RJ was therefore forcing us to work late nights in order to come up with an amazing season premiere. This made the writers angry and resentful, yet they were too scared of losing their jobs to do anything about it. They began to treat one another even worse than they treated me, pissing all over one another's ideas, saying sexist things that they would have been fired for saying in any other workplace. They discussed how and where in their offices they masturbated and who in the cast they pictured when they did it; they mocked their husbands' penises and their wives' breast implants; they described even the size and texture of their own excrement.

"I'm having a real cunt of a day," announced one writer, glaring at the snakewoman after she mocked his story pitch.

"I think I just found your dick," she said, holding up a golf pencil.

"Can you say that again but with your tits out?" said the man. "At least then it might be vaguely entertaining."

The studio lawyers, throwing up their hands and turning their backs, had simply made us all sign waivers in which we acknowledged that lascivious behavior and crude language in the writers' room were essential to the creative process. According to the waiver, whose legal value was highly dubious, not only did we agree to tolerate this behavior, in fact we "welcomed" it. The writers had therefore taken to saying, whenever anyone protested their offensive jokes, "Oh, fuck off, you welcome it!"

MISTY, who everyone suspected was now sleeping with RJ, had been burdened with the task of planning a party to celebrate the airing of the season premiere two weeks away, despite the fact that it hadn't yet been written, never mind shot. She had since become obsessed with planning the party of RJ's dreams. For the past several days she had been endlessly popping her head into the writers' room to ask RJ for decisions regarding mundane party details he had no interest in: invitations or e-vites, food stations or buffet, karaoke or band.

"Misty," RJ said vacantly two and three times a day as she stuttered into silence, the writers looking on dumbly, "what the fuck are you even talking about?"

She fled the room in tears nearly on the hour.

"Wow," the snakewoman said finally one day, turning to face me squarely at my little desk, where I sat, ostensibly taking notes for them. "If only someone was available to help her. And if only that someone would offer to help."

I was still on thin ice at work. In the wake of all the drama with the network and the season premiere, RJ had somehow forgotten about our argument over Attila's death, as well as his idle threat that maybe I wasn't working out. But I was scared he might remember and focus his laserlike hatred on me again, so I was trying to make myself still more invisible. I hid at my little desk and did my humiliating tasks—going out to Starbucks for the writers' lattes, making sure their cabinets were stocked with their favorite Trader Joe's chocolates and plenty of Emergen-C, taking their cars to get them washed—with no complaints or attitude. I fantasized daily of quitting, but we desperately needed the money. And besides, given the state of my marriage, life seemed difficult enough without throwing unemployment into the mix.

Now I looked up from downloading lunch menus. (I had long ago stopped taking notes; in lieu of pitching stories for the new season, the writers had been debating which agency in town had the least attractive agents. This controversy had engrossed them more than any story line ever could: they had created charts and graphs; calculators and spreadsheets were involved; a superagent at CAA had somehow rated a negative 11.) "I'll help Misty if you want me to," I said.

RJ nodded at me firmly, as if he were a drill sergeant.

I went downstairs. Misty was at her desk, crying.

"Hey," I said.

"Hi," she said, sniffling.

We had warily become friends over the past several weeks—well, perhaps *friends* was too strong a word, but in any event we had banded together, mainly to protect ourselves from RJ and his evil army.

"What's the matter?" I asked.

"I can't say," she said.

"Why?"

"I'm embarrassed," she said.

I stared at her without saying anything. This often worked with Misty. She had an extremely low resistance to pressure combined with a stunning inability to refrain from filling a void of silence.

"Fine," she said crossly after a moment. "I booked the season premiere party at the Magic Castle."

"Oh," I said. That was a mistake. A big one. The writers would be mocking her for the rest of the season. The Magic Castle was a cheesy club in the Hollywood Hills where you could go see amateur magic acts and eat a greasy forty-dollar steak dinner. I had never been. No one in Hollywood had ever been. It was like Disneyland; one did not go unless one was a tourist.

"I told RJ," she said, and I cringed. "And he told me to cancel and book the Viceroy instead."

"So did you?" I said.

She ignored me. "I managed to get us in there, and this is the thanks I get," she continued defiantly, blowing her nose. When I did not respond she added, "Apparently it's a big deal to get into the Magic Castle, you know."

I opened my mouth to disagree but then I changed my mind because I could see that she was skirting the margins of a nervous breakdown.

"Anyway, what do you want?" she said.

"I want to help you," I said.

"Oh, now you want to help," she said, crossing her arms. "Well, I'm not going to cancel it. You go ahead if you want to."

I called the Magic Castle. We could not cancel. If we did, we would forfeit the ten-thousand-dollar deposit that Misty had somehow agreed to hand over without first consulting RJ.

"Uh-oh," I said.

Now Misty dropped the defiant act and looked scared. I didn't blame her. "What do you think he's going to say?" she said nervously.

We found out that afternoon, up in the writers' room, after RJ banged his fist on the table in front of everyone and then stared at her for a full minute without saying a word: Misty was fired.

BACK AT THE RANCH, therapy was not helping. Perhaps it was because I had been the one to force the issue of going, but Toby appeared to feel empowered to say whatever he wanted. And in the back of my mind I knew it was because he had already moved on. Now he would have to say the things that would hurt me, the things that I would not be able to forgive.

"Your homework for the week is to go home and have a lot of sex," announced Ira cheerily at the end of one session. Toby and I had not slept together in over a month.

Now Toby surveyed me as if I were a fish in a tank he was considering buying. He turned back to Ira and shook his head. "I'm not attracted to her anymore," he said, as if he had just come to that conclusion. I wondered if it was the way I was wearing my hair that day, or the nubby pills on my favorite pink sweater, or perhaps it was my eyes, red and swollen from crying. "I think of her more as a friend," he said, as if I wasn't in the room.

The following week we had not done our homework.

"And why not?" scolded Ira, and I considered punching him.

"I want a Jewish kind of love," Toby announced unapologetically, and my instinct was to call him—what?—anti-Catholic? Xenophobic?

But deep down I knew what he meant. Though I had often felt like his mother—cooking his meals, washing his clothes, sitting at my desk working while he lazed on the couch watching cartoons—I could not give him the unconditional love that his mother did.

He wanted a mother, but I wanted a man, and I had been growing angrier all the time that I had married a boy. This anger had been seeping out of me, and I knew it.

"Why don't you go away for the weekend?" suggested Ira. "Maybe a nice B and B?"

Toby snorted, as if the suggestion was absurd, then shook his head. "I feel like a dog that's been whacked on the nose too many times," he explained, crossing his arms on Ira's couch.

Later that night, at our weekly dinner, I chucked a lime at Toby while he sat on the couch watching television. He caught it in his hand without looking up. "Nice try," he said, staring into the TV set.

THE MORNING AFTER Misty was fired, she came in to work and took her usual place behind her desk, just outside RJ's door.

"Um?" I said, when I saw her there around 9 A.M.

She was defiant. "My contract says I can keep working for two weeks after being terminated."

"And you're *going* to?" I said.

"I have to keep this job. I need the money. And besides," she added confidently and somewhat mysteriously, "I think I might be able to change RJ's mind about firing me."

"Really?" I said, curious. "How?"

"The party," she said.

"You mean the one that got you fired in the first place?"

"I'm going to fix that," she said, and a strange determined look came over her; it was clear she had a plan. "I'm going to make this the best launch party ever," she vowed vehemently, looking off into the distance.

I was slightly taken aback; I sensed that she had weighted this decision, and this moment, with more drama than it perhaps deserved. I got the feeling that in her mind she was playing a part akin to a fallen cheerleader in a teen movie: cast out by the cool kids, she must now redeem herself by planning the absolute best prom ever (set to a music montage) or face a future of unpopularity. Misty had grown up in Olathe, Kansas, before coming to Hollywood a year earlier to make it as an actress. Her biggest dream was that RJ might give her a walk-on role on the show that would launch her career. Obviously, that would never happen now.

"Look, Misty," I said, "I didn't want to mention it, but if you really want to stay at this job, then, well, didn't RJ sleep with you?"

She narrowed her eyes at me. "*I* slept with *him*," she said. "He didn't do anything to me. And besides, that was weeks ago."

"What happened?" I probed, feeling guilty for doing so. "Why did it end?"

"The sex was too good," Misty said mournfully. "He said he couldn't focus at work."

I studied her; she was serious.

"Well, whatever happened," I said, "you have a sexual harassment claim right there. He can't fire you."

She laughed hollowly and looked at me as though she felt sorry for me, as though I was the most naïve person she had ever laid eyes on. "You're kidding, right?" she said. "You know what would happen to me in this town if I did that, right?" Then her eyes narrowed even further. "You're not going to say anything to anyone about it, are you?"

"No." I sighed. "But I don't get it. Why would you want to keep working for him? Get out while you can."

"No, you don't get it," she said, and she smiled, that strange determination glowing again in her eyes. "This is Hollywood, Lacey. If you can make it here, you can make it anywhere."

THERE WAS A LAYER of dust over the glass shelves full of glass knickknacks in Ira's dark, sleek, glass office, which was at the top of an office tower on Sunset, near the nightclubs on the Strip. Toby and I had to park in an underground garage and then take the elevator up. We usually arrived separately and met in Ira's ominous waiting room. Then we greeted each other with a hug. "Hi, Smooch," we would both say. Sometimes I had a bill to discuss with him, or mail to give to him. Then we usually sat in silence, waiting.

We were afraid of therapy, a little. Usually in the session Toby would say something harsh and mean, something that pulled no punches—and then I would start to cry and then he would feel guilty and get angry at me for making him say those things and then I would say something harsh and mean, and he would say to Ira, "See?"

But strangely, afterward, riding down together in the elevator, we would often glance at each other and smile guiltily like children, out of awkwardness, or shyness after having been so open with each other, embarrassed by what we had said and done to each other. It was then that sometimes I felt hope. Perhaps in Ira's dark, serious office, we were pretending to be adults, saying adult things, hashing it out like we imagined adults would, but in the elevator we could be ourselves, our silly, childlike selves, and perhaps we could be saved.

One day, sitting far away from me on the couch, Toby told Ira that he was tired of staying at Rob's, where he felt that the demise of our relationship was not treated with the respect it deserved.

"I wonder why no one is grabbing me by the lapels and shaking me and saying, 'What the hell are you doing?' " Toby complained, while I sat there watching. "Over at Rob's my friends just shake their heads and say how terrible it is that Lacey and I are breaking up. Then they just get stoned and turn on the TV and forget about it. I kind of want someone to talk some sense into me."

"Well, you know who you're really talking about, right?" said Ira, leaning suddenly forward in his chair and looking at Toby intently. "You know who you really think should turn off the TV and grab you by the lapels and talk some sense into you, right?"

I did not know, and I looked to my husband. Did he know? Because perhaps I could get that person over here right away and they could do that.

"Me?" said Toby.

Ira nodded sagely. "You."

My husband looked at Ira and nodded back as if he had finally said something very wise, and in the weeks that followed I waited and I hoped and I watched, but my husband never grabbed himself by the lapels and talked some sense into himself. There were others who tried—my father for one, his mother, me—and there were times when I thought I saw Toby mustering up the strength to try to do something to change everything, but in the end, he never actually did.

A FEW DAYS LATER Misty came into my office, crying yet again, and angry at me. She had just received a call from the studio's human resources office. Someone had reported her liaison with RJ; now they wanted to talk to her about it. After a half hour, I finally convinced her it wasn't me. "They've been hearing about other things, too," she whispered. "They're coming over to sniff around. If I were you, I'd keep my mouth shut."

The studio execs began to drop by, pretending to be interested in the season premiere, but it was clear to all of us that they were in fact attempting to suss out whether the show's dysfunctional family dynamic, starring RJ as the abusive father, would affect the show. RJ refused to meet with them, and so they wandered the lot unchaperoned, noting our many transgressions, whispering into their cell phones, smiling fakely if we ran into them on the stage.

"Hmm," they commented studiously, as if observing animals at a zoo, when they came up to the writers' room, where everyone was gossiping instead of working, where the snakewoman was flirting with the PA in the kitchen. When they happened to see RJ slam the door in the face of a tearful Misty—who, incidentally, was wearing a gold lamé spaghetti-strap top, white short shorts, and metallic gold wedge heels—they raised their eyebrows and kept walking.

But there soon came a rumor: they were thinking of taking drastic action against RJ. The writers' room was abuzz with speculation. Sometimes a studio hired a TV veteran to serve as a co-showrunner, or they brought in a studio exec to babysit the showrunner for a few weeks. As a last resort, they might fire a showrunner off his own show, even if he had created it, as RJ had. But none of those options seemed likely. I couldn't imagine RJ sharing his job with anyone, and I definitely couldn't imagine him being fired. "I'd like to see them try," he said.

IN THE MEANTIME, Misty was still showing up for work, and RJ was pretending that she no longer worked for him, even though she was still acting as his assistant and he hadn't hired another one. He ignored her when she passed him his phone messages in the writers' room, swiveled his chair around when she entered his office to bring him his lunch. Yet most of the time I thought I could see regret in his eyes; I had the distinct impression that he wished he could take back Misty's firing but was not sure how to go about it, how to admit that he had made a mistake.

Misty had one week left, and she was growing more and more desperate to stay. She had whipped up all sorts of surprises for the party—a magician, a chocolate fountain, an ice sculpture in the shape of RJ's head—hoping its success would push RJ over the edge and he would grant her a reprieve.

"Why don't you just ask him to reconsider?" I said. "I bet he would."

"No, no, no," she said. "He's a *guy*. He has to think it was his idea."

"I WANT TO HAVE A BABY," I announced one day in therapy. I was not sure that this was true, but I was not sure that it was untrue either.

"Do you think this is the best time to do that?" Ira said gently.

"No," I said, "but it's never the right time, and sometimes you just have to . . ." I trailed off. I knew that I was being irrational, that this was the opposite of the right time.

"Why do you want children?" Ira said.

"I want a family," I said. "My own family. A normal family. Toby and I come from divorced families, and I think that's part of why we're here right now—"

"I don't know if I even want to have children," Toby broke in.

"You don't want children?" I said. "You never told me that."

"Well, I don't know if I want them with *you*."

"What? Why?"

He stared at me for a minute. "Because I don't know if you'd be a good mother."

I stared back at him. I couldn't breathe. It was if I had just been socked in the chest.

Toby looked a little ashamed for having said it, yet he closed his eyes, took a breath, and continued. "For instance," he said, "if our children got sick with the flu, or had some other problems, I don't know if you could take care of them. I bet you'd just get angry at them, and be harsh and cold."

I burst into tears, yet I was aware that I was crying because I was afraid that what he had said was true. He had just spoken aloud my greatest fear. I could not agree with him, yet I could not in all honesty disagree either. I didn't know if I would be a good mother. I had no role model. There was no way to tell. I felt I would be acting in a void of knowledge. Then I thought hopefully: perhaps, having no role model, I would be free to parent as I saw fit. Perhaps I would not repeat the mistakes my parents had made with us. But I knew this was a delusion. Toby and I had said we would never get divorced, as our parents had, and yet here we were—trying to steer the car off that course. What if I had children and then felt nothing for them? What if I left them as I had been left? Were my children doomed to end up like me, here, in a therapist's office, trying to save themselves?

I looked up at Ira. Perhaps he would make sense of all this.

"Well," he said, rising to his feet, "that's all the time we have for today."

SEVERAL DAYS LATER, as the rumors about what the studio might do to RJ reached a crescendo, there was a knock at the door of the writers' room.

"What," barked RJ, as if the intruder had deigned to interrupt the writers in some kind of creative reverie. (In fact they had been arguing all morning about whether to order In-N-Out or Baja Fresh for lunch.)

The door opened, and one of the studio executives, a strong southern blonde known for her incongruously high-pitched voice, entered, accompanied by a pale, short man, leprechaun-like, with a red beard.

Misty trailed behind them, cowering in the background. "I tried calling your cell phone to warn you they were coming up," she stage-whispered to RJ. "It must be on vibrate."

"Shut up, Misty," RJ said without looking at her, but Misty broke into a grateful smile, clearly thrilled that he had finally chosen to acknowledge her again.

RJ kept his eyes on the network exec. "To what do I owe the pleasure?" he said.

"You haven't returned my calls," said the exec.

"I've been busy," RJ said, nodding at the whiteboard; it outlined a story he and the writers had developed yesterday and hadn't glanced at since.

"Your agent hasn't returned my calls," she said.

"I can't control my agent." RJ smirked, making it clear he absolutely could.

That pissed her off; her anger refreshed, she forged ahead. "Anyway," she said, gesturing toward the red-haired man, "this is Alvin."

"Alvin," RJ said.

"He's a life coach," she said.

"Excuse me?"

"It's a new thing studios are trying," she said. "You haven't heard of it?"

RJ stared back at her blankly.

"Remember when James Cameron was such an asshole on the set of *Titanic*?" she said. "Or when Russell Crowe threw that phone at that hotel clerk because he couldn't get through to his wife? You know who worked with both of them?" She nodded at Alvin, who blushed and looked at the ground. "He's that good. And now he's going to help you sort through some issues on the show."

"Nice to meet you all," said Alvin.

"You must be joking," said RJ.

"Try me," said the exec, and her high, cartoonish voice turned flat and serious. "I've had enough of you."

"You can't talk to me that way, Hadley."

She laughed. "Right, asshole. Now listen to me, prick. This show was on the bubble. The network nearly canceled it last year, and I fought like hell to have it picked up for a third season. I won't have you run it into the ground."

"I think you're forgetting who created this show," RJ said.

"And I think you're forgetting who's paying for it."

"You buffoons may write the checks," RJ said, smiling, "but you can't write the scripts."

"Oh, but we'll find someone who can," she said, "and I promise you their scripts'll be a hell of a lot better than the crap you people tried to pass off as a season premiere."

"Are you suggesting that the network would even entertain the thought of replacing me?"

"You know as well as I do that I can fire you in two seconds. All my other shows are Top Ten shows, RJ—the network thinks I walk on water. I'll have Jack Rudolphi send a moving van over here faster than you can pick up *Variety* and read 'Asshole showrunner fired off his own show.' Now, this ship needs to be shaped up. Either do what Alvin says"—everyone looked at Alvin, who actually waved—"or you're done."

She turned and left. "Good luck, Alvin," she called from the hallway.

Alvin took a seat in the back of the room, outside the ring of the conference table. "Don't mind me," he said, taking out a notebook. "Just pretend I'm not even here."

RJ snorted in disgust, let out a strange, stifled laugh, and left.

"Oh, this is going to be fun," Alvin said, and followed.

THAT NIGHT TOBY CAME to the apartment. He stood down on the street below, picked a lime off the tree out front, and threw it up at the windows. It connected with a loud thump; a huge crack spread instantly across an upper pane of glass. I was on the couch reading, and I looked up from my book, startled. I went to the window, opened it, and found Toby standing below, a guilty look on his face.

"Sorry," he said.

"It's okay," I said. "What's up?"

"I can't come to dinner tomorrow," he said.

"Why not?" I said. "Ira said we shouldn't skip a week."

"That guy?" he scoffed. "Please."

Before I could point out that if he did not respect our marriage counselor, perhaps we should find another, he told me that there was a *Star Wars* marathon the next night and all his friends were going to watch it at Rob's. Did I mind if he did, too?

"Fine," I said sullenly.

"Fine," he said back, and I could tell he was annoyed that I was not more understanding. "Sorry again about the window," he added curtly, and left.

I felt strangely guilty, as though I were a controlling parent. My husband was still a child, a teenager in a basement getting high with his buddies; how could I ask him to give up his pot and his TV and his *Star Wars* movies? I realized then that I was playing a mother role—not the loving mother I would have hoped to be but an angry, punishing mother. Toby did not want to have children with me. How could I blame him?

HOME ALONE THAT NIGHT, I idly cut up limes. I squeezed their juice into a wine glass; it was faintly green and cloudy. I stirred it with a spoon and considered adding sugar but decided against it. When I raised the glass to my lips, I wondered what I was doing and why. It occurred to me that I might finally have to consider myself unhinged, and I wondered if this was the first step in some kind of mental decline, if this was what it felt like to lose oneself. Yet I drank. The juice was the real thing; it was bitter, as I expected, and then tart, and then, patiently, irrationally, I waited for the saccharine ending I expected, the sweet aftertaste of a lime-flavored soft drink that never came.

RJ WOULD NOT SPEAK to Alvin, and so Alvin was trying to break him. He had camped outside RJ's closed door. For two days they had been in a standoff. RJ had a full bathroom, a refrigerator, and a liquor cabinet in his office, and no family to go home to. He did not need to leave. He took his calls in his office, showered, ate, slept there. Still, we all wondered with exhilaration, how long could he survive? How long could this go on?

For his part, Alvin did not seem likely to break. He ordered dinner on his cell phone, slept on the couch outside RJ's office, did yoga on a mat in the waiting room, and when he had to pee, he literally sprinted to the bathroom down the hall, then sprinted back.

Finally, one evening, there was movement in the plot. The door to RJ's office opened and he strode out. Alvin followed him with his eyes. Then RJ stopped. He did not look at Alvin.

"Tomorrow," RJ said. "Nine A.M." He left.

Alvin visibly exhaled, packed up his yoga mat, and left, too.

The next morning we were all there, peeking around corners, as RJ entered his office at nine. Alvin followed him in and shut the door.

From then on, several times a day, behind the closed door of his office, RJ's yelling would build, then explode ("My mother did so love me!"), and the door would fly open and he would storm out. Alvin would trail him as far as the door and then lean against the doorway watching him go, smiling serenely, as if he knew a secret no one else did.

We were skeptical of their progress at first, yet after a time we began to notice a small difference in the writers' room. RJ still yelled at us, and he was still breathtakingly rude to everyone, but there were times when he actually acted like a human being, tearing up when someone pitched a schmaltzy story idea, and telling us revealing stories about his childhood. His mother, apparently, had favored his older brother, while his father had spent all his time in the basement raising terrier gerbils.

As THINGS AT HOME rapidly declined, I began to spend a good portion of each day in my office crying. When RJ and the writers wanted me to take notes for them or order lunch, I went upstairs to the writers' room, my eyes red, my face raw. They now knew what was happening because of a conversation that occurred one day when I couldn't prevent my tears as I typed.

"From the looks of things, I believe Lacey has something to share with us," said Alvin. This was Alvin's thing. Sharing.

"No, I don't," I whispered.

"Then what the hell is wrong with you?" said RJ, turning impatiently in his chair.

"Ronald," chided Alvin. RJ's real name was Ronald, a fact that gave me inordinate pleasure.

"Sorry," RJ said.

"Please rephrase your question so it sounds more caring," Alvin said.

"Lacey," RJ said politely, "would you like to share with us what is wrong with you?" I listened for the sarcasm, I practically fell over in my chair trying to hear it, but it wasn't there.

"Nothing's wrong," I whispered.

"Well, you're making quite a scene about nothing then," snapped the snakewoman.

"Question for the room," announced Alvin. "Does anyone think that's an appropriate response to a colleague's pain?"

"Well, I wouldn't exactly call her a *colleague*," the snakewoman said. "She's an assistant."

"Lacey," said Alvin, "why don't you share what's wrong? This is a safe space."

I was literally cowering in the corner, my arms wrapped around myself. I looked back at Alvin. He seemed to realize that he needed to do more to convince me.

"I promise everyone will behave," he said, glaring pointedly around the table, "or the studio will certainly hear about it."

"Fine," I said, suddenly irritated. Why did I care what these people thought about me anyway? "I think my husband is leaving me." Then I surprised myself: I started to cry, hard.

There was silence in the room.

"Would anyone like to try to comfort Lacey?" said Alvin.

It was RJ who finally broke the silence. "I'm not surprised," he said, musing. "He's a comedy writer, right? They like to make people laugh, sure, but underneath it, comedy writers are always assholes."

"Yet underneath that," Alvin noted, "they're often in pain, suffering from some kind of childhood loss or trauma."

"Cry me a river," said RJ.

Now the snakewoman turned to me impatiently. "People don't just leave," she said. "What happened?"

"I don't know," I said.

"Nothing good," RJ said ruefully. "Nothing good."

"DID YOU SUFFER a childhood loss or trauma?" I asked Toby at our next session.

"No," he said.

"Didn't your father leave when you were like ten and move to Israel?"

"What's your point?"

"Yes, what is your point, Lacey?" said Ira.

"That he might have some shit to work out."

"Oh, *I* have some shit to work out?" Toby snorted. "I do? That's good."

"I'm not saying I don't. I'm just saying you might, too."

"Who doesn't?" said Ira cheerily.

At this point Toby announced that he did not want to come with me to the season premiere party at the Magic Castle.

"And why not?" said Ira. "I've heard very good things about the Castle. Except for the food. The food there is not good, apparently."

"I don't think it's appropriate," Toby said.

"I thought we were trying," I said.

He gave me a disapproving frown, as if I was living in a dream world. "I can only try so hard."

"I don't want to go alone," I said. "Please come."

"*Oh*-kay," Toby said with a sigh, but there was an ominous tone in his voice, as if he had warned me up front that this was not going to go well, as if I had just cashed in all my chips, as if this was the last thing he would ever do for me.

FINALLY, ONE NIGHT, sitting on the side of the bathtub, I took off my engagement ring and hid it away in a jewelry box. I could not wear it anymore. I did not want to take it off; taking it off was a sign that things were past the point of no return, that I was giving up. But I physically could not bear to have it on my finger anymore. It was a reminder of a happier time, of the day we became engaged, the party in SoHo that night, and the morning after, when I woke and zoomed my hand to my face, staring at the ring, making Toby smile next to me in bed. Now I felt the ring mocking me every time I looked at my hand. It was painful to take it off—I loved that ring, it was the most beautiful ring in the world—but not as painful as when, some days later, I removed my wedding ring as well.

"You're not wearing your wedding ring?" Toby noted one day as we sat on Ira's couch.

"I don't feel like we're married anymore," I said.

"That says a lot," Ira pointed out.

Thanks, asshole, I thought. *You know what, Ira? You really fucking suck at your job.* But I knew he was not to blame.

At the next session Toby had removed his ring as well.

"Well, she took hers off," he said.

And on and on we went. That is how a marriage ends. Those are the steps, the moments that you think can't happen, but they do, and when they do they are smaller than you think, and then there is no turning back and there is nothing to be done about it.

TOBY ASKED for a private session with Ira.

"I don't think that's a good idea," I said, but Toby insisted.

Afterward, Ira asked for a private session with me.

"I don't think that's a good idea," I said, but Ira insisted.

When I came in alone and sat down, Ira looked at me regretfully. I got the distinct sense that he knew something bad.

"What is it?" I said. "What did Toby tell you?"

Ira smiled faintly and waggled his finger at me, as if I were a naughty child. "You know I can't tell you that."

"Fine," I said, crossing my arms and looking away.

"How old are you?" Ira said.

"I'm thirty-one," I said warily, wondering where this was going.

"Hmm," Ira mused. "Well, you have time, but not a lot."

"What do you mean?"

"I mean, if this isn't going to work out between you and Toby, and if you want to have kids, we need to get you back out there so you can meet someone else. You're going to be thirty-five before you know it."

I sat, stunned. "What the fuck are you talking about, Ira?" I snarled, instantly regretting swearing at my marriage counselor. Then I said quietly: "I'm here trying to save my marriage."

"Yes," Ira said. "Well, we may want to rethink that goal."

ON OUR DATE that night, Toby would not tell me what he had said to Ira. When I questioned him, he looked at me the same way Ira had, as though I had misbehaved and should be ashamed for even asking.

"I think we should find a new marriage counselor," I said, "someone who's going to at least try to save us before pawning me off on the next man."

"Oh, come on, Smooch," Toby said. Then he said good-bye and left for Rob's.

On the way out he chucked a lime, hidden in his sleeve, at me: it landed lightly in my lap just as the door closed.

THE NIGHT of the season premiere arrived, and the Magic Castle loomed before us, dark and mysterious in the Hollywood Hills. We twisted and turned through the tiny winding streets, and shot up the steep driveway; the valets descended upon us and took the car.

The hostess greeted us in a small, dimly lit room with no doors. "Go to the owl on the bookshelf and say, 'Open sesame,' " she said. We did and a secret door swung open, revealing an elegant bar paneled in dark wood, filled with people from the show talking and laughing.

It was clear from the moment we entered that Misty had succeeded. The party was in full swing. Magicians wandered the crowd, pulling birds from their sleeves and making people disappear, while RJ held court in a corner.

Misty was rushing around like an insane person, and she accosted us as soon as we walked in. "Have you seen RJ? Do you think he's having fun? Are you having fun? Tell me you're having fun."

I reassured her, and she ran off to check on the sushi bar. Toby and I got a drink, I looked around for someone to talk to, and then suddenly Liam, the costume designer, a gay Scottish guy in his mid-thirties, rushed up to us and threw his arms around me. He was wearing a kilt and was obviously drunk.

"You," Liam said, slurring. Over my head, he spoke to Toby, still clutching me. "She always sneaks me the outlines early so I can plan my budget. She rocks. You're a lucky man."

"Thanks, Liam," I said, trying to extricate myself as Toby looked on. I could not make out Toby's expression. *Is he jealous?* I wondered hopefully.

Finally it was time to watch the season premiere as it aired on TV, on a screen as big as a movie theater's that Misty had had brought in. RJ had written the script himself, and I had heard from the writers that it was actually not bad, a huge compliment coming from them. RJ had directed it, too, and I was stunned when I saw what an amazing job he had done, how powerful the acting was, how clean the dialogue. He had answered the studio's dictum to pump up the drama; we had moved forward in time from the fifties to the sixties and there was lots of sex and drugs and some amazing rock and roll, but the highlight of the show was a heart-wrenching scene where one of the young male stars says good-bye to his family as he leaves for Vietnam. I cried while watching it, and when I looked around the room I saw that everyone else was crying, too. We would know the ratings tomorrow morning. Whatever happens, I thought, RJ should be proud.

Later we saw the gag reel, a twenty-minute tape of outtakes from the show and silly jokes people had caught on tape over the past couple of months. There I was with Misty in one shot, giggling while we poured sugar from a container we'd marked with a skull and crossbones into RJ's coffee. And there was RJ, unknowingly drinking it while we rubbed our hands gleefully, peeking out from a doorway.

Watching it, everyone in the room laughed, and afterward people came up to congratulate Misty and me. "Great idea," they said. "So funny."

Toby seemed annoyed. "You never told me about that," he said.

"That?" I said. "It was nothing. We just came up with it one day."

"You never told me you had all these friends at work," he said.

I looked around. I had never thought of them that way. "They're just work people. Anyway, the writers hate me, and that's what matters."

As if to disprove my point on cue, a gaggle of writers came up just then and congratulated me on how funny the coffee thing was.

"Great work," said the snakewoman. "Really funny gag about RJ."

"Yeah, really funny," intoned RJ darkly, suddenly behind us.

We all fell silent.

"So," he said, "this is the infamous husband we've been hearing so much about?"

I nodded and introduced them.

RJ looked Toby up and down. "I hear you're a real hell of a guy," he said.

"Funny," Toby said, equally aggressively. "I hear the same thing about you."

"Yeah?" RJ said.

"Yeah," said Toby. "Sounds like you don't give Lacey much of a break."

"Funny," RJ said. "I hear the same thing about you."

"Toby," I broke in desperately, "can you get me another drink?"

"Sure," he said evenly, and walked off toward the bar, but not before whispering, "What an asshole."

As soon as he left, RJ turned to me accusingly. "Why the fuck did you marry that guy?"

"He's actually a nice person," I said. "He's just, well, kind of a child."

"No shit," RJ said.

"He's trying to grow up," I said. "And it's not like I don't have my problems, too."

Suddenly something struck me on the cheek, hard, and I bit my tongue. Tears came to my eyes. I put a hand to my cheek and looked around.

"What the fuck?" RJ said.

Toby approached with our drinks. Mine was missing its lime. "Gotcha," he said.

I could not speak because of my bitten tongue. Tears welled in my eyes.

RJ looked at me, then turned to Toby, outraged. "Did you just throw a lime at her?"

"It's a game we play," Toby said.

"Some fucking game," said RJ.

"It's none of your business."

RJ inspected him, looked him up and down in the same way he did with actresses who auditioned for the show. "Dude," he said, shaking his head, "I hate to say it, but I think I'm going to have to ask you to leave. This is my gig and you're not welcome."

"Damn," Toby said dryly, exaggeratedly. "What a bummer."

"Now, wait just a minute," RJ said. "Are you saying you don't want to be here?"

"You're smarter than you look," Toby said.

"This is a nice party. These girls worked hard on it. Your wife worked hard on it."

"I didn't really," I said, more to RJ than to Toby. "It was all Misty's thing."

"Let me tell you something," RJ said to Toby. "I used to be all fucked up, too. Like, three weeks ago. Then I got some help and now I'm fine. You should get some help."

"We don't need your advice, thanks," Toby said.

"I wasn't talking about her," RJ said. "I was talking about you."

Now Toby looked at RJ curiously. "Are you in love with my wife?" he said.

"What's it to you if I am?" RJ said. "You're not in love with her anymore, are you?"

Toby looked at me. I stared back, waiting. He opened his mouth, but he didn't say anything. Then he looked away.

"I think you should go," RJ said to Toby.

"I'll meet you at the door," Toby said to me, and walked away.

I stood alone with RJ. I couldn't really speak.

"Thank you for that," I managed after a moment.

RJ snorted. "Don't get any ideas, sweetie," he said. "I am so not in love with you." And then he walked off, too.

On the car ride home I told Toby that I didn't want to go to therapy anymore.

He said he didn't either.

And then, staring straight ahead, the car rushing us forward into darkness, we agreed that we were done.

THE RATINGS the next day were amazing, miraculous. The critics even took note, calling the show "back from the dead" and a "hit," an extreme rarity for a show in its third season. RJ swaggered into the writers' room and all the writers talked excitedly at once as he sat proudly at the head of the conference table, a king returned from exile. The studio exec called to congratulate him, and Misty patched her into the writers' room via speakerphone.

"Nice work," the exec said sheepishly. "I guess I owe you—"

"Fuck you," RJ said, and slammed down the phone.

Alvin entered gaily, ready for the day. "Congratulations," he said, beaming at RJ. "I do hope our work together played some sort of role in this."

"Get out," RJ said. "You're fired."

He picked up the phone and roared, "Misty!"

She appeared almost instantly at the door.

"If you can stop being such a goddamn ditzy fool, you can come back to work."

"Thank—"

"Venti chai latte," he said. "Now."

And then, for the rest of the day, I sat and took diligent notes as the writers debated whether studio executives, therapists, or assistants had the smallest brains.

THE LAST TIME I saw Toby was later that week on Sunset Boulevard, outside Ira's high-rise office building, traffic zooming by in the morning sun.

We had met upstairs in Ira's waiting room and, without saying a word to each other, went inside Ira's office, sat down on his couch, and told him we were giving up. I felt naked and trashed, officially ending my marriage in front of a stranger.

"I'm sorry," Ira said, and it seemed like he really was. He did not try to stop us, to convince us to rethink it, to give it one more chance. Then the three of us stood up again awkwardly. Ira shook our hands. "Good luck," he said, and I felt the inadequacy of those words, sending me out into the world, my marriage over. I felt like I was being pushed off a cliff and wished luck on the fall.

"Good luck to you," I said stiffly back to Ira, and I wondered how often this happened to him, and how he felt at these moments, if he thought that he had failed.

As Toby and I descended together in the elevator, the silly childish hope I used to feel in that comforting space was dead. There was only one moment, when I glanced over at Toby, my young, funny, sweet, childlike husband, who had once been mine for the rest of my life and now was not mine at all, when for one flash of one second, I wanted to pull us back from the edge, to take his hand and say, *Wait, no, stop, we can fix this, let's try one more time, we know better now, let's not give up yet, this can't be it, this can't be the moment we say there's nothing more we can do, because then it will really be over.* I opened my mouth to say something, but Toby was staring straight ahead, shifting his weight like he couldn't wait to get downstairs and outside, and I knew there was nothing left to say.

Outside, down on Sunset Boulevard, my husband handed me a brown paper bag filled with CDs that had been in his car. I don't remember if we hugged. I think we did, but then I can't imagine that we did. In either case, we got into our separate cars and drove away, Toby back to our apartment, which I had recently vacated, me to a tiny bungalow I had rented in Venice Beach.

And that was the end. I was alone in L.A. We had been married for ten months. Some months later I filed for divorce, and some months after that we actually were. Our recent past seemed like someone else's. I remembered it as you might a movie that sticks with you long after you leave the theater. Once we had been married, I told myself with surprise. Once, I told myself, on a perfect summer day, on a farm in Vermont, in a green field ruffled by a gentle breeze, we had been married. It was only at the end of my daydreams that I remembered the lime, whizzing at me out of nowhere, a slap in the face, a wake-up call.

Part Two

Baby

WHEN I PULLED UP to the house in Topanga, I could see that the garage door was open to the dirt road. Catherine's husband, Henry, was in there, building something huge and incongruous out of wood. It didn't look like anything a baby could use.

"Hey," I called, climbing out of the car, as the dust I'd kicked up settled around me.

"Hey," he said, with equally false enthusiasm, and he hugged me. His shirt was damp and he smelled sour. I could see that he had been at this for some time, this project.

"It's a surprise," he said when he noticed my glances at the hulk of nailed-together blond wood. "For Catherine."

"That's nice," I said, though in reality I thought the whole thing self-indulgent and absurd. The last thing Catherine needed was another surprise from him. And Henry should be inside helping with the baby, I thought, not hammering away at some toy like a little boy.

"Congrats on the script," he said.

After I'd worked as a writers' assistant for a year and a half, I was finally going to get to write an episode of the show. "Thanks," I said now. "It's great but it's a lot of pressure, too."

"I can imagine," he said. "Anyway, Cath and the baby are inside."

"I'll go in then," I said, and he nodded and went back to hammering.

Inside, Catherine had the baby at her breast. She took one look at me and burst into tears.

Things between Cath and Henry had been bad since Matilda was born three months earlier, but I wasn't supposed to let on that I knew, at least not in front of Henry. He had asked Catherine not to discuss their problems with me lest I think less of him, which was ironic, considering his request had only made me do exactly that.

Catherine told me everything anyway, of course. Despite the fact that they had suffered and grieved a miscarriage before successfully conceiving Matilda, apparently Henry was now scaring Cath with his rabid lack of interest in being a father. He was sulking around, complaining that he could no longer go out on weekend nights, or sleep late anymore, and the baby didn't pay any attention to him anyway.

I had seen this type of thing happen with several husbands of other friends, whose reactions, upon the births of their first children, were to throw themselves headlong into midlife crises. One had actually gone out and bought a red Porsche, while another had stayed out doing coke until 5 A.M. every weekend night for a month.

Henry was aware that he was being an asshole. But he only copped to so much. "At least I'm not acting like Lacey's brother" was his most recent comment, which obviously infuriated me, though I had to admit there was truth to it. At least Henry had not out-and-out left his wife and child.

I had finally heard from Sam about a month earlier, after years of radio silence. He'd sent me a postcard, postmarked from India: *Hey. I'm alive and well. I wanted you to know. Will fill you in on everything down the line. I miss you. Give my love to Mom and Dad.*

Great, I thought. Do that. Fill me in on everything. Fill me in on why you missed my wedding, my divorce, and the birth of your child. There was, of course, no return address. No word about his child or his girlfriend. What the hell was he doing in India? Was there even skiing in India? Maybe in Kashmir? If I had known where he was, I would have flown there to track him down—and maybe I'd get some insight into Henry, too.

———

HENRY HAD TOLD CATH that the pregnancy and resulting baby had come too soon. He wasn't ready to be a father. He wasn't even ready to be ready to be a father. He'd had his whole life ahead of him, but now, with the responsibility of a child, he felt trapped. Cath pointed out that he might have thought about all this before she'd gotten pregnant, but Henry said that wasn't fair: he hadn't known it would be like this.

After he quit his job with the agent, Henry had actually done as he'd promised. He had finished *Beating Dad* in six months and gotten an agent. When the agent went out with the script to studios and production companies, Henry was so tense I was actually afraid he might have a heart attack. "If it sells for over five hundred thousand dollars, I get a private lunch with Robert McKee," he kept saying. "It says so right in the seminar contract. A private lunch." And then, to our delight and disbelief, the script actually sold— but not for the over-$500,000 figure Henry had dreamed about. It went to an independent production house for $35,000.

We were all deeply impressed that he had sold it at all, but the fact was that after taxes and his agent's 15 percent fee Henry was left with only $18,000— obviously not enough for him, Cath, and the baby to live on, and so in a somewhat sordid turn of events, as the money quickly dwindled to nothing, Henry had been forced to take a job answering phones for his own agent.

Henry's disappointment was sharp. He threw away all of McKee's books and sent him nasty, blaming letters. Eventually, to try to take his mind off things, he signed up for a weekend woodworking class, and it seemed to me he enjoyed pounding the nails into the wood a little too much. However, as time went on, it became clear that there was something pure and simple about the labor that affected him. Lately he'd convinced himself that the paltry amount he'd received for the script was actually a good thing, proof that he hadn't sold out to Hollywood. He'd gone and had his ear pierced and had begun wearing a Rasta cap and going to evening self-esteem seminars about how to awaken the artist within. "I have a responsibility to myself now," he said when Cath asked him to stay home instead. "I have to envision living the life of an artist."

"You have a baby now," Cath replied dryly. "Envision living the life of a father."

I TRIED OCCASIONALLY to look at it from Henry's perspective. I was sure that being the sole breadwinner for a family was quite stressful. But still. That was what you signed up for when you made the successful transition to adulthood, even if you did wake up one day and realize that marriage and children might be what most people wanted, but not what you wanted. Well, too late. You can't take a marriage back, and you sure as hell can't take a child back. *Grow up, Henry,* was what I thought. *Grow up and be a man and live up to your responsibilities.*

This kind of thing wasn't happening to my friends back home. On the East Coast my friends' husbands seemed to be taking adulthood in stride. They weren't leaving their spouses or their commitments. They were rising up in the ranks of their law and investment banking firms, staying married to the same people, buying homes in the same suburban communities where they had grown up. They were not going around acting like Peter Pan, pretending to be children forever.

I considered my ex-husband, for instance. Toby had moved out here from Philadelphia five years earlier, and in that time he had married and left me and, according to reports from mutual friends, was now spending all his time with a friend from childhood who had also recently divorced; the two of them stayed up until 2 A.M. playing video games, and spent their Sunday afternoons on twin Barcaloungers watching the NFL.

While we were splitting up, I'd thought Toby was careless. Why had he married me, I asked him, if he was only going to turn around and leave a year later? He didn't understand my question and looked at me blankly for a moment. "Well, I wanted to at the time," he said, as if that explained everything.

Perhaps, I realized then, it had less to do with carelessness and more to do with L.A.'s love of change, its quest for the next new thing. When a friend's wife left him she explained it this way: "The passion is gone. It's not the same as it was at the beginning. I want it to be new again."

Or perhaps there was no logical explanation. Maybe Toby's and Henry's bad behavior had simply to do, as some hypothesized, with the Santa Anas, the winds of anxiety. Maybe it was about the possibility of an earthquake at any moment. Or maybe it was just the decadence of the climate, the way the sun shone eternally in the sky like a bright yellow Prozac pill. In any case, I had noticed that people tended to blame the town's moral faltering on the elements: the heat, the wind, the water. "Can't you feel it in the air?" I once watched a famous actress say to a TV reporter, looking nervously around, before leaving town for good.

IN SPITE OF CATHERINE'S troubles at home, I was still sometimes envious of her. She got to step off the work cycle when she had Matilda, and no one expected anything from her career anymore. As a childless single woman in my mid-thirties, I still felt I had to prove that my higher education had not been in vain. But the truth was, sometimes just driving to work felt like a lot to ask. Why do I have to drag myself into an office and try to make something of myself, I thought, while Catherine gets to stay home and take care of the people she loves?

At the same time, I admitted to myself that I sometimes felt I was better than Cath. Since high school we had had plans to be successful, to have creative lives. Now she appeared to me as suspect. "I never liked social work that much anyway," she said when she quit her job right before the baby was born. Had she only been biding her time before she could marry, change her name, have children, and stop reading the newspaper? I felt, in the simple act of going to an office every day, that I was a feminist.

This was ironic because at the time I was acting like anything but.

After my split from Toby I had accepted RJ's apology for being rude to me at the party at the Magic Castle—"I shouldn't have said I wasn't in love with you. Even though I'm not. Still, it was poor timing for me to say that"—and I'd tried to ignore the fact that my divorce seemed to be provoking in him some kind of rescue fantasy.

The writers had softened quite a bit toward me in the wake of my split from Toby, but if they so much as asked me in a peevish tone when lunch would arrive, RJ glared at them. If they talked about setting me up on dates, telling me it was time to get back out there, he told them to leave me alone. When I e-mailed the notes I'd taken for the day to him and the writers, he'd write back to say I was doing a good job. It unnerved me a little at first, but the truth was, his protection was comforting.

After Toby and I separated, it was all I could do to haul myself out of bed and into the office. I had begun to think about seeing a therapist, but after the Ira debacle, I wasn't so sure it was a good idea. Instead I spent a lot of time curled on the couch in my little house in Venice, or sitting out on my patio, drinking wine and chain-smoking. Looking at my wine-store bills, I had begun to think Toby was right, that maybe I did have a drinking problem.

My mother had flown out to Los Angeles right after the split (I had met her at the airport, and once again the sight of her familiar face, her dark hair, her soft smile hit me with a rush, and I felt weak from how much I loved her). She whirled in, taking charge and setting up shop. She outfitted the house with chic modern furniture, colorful new dishes, fresh sheets and towels, and a month's worth of groceries. It broke my heart the way she wanted to do everything for me. She cleaned my little house and got a handyman in to fix things, but whenever she stopped to rest, to sit down on the couch for a moment or stand by the sink for a drink of water, she lost herself in despair. "I just don't know how this could have happened to you," she kept repeating, her voice dropping to a whisper, her hands shaking, and I did not know what to say to that. In the back of my mind, and deep in my bones, I knew that she had something to do with it, that her leaving when I was a child had made me afraid to love Toby or anyone else, but I didn't know how to express that. It seemed too huge and painful to even think about, much less absorb. When she left I cried, wanting her to stay.

Several weeks later my father flew out to L.A. and took me to dinner at Valentino, a New York–style Italian place. He told me that I would be okay, though I felt otherwise. When he saw my timid eyes, heard my trembly voice, he was taken aback. "Do not let this damage you, Lacey," he said sternly, looking at me intently. "You are going to get over this. Do not let this crawl inside you and shake your sense of yourself." He encouraged me to come home to New York, but I said no, I'd had too much change in my life already; I had a place to live and a job, and that was stability for me right now. He hugged me and said he understood.

In the familiar balance of my two parents I felt something akin to being taken care of. But I knew I had to deal with my life on my own.

The only place where I felt I could escape from my feelings was work. RJ was acting like my protector, so I felt relatively safe there. I still remembered how he'd gotten so upset when Toby had thrown the lime at me. Still (and perhaps I was so distracted by depression that I was naïve), when RJ made a pass at me three months after the party, I was surprised.

He called my office at around seven one night. I was there late, doing research for the writers, avoiding going home to my empty house.

"I need a huge favor," he said.

"Sure," I said.

"I need a script. I'm on a deadline rewriting for the studio, and I forgot one of my scripts."

"Where's Ralph?" Ralph was the PA whose job it was to deliver scripts to people's homes, that is, when he wasn't sleeping with the snakewoman.

"He's in Burbank dropping off the studio's scripts, and he says he can't be here for another hour because of traffic."

"Where are you?"

"I'm at the Beverly Hills Hotel, working in the bar."

"Oh. Okay."

"Can you leave now?"

"Sure," I said hesitantly.

I hung up annoyed. I couldn't say no to the showrunner, and yes, he had been very nice to me lately, but this wasn't my job. It was the PA's job. Delivering scripts was the lowest of the lowly jobs, in my opinion. It was worse than getting coffee. God, what was I still doing in this godforsaken town as an assistant at this age?

Outside, it was raining. I got into my car, threw the script onto the passenger seat, and crept along in the traffic to Sunset Boulevard and up the driveway of the huge, iconic hotel, palm trees waving against its spotlit sign. I left my car with the valet. I walked down the hotel's long red carpet and through the lobby and stopped for a moment at the door to the Polo Lounge, where I took in the scene. The legendary restaurant was for me the epitome of Hollywood glamour. Humphrey Bogart and Lauren Bacall had had drinks here. The bar area was quiet, maybe because of the rain; only a few people sat in corners in the dim light of candles. RJ sat in one corner, a scotch in front of him, marking up a script with a red pen. The room, and even RJ, seemed suffused with the glow of the past.

"God, these writers," RJ said loudly as I approached, his irreverent voice booming in the hushed setting, shattering my reverie. "I'd be better off having you and Ralph write the scripts."

"Gee, thanks," I said dryly. I handed him the script. "Here you go."

"Ah, great."

You're welcome, I thought. "How's the work coming?" I said.

"It's coming," he said.

"Well, I won't keep you. See you tomorrow." I turned to go.

"Wait, Lacey," he said, looking around the room for something and finally landing on me. "Stay and have a drink with me."

A drink? With the showrunner? With RJ? "No, no, I couldn't," I said.

"Come on," he said.

"I can't," I said. "You're on deadline. You have to get back to work."

"I could really use a break," he said. "Just one drink."

I couldn't see a way out of it. "Okay," I said, and when I took a seat I was surprised to find I was blushing.

We had a drink. RJ seemed distracted. To fill the silence I asked him questions about the studio execs, his job, how he liked the actors. He loosened up and did all the talking, answering my questions with stories and gossip. I was relieved when we'd both drained our glasses.

"One more?" he asked.

"No thanks," I said. "I'd better let you get back to work. Thanks so much for the drink." I stood, clutching my purse.

He stood too. "You know what?" he said. "I think I'll get going, too. I'll work better from home."

"Okay," I said uncertainly.

He waved to the waiter, who brought him the check. In the silence as RJ counted out cash, I felt uncomfortably like we were on a date; I stifled an urge to offer to split the check. Then he grabbed up his things and we walked through the lobby and out to the valet.

It was still raining. We stood under the awning that covered the red-carpeted stairs that led into the hotel. I found my valet ticket, and RJ immediately took it from me. "I'll take care of that," he said, walking to the stand and paying the eight-dollar fee. Both our cars were parked nearby; the valets brought them to us. RJ drove a silver BMW M3 convertible; I drove a 1999 black Jetta that Toby and I had bought at a used-car lot.

"Well," he said.

"See you tomorrow," I said. "Thanks for the drink."

"Okay," he said. "Anytime."

We got into our cars and he pulled out ahead of me, both of us driving slowly because of the rain, our wipers going madly. The hotel driveway was curvy and narrow and surrounded by dense foliage. Toward the end, before we reached the street, RJ slowed and then stopped. His brake lights stayed on. He was blocking me. *Now what?* I thought. After a moment his door opened and he jumped out, grabbing the collar of his jacket and pulling it up over his head. He ran back to my car and stood by my window, waiting. I quickly put the window down.

"Hey," I said, confused.

He stared at me for a second, and then he leaned into my car and kissed me. After a second I kissed him back. He smelled clean, like soap, not at all what I would have imagined, had I ever imagined getting close enough to RJ to smell him.

It felt strange to be kissing someone again, someone different from Toby. I didn't feel much at first beyond the recognition that I had finally kissed someone else, that I had passed a milestone in my divorce. But after a little while RJ put his hand on the back of my head, and I felt something stirring in myself, and then, after another little while, before it got too heated, he pulled back. He looked at me with a big smile on his face.

"Good," he said, nodding. "Good."

He backed away from the car and I waved and he ran back to his car and honked at me and turned right. I turned left and drove toward home, wondering what I had just done. A few minutes later my cell phone rang. It was RJ. I didn't know how he'd gotten my number. "Was that okay?" he said. "Are you okay?"

"I'm okay," I said. "Thanks for checking."

"Okay, good."

"But I don't think we should do that again," I said.

"No, you're right," he asked. "I agree."

The next day at work he followed me down to the set when I went to deliver some scripts, and when no one was looking he steered me toward a darkened wing of the fake suburban house where we shot most of the show's scenes. He pushed me against a bureau in the room of one of the teenage characters. It was supposed to be her hideaway; the room was cozy with a white shag rug and a lava lamp on the desk; there was a poster of a peace sign on the wall, a pink bedspread on the bed.

As RJ put his arms around me I felt something stirring in me again and I fought it, turning my face away when he tried to kiss me. But he was a director; he was used to telling people what to do. "Kiss me," he commanded.

"No," I said. "We can't. Last night was nice, but we can't do this. You're my boss. I'm an assistant. Someone will find out and we'll get in big trouble."

"Let me worry about that," he said, and for a moment I melted. It would be so nice to let someone else worry about things. But he was the show-runner. It was illegal and immoral and against the rules in about nine hundred different ways.

"No," I said. "We can't."

"Don't say no anymore." His hand was already up the back of my shirt. "No one's going to find out. You're free again. You're single. You need an adventure. Say yes. Say we can."

I opened my mouth to speak. I couldn't say yes, yet I couldn't say no. I was so tired of being afraid to love someone, even my own husband. I didn't want to keep saying no to everything in life. RJ pressed against me, hard and insistent. Well, maybe he was right, I thought then. Toby was gone. My family and most of my friends were back east. I was trying to make it in Hollywood alone. What did I have to lose?

I HAD COME UP to Catherine and Henry's place in Topanga for the day to take Catherine out for lunch, to force her to take a break from the baby. Now I sat on the couch. The baby turned away from Catherine's breast and looked up at me with her wide eyes, which hadn't yet decided on a color. "Hi, baby," I said. "Hi." Then to Catherine I said, "Hi, my love," and I held her hand. She sniffled.

"This morning Henry slept in and then worked out," she said. "Do you know how badly I want sleep? How badly I need to work out? Do you see this body?"

Her breasts were enormous; they were crazy double-E breasts. The folds of her stomach lapped over the lip of her pants.

"Then he came home and tried to give her the bottle for all of three minutes," she said. "And now he's been out there hammering all day, and all day yesterday, too."

"He probably just feels rejected because the baby's more comfortable with you," I said, remembering a book on motherhood I had read when I was engaged. "It'll pass."

But even as I said it I knew with an instinct that came with experience that it wasn't true. In the past year I had started to see that as you got into your thirties things really did get gray, and there was heartache, and bad things happened like affairs and career failure and babies born with problems. In the same way I knew that my husband was going to leave me I knew that with Henry there was something else going on, something sadder and more sinister.

"He doesn't want to sleep with me anymore," she said.

"Don't be ridiculous," I said.

"And if we do have sex, he closes his eyes now," she said. "He used to watch me."

"Well, you just watch him instead," I said.

RJ WANTED TO SLEEP with me every day. And each time he came to me, I found I wanted him more and more. This was strange, because as things progressed between us, I began to like him less and less. If I'd imagined our kiss in the rain as evidence that he was a closet romantic, I'd been wrong. As paramours go, he was toxic. He had, for instance, a pathological propensity to lie. He lied about his past, he lied about other women, and he lied about why he had to break our dates.

"I have a meeting at Touchstone," he'd say.

"At ten P.M.?"

"I'm a very busy man, Lacey," he'd say, as if he was hurt that I didn't believe him. "I'm trying to run a show here."

But after a time I found I really didn't care what kind of person he was. I wasn't looking for a boyfriend; I was looking for a distraction. It was his power that turned me on, plain and simple. It was a time in my life when my judgment felt broken and I needed direction; I preferred to pretend that I was an actor in one of his shows. In bed he told me what to do and how he wanted it done, and I did it, often in risky locations like on top of the big mahogany desk in his office, or once, early in the morning, in the office elevator, he pressed the red "stop" button and laughed when I looked nervous. "My show," he said, "my elevator."

Sleeping with RJ made going to work more fun—it was reminiscent of the thrill of seeing a crush every day in seventh grade—but I was starting to feel that the high wasn't worth the low-grade fever I got from the fear of being found out. Misty looked at me suspiciously sometimes, and I thought the writers did, too. I lay awake nights wondering if they knew, but it didn't really matter, because I knew that one day it would all come out, and I would lose my reputation once and for all, and all the colleagues in Los Angeles I had worked so hard to cultivate would turn away from me. No one in Hollywood would hire me again, and I would have to go back east a failure: divorced, childless, without a career, untrue to myself, and, if I was being honest, something of a whore.

The money thing happened because RJ was trying to help me with my career, which was nonexistent. I was an assistant on the show, but I needed to write my own scripts so people could see I could do it. I'd given him a movie script I'd recently started writing, about a superhero who fixes broken hearts, and he'd read it and called me into his office.

"Hey," I said. I saw that he had my script in his hand.

"No," he said, and dropped it into the garbage. "No, no, no."

"Thanks," I said stonily.

"Delete it from your computer immediately and never show it to anyone again."

"Fine." I started to walk away.

"You're writing about something that means nothing to you," he said, and I stopped, "and I can feel it in the writing. You don't care about your characters."

"I should care about a superhero?"

He sighed. "That's your problem, Lacey. You keep everything at a distance. Yes, you should care about your characters. In fact, you should care the most about them."

"Like you care about anything?"

He raised his eyebrows at me. "This whole show is based on me and my family growing up in the 1950s and '60s. Every time I direct an episode, I care so much about it, I get an ulcer. I care more about this show than any person, place, or thing I have ever loved. This show is all I have room for because I care so much. It's why I can't care more about you."

"Good to know," I said. Why was I dating him again?

He ignored me. "Don't be like that. Don't give up. Care. Dig deep and write about your own life."

Even though I hated him right then, even though he sounded like a character in one of the melodramatic scenes in his show, I felt slightly humbled by his words. He had written something he cared about. I had not, but I had my reasons.

"I'm trying to write a summer blockbuster that will sell," I admitted meekly.

He laughed. "Are you kidding? You're young, just starting out. First you have to write something good, and prove you can do it—then worry about selling it."

"Easy for you to say. I need money." And I did—badly. I was running out. Toby had given me fifteen thousand dollars as a settlement, money that he had borrowed from his mother, and I had already spent more than half of it on a security deposit, first and last month's rent, and car payments. Now, alarmingly, every month my bank balance grew smaller. I had started using my credit cards, hoping to stave off the squeeze. I couldn't ask my father for help: he didn't have any money right now (though, he took pains to tell me, he did have a deal closing soon, and then he'd be able to give me whatever I needed). My mother had helped me already, outfitting my house with furniture and dishes; I was embarrassed to ask for more.

"Money?" RJ said incredulously, as if it were air or water, as if he couldn't imagine someone not having enough of it. As the creator and executive producer of the show, RJ would make a million dollars that year, as he had for the past two years. "Is that all?" he said. "That I can give you. I'll write you a goddamn check right now."

"I can't take money from you," I said.

"*I'll* decide what you can and cannot do," he snarled.

The next day he called me into his office and told me he wanted me to write an episode of the show, a little gift that paid thirty thousand dollars.

I shook my head. "I can't," I said.

"I thought you wanted to be a TV writer."

"I do, but not this way. It would be wrong."

"Please," he said. "Save the drama for the script. Assistants get to write scripts all the time. That's why they bother getting coffee for a year."

"But you never let your assistants write scripts."

"That's because anyone who would get coffee for a year is a fucking idiot. No offense." RJ studied me for a minute. "I know what this is about. You're afraid. You're afraid you'll write a crappy script and everyone will know you can't write for shit."

"Fuck you," I said.

"Then write the script."

"No. I can't."

"You can, and you will, or you're fired."

I sighed. I knew that RJ wouldn't fire me. But I also wanted to write a script. I wanted to prove to him and the writers—and myself—that I could write. Plus, after all I'd been through, I felt I deserved the chance.

"Fine," I said. "I'll do it."

"Thank you so much for agreeing to accept thirty grand from me," RJ said sarcastically.

"You mean from the studio," I corrected him. This was technically true, but I left his office feeling dirty, aware that I had just struck a pretty shady deal.

Catherine was in thrall to the cliché of it all.

"So it really is like that in Hollywood?" she asked. "You can get ahead just by sleeping with someone?" She wanted the details. "Was it like, he said he'd only let you write it if you had sex with him?" I smiled at her naïveté, her sheltered life. But often, during the day, if RJ came into my office and locked the door, I pictured Catherine at home, safe and secure, rocking Matilda to sleep.

NOW CATHERINE dried her tears. She tried to sound okay. "So how are you?" she asked. "Have you broken it off with the boss man yet?"

My friends knew that my affair with RJ was a bad phase, some kind of manifestation of the self-esteem dip I was experiencing in the wake of my split from Toby. For the most part they kept their mouths shut, not wanting to criticize me, waiting for it to run its course. Still, as much as everyone was trying to be patient, there were times when their indignation erupted and they tried to talk some sense into me.

"He's not so bad," I said meekly.

"Lacey," Cath said now. "When are you going to give him up and move on? He lies to you, he's almost certainly seeing other people, and you want someone you can have kids with, don't you? And," she added, "he's such an asshole."

"I don't know," I said. "I think I might be falling in love with him."

This wasn't true. I didn't know why I'd said it. RJ lied to me all the time, and I had to lie so often at work to cover things up with him, I didn't know what the truth was anymore. There were days when I barely uttered one true thing before lunch, even when responding to the simplest of questions. What had I gotten up to last night? *Oh, stayed in, watched a movie.* (I'd gone with RJ to a party at Aaron Sorkin's house.) Where were you during the meeting? *Oh, doing research downstairs.* (Making out with RJ in his office.) Have you heard anything about my script? *Oh, I don't think he's read it yet.* (He read it and he hates it—he told me last night in bed.)

"Well, do you think he's falling in love with you?" Cath said.

"No," I said. This was true. He loved his show, and he had loved his dog until he'd had it put down, but that was all he had room for.

"Lacey," she said firmly. "You're not in love with him. You wouldn't want to have kids with that man."

"It doesn't matter," I said. I was becoming annoyed with her tone, as if she knew what was best, as if any of us knew what was best for ourselves anymore. "I don't even know if I want kids anyway."

She looked surprised. "Since when?"

"Since lately, I guess."

Catherine looked down at Matilda, then looked up at me intently. "This will all pass," she said. "Henry's going to get over it. You're going to get over it."

I nodded as if I believed her, but I did not.

There are things we don't get over, despite what well-meaning friends and self-help books would have us believe. In California people will tell you that you can reinvent yourself and start anew whenever you choose, but after my divorce I found that this was not true. Being divorced was just like losing my family again, and despite my best efforts, I felt I was never going to escape from the pain of what had happened in my marriage or my childhood. And yet in a strange way this realization was comforting, despite all the bad that had happened. Knowing I could not wipe the slate clean helped me to see that my history, however flawed, was my own. My past was etched upon me as if on a gravestone, and the things I did, the choices I made, mattered. I could not simply shake off my self like water from a dog, no matter how much I might have liked to.

Catherine and I sat and gazed at Matilda as she sucked at Catherine's breast. She looked so much like Cath it choked me up. They had the same wide mouth that turned down at the corners, the same long eyelashes, the same pink cheeks. It was like there were two of Cath now.

We suddenly heard the sound of Henry's crazy hammering.

"What the hell is he making out there?" I said.

Catherine rolled her eyes. "He won't tell me. It's something for the baby."

"Huh," I said. "Just now he said it was for you."

She shrugged.

"Maybe it's an adult-sized crib," I said.

"Sounds perfect for him," she said, and giggled.

She called out the front door to him that we were ready to go for our lunch so could he come take Matilda, but he called back to say he needed twenty more minutes. The baby started to scream. "Will you give her a pacifier?" Cath said to me. "There's one in one of those drawers."

I began to open drawers. In the second was a DVD marked "Birth," with Matilda's birthday on it.

"Cath?" I said. "You recorded it?"

She turned and looked at the DVD. "Oh," she said. "Yeah. Well, my doula did."

In recent years Catherine had fallen into the more natural lifestyle of her neighbors out here in Topanga. She had insisted on childbirth at home, with a midwife and a doula, without any pain medication. She said it was something her body had been built to do, and women had done it for thousands of years, and she wanted to share in that tradition, she wanted to live her life with the knowledge of that accomplishment. I was in awe of her; I could handle emotional pain, had dealt with it enough to know that, but enormous physical pain like childbirth, without any medication? I imagined that I'd take divorce over that any day.

Catherine took the DVD from my hands and put it back in the drawer.

"Can I watch it?"

She hesitated, then sighed. "Do you think you can handle it?"

"Of course I can," I said, but as soon as I said it I wasn't sure.

We found the pacifier and the baby calmed down and I put the DVD into the player and went to sit on the couch and immediately there came from the TV a terrible, eerie, wolflike moaning. I whipped around, and there on-screen was Catherine, lying on her back, her legs in the air. She was crying, and her legs were shaking, and she was trying to reach down between her legs, apparently to get at whatever was causing this torture. Her moaning was unbearable. The pain she was in seemed unimaginable. The scene was even more frightening than what I'd imagined childbirth to be. Tears immediately flooded my eyes.

"Oh God, Cath," I said, sinking to the sofa.

She watched herself on-screen. "It wasn't that bad," she said. She looked down at Matilda. "I'd do it again in a second."

But now, on the TV screen, she was unmoored, unable to even move from the pain. *"Uuuuuuuuuuuuu!"* was all she could say. Then the camera focused on what was happening down below. I couldn't believe a woman could open so wide. It seemed physically impossible. After a while something black appeared, oozing out of Catherine.

"Henry!" the midwife cried excitedly. "Get ready to catch the baby!"

They all crowded around, and suddenly the baby's wet, shiny head popped through, and then Catherine gave one last push and the baby came out, along with a wash of blood and gore, landing in Henry's outstretched hands. Henry lifted the baby up onto Catherine's stomach, but the cord was still attached, so Catherine had to sit up to be able to reach it.

"It's a girl," Cath said, sobbing, and a joyous smile came over her.

I knew that Cath and Henry had expected a boy. They had never confirmed the sex with a doctor, but they had played some superstitious game where they had hung a crystal from a string and dangled it over Cath's belly. Counterclockwise would have meant girl, but the crystal had moved in a clockwise direction, so they were having a boy.

Now, on-screen, Cath held her daughter and laughed, and then she burst into happy tears. You could hear the doula, who was recording, crying, also.

I was crying now, too, watching the whole amazing event, new life entering the world, but it was slowly dawning on me to wonder where Henry was in this whole scene. Apparently it occurred to the doula, too, because the camera swept the room.

"Henry?" she said. "Where'd you go?"

"Yeah, I guess I got nervous," Henry said, and suddenly I jumped. He was standing behind us at the door, his hammer in his hand.

"Henry?" the doula called on-screen, as Catherine's sobs, also on-screen, filled the room.

"Here I am," Henry said on-screen, as he returned to the frame.

Now I stared at Henry on the TV as he watched himself meet his daughter.

"Is that what this is about?" I said without thinking.

"What?" he said.

"You wanted a boy?"

"What what's about?" he said.

"Is that why you're sulking around like a big baby? Because you didn't get what you wanted?"

Henry turned to Cath. "What did you tell her? That I wasn't being a good father?"

Cath was silent.

"I'm sorry, Cath," I said.

"Yeah, well, at least I'm still here," Henry said.

"You're a husband and a father, Henry," I said. "You're supposed to be here."

"Like you know anything about it?" he said, turning to me. "Your husband left you. Your mother left you. Even your brother left. You don't know what it takes to stick around."

"Stop it," Cath said.

Suddenly I felt tired. Henry was right. I didn't know anything about the sacrifice it took to stay when you wanted to go. "You're right," I said. "I don't know. But you should still stay."

"Oh, I'm staying," he said. "I'm not going anywhere."

We all stopped, and the baby lay against Catherine's neck, worn out.

"Henry, what are you building out there?" I said.

"It's none of your business."

"Did you want a boy?" Catherine said.

"I don't have to answer that," he said.

"Why are you out there at all hours building whatever the hell it is you're building when you have a new baby and a wife who needs help?" I said.

"Did you?" Cath said.

"When I imagined a baby, I may have imagined a boy," he said to Catherine.

"Get used to reality," she snapped.

"I'm building a boat," he said to me.

"A boat?" I said.

"A boat?" Catherine said.

We were quiet for a moment. "Where are you going?" Catherine said.

Suddenly he looked ashamed. "I don't know," Henry said, and then he couldn't look at us. The baby started to scream.

Out of Body

FIRST YOU WILL NOTICE that your period is late, and your breasts are a little sore. Then, on a rainy Sunday night, when all the drugstores are closed except for the twenty-four-hour Rite Aid, after you've gone out for Chinese with friends, barely able to speak you were so distracted, you'll force yourself to get back into your car and drive over to Venice Boulevard to buy a pregnancy test. No, two.

You will come home and sit on the toilet, the bathroom so small the door nearly grazes your face when you close it, though there is no one else in the house to hide from. You will read the test's instructions twice before peeing for thirty seconds on a strip of material encased in a little window on a beige plastic stick. These instructions, folded tightly as origami and stuffed in the box like a secret, will lie when they tell you you will have to wait as long as three minutes for the results. The results will come instantly, almost as soon as you pee. You will close your eyes and then open them, and in the stick's window two twin pink lines will have appeared. One line by itself would have meant no, but you will have two lines. You will definitely have two. This will be hard to believe, so you will open the second box and pee on a second stick. When the two lines appear again, a little pink highway leading to your future, your heart will begin to beat fast. It will beat so fast and so loud that you will put a hand to your chest. And you will keep it there, you will hold on to yourself. The beat of your heart will be like company: you are not alone.

YOU WILL GET UP EARLY the next day and bike through the streets of Venice, as is your habit. You will follow the route you follow every day: down the length of funky Abbot Kinney Boulevard, its stores shuttered, only a few early risers standing outside the coffee place. You will head down to the boardwalk that runs alongside the beach, past the homeless with their shopping carts, the junkies asleep on the sand, the runaway kids looking for somewhere safe to sleep, the men lifting weights in the dawny gloom at Muscle Beach. Coasting home along Venice Boulevard, you will watch as people yawn in the sunshine and walk their dogs, as they do every day. You will try to go numb and vacant, to let the buzzing whir of your turning wheels drone out your thoughts.

Then you will go to work. You are under a lot of pressure at work. You are currently writing an episode of the show—a little gift from your boss, RJ, that happens to pay thirty thousand dollars—and you have a lot of work to do. The script is due in fourteen days and you know it will make or break you in terms of your reputation among the writers. You saw their looks of surprise when RJ told them you were writing an episode. They are not sure if you know how to write a TV script—and the truth is, neither are you, but you know that if you can focus over the next two weeks and write a good script, then perhaps they will take you under their wing, mentor you, help you get a job as a full-fledged staff writer on the show, making a salary of ninety thousand a year. Because RJ has made it clear—he gave you the script as a gift, sure, because you told him you needed the money, but if it is not good, he will not even think about hiring you as a writer. Not for one second. You could very easily remain an assistant forever if the script is not good.

Yet the script will be the last thing you want to think about right now, and so you will not. Instead, in your little office, you will close the door, dial the local Planned Parenthood, and murmur a request for an appointment.

"Sure," the receptionist will say. "How can we help you?"

"I'm pregnant," you will say aloud, for the first time, to this stranger.

"Are you sure?" she will ask.

"I took a test," you will say. "Two."

"Well, still, you never know," she will say. "You'll need to come in for a professional test to make sure you're pregnant before we can refer you to any services."

"Okay," you will reply, and hope will bloom in your heart.

YOU KNOW THAT this sounds crazy, but you do not feel you can tell your therapist. You have just started seeing her, you barely know her, and more importantly, you feel too ashamed that you have allowed this to happen to yourself.

Perhaps crazier still, you do not feel that you can tell your gynecologist. She knows everyone in Hollywood, and you are irrationally terrified that she will let it slip, that someone will piece it together, that somehow it will all come out—the affair with RJ, the pregnancy, what you are planning to do about it. You have seen the ads for Planned Parenthood on the buses that pass you as you bike along Venice Boulevard in the mornings.

You feel a need to keep this off the grid, outside the boundaries of your real life, so that when it is all over it can be as though it never happened.

You would tell your brother, who has a child but who apparently fled before it was born. If he were a father, a participating father, he might understand your feelings of fear, he might be able to relate and make you feel less alone, but he is still missing, and you have not spoken to him in almost three years.

You know that if you told your mother, she would book you into the best hospital in Palm Beach, where both your stepfather and the governor have been treated for prostate cancer. You could have a three-thousand-dollar abortion.

You know that if you told your father, he would somehow scramble together money and come out to L.A. and take you to dinner so you could have one of your heart-to-heart chats.

But you will not consider telling your mother, or your stepfather, or your father.

And you will not consider telling RJ. Will they ask you to name "the father" when you go in for your appointment? You would prefer if they did not. You have trouble reconciling RJ, lover of pit bulls, with the image of a father. "Kids," he said once in the writers' room, "are for people who give a shit."

THERE WILL NOT be a back entrance to your local Planned Parenthood office. You will realize this when you are forced to walk through its front door, right on Main Street in Venice, steps away from the neighborhood place where you get your coffee every morning.

Inside Planned Parenthood, you will provide a urine sample, and your counselor will take it away for the test. When she returns, you will know the results from the look on her face.

"I'm sorry," she will say softly. "You're pregnant."

"I know," you will say, and you did. But still, the tears will come. Trying to swallow the enormous lump in your throat will make you consider how painful giving birth must be.

YOUR ABORTION will cost exactly $390—payable in cash only—and your doctor will be a slight Indian man. You won't have met him until the day of the procedure, but you will have heard his voice on the phone two weeks before, when you went to your abortion clinic for state-mandated "informed consent" counseling. As you sat around a table with six other girls—mostly young and mostly minorities—your doctor called in and spoke to you for about three minutes from a speakerphone in the center of the table. He spoke rapidly, with an accent that you found soothing and intelligent-sounding, and he ended every sentence with "Okay?"

"You have other options, this is not the only one, okay?" he said. "You can have the baby, you can give the baby up for adoption, okay?"

You will choose from among other options that day. You will choose to be knocked out when they perform the procedure, rather than remaining awake; you will choose to have your abortion in two weeks, the earliest they can fit you in, rather than waiting a month or so. And you will choose to go alone.

YOU WILL BE PREGNANT for twenty-one days. During those days, you will begin to rise earlier and earlier in the mornings, in order to bike farther and farther and longer and longer. You will bike along the Venice canals before anyone else is up, turning and twisting through their skinny maze of sidewalks, the houses alongside it huge and silent in the morning gloom, your bicycle coming dangerously close to the water's edge. Then you will point your bike to Marina del Rey and watch as men launch their shells into the water and begin to row, first as pairs, then all together, eight oars carving below the surface, the coxswain's voice carrying across the water: "Do you want it? Come on! Push!" Biking along the walkway that runs next to the sea, you will choose a boat and follow it; you will be its shadow, keeping pace, letting the crew warm up as they ease into their strokes. Soon they will start to row in synch, and when they hit their stride you will race against them, faster and faster until your bike almost lifts from underneath you. You will pass them and you won't look back.

WHEN YOUR EX-HUSBAND calls for the first time since your divorce went through six months ago, you will not recognize your old home phone number on caller ID. You will pick it up while sitting on your couch at home alone at 8 P.M., expecting it to be someone from work. Instead:

"Hi," he will say. "It's me."

"Hi," you will say back. You have imagined talking with him again after all this time. Now you are too distracted to really care.

After silence settles, he will begin. "How are you?"

"I'm good," you will say, and you will wonder whether he can tell that something is wrong. "You?"

"Good," he will say. "Good."

More silence.

"Listen," he will finally say, "I can't find my gray sweatshirt. The Andover one. Have you seen it?"

You are not sure what he is asking. "You mean, do I have it?"

"No, I mean, do you know where in the apartment it could be?"

You can picture the apartment perfectly; you feel you know it as well as the house you grew up in. "I guess you could check the hall closet, behind your sweaters," you will say.

"Okay," he will say. "I will." Then: "So, what's new with you lately?"

"Not much," you will say. Your throat is so tight you can barely spit out the words. Once he was your husband. Then he left you alone to fend for yourself in a strange town you had no business staying in without him, left you in such a vulnerable state that you allowed yourself to be preyed upon by this manipulative older man. *See what happened?* you want to say to him. *See what you did?* The inexpressible pain of what you have lost has never felt so throbbingly real as right then.

"I think of you," he will say.

"Yeah," you will manage.

"The other day at Nordstrom's I ran into the guy who sold us my wedding suit," he will say. "It was weird."

"That is weird," you will say.

"Did you realize that last week would have been our second wedding anniversary?" he will say.

"No," you will say, and you didn't.

"So anyway," he will say, "I've been thinking. Do you think we made the right decision?"

You will not answer. This is a question that for months you have been hoping he would ask, proof that he has questioned the decision himself. Yet now you are pregnant with another man's child. The decision to divorce was never yours to begin with—it was his, you were never given a choice—and now it seems a lifetime ago, a simple time when you were young and innocent and pure, if damaged. You will remember how you looked at babies longingly when your marriage was ending, how you saw them everywhere: in airplanes, at the grocery store, at your favorite brunch place. When you thought of your own baby then, you always pictured a little boy, with your ex's dark hair and sad eyes.

"Good-bye," you will say.

"Okay," he will say.

YOU WILL BEGIN to show up for work later and later. You will start to write one or two pages of your script a day. You will need to write sixty before the two weeks are up. The writers will eye you when you come in late, and they will eye you when you leave for the day without discussing the script with them, but they will not say anything. They will not have to. "What's the matter with you?" they will overhear RJ say to you one day in the hallway. "Why aren't you further along with this? Don't embarrass me here."

YOU WILL NOT TELL RJ, but he will find out anyway.

One night before bed, while you are in the bath, having left him alone in your bed, he will go through your things. Searching, he will later claim, for the book on how to write a TV script that he gave you for your birthday, he will go through the pine chest at the end of your bed, where he will find your diary and read it: the details of the sex the night it happened; how stupid you feel for letting him pull out instead of using a condom; your plans for the abortion; the blame you place on him; your fantasies about screaming the truth at him just to hear him tell you, just once, for all the things he has done to you, that he is sorry.

But after RJ reads your diary, he will not be sorry. He will confront you when you come out of the bath, light-headed from the heat and softly fragrant with rose oil. He will claim that he had a right to know, that he would have wanted to be a part of it, to *share* in it with you. He will even allow tears to roll down his cheeks. This uncharacteristically sappy response from him will make you mad—insanely, perversely mad. He has no right to cry over this. He has no right to claim any stake in this. You will walk out the door and climb onto your bike, and you will pedal along Venice streets that have seen so much worse, and you will be soothed.

Eventually you will come home, realizing that you are being unfair. RJ will be nicer to you that night than he ever has been before or since. He will hold you all night and smooth your hair back over your forehead over and over and over, and he will even talk about whether you should have it. You will cry and cry and cry. But you will not consider having it.

The next night he will surprise you by taking you to dinner at the fanciest place in Los Angeles, the most beautiful restaurant you have ever seen, with sterling silver place settings three deep, and pale pink walls, and seven courses. He will spend four hundred dollars on dinner and white wine. This will strike you as a strange reaction to an abortion, and also as something of a payoff—the procedure will cost about four hundred dollars, too.

Over dinner he will tell you that now there is a bond between the two of you forever. What kind of a sick person would say something like that? you will think. You will not want a bond with him; in fact you never really wanted anything more from him than a little attention, to curl into a warm body at night, to feel someone want you again after your divorce.

But still, you know that RJ is right; the event will tether you to him, an invisible, unspoken tie made all the more intimate because only the two of you will know about it. This will be the part that will frustrate you the most: you will want nothing more than to break this secret bond with him by including others in it. But you will be unable to. For a long time you will not consider telling anyone else. Then, eventually, cautiously, many months later, you will tell some friends. Their reactions will be sympathetic, supportive, what you had hoped for. But even then your hidden bond with RJ—breakable, in your fantasies, by revelation—will remain.

As you grow older, as the months and years after your abortion pass, you will meet other women who have had abortions. You will be stunned by their honesty, their openness, by the way they tell you in passing, after they have only just met you—in work cubicles, during exercise class, at book clubs and dinner parties—as if there is nothing to be ashamed of, as if abortion is as common as sex, as if it is something every woman has gone through, and after a time you will realize that a lot of women have. And soon you will become almost comfortable with it. You will talk about it as if it is simply another part of your past, another part of who you are, and after a time it will be.

But all through your pregnancy you will be ashamed. You will feel as though you are harboring a dirty secret no one can know. You will feel spoiled, unclean, marked, ruined. You will feel less like who you are and more like who you never wanted to be.

RJ WILL SAY that he wants to go with you. He still talks about the possibility of you keeping it. But when you picture what is growing inside you, you sometimes imagine horns. You are honestly afraid that RJ might stride into the room during the procedure and order the doctor to stop the whole thing. No, you will tell him firmly, he cannot come. You will tell him that it is your body and your decision. You will be surprised at how quickly he backs down.

THE MORNING of your abortion, you will go for a bike ride at six o'clock. No one told you not to. And what more damage can you do to yourself? You will ride and ride through the empty weekend streets, Venice tucked away, sleeping on and on, innocent, unaware, unconcerned. You will coast home, resigned, ready.

YOUR ABORTION CLINIC will turn out to be only five blocks from your house in Venice—you will bike by it at least once a week for the rest of the time you live there. It will be on the third floor of a dumpy office building that looks as if it might have once housed a sweatshop. When you arrive by bicycle at 7 A.M., there are other girls waiting outside the building for the doors to open. You try not to look at them. You feel exposed; anyone you know could drive by and ask what you're doing there.

Inside you will wait and wait and wait. The waiting room is huge and quickly becomes packed. There must be fifty women there. They are young and old, black and white, accompanied and alone. They doze, read magazines, murmur. You don't know where to look. You feel naked, as if you should cover yourself.

Three hours later, your name will finally be called. You will be taken to a locker room, where you will change into a robe and slippers that you brought with you, as requested, leaving your clothes in a locker. You will be taken to another room, which will be dimly lit, with armchairs and only four other women.

You will wait there for another three hours.

Outside, from another room, you will hear the sounds of nurses waking other girls from their anesthesia. "Sherry!" they will call. "Can you hear me? It's all over! Wake up!"

At first you are afraid, but as time moves on, your fear lessens and your impatience grows. You want this over with. You have now been waiting, by yourself, among strange girls, for over six hours. You long to be that girl, the girl they are trying to wake in the other room.

Finally, your name is called, and you are taken by wheelchair into an operating room where a nurse says hello and calls you by your first name. You are asked to lie on a table with your feet in stirrups. The doctor comes in and waves down at you; he is what you pictured, brown-faced and smiling, distracted and focused at the same time. An anesthesia drip is placed in your arm, and the nurse asks you to count backward from ten, and the last thing you remember is staring up at the nurse, and ten, nine, eight . . .

And the next thing you know your name is being called out again—so much calling out of your name in this place!—and you wake slowly. Woozy, you drink apple juice, still more girls all around you, waking, recovering. You haven't spoken a word to one another all day.

After you lie and say your boyfriend is waiting downstairs to drive you home, you are let go. You can go back to work as soon as Monday, they tell you, the day after tomorrow. But no bike riding for a week.

You walk your bike home along Venice Boulevard in the August sun. You are too hot with your long-sleeve oxford shirt over your tank top, but you have cotton balls taped to your arm from being stuck with the anesthesia needle, and you don't want people to notice. Suddenly you think you might faint. You stop to rest on a fire hydrant.

"Are you okay, miss?" someone asks.

You smile weakly and nod. You make it home.

For a few days, you won't want to get out of bed. But you will. You will go to work on Monday, and you will watch the writers and RJ as if from a distance. On Tuesday you will stay up all night finishing the script, and you will hand it in a day late, on Wednesday, and you will know that it is good, that you have made RJ proud. On Thursday you will break up with RJ and quit your job, and on Friday you will go in for a checkup at the clinic, and everything will look fine.

A week later, you will go back to riding your bike. You will punch and punch at the ground with your legs, trying to tire yourself out. Soon your morning ride will not be enough. You will begin to ride after the sun goes down, too, into the evenings. Long rides, aimless. You will stay out later and later, into the hot summer nights, and you will begin to stray from the streets you know into the city's margins, its dark corners. Your own neighborhood, quiet after midnight, borders a poor neighborhood where long past bedtime children still play in the streets, women sit on stoops, men stand near bodegas. Delirious, sweaty, you will glide through their streets, an angel, omniscient, untouchable. No one will stop you or bother you. You will keep going, night after night, later and later, deeper and deeper, the people you pass a blur, loud, alive, awake, unchanging. You will pump and pump, and then you will pick your feet up off the pedals and you will be soundless, weightless. You will open your arms and close your eyes and, unseeing and unseen, you will rise up and fly. From a distance the world will look like home.

Love or Something Like It

AFTER RJ, I slept alone for three months. And then I didn't want to anymore.

Rich, the first, was an agent who wore black even to the beach. He was having lunch alone in a suit and sunglasses at the Viceroy pool; I had snuck in for some sun. He talked me into a drink that night, which turned into another, followed by dinner and, eventually, breakfast. Apparently, however, he preferred his clients. He listed them off as though I'd be impressed. "Paris Hilton slept in these sheets," he told me as we lay in bed. "I haven't washed them since."

Jake, the second, was just a fuck. He was a soap star with a great body and nothing to say. We met in line at the Coffee Bean on Sunset; his line was *Are you by any chance an actress?* Back at my place he wanted to take it slow, see where things with us could go, but I kissed him hard and moved my hands and things went from there. "I really needed that," I said when we were done. He stayed over, sleeping soundly in my white sheets. All night I felt like a guy: I lay awake, willing him to leave.

Nick was British and blond and too hip for me. He liked my smile; they always like my smile. At the bar in Hollywood he took me into the bathroom so he could do some coke. The room glowed small and red, the muffled music thumped at the door. He did it fast; I never even saw the stuff. Then his eyes flashed and he came toward me. "What else can we do in a bathroom?" he said, his arm already around my neck. Back outside I lost him in the crowd.

With David, I burned my hand on the oven at a dinner party in Los Feliz. "It hurts me that you're hurt," he said when he saw the ice melting over my knuckles. I still have the scar, light brown and curved, like a muddy river. We'd met months earlier with friends at a resort in Cabo. It was hot there at night, breezy, lonely. I'd sit up late on my patio, smoking; he said he'd fantasized about me knocking on his door in a black negligee. But back in L.A. he couldn't get it up. "Prozac has its downside," he said, turning his back on me in bed.

Bobby's mother was dying. At the wedding where we met, he didn't want to leave her side. But he was twenty-five and hot; it was bursting out of him. By the shore in Carmel, in the attic room of an old inn, he took off my clothes, and my single bed creaked, the sea roaring gray below us. We were like teenagers, insatiable. "That was nice and all," he text-messaged me the next day. "But my mom's my priority right now."

I CALLED THEM BOYS. It helped me forget they were men.

IF IT WAS A DATE then they came to the door to pick me up, never with flowers, but looking nice, with a glow, eager. Blind dates always seem relieved that I put effort into it—jeans and sandals and a sleeveless white top, my long hair brushed, shimmery pink lipstick.

Jason #1 was my first blind date. He had glasses and a beard, and seeing him, I silently asked the friend who'd set us up why. But he was an advisor for Schwarzenegger, and we had fun talking politics and smoking cigarettes. He called the next day and went for it, asking me out for Saturday night. I told him I was getting over my divorce and not yet ready for a relationship, which certainly wasn't untrue. "Then why'd you bother going out with me?" he snapped, hanging up.

There was Jason #2, the network executive with connections and power, forty-three and never married, high-voiced and possibly gay. I went out with him once, and then I went out with him again, because, well, you never know. He tried to kiss me at the end of the night; I didn't handle that well. When he drove away, he peeled off.

When Jason #3 walked into the room, I thought, This is it. I've met him. Only a year after the divorce—and look at that! I've already met him. He was my age, a movie writer, with dark hair and flashing blue eyes, from the East Coast like me. He wore a blazer and Stan Smiths to our first date. It took him three dates to kiss me, which was sweet but weird, and when we finally made out he was sloppy, like a dog. You can fix that, my married friends said, and anyway, kissing's not that important in the scheme of things.

SOMETIMES IT WAS FUN: intimate and sexy and sweet and hot. And sometimes, lying in a foreign bed at 4 A.M., a boy breathing rhythmically beside me, the night silent and powerful, the city outside deserted and desolate, I could not sleep and then I was lonelier than I had ever been. The tears threatened, my throat closed, and I resisted an urge to flee with every muscle in my body, stiff with the stillness of trying not to wake a stranger.

IF I THOUGHT they could be the one, and I always thought that at some point in the night, then eventually I also thought, *But I was already married to the one.*

Sometimes I compared them to Toby, and then no one could measure up. On our good days he had been funnier, sweeter, more insightful, more talented than anyone else. He had understood me like no one else, he had been *my family* for a while, and there was something permanent and deep, a connection—it was something that no one can name because it is unnamable—and I was never going to get that back or find it again. And sometimes I wondered what he would say about the guys I was dating. I imagined the two of us discussing them, the way we used to deconstruct parties on the way home. I knew he'd think Nick was a phoney, that Jake was a nice guy but cheesy, that David took himself too seriously. But he'd have hit it off with Jason #3, I was sure—he would have invited him to our dinner parties, and we all would have been friends.

I MET A BLIND DATE at a bar in Venice Beach. He was blond and cute and I could tell that he was satisfied with me, too. But when we got to talking, we strained to find common ground. He was spacey, very Southern California, a surfer guy. Fumbling for words, thinking he was a touchy-feely type, I let it slip that I was once married, that I was in therapy, that I sensed I still had quite a bit to figure out about myself. I could tell instantly that this was a mistake. This was the first time I saw the change in someone's eyes when I opened up about my divorce. If we had been finding it difficult to relate before, now he was utterly silent, his eyes glazed over. We'd had only one drink; our glasses were drained and I prayed he didn't want another—what would we possibly talk about?—but when he signaled for the waitress and turned to me and said, "You ready to get going?" my feelings were hurt. And the next day, when he didn't call when he said he would, my feelings were hurt again, and then, later, when he failed to call, ever, my feelings were hurt again, and again, and again.

MY MARRIED FRIENDS had vicarious questions. Their husbands had more. How is it being back out there? *Similar to being kidnapped,* I thought, *and dropped into enemy territory.* Is it strange to be sleeping with someone else after you thought you'd never sleep with anyone else again? *Well, yes. But not in the way you mean.* My friends wanted me to celebrate the sex: the one perk, they imagined, of divorce. The problem was, however, that I went from belonging to someone to belonging to anyone, from the sanctity of home to the insanity of bars, and I had not yet reached the place where *I am woman.* I told my body to feel something for someone, anyone, but it wouldn't obey.

THERE WAS a female therapist on TV who analyzed women's problems.
"She says all women have wounds," I told Cath.
"Yeah, they're called vaginas," Cath said.
"She says we use men to fill our wounds."
Cath looked at me. "Did you hear what you just said?"

"She says we have holes and hungers," I said. "And we use things like sex and attention from men to fill them up."

"Well, what the hell else are we supposed to use?"

"Work," I said. "Hobbies. You know, interests."

"Yeah, well, tell her I don't have time for that shit," she said. "I have a pain-in-the-ass husband and a kid."

"So what happened?" my dates inevitably asked, as if there was an answer, a moral to the story, a tidy explanation. *Please tell us why your marriage failed in three sentences or less.* But I did not blame them. They wanted to get it out of the way. Clear the air. Make sense of me. Besides, to be fair, I believed deep down that there was an explanation, too. I believed that there would be a moment, an epiphany, a sudden bright light—one turn of the key and all would become clear. And so I told each boy a story, and I told it to myself at the same time. "We felt trapped," I said. Or "There were issues we never addressed, and once we got married, *boom.*" They nodded nicely, and they smiled sympathetically, and they acted like they understood, like it was all in the past, like I was over it, and so I did, too.

If I passed a wedding-dress shop in Beverly Hills, I might stop and stare if I liked a certain dress. But I always tried to hide on the sidewalk, as if I expected someone I knew to spot me and yell out their car window, "You already did that!" Putting on a white dress, walking down the aisle on your father's arm—you can only do those things for the first time once. The second time, I suspected, if it happened, would be something different, something grown-up, something jaded and mature, something that lacks that sweet faith, the faith you have because you don't know any better, the faith you need to sustain a marriage, the innocent belief that nothing could go wrong, that this *will* work, of course it will, *how could it not?*

At our age half my friends had fertility problems. They were all on Clomid or doing IVF, scared it would never happen for them. They drank green tea and quit drinking and got shots in the ass from their husbands.

THERE WAS SOMETHING about sex that worked for me. It was as deep as I could go. My eyes stared blankly during the act. Yet during it there was, at least, the illusion of intimacy.

I WANTED to go back to my twenties, to flirting in a bar, to going home with someone at 2 A.M. and just having fun, but I couldn't. Now I had to focus, to try to find *the one*. I tried for a while and then sometimes I forgot and that's when I found myself in a stranger's house without my clothes on.

MEN IN OTHER CITIES hooked onto the California thing. The Hollywood thing. The beach-blonde thing. Their own fantasies came to roost in me. "I didn't expect an L.A. blonde," said one guy, apparently pleasantly surprised after a setup in San Francisco, where the girls all seem to wear fleece and ride mountain bikes. "You hot little California hottie," another e-mailed me from the East Coast, after we did, admittedly, have pretty hot sex. "Hello my California girl," e-mailed yet another East Coaster, inappropriately, since I was not his anything. Never mind that I was from New York, and the blond was all fake.

IN THE END, I thought sometimes, I should just pick someone at random and get on with it. In the end, I thought, it doesn't matter whom you marry—the janitor, your priest, your high school sweetheart, the man sitting next to you on the subway—as long as you commit to sticking it out. There will be good times and bad, whether you're with one person or another, whether you're married or single. A lot of life really is attitude. *If you're going to play, then get in the game,* is what I thought. *Don't walk away. Don't sit on the sidelines. Play.* And then I thought, *When the fuck did I become one of those inspirational posters on my dentist's ceiling?*

MY JUDGMENT felt broken. If I thought a guy was cute up close, as soon as I pulled back, not so much. When I introduced Bill to my friends, they were not as enthusiastic about him as I was. He was from Cleveland, mediocre-looking, a struggling screenwriter; his father drove a taxi for a living. I didn't know that that stuff mattered anymore—wasn't it about what he was like inside? At dinner he told Cath how much he liked me, and she leaned over to me and whispered, "At least he knows he's dating up." When I looked back up at him, my eyes narrowed, and suddenly I saw him clearly.

ON PLANES, in the gym, at bars, I was always aware of the men around me, of who was wearing a wedding ring or checking me out. If they came at me too strongly, then I knew they did that with everyone and I felt like I could be anyone.

I WAS GUN-SHY. If they made a sarcastic remark, a little nothing joke, I took it personally and picked a fight, and then as soon as I felt like they might leave, all I could think about was getting out of there first.

SOMETIMES they hurt my feelings, sometimes I hurt theirs. They did not call or I didn't; I told them my divorce was too fresh, they told me their career was too unsettled. I said one thing and they heard another, or they said one thing and then did another, but by this, at least, I was never surprised—after all, my *husband* left. There was always another one around the corner anyway, and all it took to change everything was one hello. There were more boys than I knew what to do with, sometimes. Soon I had them stashed across the city. They came and went, new ones took their places. They blurred together and I forgot how I met them or what they did or why I cared.

"BUT DON'T YOU WANT to try to meet the father of your children?" a friend from back east asked, concerned, when she heard about all the boys. "When are you going to have a baby?" her four-year-old daughter asked, and this focused me for a while, sent me off in a new direction. I agreed to another round of blind dates, I went to parties, I smiled and looked around for him, the one, the dad. No more boys, I promised myself. Men.

IN A MARBLE outdoor courtyard, at a fancy cocktail party in Malibu, I had another blind date. I was feeling attractive on this night, and fearless, as though I would always be single and love it. There was wine and music and rare roast beef. There were opera singers. Here I was meeting the kind of L.A. men who have so much money they need to come to a party like this to be reminded just how much, to be sucked up to by the men who manage their careers, to nod to the others at the event, saying, *Yes that's right, I belong here, too.*

My date, Matthew, fortyish and divorced, a well-known film director, was this kind of man, the kind of man who, when I told him I found Malibu to be impenetrable, reacted as if I'd called Pamela Anderson hard to get.

"Malibu?" he sputtered. "Perhaps," he said ridiculously, "you feel that way because it's a small town and you don't yet know the locals. For instance, just the other night I went down to Nobu at eight o'clock without a reservation, but Linda knows me so she got my friend and me right in. And it was a Saturday night, too. That would never happen outside of Malibu."

I wondered for a moment whether he actually believed himself, because I hadn't yet gotten to know him, a process that took less than five minutes, when he continued: "Of course then we ran into Fran Drescher and Cheech, and they didn't have a reservation, so then we were a party of four, and then we ran into Marty Sheen, you know Marty?" he asked another man standing with us—of course this man knew Martin Sheen, all real men know the right men—"and they didn't have a reservation, so then we were a party of six." He went on like this, expanding the tale as more and more Malibulian celebrities showed up, like clowns climbing out of a car, without reservations, at the local dive known as Nobu, in the small town of Malibu—until they were, finally, a party of ten. *"Ten,* can you believe it?" he said proudly. "And Linda still seated us because she knows us. That's Malibu."

Yes, I'm sure it is, I started to say, *but I wouldn't know because I don't have that kind of access, which was exactly my point.*

But he was not finished; he would not be finished until you were aware that somewhere along the journey of life he became good friends with Bono, and that he was given ten front-row tickets to the U2 concert last time they were in town, but he gave them all away, and that you must get your wines from the Woodland Hills Wine Company, because they are excellent at ferreting out good wines before that loudmouth Robert Parker tells the rest of the country about them. No, he would not be finished until he had the chance to tell you—so that you *understand* what kind of person he is—that he takes every meeting at the house in Malibu, because if someone is not willing to take the time to come out to the house and talk for two or three hours about his vision for a film and then go for a walk on the beach and then go to lunch, well, then he doesn't need to meet with them, because, let's be frank, he doesn't *need* to meet with anyone. Now, chuckling, he interrupted himself to say incongruously to his friend: "Steve, will you please tell her how much you paid for the wines at that charity auction, and how I told them to ten-X the price before charging your card?"

"That *was* a laugh," agreed Steve, a movie producer, also single, with a proud grin. When I wondered at the phrase "ten-X," he eagerly explained: "Instead of two thousand dollars there was twenty thousand on my credit card receipt when I got home."

"I felt he had underpaid," said my date, Matthew from Malibu, winking at me, and now he acted as though he had done this Steve a favor, giving him these wines for only twenty thousand dollars. "There was a very nice super Tuscan that I think will be drinkable soon," he said—and then I was done. I could no longer stand there without rolling my eyes. These were men I could no longer find interesting, or redeemable, or even at the very least windows onto an interesting world I knew nothing about. These were men who could spend three thousand dollars on a single bottle of wine, who could spend significant portions of their own intellect, time, and passion on things such as wine auctions, wine tastings, and intricate wine discussions, and find nothing distasteful about it.

"I'll call you," said Matthew from Malibu, and then he didn't.

I TOOK A BREAK. I swore off blind dates, I went to bed early at weddings, and alone. And when people talked about sex, I said wistfully, with a far-off look in my eyes, "I remember sex." I joined a soccer team, I traveled, I learned to play the piano. I watched my friends with their husbands and their babies and no careers and I watched their marriages and their spats and their domestic routines and I thought, Is this really what I want anyway? But deep down I knew there was something to it, to married life, something pure and whole, something rich and simple at the same time, like a good carrot soup.

And I wondered if it would ever end, this searching again for a life that I both wanted and did not want, and sometimes I felt exposed, threatened, vulnerable, left alone in the wilderness. I felt like anyone could just come along and snatch me off the street, and then I prayed that someone would. I started to feel less like a hole that needed filling and more like a ball bouncing into traffic. Alone, I was untethered, unpredictable, unknown. I was a wild boom, a lightning bolt, a tree about to fall in the forest.

Postcard from Nebraska

I DECIDED TO GO TO NEBRASKA because I didn't know what else to do. Though I did not share this with anyone, I felt I was on the verge of a desperate time. My husband had left and the president had lied to us, and I hadn't been able to stop either of them, and out of the corner of my eye I was aware that I was beginning to care less and less about what might happen next. It had been over a year since the divorce, and I felt ensnared by the stubbornness of grief, yet rather than shake myself out of it, I seemed to be melting into it. I pictured myself as a dingy brown puddle on a dirt road. I was unemployed and uninterested and unmotivated. What I was mostly doing these days was sitting at home, growing fat and slow, chewing my way through RJ's thirty thousand dollars like a caterpillar eating a peach.

If you do nothing, I warned myself delicately, *nothing will change.*

"Nebraska?" said Cath. "What's in Nebraska?"

There was an artists' colony, in a little town outside Omaha. A painter friend had told me about these places: it was like a paid vacation for artists; they put you up and gave you a studio in which to paint or write or whatever it was you did.

True, I was not an artist. I was an unemployed writers' assistant. But spring was approaching, and I knew I could not face springtime alone in L.A., not with its empty, perfect, Prozac weather. Sunshine felt too sinister in the face of war, as if the president had manufactured it, too. Everything was going to be okay if we just stayed the course and kept shopping, he promised with a wink and a smile, but I knew it wouldn't. I had lately been waking in the middle of the night with nightmares of falling off the cliffs of Malibu into the sea. The idea of snuggling myself into the middle of the country, like crawling into the center of a big cottony bed, was comforting.

So I quickly took twenty pages of a film script that I'd been writing for the past few months, disguised it as a one-act play, and sent it off to a few of these midwestern artists' colonies, requesting entry as soon as possible. To my deep, deep surprise, the one in Nebraska accepted me. My residency as a playwright would begin the following month.

It was called a colony because you were supposed to live with other artists, isolated in a hothouse environment, exchanging ideas, intermingling your creative juices, perhaps becoming part of some sort of artistic *movement*— but when I arrived, having flown into Omaha via Denver and driven a rental car from the airport, I found I was to be the only one there for the entire month.

"We had very disappointing applications this year," explained the director as he showed me around the colony's old Victorian house. "Hardly anyone applied," he added. "I was just glad to get a warm body in here."

I looked at him; he had no idea he was offending me. He was short and stout, with a comb-over, the outlines of his wife-beater showed through his threadbare white oxford shirt; his khakis were hiked up, a brown belt cinching his middle too tightly. He was actually the interim director. The real director had quit the month before to take a job at a more prestigious colony in Colorado. Colorado sounded nice, I thought. Mountains and fresh air, hikes.

It was early April in Nebraska, a seasonless time between winter and spring. They had had a blizzard and four feet of snow two weeks earlier, but it had since melted and the trees outside my window were bare and the grass was gray and scrubby with bits of trash hiding in it.

My mother was worried. She called twice a day, wanting me to go back to L.A. "Won't you get depressed there all alone?" she said. "What will you do by yourself every day?"

"Eh," I said into the phone, shrugging. I settled in. I hadn't expected much anyway, and now I simply recalibrated those expectations. I had planned to read and drink wine and hang out with artists and hope that I felt better. Now I decided I would just read and drink wine and hope for something.

For the first few days I enjoyed just being away from my life in L.A., away from my friends and my neighbors and even my therapist, with all her probing questions, who forced me to think about myself and Toby and my family, constantly trying to make me into a better person. In Nebraska I guiltlessly thought about nothing. I let myself go, even more so than I had in L.A., where people had been checking up on me.

In the mornings I lay around the old house reading, alternating between back issues of *The New Yorker* I'd brought with me and romance novels I'd found in the apartment's bookshelves. Around eleven or so I'd pull myself off the couch to go shopping on Main Street. The colony had given me a stipend of two hundred dollars a week, a princely sum in this little town, so I felt quite rich. I bought trinkets at the little antiques store, an old rhinestone ring for four dollars, and tea towels for twenty-five cents, and I became a regular at a little lunch place on Main Street, two blocks from the colony, patronized exclusively by people over the age of eighty, where I ate iceberg salads with radishes, and coconut cream pie. I sat alone at a table by the window, gazing out at the passersby but listening to the conversation inside: *And how's Marge today, Irv? Weeeeell, she's a little bony, Lou, thanks for asking. Feels it all in her joints, too. But she's up and around, so we'll take what we can get.*

In the afternoon I was often tired from my listlessness, and I took breaks from doing nothing to stare lazily out my window. There was a war of seasons: one day it would be warm and breezy, the next rainy and freezing, and there was even hail—big pellets of ice bulleting down on my roof. I enjoyed watching the trees and buds and grasses struggle to understand their mission: stay buried or burst forth? It was heartening to see nature going through what looked like a rough time, and surviving.

In the evenings I took walks around town in the twilight. Main Street, wide and open, was so authentic it reminded me of a Hollywood movie set of an old western farm town. It was lined with halfhearted businesses: an intimidating bar called the Chase Around, ill lit and smoky and full of farmers; a western shop that sold cowboy boots and spurs; a sad little pharmacy with old people's apparatuses in the window; tiny hair salons with names like Curl Up and Dye—and then, spreading out around it, little white homes that all looked the same for blocks and blocks in every direction. Friendly dogs roamed aimlessly, having little wrestling parties on the grass and then moving on; children left their bikes where they fell in their yards, wheels spinning. You never saw a police car, anywhere. In the real estate section of the local paper, the houses were selling for $79,000.

"I might move here," I told my mother. "It's not so bad."

"Oh, honey," she said. "Please. Nebraska? You wouldn't last ten seconds."

But perhaps I would settle here—I could get a job at the movie theater or the cable TV company, the only work for which I felt qualified. I would buy a little house and a dog and just let my days peter out as they would. Life, I had noticed, just kept going. It didn't really care where you were—things would happen to me in this town if I stayed, I knew. I would meet a man, perhaps a hardworking farmer who didn't talk much, just loved me silently yet strongly. I would get married again; we would raise our children here. And wherever my children went in life, whenever people asked where they were from, they would say, "Nebraska." Nebraska! Ha! *My* children! I had barely been aware of the state's existence a month ago, and now I had ghost children here.

But I knew now that this was how life worked. One could change one's life in an instant just by speaking a desire aloud. "I don't want to be married anymore," Toby had said, and now, a year and a half later, I was still having trouble getting over the shock. I wondered at times if I ever would. I had come here, I supposed, to try.

I liked to think about the fact that I could settle here in Nebraska if I wanted, that I, too, had control over my destiny. The possibility of creating a future for myself, of driving my life forward with purpose and direction, just like that, made me lust for everything that I wanted in my life to happen, and for it to happen *now.* But it couldn't, because I didn't know what it was I wanted in my future. Did I want to be married again? Have children? A career in TV? A career in something else? Should I stay in L.A.? Should I move somewhere else? I didn't know. All I felt was just a sharp, yearning feeling of *I want.*

On my fourth day in Nebraska I went out to the town's graveyard. The stones were whitish gray, old and worn. The town's founder, J. Sterling Lanier, was buried there. He had died in 1902. His gravestone was a simple, humble thing, like the town he'd founded, the marker just barely readable.

———

HUSBAND OF CAROLINE, it said. A sign nearby explained that he had been dev-astated by her death, forty years before his own. He had planted a huge Burr oak tree near her grave to shade and shelter her. Now it towered over the site, strong and silent, a picture of devotion, a tiny town's Taj Mahal.

What luck I had had, I thought for a moment, standing there as the rows of graves spread out before me. Everyone I had ever loved was still alive. But then again, what was it my old widowed aunt had said to me after my husband left? *I imagine it's like death,* she had said, *only worse.*

ON THE FIFTH DAY there was a tornado watch.

"I wouldn't worry about it," said the colony director, leaving early for the day. "We don't take them too seriously. Then again, I wouldn't venture too far from the center tonight. You'll want to get down to the basement right away if the sirens go."

Around 8 P.M. the wind picked up, and the building creaked, and the sky was a brassy yellow color that then turned dim and dismal and wan, becom-ing almost luminous, like the palest sunshine. A sickly greenish cast came into the clouds, and they turned darker and darker until they became a ghostly gray, and then I heard a crashing din, like a river rushing. Suddenly the town's sirens screamed above it all, and I ran down to the basement.

I was scared—the wind and the crashing had been quite dramatic—but I knew I was safe down below. The cement room was outfitted with cots and bottled water and a radio, and now I turned the dial on the radio until I landed on a local station.

I was surprised to find that it was still playing a regularly scheduled show that I'd heard the other evening in the car at this same time. It was called *Swap Meet,* and it was simply people calling in and describing things they wanted to barter—tractors, egg beaters, video games, railroad ties.

Apparently the town's residents were so unfazed by the tornado that they were simply going to continue to call in. I found this comforting. I lay down on a cot, covered myself with a woolen blanket, and listened, staring at the radio's speaker. The host was a pleasant guy with a voice like an old-time radio announcer.

"And what've you got for us this evening, friend?" he said to the caller. "By the way, I sure do hope you're underground right about now."

"Yes, sir, I am, I sure am," said the man. There were children in the background. "Sir, I have two black-and-white TVs. One is a sixteen-inch and the other a twenty-inch."

"And what are ya wanting for 'em?"

"Sir, I'd take a set of curlers for my wife here, or a ten-pound bag of fertilizer."

"All righty then," said the announcer. "And what've you got for us, young lady?" he said to the next caller, a grandmother trying to trade some old jam jars.

I fell asleep to his soothing voice.

BY FRIDAY I had been in Nebraska a week and I hadn't said more than a few sentences to anyone. Wandering the huge, fluorescently lit grocery store that night, way out on the commercial corridor by Burger King and the auto shops, I couldn't think of what to make for dinner, and suddenly I was hit by a wave of homesickness so deep and sharp it made me wonder if I shouldn't just pack up my things and leave that very night. I missed our shared little apartment, down to my bones, and I missed our white sheets and our monogrammed towels and our wedding china—until I remembered that I had moved out and he had kept the sheets and towels and I was living in a house by myself now. As I searched up and down the grocery aisles—for what, I did not know—I realized that being homesick was quite like being heartbroken. The difference, I thought, was that when one was homesick one held out hope of eventually seeing home again, while with heartbreak, no matter how the heart yearns to go back, it cannot.

THAT EVENING I went for my walk. It was that lovely time of year just after daylight savings, when it stays light until you think it can't anymore. The sun had set and the moon was just a smudge of white cloud in the sky, as if someone had tried to erase it and failed.

Main Street was busy—it was Friday night and spring was coming, and everyone was out and about, nodding at me as they walked by. The teenage boys in their pickups cruised the street looking for girls, gunning their engines in an old-fashioned small-town ritual.

Passing by the Chase Around, I heard the clink of pool balls and the low murmuring laughter of women with men, and the lurid lights shone through the screen door, beckoning me. My loneliness from the grocery store lingered—should I go in, have a drink and a chat? But I walked on. I was a woman alone in a strange town. No one would be coming to rescue me here.

ON SATURDAY I woke to spring. Everything—the grass, the leaves, the flower buds on the trees—was suddenly green, and for the first time I noticed that birds were building a nest in the big oak outside my window. Their chirping was a rasping, rhythmic one that sounded like the hinges of a bed squeaking. I realized then how little I'd thought about sex since I'd been in Nebraska. That part of me felt dead. I couldn't even get myself to respond at night. I knew I could wake myself if I wanted, by thinking of my ex-husband—I could call up our sex behind my eyes in an instant—but I had, long ago, decided not to give in to that. It felt too sad and sick when I came up for air on the other side.

There was a reception that night for the trustees of the colony. I was not looking forward to it; I was anxious. Normally I was quite a sociable person, but I was afraid that in the past week I had forgotten how to say light conversational things in response to other light conversational things. Still, as the only colonist in residence I felt I should go, and so that evening, craving a glass of wine anyway, I went downstairs, where the reception was being held.

I was relieved to see the director, the only person I knew, when I walked in. He was talking to a cute guy in his twenties who was wearing a tie and a wedding ring.

"Hi," I said.

The director introduced us. Sterling Lanier IV was his name. "Sterling is the great-great-great-grandson of the town's founder," said the director.

"I'm also running for mayor, and I'd love your vote," said Sterling.

"Oh," I said. "Well, I don't think I can—"

"Ah, you're one of the artists," he said. "What kind of art do you do?"

"I'm a, um, poet," I said, squelching an absurd urge to look furtively around to see if anyone from L.A. had overheard.

"I thought you were a playwright," said the director, eyebrows raised.

Damn! Playwright! I was supposed to be a *playwright*.

"Yes, I am that, as well, but I'm, uh, branching out while I'm here. Into poetry."

"Huh," the director grumbled and walked off. Out of the corner of my eye I watched him approach another little group. Were those the trustees? Was he going to tell on me? Could they kick me out of the colony?

"You won't believe who came into the bookstore the other day," said a strange woman suddenly standing in front of me. "You'll love this."

"Who?" I did not know this woman, so I did not know how she would know what I would love.

"Ted Kooser."

"No," I said, faking disbelief. Who was Ted Kooser?

"Yes," the woman said in her flat nasal voice. "I know."

"You know . . . what?" I said. "I'm sorry?"

"I know how excited that must make you."

"Oh, yes, very," still trying to bluff my way through. "When will he be back?"

"I don't know, silly," she said flatly. "He just wandered in. I just stood there behind the counter in shock. Finally I went up to him and I told him my favorite book of his was the one where he wrote a poem every day on a postcard and mailed it to his friend. And you know what he said? 'Thank you,' he said. 'It's one of my favorites as well. It was very helpful to write those postcards. It was a difficult time in my life. I had cancer and I felt very alone.' " The woman glowed. "It was the greatest moment of my life."

So this Ted Kooser was apparently a poet, and this woman, whose name turned out, oddly, to be Jane Austen, apparently worked in the town's bookstore, and the greatest moment in Jane's life up until now had been meeting this man.

Must be some poet, this man, who wrote a postcard every day to his friend. I chided myself for being snappish, then realized, with a bit of a confused jolt, that I was envious. I didn't know what to do with this feeling, where to put it. Why was I envious of someone for doing something I was only pretending to want to do?

"Hey," whispered J. Sterling Lanier IV, tugging at my elbow. "Wanna get out of here?"

I looked at him skeptically. "And go where?"

"The Chase Around. I'm having a mayoral fund-raiser. All my buddies'll be there."

"Are you serious?" It sounded like heaven compared with worrying about being interrogated by the director and his entourage of trustees.

"Deadly," he said, staring at me. "Like a python."

I nodded. "I'll meet you there."

Now a priest and a homely woman walked up to our little group.

"God be with you," whispered Sterling IV, and he left.

The priest, an Episcopal reverend, was gray and overweight, and his name was Kermit. The woman was his wife, Lillian, and she had the same short, feathered haircut as every other woman in town, and a melodious voice. They had been married for twenty-three years.

"Oh yes, we nearly divorced our first year of marriage," said Lillian, as if somehow picking up where she'd left off. "But I didn't want to give my mother the satisfaction. My mother had been divorced, you see, and I knew that if I did, she'd make me her little pal in disappointment—'See, now you understand, isn't life awful?'—that kind of thing. Oh no. I would have sooner killed Kermit than divorced him."

"I was lucky to escape that year alive," the reverend said with a chuckle. "My marriage is the only relationship I have that has a transtemporal quality to it," he mused. "I simply cannot tell how long we have been married. Sometimes it feels like a month, sometimes my whole life. It is the only relationship that I have ever had that does this to me."

"Finally, we went to a marriage counselor," Lillian said, as if her husband hadn't spoken, "and this man said, 'Do you like to do things together?' and we said, 'Well, yes, we do everything together.' And he said, 'Then you're fine.'"

"And, after a while," Kermit said, "we were."

"Isn't that always the way?" said Jane Austen cheerfully.

"Well, no," said Lillian flatly. "It isn't. Half of all marriages end in divorce." Now she turned to me. "You know," she said, with blame in her voice, "they never show that on TV. They never show the people who struggle to work it out. And in every single marriage there comes a time when each partner asks themselves, 'Is this really the only life I'm going to have? Am I really never going to sleep with anyone else, never be attracted to anyone else?'"

At this Kermit nodded solemnly, closing his eyes while munching an olive.

"It's quite existential, when it comes down to it," Lillian went on. "It's all about the narrowing of choices, down, down, down, until you die. Being confronted with a choice and realizing we must decide it, makes us aware that we don't have all the time in the world to do other things. The very act of making a choice makes other choices, other paths, impossible."

And she walked off to get a stuffed mushroom.

"Yes, well, one can't help one's attractions," said the reverend. "I'm sure quite a few fellows have been attracted to my wife, and there's not much I can do about it."

"I was once attracted to J. Sterling Lanier," said Jane Austen in her flat voice. "It was all quite torrid, though of course it never went any further than my imagination."

"You mean . . . the town's founder?" I said, confused. "But isn't he dead?"

"I know," said Jane, shaking her head in wonder. "And he has been for a hundred years."

ON MY WALK to the bar I passed the local bookstore, where, looking in the window, I stopped short. It seemed a strange coincidence, but when I thought about it, of course it wasn't. In the window were two books by "Pulitzer Prize–winning Nebraska poet Ted Kooser." So the guy was not only a poet, he had won a Pulitzer. One was the book of postcards he had written to a friend, and the other was something called *The Poetry Home Repair Manual.* I peered in at it. Apparently it was meant to help young people write poems. Well, maybe I would buy it. I should do something with myself while I was here, I thought. I should stop pretending.

AT THE BAR, all of Sterling IV's friends had shaved heads. I was afraid I'd stumbled into a neo-Nazi meeting in the heartland, but it turned out they were Marines. They had all done ROTC together at the University of Nebraska, and they were shipping out to Iraq in a couple weeks. I had some fun for a while, telling them some good places to go out in San Diego, where they'd be stationed before going overseas, but soon they started drinking too much and that scared me a little. Then, on top of that, their alpha-dog sergeant arrived.

"Hey, Sarge," they said, and he nodded back.

Slightly tipsy, I saluted him.

"And you would be . . . ?" he said, standing at the bar, looking me up and down.

"Not interested," I said.

"Ha," he said without smiling. "Ha."

I ignored him. I ordered a shot of tequila and shot it.

"Cute drunk women ought to be more polite in strange towns," he said.

"Macho local men ought to be less macho," I said. "And get better pickup lines."

"You annoy me," he said.

"Just wait," I said.

"Sarge!" Sterling said, approaching. "Mind relinquishing this little lady for a minute?"

"Not at all," he said, scowling at me. "It would be my pleasure. My *extreme* pleasure."

Sterling and I walked over toward the pool table. He got me into a corner.

"So, here's the deal," he whispered. "My wife is out of town. But I'm Catholic."

"Me too!" I whispered, unaccountably happy.

"Well, yeah, that's great and all, but it's not like they cancel each other out."

"Um, I'm sorry, what are you talking about?"

"Like this wasn't going to happen from the moment we met?" he whispered fiercely, getting his face in mine. "Like you didn't feel the connection?"

"You're joking, right?" I laughed and then stopped. It was like he was quoting from the movies or something. This couldn't be more manufactured. There had been zero chemistry between us at the reception. He was good-looking, but that was it. On top of that, the wedding ring obviously killed it for me.

"Look, if we don't actually have sex then I think we're okay in the eyes of the church," he said. "What does your priest count as adultery, do you know?"

"No," I said. "Anyway, it was nice meeting you. Good luck with the election."

I went back to the bar to settle my tab.

"I already got it," said the sergeant.

"Really?" I said, looking up at him.

"Really," he said.

We spent the rest of the night walking the town and talking. The streets were quiet, their homes small and white and tucked away for the night, lamps glowing yellow and warm behind unlocked doors. Later we headed out beyond, to the dirt roads, by the farms and the rolling fields, where it was silent except for our footsteps and the low murmur of our talk. He talked to me about war and duty and loyalty and commitment. It was so dark we could see the Milky Way. Toward dawn we went down by the river. The green grass was firm and new. Afterward, he kept me so warm, it was like he had a skill for it. Then we watched the sun come up. I hadn't done anything like it since I was a teenager.

I told him that, all of it. I said I would never forget him.

"You know," he said, looking at me intently, "every man who's ever passed you on the street and kept walking is an idiot."

I was about to make another crack about pickup lines, but stopped.

"Where do you think you're gonna be when I get back?" he said. "I mean, what is it you want out of life?"

I was touched by the question but felt it was too late to ask it. Whatever I'd wanted—well, I hadn't gotten it. Ten years ago, or even five, when I was in my twenties, I'd had time to figure out what I wanted. But now, at thirty-three, there wasn't any time to think about wanting; I had to go ahead and get it. And suddenly I realized I couldn't say what I wanted from the future, because the future and I were at the same place. Whatever I wanted from the future, I was living it right now.

"I guess I want this," I said happily, hugging myself, exhilarated by my realization. "A night like this. More nights like this."

He smiled. I knew he thought I was talking about him and that was okay.

We said good-bye as the sun rose higher, the river rushing clean and loud beside us.

He was flying out that day for Camp Pendleton, and then for Iraq. We wouldn't see each other again. Part of me felt sad, and another part was already imagining a hot shower, the book by my bed, whatever came next. This was just a good-bye, the things you said.

"I'll write to you over there," I said. "How often do you get mail?"

"We have e-mail now."

"Oh," I said, disappointed. He might as well be in Omaha if we were just going to *e-mail*. Still. He was going to war. Over there, he was going to be feeling what I'd felt in the grocery store the other night, only multiplied by ten thousand. He would be heartsick and homesick, with no assurance of ever coming back again.

"I'll be home in eighteen months," he said. "Will you wait for me?" When I hesitated he blushed and added, "We can get married if you want."

Stunned, I stared back at him. Sure, I felt something for him, a little of that glowy affection that comes when you spend the night with someone, and, yes, I admired him for where he was about to go and what he was about to do. But in truth my happiness right then was more a joy of my own, a gratitude to the world for finally giving me a night like this and, with it, the assurance that there would be others.

"What do you say?" he said with a sheepish smile. "Will you marry me?"

"Oh, Sarge," I said, grabbing him up in a hug. "You know we can't."

"I don't see why not," he said, pushing me away.

"Don't be like that, Sarge," I said. "I'm going to write you every day." Well—was I, *really*? Maybe a postcard every day anyway. I could just get in the habit, in the mornings, of jotting off a little note to him, a poem even—

"I just want to feel like I belong to someone while I'm over there," he said miserably.

"I understand," I said, and I did.

"I don't know if you do," he said.

I had been a child bride once, when I was about six years old. I had married my next door neighbor, also six, in a little make-believe ceremony in the backyard. It was back in the late seventies, and I had worn a white eyelet nightgown and a crown of daisies in my hair. I was still very close to my neighbor-husband. He was married now, with a child of his own, but sometimes we wrote to each other, or we talked on the phone.

Now I took my man's hand. I made him look at me. I remembered the ceremony by heart.

The Perfect Stranger

THE SHOW WAS CALLED *Inconceivable,* and the joke among the crew was that it was inconceivable that the network had actually decided to produce it. It was a nighttime soap opera set in a fertility clinic with a crappy script and a low-rent cast; its stories centered on such tired ideas as nurses switching sperm samples and white women giving birth to black babies, and absolutely no one thought it would go more than a few episodes before being canceled midseason.

Still, until it got killed, the studio needed stories, which would have to be pitched, and scripts, which would have to be written, and dailies, which would have to be shot. And so, near the end of May, at the beginning of the Valley's laser-hot summer, I halfheartedly reported to work on the Disney lot in Burbank, a huge green sanitized campus whose aesthetic was one of artificial celebration. They had glossed up the Disney characters in a dubious effort to make them palatable to adults. The seven dwarves had been maniacally carved into Roman columns, staring down at us like comic gargoyles; a huge shrub at the lot's entrance had been carefully trimmed to resemble Goofy; electric golf carts bearing Cinderella flags whisked along paved paths with names like Dumbo Drive and Mickey Lane. I felt humiliated just walking around the place.

There were times when I wondered what I was still doing in Hollywood, in this town, this playground for adults—I was too dark for its light, too serious for its frivolity. There were times when I questioned my decision to stay as ruthlessly as I had any choice I had ever made.

Over the past several months I had considered settling in Nebraska or moving back to New York or to someplace exotic like Morocco or Mozambique, where I could lose myself and then find myself again, but I did not go. I felt strangely bound to L.A., as if I had to hold on to something in lieu of a husband, as if my relationship with the city was now the marriage I had to save. I had the sense that if I could do it slowly, if I could enmesh myself in L.A.'s fabric, then I could come to learn the secret of myself by becoming part of a place. I imagined myself as a surfer, one with the sea, inside the wave.

And so I did the opposite of leaving: I committed. I renewed my lease, gave my walls a fresh coat of paint, and planted a garden in the front lawn of my little house. My neighborhood, Venice Beach, was starkly different from the trendy, concrete, buzzing scene of Hollywood where I had lived with Toby. My bungalow had driftwood beams across its ceilings, a fringe of pink bougainvillea hanging over its white picket fence, and a little backyard. It was a block from the beach and everyone in the neighborhood rode beach cruiser bikes and wore shorts and flip-flops. I rode my bike along the strand every morning and watched the surfers wait for waves. I quit smoking and ate more vegetables and bought a yoga mat and went to class every day; I did not understand what it was all about, but I knew that if I stuck it out, I would.

Come home, urged my friends back east. *Come home and shake off this whole horrible mess and move on,* they pleaded, with a slight hint of desperation in their voices, as if they could not for the life of them understand my intentions, as if the town itself had rejected me along with my husband, as if by staying out west I was tightening the screws that would seal my unhappy fate. But I could not go. I would not go until I felt I could leave L.A. on my own terms.

STAYING MEANT I needed another job, and so, after I got back from Nebraska, I'd gotten one. Stunningly, it was the snakewoman on RJ's show who helped me. I ran into her at a party, and she went out of her way to be nice to me. "I treated you so badly," she said. "My husband was cheating on me, and

I had an affair with that loser PA to make myself feel better, which obviously didn't work. So I took it out on you and everyone else. But you didn't deserve it." I nodded at her and said I understood, and she nodded back, and suddenly we were women on equal terms, just like that. She called up some producer friends, Carl and Bert, the ones who'd created *Inconceivable*; they were a campy playwright couple, famous in New York theater circles for their risqué plays but largely unknown in Hollywood, and they hired me to do research on infertility.

The main thing I learned from the hours I spent online, the books I read, and the experts I spoke with was that, at thirty-three and husbandless, I'd better hurry up and freeze my eggs—then at least I'd have a chance at in vitro if I ever met anyone normal. Apparently Ira had been right about my need to hurry up and get back out there. Yet I did not seem to care. Each day I faced my own declining fertility (along with written accounts of women whose "wombs ached" upon reaching their thirty-fifth birthdays, who did in vitro four and five times without success, who had never considered the possibility of not becoming a mother until they were told it would not happen) with an indifference that shocked me. Did I even want to have a baby? Did I see myself raising a child for the rest of my life, seeing as I could barely take care of myself? I did not know. This felt like number eighty-eight of about one hundred things that I still did not know about myself.

I HAD NOT SEEN or talked to Misty since I had quit working for RJ several months earlier. Then one day she showed up unannounced at my office on the Disney lot, having tracked me down via the snakewoman. Standing in my doorway, she said she had done a lot of soul searching, and had come to the conclusion that no one in L.A. really cared about her. Her manager had hit on her, her agent was pressuring her to do a horror film about prostitutes, and her trashy friends were always talking about her behind her back. She wanted to be friends with someone who respected her.

"I want to be friends with *you*," she said.

"Okay," I said, slightly stunned.

"Excellent," she said, and then plunked herself down on the couch in my office, put her feet up, and studied her nails, as if we were simply resuming a conversation that had been interrupted a few minutes ago. "You know,

Lacey," she said, shaking her finger at me scoldingly, "I would have told you not to sleep with RJ if you'd asked me. But you were so secretive about it. I didn't even know about it until after you left."

"Who told you?" I thought RJ and I had been so good about hiding it.

"Oh, no one told me. I hacked into his account and read all his e-mails the day before I quit—he uses the same password for everything, by the way, *Ronald Rules,* God, what a dork—because I wanted to have some dirt on him if I ever needed it. And boy, did I ever find some, by the way. That man is sick."

"Well, I feel really guilty, Misty," I said. "I was always telling you to get another job because he was such a jerk, and then I went ahead and had a relationship with him."

"Yeah, well, live and learn," she said, lolling on my couch. "You know, it's funny, you were always telling me that I deserved better, that I shouldn't let him treat me that way. And I was always ignoring you."

"I remember it well," I said.

"But then after you left, there was no one telling me that I deserved better. And so eventually I guess I started to feel, well, that I deserved better."

"Wow. Well, Misty, honestly, I'm impressed that you're giving yourself more respect."

"Also, I told RJ if he didn't give me a part on the show, I'd quit."

"Good for you."

"And he said that even if the show went into syndication for fifteen seasons and I was the last actress in Hollywood and he had to use a robotic mannequin instead, it would never happen."

"Harsh."

"I know, right? So I left."

Thus unemployed, she had decided to focus on forging a friendship with me, and jump-starting her acting career. Between auditions she began regularly hanging around my office, which happened to be close to many of the casting offices in Burbank. She napped on my couch, read *In Touch* magazine aloud to an unwilling audience of one, Googled boys she was interested in, and endlessly asked me to read lines with her.

Finally, in large part to get her out of my office for an afternoon, I got her an audition on *Inconceivable.* It was for a minor part—a nun who somehow gets pregnant—but when she came in to read for Carl and Bert she thought she was reading for another part—a prostitute who can't get pregnant—and so she inadvertently did the whole nun reading in the character and costume of a prostitute.

Carl and Bert, instead of feeling that her reading was totally off, not to mention wildly inappropriate, somehow thought she'd had a "charming" take on the nun. They spontaneously asked her to read for one of the leads—a woman who has a bizarre medical condition that makes her pregnant all the time—then offered her the part on the spot. An eternally pregnant Misty would now be starring in the show alongside three famous actors; she would be making twenty thousand dollars an episode; a billboard that included her image would go up on Sunset Boulevard, near the Chateau Marmont.

It was—and this was even understating it—her monumentally big break.

"I guess I owe you, Lacey," she said bitterly when she came by my office to tell me.

"You don't seem very excited," I said, still reeling from the news.

"I play a pregnant person," she said. "I have to look fat all the time. How do you expect me to feel?"

CARL AND BERT, as it turned out, were having a baby. Their real-life struggle to have this child was, of course, how they had come up with the idea for the show. They had spent two years and $175,000 in legal fees in their quest for an egg donor and a surrogate to carry the baby. Finally, when they were on the verge of calling it quits, they had found and hired a willing surrogate in Indiana. Her name was Arlene and she was a Methodist and a cashier at Kmart, married with four children of her own. Her small town was religious and conservative and her neighbors disapproved of her having a baby for a gay couple, but Arlene was a strong woman and she believed that Jesus would have done it in his time. After meeting Bert and Carl and becoming overwhelmed by how lovely they were, she had further agreed to donate the egg, too. But the other half of the child's DNA would be a mystery. Carl and Bert did not know whose sperm it was, and in fact even the doctors did not know. This was because both Carl and Bert had donated their sperm into several separate vials, and then the doctor had placed all the vials in a diaper bag and Carl and Bert had closed their eyes and picked one at random.

The baby was clearly going to be a completely different person depending upon whose sperm they had chosen. Carl was tall, blond, totally gorgeous, crazy, campy, and very funny. He was loud, and he would pitch any idea and do anything to get a laugh. Bert was shorter and gray-haired with round wire-rimmed glasses and shy eyes, and he was soft-spoken and brilliant. When he said anything in the writers' room, everyone leaned in close. Every day I felt differently about it: one day I hoped they had chosen Bert's sperm, the next, Carl's.

MY OWN PARTICULAR STRUGGLE around this time had more to do with feeling that I had "plateaued" in therapy. I had been divorced for over a year and a half, and in therapy for about a year, and I'd been making progress, I felt—until now.

I'd found my therapist, Eleanor, through Cath, who was in couples therapy with Henry.

Henry, who had not sailed away after all, had fallen head over heels for Matilda one weekend when Cath had the flu and he had been forced to take care of the baby for forty-eight hours straight. (It helped even more a few months later when Matilda started saying "Da" whenever she saw him.) Cath had gone back to work part-time and seemed almost relieved to be at an office again, helping to bring in money, although Henry said she might not have to worry about that for long—he had written another screenplay, and it looked like it might sell to Miramax. Cath said that Eleanor was responsible for a lot of the changes; she'd helped Cath deal with her mother and Henry with his dad. She was a somatic therapist, meaning she focused on using awareness of the body to release tension and pain. It all sounded a little bit hippie-dippy California to me, but I figured at that point that anything was worth trying.

Eleanor's office was attached to her home, at the top of a winding road in the Palisades, with a view of the ocean. The first time I met her, I walked through a rambling rose garden in her backyard to get to her office door, which was painted fuchsia. I knocked, and she opened it; she was in her forties with dark hair and glasses, a womanly figure, and a wide smile. She was beautiful in a Mother Earth way, and spiritual in an L.A. way, schooled in both Buddhism and Hinduism—she had a guru, no less. She dressed in flowing monochromatic outfits, with jewelry that looked like it came from exotic places she had probably visited in her quest to find herself. I had no doubt that she had already found herself: she was the epitome of the word *peaceful.*

We held that first session in her garden, two chairs facing each other.

"Let's sit in silence for a few minutes," she said. "And just pay attention to your body."

"I guess . . . I don't know how to do that," I said.

"Notice your heartbeat, how fast or slow it is," she said, "or your breath, whether it is short or deep, or your chest, whether it is tight or expanded."

"Okay." I was skeptical, but I did it. I noticed that my heart was beating fast. I willed myself to relax, but my breath was short and my chest felt tight. I tried again.

"Don't fight yourself," Eleanor said. "Just let whatever feelings you are having today rise to the surface."

I didn't know what she meant, but I sat there awkwardly for a few minutes. My chest was tight and then I felt like I was holding something in, and then my throat closed up.

"Let yourself go," she said. But I couldn't. The lump sat in my throat, refusing to move.

"I'm sorry," I said finally. "I can't do it."

She smiled. "That's okay," she said, in a way that felt like it was. "We have next week to try again, and the week after that, and the week after that. I'm not going anywhere." And that became her sign-off every week: *I'm not going anywhere.* It reassured me.

Eventually, as time went on, I'd been able to breathe, I'd been able to talk about my feelings. Yet lately it felt like there was a wall up, a certain point I couldn't get past. Eleanor tried to help. She asked me questions about my parents that I could not answer, and I wrote down everything. Why had my mom left us? Why had my dad cheated on my mom? Why was my dad addicted to gambling? Did my mom regret leaving us?

Finally, Eleanor suggested I ask my parents these questions. I decided she was right. I invited my parents to come out to L.A. for a weekend. Both of them at the same time. Like an intervention. We had a few things to discuss.

"No," said my mother. "Not if your father will be there."

"You owe me," I said. "You left me when I was seven years old. I am all fucked up because of you."

"Fine," she said stonily.

"Sure," said my dad cheerily later that day.

"Oh," I said, "I forgot to tell you. No gambling, no phone calls to weird people who might be gambling, no discussion of deals that may or may not be closing Tuesday."

"You know what?" he said. "Can't make it. Wish I could."

"Let me know your flight info and I'll pick you up." I hung up.

Misty, who, to my chagrin, continued to spend all her time between scenes in my office, was envious of all the progress I had made with Eleanor.

"*I* want to deal with the pain of my past," she said, pouting.

"Please," I said. "You were Miss Teen Kansas. Your parents are still married. You wouldn't know pain if you fell out a window."

"I did so have a painful childhood," she insisted. "My horse died when I was eight."

"So go to therapy," I said.

She snorted. "I'm not *crazy*."

I raised my eyebrows at her.

"Plus," she added, ignoring me, "I still have my midwestern values. You can't pay for advice where I come from."

"Well, then, where are you supposed to get it?"

"From your friends and neighbors. Over the back fence, that kind of thing. I get my therapy from talking to you, for instance."

"Yeah, that seems like a wise idea."

"You know, Lacey," Misty said, "I thought therapy was supposed to make you nicer."

A FEW WEEKS into the show Misty started falling for one of her co-stars, and he for her. His name was Nick Newton; he was very good-looking, he was known for having dated Julia Roberts for a time, and he was the nicest star I had ever worked with. When people brought their families to the set he made a point of talking to them and taking photos with them; he was unfailingly on time for call and always knew his lines; he remembered every single crew member's name.

He treated Misty like gold—sending flowers to her trailer, calling her all the time, taking her to the nicest places in town—yet she remained in a constant state of anxiety, endlessly coming up with new and ever more bizarre reasons to mistrust him.

"He dated Julia Roberts," she complained one day as she lounged in my office; she was between scenes, wearing her ever-present fake bump. When I didn't respond she said, "*Julia. Roberts.* How can he possibly like *me* after dating *her*?"

I was sitting at my desk; I idly IMDB'd him. "He's also dated Kate Winslet, Drew Barrymore, and Jennifer Aniston," I reported from my computer.

"Don't you think I'm aware of that?" she said, looking at me hatefully. "God, Lacey, why would you tell me that? Isn't my self-esteem low enough already?"

"Why are you acting like an insane person? Nick likes *you* now."

"He can't like me," she said. "I look fat ninety-nine percent of the time he's around me."

"It's called a costume."

She ignored me. "I wouldn't blame him for leaving me. I would leave me if I looked like I do." She stood and turned in her costume, eyeing her false stomach from all sides. "Maybe I should get a tummy tuck."

As ARLENE'S DUE DATE approached, Bert and Carl constantly worried that if they did not fly to Indiana soon, they might miss the birth altogether. They intended to be present for their child's entry into the world—they were very clear about that—yet they were reluctant to leave the show if the baby wasn't going to arrive for several weeks. They debated it constantly in the writers' room.

Two weeks before the due date, Bert, mellow and thoughtful, was in favor of just going to Indiana and waiting it out, while Carl, high-strung and sarcastic, preferred to wait in L.A. and jump on the first flight out there as soon as Arlene went into labor.

"We should just go there and settle in," Bert urged. "Let the baby feel that we are settled, that the universe is settled, that we are ready and waiting patiently to receive him or her."

"And do what while we're there?" argued Carl. "Wait for two weeks at a Holiday Inn in Terre Haute? Last time we went I got an all-over body rash from sleeping in those sheets. I am telling you that the thread count of their linens cannot be higher than forty."

"This is the miracle of our child's birth. Who cares about thread count?"

"Bert," Carl said, suppressing a smile, "when you say things like that I begin to wonder why I married you, never mind agreed to have a child with you."

In the end they could never decide to go, and so they stayed.

TO COMPENSATE for her pregnancy costume, Misty began showing up at work in ever more revealing outfits: a slinky red top cut down to her stomach; jeans riding so low that her purple thong peeked out; a skirt so short it literally didn't cover the back of her black lace underwear.

I told her to stop it, and finally Nick Newton did too, asking her to dress more modestly, saying he didn't like the crew ogling her.

"You see?" she said fervently. "He's trying to keep me down."

"Honey," I said, "he respects you, and he wants you to respect yourself."

"I can't *respect* myself," she said. "Not after he dated Julia Roberts."

I told her to stop talking to me about it, because it was clearly making her crazy. She said she was only talking about it so I could help her decide what to do about Nick and his cheating, tomcat ways. "You have Eleanor to talk to," she said. "If I can't talk to you about it, I have no one."

"But Nick has never cheated on you," I said. "He has a reputation in Hollywood for being a good guy."

"He hasn't cheated on me *yet*," she corrected. "But in five, ten, twenty years, who knows?"

"Stop," I said. "We can talk, just not about him."

"Fine," she said. "Then I have no choice but to cut you off." She crossed her arms and turned her back on me.

"Cut me off from what?"

"You're dead to me now."

I sighed. "Fine, crazy person," I said.

"Dead people don't talk," she said.

THE NEXT DAY a very pregnant Misty came rushing up to me on the set.

"Look," she said breathlessly, thrusting a piece of paper at me.

"I thought I was dead to you," I said.

"Huh?" she said, looking genuinely confused. Then she forced the photocopied paper on me. "I found this on the bulletin board at Whole Foods last night."

I looked. There was a photo of a woman wearing heavy makeup and a scarf around her head; a caption beneath identified her as Shana Starr. "I am NOT a therapist," it read. "I am the Perfect Stranger. I am the perfect person to listen to your problems and offer solutions without judgment. $20 a call. One problem per call, please." And it gave a local phone number.

As usual with Misty, I didn't know where to begin.

"What the hell is this?" I said. "A psychic?"

"She's not a *psychic*," Misty said. "She's a healer. And I talked to her this morning for like an hour and she was great."

"About Nick?"

She nodded. "I feel soooo much better."

"What did she say?"

"Oh, you know, she told me what she sees happening in our future, she interpreted the vibrations in my voice, she told me all about Nick's past lives."

"And what was Nick in his past life?"

"Some kind of king in Asia, then some kind of artist in Paris, that kind of thing. But the kicker was, he had issues with commitment even then. So now I know."

"Well, that's great," I said, unwilling to go there. "At least now you know."

"We're going to fix them, of course," she said.

I looked at her blankly.

"Nick and I are going to have our past-life agreements amended," she said. "Tonight."

"Excuse me?" I said.

"And you're coming."

"Ha," I said.

"Don't be such a downer," Misty said, and she got that familiar faraway look in her eyes. "Tonight, we're going to shift the train tracks of karma."

As THE WEEKEND with my parents approached, I began to wish I had an ally, someone on my team, someone who could convince them to give me the honest answers I needed to figure myself out. I considered calling Toby, but that seemed too masochistic. When the answer finally dawned on me, I felt like an idiot that I hadn't thought of it before: my brother, Sam.

Still, there was quite a large barrier to this plan. I did not know how to get in touch with Sam. My mother had tried sporadically over the past three and a half years, sending letters to his last known address in Zermatt, with no re-sponse, and calling Olivia's number, which was disconnected. I had never once, since he had cut us all off, tried to get in touch with Sam. I had been so angry with him for cutting us off that I had decided to cut him off, too. I could have made an effort to reach out to him when his girlfriend had gotten preg-nant and he'd freaked out, but I hadn't. *I guess that's what happens when you cut someone off and mean it,* I thought ruefully.

I decided to send an overnight FedEx envelope to Zermatt, using the Dis-ney account. I wrote Sam a note and put a fifty-dollar bill inside. "Please call me anytime, day or night, as soon as possible. I really need to talk to you. I love you." I added my cell phone number, signed it, and sent it off.

MISTY'S MEETING with destiny was held in a shitty ranch house in Tarzana, a relatively undesirable part of the Valley. We drove over there after shooting ended for the night, around nine o'clock.

Shana Starr greeted us at the door. She was wearing all the psychic glitz—a patterned scarf around her hair and a flowy Indian-print skirt, her feet bare ex-cept for an elaborate gold chain with tinkly gold bells on it that wound from her ankle to each toe. There was incense burning, and velvet cushions on the floor, and chantlike music turned down low.

She spoke in a hushed voice. "Welcome," she said, "to the most transfor-mative night of your lives."

I rolled my eyes, but Misty hugged her out of excitement, and Shana hugged Nick, and then me, and then Misty hugged Nick out of excitement, and then Nick hugged me, just to be funny, which made me laugh.

Shana and I sat cross-legged on cushions on one side of a low table; Nick and Misty sat on the other side. I looked across the table at Nick. I felt like he and I were the two normal people in the room. I wondered how he was going to handle this. He seemed to find Misty charming; he made room for her silli-ness because she was young, and a girly girl. I liked that he liked all of her, but I worried that it might wear off, that he might grow tired of it. In feeling this, I noticed with a jolt that I no longer looked at Nick as Nick Newton. He was a celebrity, yes, but he was also just my friend's boyfriend, a normal person. I thought about how far I had come since the Summertime Party and my friend-ship with Charlotte and Jack. I wasn't sure what had changed, but I liked it.

Shana rang a small brass bell and bowed. "Are we all ready to leave the normal world and enter into the paranormal?"

"Yes," we all said, and Shana Starr closed her eyes and took a deep breath. After a few moments, she spoke, her eyes still closed.

"We all made prior agreements with the universe to live according to our pasts. What happened in the past dictates how we live now. What we want to do tonight is to change those agreements. You are responsible for your own future. No matter what happened or what agreement you made in the name of karma, tonight we can amend it. The way we are going to do that is by focusing on the one person in your life who has impacted you the most, whose impact you still need to deal with."

"Nick," she said, "I am hearing from a woman whom you once dated. She is someone who has garnered great acclaim for her work, just as you have. She says that she is now happy with someone else. She is telling you to go on and be happy with someone else, too. She is saying that your past-life agreement, in which you were bound to her and her alone, has been severed. She has set you free. Go forward like a swan in search of your new mate."

Oh my God, Misty had actually asked this woman to try to channel Julia Roberts. I glanced at Nick, who was looking at me with his eyebrows raised, and I felt like we were back in a classroom in junior high. I mouthed the word *swan* and pointed at him, and then I had to work so hard to stop from laughing I thought I might explode, and I could see that he was fighting the same battle.

Misty, Shana said now, was being hindered by her past relationship with a high school drama teacher. "He said you weren't good enough," she said. "He told you you'd never amount to anything, and deep down you still believe him. Let go of that belief. Let go of the chains that bind you to his criticism. His opinion is meaningless and has no bearing on you and your success."

I had heard Misty talk about this teacher, who had treated her very cruelly, and when I turned to her, to my surprise she was crying a little. Nick hugged her, and after a little while she seemed okay.

Shana Starr, her eyes still closed, now turned toward me. "I am now hearing from someone important to you," she said, "but someone who is missing from your life. He was once a large part of your world but now is completely absent."

So Misty had told this crazy woman all about Toby, and now I would have to listen to her talk about him and his impact on me. Okay, I thought, I can take it.

"You feel a void in your heart because of that. Perhaps you can find a way to reach out to him. He says he misses you. He wants you to love him again. I love you, LeeLee, he says."

My heart started beating very fast. LeeLee was the name that Sam had called me when we were small. I had never told Misty. How would this psychic know this?

"You must act to reach out to him," Shana said.

"What can I do?" I said.

"Do?" Shana Starr said calmly, still apparently in her trance.

"I mean, how can I be in touch with this person?" I asked.

Misty and Nick both turned to me, clearly surprised.

"Think positive thoughts about him," said Shana Starr, her eyes still closed. "Assume the best about him. You have been assuming the worst; now assume the best. Your expectations will be fulfilled. I hereby sever your past-life agreement with this person tonight, in the name of fortune and all that is love, and I leave you open to a new future with him."

At that, her eyes flipped open.

"Wow," I said to Shana Starr. "Thank you."

"And you mocked it, Lacey," Misty said to me. "See that? Did that switch up your karma or what? Am I a good friend to you or not?"

We said our good-byes to Shana. "Our regular time tomorrow then, Misty, my dear? All right then. Good night, Nick, lovely to meet you. Good night, LeeLee, lovely to meet you."

I froze. Had Shana simply misheard my name when Misty introduced us at the beginning of the night? Was that why she had called me LeeLee, and not because she was communing with Sam? I supposed it didn't matter; she had heard LeeLee somehow, and it was still a sign of some sort.

I SAW ELEANOR the following day. I told her what had happened with Shana, expecting her to laugh, or to look at me out of the corner of my eye, wondering why I'd gone to a psychic. She did neither.

"The memory that this woman stirred for you was a childhood memory, right?"

"Yes, LeeLee was the name my brother called me when we were kids."

"Do you think you feel guilty for not taking better care of your brother when you were young?"

"What do you mean?"

"Do you feel responsible for him being lost to the world and out of touch with your family? Do you think you could have prevented this if you'd been a better sister?"

"Yes," I said. "I think he's all messed up and confused because I didn't make sure he was okay. I had books and school, and he had nothing. And then I went off to boarding school and left him."

"But you weren't his parent," she said. "It wasn't your job to take care of him. It was your parents' job."

"I know that," I said.

"Your mind may know it, but your body does not."

I looked down at myself: my chest was constricted, my knees were so tight they were tapping together, my shoulders were hunched up around my neck.

"This is one part of why you feel so closed up about your parents," she said, "because you feel guilty about your brother. We want to work to get your body to release this tension."

"I can't let it go," I said.

"You can," she said softly. "By being aware of it, and by breathing."

But I couldn't.

"It's okay," Eleanor soothed, as she did at the end of every session. "Remember, I'm not going anywhere."

TWO DAYS LATER on the way home from work my cell phone rang. It was Sam.

"Hey," he said. "It's me."

"Sam?"

"It's been a while," he said.

"Sam?" I said.

"Yeah, your brother."

"Oh my God," I said. "Oh my God."

"I know," he said.

"Oh my God," I said again.

"Lace?" he said. "Are you okay?"

"Where are you?" I said. "Where have you been? Are you in Switzerland?"

"No," he said. "A friend staying in the apartment in Zermatt opened your FedEx letter and e-mailed me your number."

"Where are you now?"

"India."

"India?"

"I live here now. I came to lead a ski trip in the Himalayas two years ago and never left."

"There's skiing in the Himalayas?"

"Up near Tibet."

"Wow, I guess you're so good, you can run a ski business anywhere."

"Well, actually, I've kind of put the skiing aside."

"Really?" I was intrigued. Skiing had been his life for so long. "What are you doing now?"

"Studying Buddhism."

I was silent.

He sighed, as if he was afraid I was going to judge him and he shouldn't have told me.

"That's weird," I said. "I've been learning about Buddhism, too."

"Come on," he said. "You have not."

"I have," I said. "I've been trying to feel things in the moment instead of holding on to them."

"How did you get into it?"

"My therapist. It's a long story. What about you?"

"Long story," he said. "I don't want to get into it."

But I wanted to hear it. I wanted to hear everything he had been up to, and I told him that, and finally he started talking. It turned out that two years earlier he'd led a ski trip in Himachal Pradesh, in the north of India, and had gotten stuck on a broken lift for several hours with a client who was a Buddhist. They talked for three hours, and by the time the lift was repaired, Sam was well on his way to becoming a Buddhist himself. Since then, he had become so interested in Buddhism, he was actually trying to become a Buddhist monk. He lived in a monastery with thirty other novice monks. He'd shaved his head, and he spent his days with the other novices, reading, chanting, and meditating.

I could hardly believe that this was my brother, yet he sounded happy and healthy, so I was relieved. I longed to ask him about his child, and Olivia, but

I felt afraid. The conversation was going well, and I didn't want to stir up any anger or hurt in him. He was living with thirty other guys; perhaps he was gay. Who knew at this point?

I told him about the meeting I was going to have with our parents. "Maybe it could help you, too."

"Nah," Sam said. "I'm trying to detach myself from that kind of stuff. I've kind of moved past our past."

"I really want to see you," I said.

"Come out here for a visit," he said. "It's amazing. I could even play hooky from the monastery for a few days and we could go skiing."

"Okay," I said. But I thought of the last time I'd been skiing with him, when I'd left Deer Valley shaken by his words.

"That didn't sound very convincing," he said.

"I'd like to see you," I said. "I don't know when I'll next be in India though."

I thought he might get mad then, that I wouldn't come see him, but he didn't. "Maybe I'll come see you then," he said. "It seems fair. I'm the one who dropped off the face of the earth."

"Why did you do that, Sam?" I said.

"I'll explain when I see you in person."

I told him about our parents' visit again. "Why don't you come? I could really use you here."

"I really don't want to deal with them, Lace," he said, a little angrily. Then he relented. "Listen, I'll try. But if I don't come this time, I'll come another time, I promise."

"Okay," I said. He was in India, after all, on the other side of the world. He had said he would try; that was more than enough. I could force my parents to come and answer for their actions, but not my brother.

I opened my mouth one more time to ask him about his child, but I didn't. Had he wanted to tell me about it, he would have. Next time, I promised myself. I'll ask him next time we speak.

Sam and I exchanged all our contact information, made a weak vow to stay in better touch, and said good-bye. I wanted to feel better having talked to him, and in a way I did. I had heard his voice; I knew he was alive and well. But in another way I felt even further from him. Apparently this was how it was going to be for the rest of our lives: conversations once every few years, rarely if ever seeing each other face-to-face, growing more distant with every passing year. I thought back to when we were children, when he had slept on my floor and held my hand on airplanes. He'd understood me so well back then, it was like he was another part of me. But those childhood images were fading, and I knew that soon I wouldn't be able to recall them at all.

ELEANOR HELPED ME prepare for the meeting with my parents as if we were preparing for World War III. She promised to be on call all weekend. We worked on breathing through my anxiety and stress. She told me again that she was not going anywhere. I felt ready.

MY MOTHER arrived first. She called me from the nicest hotel in Santa Monica, where she'd booked a suite overlooking the beach. "I'm here," she said. "Now, what torture do you have in store for me?"

Next was my father. He was going through another down period financially, so he was staying at some crappy hotel out by the airport. "But I have a big deal closing any day now," he said, and I could hear the grin in his voice, "and then I'll move over to where your mother's staying, just to provoke her."

I invited them both to my house at seven o'clock.

"Great," said my mother. "Gives me time to go to the spa."

"Great," said my father. "Gives me time to hit the bar downstairs, meet a few people."

"Dad," I said. "Could you try to focus?"

"Lace," he said. "I was just kidding."

I WENT OUT grocery shopping for the dinner, and when I came home I saw that the little white gate to my front yard was open, which was odd. I went inside, quickly put away the groceries, and then came back outside. I had a strange feeling, like something was off, or maybe on. My nerves felt electrified. It's Santa Ana season, I thought; that explains it. I always felt weird when the winds came through. I felt a pull toward the beach, a block away, so I decided to walk over. It was a little overcast, not a great day for the beach, but I had come to feel that days like this were part of the inside experience of L.A., that they added a little gravitas to the city that outsiders didn't often see or appreciate.

As I approached the beach, I could see a tall figure standing with his back to me, facing the ocean. At first I didn't understand who he was or what he was doing, because he appeared to be draped in a bright orange cloth, like a Roman toga, which was fluttering in the wind. It was the orangest of oranges I could imagine, like the one they show you in grade school when they teach you the colors of the rainbow. He looked like a fluorescent Greek statue, or like one of Christo and Jeanne-Claude's Gates in Central Park, or—and then I stopped in my tracks as I realized—*like a Buddhist monk.*

It was Sam.

I came up behind him, my heart in my throat. "Sam."

He turned around slowly. His head was shaved, but it was my brother, with his broad frame, green eyes, and strong jaw. "Hey," he said, "it's you." He broke into a huge smile, and then I did, too. He opened his arms and we hugged.

"How are you?" I said into his shoulder.

"How are you?" he said back.

"Okay," I said, and then I started crying. "I'm okay," I sobbed.

"Yeah, I can see that," he said, and he pulled me back and looked at me and smiled. "Whatever it is, you are going to be fine."

"Thanks," I said, taking a deep breath. "I can't believe you're here. Why did you decide to come after all?"

He was about to answer, but then he looked up. "Lacey," he said—and as he spoke I noticed that a woman with blond hair and a small child were walking toward us, up from the ocean. I looked back at my brother. "There are some people I want you to meet," he said.

WHEN I THOUGHT about it later, I remembered the sea, gray, and my brother, orange, and his wife, Olivia, yellow as the sun, and then I remembered everything fading away and just seeing the child, as if he took up my whole optic view, as if he himself was a new color, and his name was Lee. "But we call him LeeLee," said Sam.

———

BACK AT THE HOUSE, Olivia insisted on dealing with dinner as I stared through tears at Lee, three years old, blond as his mother but with his father's green eyes. If I looked hard enough, I could see myself in there, too.

AFTER A LITTLE WHILE I went out to the patio to set the table but also to get some air. This was a lot to take in. Sam followed me out.

"Hey," he said.

"Hey," I said.

"I guess I owe you an explanation for everything."

"Yeah, you do," I said. "But maybe I owe you one, too."

"For what?"

"Leaving you," I said.

"When did you leave me?"

"When I went to boarding school."

He looked confused. "Lace, you were fourteen years old. Thank God you knew enough to go. It was the best thing you could have done for yourself."

"But if I'd stayed, maybe you wouldn't have gone off to Colorado. Maybe you would have finished school."

"I was sixteen and pissed off. I don't think anyone or anything or anyplace could have helped me back then."

"But then you started doing drugs. I felt like I should have tried more to stop you."

"You *did* stop me. I stopped doing coke a few weeks after I saw you that weekend in Deer Valley and you told me I was being stupid. I was afraid I might wake up in two years, homeless and a drug addict."

"Well, what you said that day stayed with me, too."

"Me? What did I say?"

"You said I was going to need saving. All this time I've felt like that was partly why my marriage failed. I felt like you doomed me. I know it sounds crazy."

He peered at me. "Do you really believe that, Lace?"

"I don't know," I said. "I guess so."

He laughed and shook his head. "The only reason I said those things was because I felt envious of how well you were doing. There you were in New York, with an Ivy League education and your whole life ahead of you, and you were complaining about a fight with your boyfriend and a new job that sounded interesting. I was stuck in Colorado going nowhere, and I was jealous."

So it had all been a misunderstanding, in a way. It all felt so pointless. But then again, I thought, maybe it wasn't. Whatever had happened, here we were.

"I'm sorry you got divorced," he said. "I'm sorry I wasn't around to help you."

"Why did you do it?" I said. "Why did you stay away for all these years?"

He shrugged. "After I went back to Olivia, I felt like I needed to get away from my past in order to be a good father. I wanted us to make our own family with no influence from my childhood. And I guess that included you, too."

"Still, Sam, you just disappeared. All you had to do was call once in a while."

"I know," he said. "It wasn't fair to you, but it felt like what I needed to do."

"So you planned all along on staying away for three years?" I said. "That's a really long time."

He looked at me. "I was planning on staying away forever," he said.

"Forever?" I said.

He nodded.

Suddenly I was enraged. "What the fuck, Sam? Forever? Why are you back here then? If you wanted to get away from me that badly, then why didn't you just stay away? Why are you here? What do you want from me?" I was yelling through tears.

"Lace," he said, "I tried to stay away and I couldn't."

He hugged me and I cried until I couldn't cry anymore, and finally, for the first time in seven years, I felt like things between us might be okay.

I WOULD SAY that when my parents walked into the house and saw Lee—both of them happening to arrive at the same time, awkwardly shaking each other's hands out front after their taxis dropped them off ("Hello, Elaine," said my father stiffly; "Hello, Lance," said my mother just as stiffly)—their reactions were similar to mine. No one could speak through tears, and Sam and Olivia just smiled and smiled, looking down at their child.

Finally my parents tentatively embraced their son, my mother first, and then my father, and then my mother again. As I watched Sam hug them back, with his broad shoulders and strong arms, I realized that the little boy in my brother was gone. He was a husband and a father now; he was a wall of protection for his family. And I thought then that I understood what he'd meant out on the patio. He'd needed to get away for the baby's sake.

DURING DINNER, in the backyard around a long table lit with candles, we got the full story. Yes, Sam told my parents, he had indeed left Olivia (who was Swiss but spoke perfect English) four years earlier, after she had told him she was pregnant.

"Fucker," Olivia said. My mother blanched, and my father guffawed.

"I didn't have any money," Sam said, "and I didn't know what to do."

"So what did you do?" I said.

"I freaked. First I went to Amsterdam and got really stoned, and then I went to Paris and stayed up all night looking at the Seine and questioning my life, and then I went to Monaco, where I spent two straight days and nights playing poker. At first I kept losing, over and over and over, but then finally I won one game, and then I won another, and then another and another, and after a while I just couldn't lose. When I had won enough at the small tables they started keeping an eye on me, and then they moved me into the high rollers room, hoping to cut me off at the knees, but I just kept winning, and when I came back to Olivia I had a hundred thousand dollars in cash in my backpack."

My father eyes bulged. "How much did you say?" he said.

"I know," Sam said. "It was like, I was on this mission, and I couldn't fail, and I just focused and it happened."

"Why doesn't that work for me?" my father said.

"Luckily, when I got home, Olivia took me back," Sam said.

"Well, who wouldn't, with a hundred thousand dollars in cash?" she said, laughing.

"Then, when I went to India and learned about Buddhism, it made sense to me. I needed something to get me on track mentally and emotionally. I told her I wanted us to live there for a while."

"So we did," Olivia said. "And while he was there we talked about the fact that he had isolated himself from his family."

"He certainly had," my mother said. I thought I saw my brother tense.

"I was angry with him for doing it," Olivia said. "I encouraged him to write to all of you. He said he needed space. But it remained something of a mystery to me."

"Why did you do it, Sam?" my mother said.

"I did need space," he said brusquely. "I needed separation from you."

"But couldn't you have called once in a while, come for a visit, shown us our first grandchild at least?"

Sam looked exasperated. "I needed to start my own family without feeling contaminated by all our problems."

I could see that he was ready to burst, but my mother wouldn't back down. "You left us, Sam, and for no good reason."

Sam quickly looked up at her and his eyes narrowed. "And I wonder where I learned how."

My mother opened her mouth, but no words came out. Her eyes filled with tears.

I glanced at my dad; he was looking at the table guiltily. What was he feeling guilty for? Well, maybe he felt some responsibility for her leaving; he had cheated on her, after all. If he hadn't done that, maybe we'd all still be together. Maybe he *had* started it. But how could anyone really say when it had started? It probably went back generations; my dad's parents had left him at a young age by dying; my mom's parents had seemed to show her love through money instead of affection. Maybe my grandparents had started the chain. But I supposed it didn't matter; now leaving was just the family way. Everyone in my family, I realized, had left everyone else. My dad had left my mom by cheating on her, and then my mom had left him, and then us. Sam and I had left our parents, and then each other. Leaving seemed to be the answer to every problem in this family. It seemed so immature and stupid, like a tantrum, a child's answer. But how could we break the pattern? How could I possibly get everyone to stay connected? It made me tired just to think about it.

My mother coughed and we all looked at her. I was afraid she might burst into tears, but instead she looked around at us for a moment. "Well, we're all together now," she said softly. "And that's what's important."

I took my mother's hand under the table and squeezed it, and she squeezed mine back. I was proud of her. What my brother had said must have been difficult to hear, and yet she'd handled it gracefully.

"Yes," my dad added, "and we've finally met the lovely Olivia and my beautiful grandson." I could see that both my parents were trying to steer us into gentler territory, and I was relieved. "What are you going to do with yourselves now, son?" my dad said. "Stay in India?"

Sam noticed their efforts, too, and helped them along, answering amiably, glancing up at my mom to include her in the conversation. He and Olivia weren't sure what they were going to do, he said. He had to finish his studies, and then maybe they'd stay in India, maybe travel, maybe start a company (apparently Sam had inherited the entrepreneurial bug from our father), maybe have another child. They were happy, though, that was clear. I listened, and all the while I marveled at how worried I'd been that my brother had gotten the short end of the stick in our childhood, that he'd been the one who was all messed up. He had indeed been lost to the world, but not in the way I'd imagined.

LATER OLIVIA said she was tired, and she gathered up Lee, who was asleep in my bed, and the two of them went off to their hotel, a little surfer place nearby.

"So," I said after they left, looking around the table.

"So," my brother said, clearly ready to help me get down to the business of interrogating my parents. "I think Lacey has some things she'd like to ask you."

But I wasn't sure I had the energy for it anymore, and I didn't know what I was looking for anyway, and I said so.

"Well, Lacey," my father said. "Whatever you want to know, I would like to tell you. My life is an open book to you and your brother."

My mother snorted.

"Excuse me, Elaine, did you want to say something?" my father said.

"No—well, it's just that—you, Lance? Forthcoming? I didn't notice you being so forthcoming when you had that affair with Suzie that ruined our marriage. Well, actually, I take that back, you were certainly forthcoming with the whole town about it. Meanwhile I was left in the dark and humiliated."

"Elaine," he said, "you and I hadn't slept together in fourteen months. I know because I counted."

"That was the problem," she said. "You were always counting. It was never about the emotion for you. It was just about the sex."

"You know, this wasn't exactly the talk I wanted to have . . ." I started.

My parents ignored me. "You left me emotionally before I cheated on you, Elaine," my father said, "because you wouldn't love me anymore. You wouldn't love me physically."

My mother appeared to be reflecting on this for a moment. "Yes," she said, "you're right. I didn't like the way you were always investing our money in strange things, and flying off here and there to hear some strange business plan. You were a lawyer, but I could never just get you to settle down and be happy practicing law."

"I was trying to make life better for us," my father said.

"Life was *fine*," she said. "It was better than fine. We had money, more than enough. We could have been happy. All I ever wanted was to be a house-wife with a happy marriage and happy children. I never wanted to peek over the fence, or around the next corner. But you always did. You were always a gambler, always looking at other jobs, other women, wondering what else was out there. You were never happy with me, with us. I could have been happy with you, though. I could have." She began to cry a little now.

"But you're happy now, Mom, right?" I was beginning to feel terribly guilty for putting her through all this.

"I guess," she said, through tears. "I have a wonderful husband and two other children whom I love very much. But I made the biggest mistake in my life, and I can't take it back. I left you and Sam."

"Why did you do that, Mom?" Sam said quietly.

She dried her eyes and thought for a moment. "I wanted a man to love me," she said. "And Richard did. And I guess, in some small way, I wanted to get back at your father for cheating on me. But if I had to do it over again, I wouldn't have done it. I wouldn't have put you through what you went through." Now she looked at Sam and me. "I'm sorry that I did that to you. I have never said this to you before, but I am so sorry."

I felt myself exhale then, I felt my whole body relax and my heart soar, and I realized how long I had been waiting for those words. Just a simple apology. Why was the word *sorry* so impactful? To have someone take responsibility for their actions? Why was this so important? Oddly, I was reminded then of Jimmy James, and of what he'd said to Toby and me at a dinner one night, oh so long ago. *Do what you say you're going to do,* he'd said. *That's the secret in life.*

And, I thought now, if for some reason you *don't* do what you say you're going to do, or you can't, then at least say you're sorry.

"I'm sorry, too, Lacey and Sam," said my father now. "And I'm sorry to you, too, Elaine. You're right. I should have been happy with what I had in front of me, but that's never been my nature, and you all suffered for it."

We all sat in a bit of a stunned silence, and then I thanked my parents for saying what they'd said. Meanwhile Sam just looked on in wonder, as though this was all interesting yet had no real relation to him. And in a way, I thought, that was true. He had somehow managed to get out from under the pain of our childhood, to make a new family for himself. He smiled at me encouragingly, and I thought for the first time that maybe I could do that, too.

IN THE END, Eleanor and I agreed, it had been a major success. My family remained in L.A. for three more days, and we had a few more dinners together. It wasn't perfect. The relief I'd felt after my parents' apologies faded a bit, and everyone got angry or hurt at different times. We yelled, cried, snapped at one another, accused one another, banged the table, and threatened to leave. But in the end we all agreed that it had been worth it.

We got to spend time playing with little Lee at the beach. Olivia and my mom cooked dinner together one night, and Sam and my dad talked about starting a company. I got to know Sam again, and I got to know Olivia, too. She was as laid-back as Sam, and as much fun, but she could be serious, too, the way he could. One night she and I sat up late in the backyard, talking and finishing our wine and looking at the stars.

"Gemini was the first constellation I ever learned," I told her. "My mom taught Sam and me how to find it when we were little. It's still the only one I know." Olivia and I looked up; there it was. "I always feel strangely comforted in the winter, when I know it's there."

"That's funny," she said. "We can see Gemini all winter long in our village, too, and sometimes Sam will go outside after dinner and stay out there for a long time, looking at the stars. Then in the summer, *poof*—they're gone."

Suddenly anxious, I looked up and searched the sky, fearful that the stars might somehow have disappeared. But there they still were, right above us, two twins holding hands.

At the end of three days, we all talked about spending Christmas together the following year in India, and then we hugged good-bye and they went off to catch their flights. And somehow, when they all left, I managed to not feel left.

WHEN CARL and Bert's surrogate, Arlene, went into labor a week before her due date in Indiana, the two fathers were in the writers' room at *Inconceivable*. Carl got the call on his cell phone.

"Oh my God," he said, jumping out of his chair. "Call the airport! Get us a ticket! Call the taxi! Get us a car! Where are the bags?"

Bert calmly dispatched everyone to help, one of us to buy the tickets online, one of us to fetch their prepacked bags from their offices, one of us to book the hotel in Terre Haute.

"Lacey," he said, "would you mind driving us to the airport?"

"I'd be honored," I said.

"Step on it!" screamed Carl as soon as we got into the car, before I'd even turned on the engine. "Faster!"

"Honey," Bert said, "we have three hours until the flight leaves and the airport is half an hour away."

"Three hours! What numbskull booked the flight? Why are we waiting three hours? Our child could be born any minute and we might not be there! Faster!"

I noticed that Bert never once brought up the fact that he had wanted them to fly to Indiana the week before, just to avoid this very situation. Instead, I noticed, he held Carl's hand, even from the back, sticking his head in between the seats and looking up at him lovingly, like a small child himself.

THE BABY was born twenty minutes after Carl and Bert arrived at the hospital. They witnessed the whole thing, and they even got to cut the umbilical cord. It was a boy. The poor child's name was Ethan Carlson Bartholomew Wolfson-Finkelstein. When the two parents arrived home a week later, baby in tow, they were ecstatic yet exhausted. They had hired a nanny who would stay with Ethan in their offices during the day, so they could visit with him while they worked, but at night they were on their own.

"I can't go on like this," Carl would say every morning, after he staggered up to the writers' room at around eleven. "I'm delirious. Get me coffee. Intravenous cocaine. Anything. Pinch me in the ass. Something."

But then they would be reminded of some cute but extremely basic thing the baby had done the night before, like smiling in his sleep, or simply looking at one of them.

"He's just the most magical thing though," Bert would begin with a soft smile.

"He is, though, really," Carl would say. "I know we're biased, but I do think he's cuter than most babies."

As for the question of whose sperm they had used, that remained unanswered. But both maintained it was the other's.

"Oh, he is so Carl," Bert would say. "He has this cute twinkle in his eye that is totally Carl."

"Nonsense," Carl would say. "It's clear to anyone who has a brain in his head that he's Bert. Anyone looking so grim at three A.M. has to be Bert."

AFTER *INCONCEIVABLE* PREMIERED, my mother, who always tried to be positive about my work endeavors, called. She appeared to be at a loss for what to say. "Um," was all she could come up with, "it was certainly interesting."

The reviews couldn't have been worse. Most of them punned on the word *inconceivable,* as in, "It is *inconceivable* that this show was even written, let alone produced and aired." The ratings were perhaps 3 million, while the hits, like *Lost,* were 12 million.

When the second episode aired to even worse ratings, the studio execs came over the next day and pulled the plug, right in the middle of shooting. Down on the set, Misty and Nick were in the middle of performing a scene when the cameras were unceremoniously turned off; the crew laid down their props and lights and tools right then and there and left for good.

We were summoned into the writers' room. "It's over," Bert said, jiggling the baby on his shoulder.

"Thank the Lord," added Carl.

Word soon came that everyone on the show was going to a Mexican place around the corner for happy hour. A few hours later, the vibe in the place was similar to prom night. Everyone was drunk, and none of us knew if we'd ever see each other again. A group in the center of the room was doing body shots, hoisting people aloft and drinking tequila from their belly buttons. Girls were hugging one another in corners, promising to stay in touch, couples who had eyed each other all season were finally making out; and Misty was mournful, convinced that her relationship with Nick would end with the show.

I was holding Ethan, discussing the pros and cons of sleep training with Bert, when Misty came rushing at me out of nowhere. "Guess what?" she cried. "I'm engaged!"

She stuck out her hand, showing me the ring. It was, of course, huge and sparkly and beautiful. Nick came over and put his arm around her.

"We owe everything to you, Lacey," Misty said. "We would like to name our firstborn after you."

"Are you pregnant?" I said, incredulously.

"Are you insane?" she said, happily.

Then someone handed us all tequila shots, and I handed Ethan back to his father, and we shot our shots and danced until the place closed. Afterward a group of us, led by Misty and Nick, went back to my place, where the party continued all night long in my backyard. At dawn I finally sent everyone home and got into bed, and just as I was dropping off to sleep, through the corner of my window, I could see that the sun was rising.

Do You Know Who I Am

THIS ALL HAPPENED because I was planning to leave L.A. for good at the end of May, and I got it into my head that I had to live every day as though it were my last. I started getting up early and riding my bike to the beach and doing yoga on the sand, and then I went to work over in Hollywood at a laid-back job on a popular show with a fantastically normal boss who asked me to do very little work. I joked around with the other assistants in the mornings, and then we had long lunches on the commissary's patio in the sun, and in the afternoons I closed the door to my office and worked with focused determination and energy on a screenplay. I ducked out of work early every evening and rode my bike to the neighborhood bar near my house in Venice where I knew the bartender, and I met my single friends for drinks and we stayed out late and had sushi delivered to our seats at the bar. I smiled at boys and they smiled back, and if they asked for my number I gave it to them and if they called I went out with them and if they didn't call I didn't notice.

At the end of every night I rode my bike home alone under the stars and the swaying palm trees, looping lazy figure eights in the middle of the street, singing along in my head to whatever song had last been playing in the bar, content that I had sucked everything I could out of the day and looking forward to doing it all again the next.

Cath and Misty were amused. They had many questions. "But how do you go out *every* night? Aren't you exhausted? Don't you want to just stay in and watch a movie sometimes?"

"I'm on spring break, people," I said. "Get used to it."

I WAS PLANNING to leave L.A. and move back to New York to become a reporter again because I had, months ago, decided it was time. I had no reason to stay in L.A. I had moved out here five years earlier to live with Toby, and I had given it a good run without him, but in the end I couldn't escape the nagging feeling that I was crashing a party. It was Toby's town. He was the performer and he was why I had come. I had never been a theater person in school; I wasn't an actor or a comedian, had never been any kind of entertainer by any stretch; in fact I am most at home in an audience.

It was time to go home. My dad was in New York, my mom would be only a three-hour plane ride away, and Sam was coming regularly to New York from India for his new import business. The reunion eight months earlier had helped us, and I wanted us to continue growing closer, to be more like a family again. I was ready to go back. Old friends, I told myself. Central Park. Seasons. Leaves changing. A sense of time passing. Snow. Fireplaces. Riding the subway and brushing up against people. Cabdrivers. Sheer humanity. I told myself I was looking forward to leaving L.A.

And yet lately the sun was shining and the beach was warm, working in Hollywood was like going to camp every day, and I was starting to feel like we were all doing our own thing out here in California, living at the edge of the earth. I was growing more and more afraid of going back to the real world.

IT WAS AROUND this time that three things happened all in one week. First, I got a call from Eleanor, my therapist, who told me she could not see me at our usual time that week because her house had burned down. Second, an agent called out of the blue and said he wanted to meet with me. And third, I met a boy named Ben.

I'd seen it on the news: a fire in the hills in the Palisades had erupted the night before at around 3 A.M. and spread rapidly down to a residential neighborhood. It happened so fast that people had been awakened by sirens as the fire ate at their roofs and broke down their doors. Some had barely escaped with their lives.

Eleanor was calling from the hospital, where she was being kept overnight for observation because she had suffered smoke inhalation.

"It was terrifying," she said, and my stomach clenched. Things were not supposed to terrify Eleanor. She was strong and capable. She knew how to handle whatever situation I threw at her. "I feel lucky to be alive," she said.

When I hung up I felt unsettled. I sat up straight on the couch in my office and put my feet flat on the floor, a technique we often used in Eleanor's office to help me feel grounded. But when I closed my eyes my chest was still tight, and even when I tried to focus on my breathing, taking it slow and easy, I couldn't release the tension. I pictured the fire creeping up on Eleanor as she slept. I thought about the fact that she could have died, and then I thought about the fact that she hadn't. My eyes flew open. I felt a strange anticipation, as if I had been jerked awake, as if the string between life and death had been pulled taut.

My screenplay was a talky little thing about a young marriage and its demise. I'd only written the first two acts, and I had no idea if I was doing a good job, so about a month earlier I'd sent the script to Jimmy James, the only literary agent in Hollywood I knew, hoping he might give me some encouragement or advice. A couple weeks later he'd called me.

"Hiya, Lucky," he said. In my mind I begged him not to tell me anything about Toby; I preferred not to know. I didn't have to worry—he cut right to the chase. "Yeah, so, listen, about your script. Can't touch it. I put it right in the shredder about five minutes after I got it."

"What? Why?"

"I don't think Toby would appreciate it if his own agent shopped the story of his divorce around town."

"But it's not about him, it's about me," I said. "And nobody who knows him would recognize him in the character. The husband is totally different from Toby in real life."

"I still don't think he'd like it. Sorry."

I sighed. "I understand," I said, and I did. "Thanks anyway for reading it."

"No problem."

I was about to say good-bye, and then I stopped. "Jimmy," I said.

"Yeah, Lucky."

"What did you think of it? I mean, do you think it's any good?"

"It was great," he said. "Really good stuff. Great arcs, good character development, nice story structure."

We said good-bye and hung up, and five minutes later I called him back. "You didn't read it, did you?" I said.

Jimmy sighed. "I wanted to," he said. "But I've been swamped. My assistant skimmed it for five seconds, and he told me what it was about. I think he liked it though, from, you know, skimming it for like five seconds."

I sighed. "Okay, thanks."

I didn't have anyone else to show it to. But I still wanted to know if I had any promise, if RJ's advice to dig deep had helped me at all, so I posted the first two acts on a website where screenwriters post unsolicited material, hoping an agent or someone with connections might troll the site and read it. Right.

Except that, one day, out of the blue, an agent called and asked for me. I felt like I was answering someone else's phone. An agent calling me didn't fit with any reality I understood. His name was Glenn Steelman, and he had that agent vibe, enthusiastic and confident, as if we were already old friends.

"Love your work," he said. "Big fan."

"Thanks," I said dubiously.

"No one else is writing about L.A. this way," Glenn Steelman said.

"You mean a dark, depressed, divorced way?" I said.

"What happens in the last act?" he said.

"Well, um, I guess everything just kind of works out for the best."

"But I mean what *happens*?" he said. "How does it end?"

"I'm still tweaking the final scenes," I said.

"Well, finish it," he said. "And hurry. I think I can sell this, and I know just who might buy it."

"Who?"

"Oh, never mind that," he said. "But to sell it, I'll need the whole thing by the end of the month. Can you finish it in a month?"

Was he for real? I was sitting at my desk at work, and I quickly typed his name into Google; I got nothing. Clearly he was just some insane person trying to screw with me.

"What's the name of your agency again?" I said.

"The Glenn Steelman Agency," he said. "We just formed."

"Huh," I said mistrustfully.

"End of the month, kid," he said. "Don't let me down. This could be our big break."

Kid? Our big break? My bet was that not only was he crazy and a scammer but, in all likelihood, a murderer and child molester too. Still, he was someone. And no one else was exactly beating down my door.

WHEN BEN walked into my May Day party, I recognized him from *People* magazine, not an uncommon occurrence in L.A., where everyone has at least one actor friend you vaguely recognize from last year's *Superman* movie, or that cell phone ad that used to be on all the time. Ben wasn't an actor though, not really; he was the host of an adventure sports show, and he was only famous for being married to someone famous. His ex-wife was an actress and the daughter of a legendary movie star. They had divorced a year earlier. Cath had brought him to the party; for some reason she thought we might hit it off. He was forty-two and he had blond hair that was gray at the temples and blue eyes and the beginnings of a scruffy beard. He was tan and his eyes crinkled at the sides when he smiled, and his smile was fantastic.

"Hi," I said.

"Hi," he said.

I had started throwing parties in my backyard about a year after I'd moved into my little house in Venice. I'd been stuck to my couch too long, unable to force myself to get out there and mingle in society, and so I thought, well, if I can't go out, then I will bring them to me. I always invited absolutely everyone, to remind myself that I really did know people in this town, even if I hadn't made it yet, and to my surprise, the parties had grown. Over the past two years everyone had shown up at one time or another. And when I say everyone, I mean everyone—Cath and Henry and Misty and Nick and Bert and Carl and even RJ and the snakewoman and the evil writers and Jimmy James and his wife. I did not know why they all came. Perhaps they simply wanted to show me some support after the divorce. Perhaps they liked me, and always had, or perhaps, after my divorce, they liked me more.

Probably because I am my father's daughter, I grew to love having these parties. I loved the chance of meeting someone new, the possibility of connecting people who might get along, the feeling that my house was filled with merriment. Often, as I was dressing for the night, or lighting candles in my backyard, or greeting the first guest, I'd think about the Summertime Party with some nostalgia, yet I was always grateful to be where I was. The scene in Venice was cut off from Hollywood, casual, homegrown. My bartender, for instance, Crystal, was my next-door neighbor's cousin. She was seventeen and a deejay at a local bar, that is, when she wasn't going to high school. In my backyard, she charged ten dollars an hour to pour drinks and spin music at the same time.

Strangers came to my parties, too. I don't know why they did, but my philosophy was the more the merrier, so I always let them in. Sometimes they were neighbors from a few blocks over whom I hadn't yet met, and sometimes they were tourists visiting Los Angeles who had simply walked by, heard the music, and wandered into my backyard. It was a funny mix of people sometimes, but I never once had a problem. I guess I hoped that by including everyone, I increased the chances of an interesting party. I enjoyed the feeling of never knowing what might happen on any given night.

At my May Day party, Ben was definitely an interesting addition. I kept him in my line of sight throughout the early part of the evening. Later, in the backyard, I was trying to start the rusty old gas grill that had lived on my patio forever. It started as usual but then sputtered and died out. Ben came over to see if he could help.

"Shit," I said. "I knew it was on its last legs."

"Can I have a look?" he said.

"I think it's dead," I said.

"Nah," he said, fiddling with its knobs, appraising it from all angles, finally getting underneath it with a wrench as if it were a car. I watched, amused.

"Got a match?" he said when he popped back up after a few minutes, wiping his hands on his T-shirt.

I gave him one, and he lit something, and a flame burst from the bottom of the grill.

"Wow," I said. "How'd you do that?"

He smiled his fantastic smile at me. And then he stood there all night flipping burgers, as if he were onstage, playing the part of a real man.

"So you're moving back east?" he said at the end of the night, when we were sitting out back under the stars, all sweaty from dancing.

"In a month," I said.

"Thirty days, huh?" he said.

I looked at my watch. The day was already gone. "Twenty-nine, actually."

"Any chance you'll change your mind?" he said.

"Unlikely," I said, smiling.

He smiled back. "But I've got twenty-nine days to try."

He asked for my number and I gave it to him. He called me five minutes later from his car.

"Do you want to do something tomorrow?" he said.

"It's already tomorrow," I said.

"Do you want to do something in like eight hours then?"

"Yes," I said.

"I knew it," Catherine said when I told her, shaking her head and smiling her own fantastic smile.

On our first date, Ben picked me up on his bike. When I wheeled my beach cruiser out, he surveyed it, then got out a little tool kit, raised the seat, and tightened the handlebars. "Better," he said.

We rode to the beach and had sunset drinks at a bar on the sand and told each other things. He was from Boston, his parents had been happily married for forty-nine years, and he had five brothers and sisters, all living back east. They were a close family. Every summer while Ben was growing up they'd pack up a minivan and take off on a six-week camping tour. Over the years they'd gone to Graceland, Monticello, and the Baseball Hall of Fame; they'd followed the Lewis and Clark trail; they'd pitched tents in almost every national park. One summer they made it all the way across the country, where they camped in Malibu, overlooking the beach. When Ben woke with the sun and saw the surfers bobbing in the water, he knew he wanted to live in California. He had come out to L.A. after college and had never looked back. Besides surfing, he was into cycling and yoga and rock climbing. He was also, he admitted somewhat sheepishly, a survivalist. He had an emergency kit in the back of his car, with water and granola bars and iodine. When he had been married, he said, and this was the only time he mentioned the fact that he was divorced, they had had a survival plan: they would meet at their house no matter what if something bad happened. I didn't ask him anything more about his divorce, and he didn't ask me about mine.

When it was time to head home, late, my bike had a flat, so we left it chained to a rack by the beach and he doubled me on his. He took off pedaling, and I slipped right off the seat.

"Whoops," I said from the pavement.

He looked back, horrified. "Are you okay?" he said.

I was laughing. I had a big pink scrape on my back. Strangely, it never hurt. But it turned white and the scar remained, growing fainter and fainter each day, a memory of the night tattooed only temporarily on my skin.

HE BIKED US back to his place in Santa Monica, a big house with a wraparound porch a few blocks from the beach. The silver ocean shimmered in the dark distance. Outside his bedroom window a towering palm tree's fronds were so huge it looked as if something out of *Jurassic Park* had exploded in his backyard.

I was moving across the country in twenty-eight days. This was no time for a relationship. "I'm in this weird place," I said, "where I can't look beyond each day. I'm just trying to be happy in the moment."

"Would it help if you thought of this as just a one-night stand?" he said.

"Maybe."

"Okay, then that's what it is," he said.

"Really?"

"No," he said.

But the next morning we woke and said the same thing: "Last night was just a one-night stand." And the morning after that we said it again: *Last night was just a one-night stand.* And it kept working for us, so we kept saying it, morning after morning.

EVERY DAY I heard Glenn Steelman's voice in my head: *Hurry up, kid.* And every morning I woke up determined to finish the script. But suddenly all the dialogue I typed felt flat. The next day it did, too. And then the next. Almost everything I wrote, I deleted at the end of the day. As the deadline approached, I felt the strings of anxiety stretched tightly against my brain. My instincts competed with themselves as if I had a devil and an angel perched on either shoulder. *Hurry up, kid, just churn out the pages,* urged the devil, wearing a Glenn costume. *But make sure it's good,* warned the angel, dressed as me.

Finally, I printed out what I had written of the last act—maybe ten pages—and I stacked the pages neatly and placed the whole thing in the bottom drawer of my desk. Wasn't that what old-timey Hollywood screenwriters did when they hit a wall? Weren't they always putting things in a drawer and forgetting about them? And then a few years later, when someone—a wife, a child, a biographer—opened up the drawer while searching for a stamp or a scissors and instead discovered the lost script, didn't it always turn out to be genius, the best thing they'd ever written? Strangely satisfied, I closed the drawer; it shut with a solid click. A weight lifted. I would look at it again in a week. Or so.

"WHY ARE YOU moving back to New York again?" Cath and Misty asked me once a week, deliberately trying to provoke me.

"New York's where I'm from," I explained each time.

"Huh. I wasn't aware there was some rule in life about moving back to where you're from."

"It's just time to go home."

"Have you considered the possibility that you are home?"

And everyone was always asking me, "Are you sure you want to go back to reporting? How are you going to afford Manhattan? Haven't all your friends had kids and moved out of the city and into the suburbs?"

I didn't know and I didn't like to think about it.

"I can't plan that far ahead," I said impatiently, frustrated that people were trying to foil my plan to live in the moment. "I'm on spring break."

BEN HAD WARNED ME, somewhat sheepishly, that the paparazzi sometimes followed him. Apparently they wanted to know what his ex-wife's ex-husband was up to. One morning I stepped out of his house and flashbulbs exploded. A few of them had staked us out. I gasped and ran back into the house.

"I'm really sorry," Ben said. "I'll walk you out."

He took my hand and led me through the small crowd of maybe six photographers. It was scarier than I'd ever imagined, threatening, as if one false move could lead to a riot.

A week later the photo appeared in "Star Tracks"—I was identified only as Ben's "gal pal"—and Toby called me.

"Sorry to call," he said, "but I saw you in *People*. It was so weird."

"It *was* weird," I said.

"So, you're happy," he said.

"Yeah," I said, and I realized it was true. "You?"

"Yeah," he said after a second.

I hadn't seen Toby in three years or talked to him in almost two, but I knew that he had met someone else, remarried, and had a child. No one had told me this. Our friends in common did not tell me any news about him. But I had felt it in my bones. He and his new wife had married on some cliff in Malibu, I was sure; she had worn her hair down; no one had pelted her with a lime. They went to swanky Hollywood soirées where they met celebrities who wanted to remain best friends with them for life, and they had great sex five times a week. They were now living the good life, I was sure, in some gorgeous house up in the hills with their Bugaboo stroller and their happiness.

The big question now, I supposed, was whether that mattered to me anymore. I could not say for sure that it did not:

"I have to go," I said.

"But—" Toby said, and I hung up.

L.A. COULD BE uncomfortably small. Cath and Henry and Ben and his ex-wife were all in the same group of friends, so Cath heard things. One day she called and said she'd heard through the grapevine that Ben's ex-wife had heard through the grapevine that he was dating someone he liked a lot.

"Oh God," I said. "That's awful." I thought about how I would feel if I had heard that about Toby. "Ugh, I feel badly. I've never been the other woman, and I don't like it."

"Well, um, and also . . ." Cath said sheepishly, and I could tell she was afraid to go on.

"What?"

"Well, it seems that she saw you guys at Rose Café last night and followed you home."

"Home?" I said. "What do you mean? To my house?"

"Yeah. And then she drove off," Cath said. "Should I not have told you?"

"Is she insane?" I said.

"No," Cath said. "I think she's sad."

ELEANOR WAS STILL in the hospital, so I couldn't call her. I wanted to, though. I wanted to tell her about Ben's ex and Glenn Steelman and especially about Ben. I practiced breathing, and feeling my feet on the floor, and having imaginary conversations with her in my head. And I thought, well, I'm going to have to do this alone in New York anyway, so I may as well get used to it.

"MAN, do I have some gossip," Glenn Steelman said when I picked up the phone one day. He had a habit, which I found endearing, of making me privy to "secrets" that everyone in town already knew. He was always on his way to a very important meeting at the studio in Burbank, and the 405 was going to be hell, and he only had three minutes to talk anyway because there was someone on the other line, but somehow he could never resist updating me on the latest Hollywood scandal.

"What is it?" I said.

"I'll tell you later," he said, but then launched into a long story that had already made its way around town several times, about how three B-list movie stars had fled their rehab clinic in Malibu, rented a suite at the Chateau Marmont, gotten drunk, and had a threesome. "Isn't that crazy?" said Glenn.

"Totally," I said, trying to distract him from asking me about my progress with the script. "And then what happened?"

He started to go on but suddenly interrupted himself. "Goddamnit, how did I get on this again? Listen, how's the script coming?"

"Great," I lied.

"Is it going to be done by the end of the month?"

"Yes," I lied again.

"Because if you can get that last act done by the end of the month, then I think I sold your script this afternoon."

I was silent for a moment.

"You're welcome," said Glenn.

"Don't fuck with me, crazy man," I said.

"Fine," he said. "But Reese Witherspoon's company is looking for their next thing and this is it."

"Reese Witherspoon?" I said. "*Legally Blonde* Reese Witherspoon?"

"That's the one," he said.

"Oh, come on," I said.

"What?" he said.

"Well, I don't mean to be rude, Glenn, but I've never heard of you. Google has never heard of you."

"You want proof?" He sighed. "No one takes anyone at their word in this town. Fine. Reese's agent went to film school with me. We were roommates the first year, and we're still tight."

"Are you serious?"

"I had lunch with Reese and Tom yesterday at her office. They've been reading scripts for the past five months and haven't found anything they can work with. But she likes what I've told her about your script so far. She's dying to read it."

"Oh, stop it," I said.

"It's true. She said it sounds like a love story."

"A love story?"

"I know. I said it wasn't, but she insisted."

"You're lying," I began, but I trailed off. Suddenly, for the first time since he'd called three weeks earlier, I believed him.

"Keep in mind, she doesn't want a regular love story," he said. "She wants something dark, but with a happy ending."

"But I haven't even written the ending," I said.

"Yeah, I'm aware of that," Glenn said, as if he feared the worst.

"Well, I'm *going* to," I said.

"When?"

"Don't pressure me."

"You said you'd be done by the end of the month."

"And I will," I said. "I hope."

"Fine," he said. "But this is your one big chance. And they need it by the end of the month or the deal's off."

"I just *asked* you not to pressure me."

"This would be the first success you've had in Hollywood, right?" he said.

"Maybe."

"It would feel good to finally make it, wouldn't it?" I could hear his sarcastic smile over the phone. "No pressure, though." He hung up.

I hung up and sat there. I opened up the document, scrolled to the last act, and stared at the blank page. A happy ending. I didn't know if I could do it. I honestly didn't know.

BEN AND I did not talk about the future or the past. We did not talk about the fact that there were now only twenty-two days left. And we did not talk about his ex. I tried therefore to broach the subject carefully.

"Were you aware that your ex is stalking me?" I said. Whoops. That had been too aggressive.

"What?" he said.

I had sounded crazy, I knew. I tried to calm down and be reasonable. "I thought you said the divorce was amicable," I said.

"It was," he said, a little defensively.

"Then why is she sad about us being together?" I said. "Did you leave her? Did you hurt her? Because, you know, I'm on spring break here. I don't want to be hurting anybody. That wasn't part of the plan."

I hadn't been able to see Eleanor in two weeks, and now I tried to picture myself in her office, my feet planted on the floor. I took some deep breaths. My chest was still tight.

"I'm sorry she followed us," he said. "I'll talk to her."

"Do you want me to talk to her?" I said.

"I don't think that's such a good idea, babe," he said gently.

"I know," I said. "You're right. But when you do talk to her, you know, reassure her. Tell her I'm just a one-night stand. Tell her this isn't going anywhere."

We looked at each other. Neither of us said anything.

"I'll talk to her," he said finally. "Now can we go to bed?"

WE WENT TO BED, having survived our first fight, and held each other. He fell asleep soundly, his arms around me, breathing his quiet breath. But I felt bad. Even though they were divorced, I felt I was somehow wronging Ben's ex-wife. I knew from Cath that she was thirty-four, my age. I didn't feel any kind of clock ticking, marital or biological or otherwise, perhaps because I'd already been married and I knew from my friends that marriage and kids weren't necessarily the nirvana that women built them up to be. But this woman probably had expectations for her life, and who could blame her? Most women weren't on spring break at age thirty-four. They were grown-up, mature; they wanted and expected things, they imagined a future beyond the next day. She had likely imagined a future with Ben, and then she'd had to start her search over again. I felt I understood better than anyone how painful that could be. But what could I do about it? Tell Ben we couldn't see each other anymore? That wouldn't solve anything. It wasn't like he was going to go back to his wife. He liked me now, and I liked him. And besides, we only had twenty-two days left anyway.

I COULD NOT write the ending. I tried every day, but when I sat down at my desk, I couldn't even bring myself to open the drawer and look at the script. Instead I pretended I had all the time in the world, and I left work early and went to meet my friends at the bar or Ben at his house, and I told myself I would write it tomorrow. I was aware that this was not the brightest plan.

WHEN ELEANOR CALLED, I didn't recognize her voice. It had become raspy and hoarse. Since the fire, she'd grown worse. The smoke had further damaged her vocal chords. She was still in the hospital; they would be treating her for several weeks. But there was something else, she said.

"There's no easy way for me to say this," she said.

What? I screamed frantically inside. "What?" I said casually.

"I've lost some of my memory," she said. "Memory loss is sometimes a symptom of carbon monoxide poisoning."

I wasn't sure what she was trying to say. "Do you remember who I am?" I said.

She laughed, which made me feel better. "Yes," she said, and I could hear her smile. "But the next time I see you, I might not remember all your history. All the things you've told me, all the things I've come to know about you—you may have to tell them to me again."

"Okay," I said.

I hung up. I thought about that for a moment. I waited to see how I felt. All the work we had done together over the past two years, a lot of it had been stored in Eleanor's head. She had heard and remembered every painful story I had to tell—about Toby, my parents, my fears, my failures. Now it was all gone. Yet instead of feeling sad, I felt strangely lightweight, almost euphoric. If Eleanor didn't remember it, had it even happened? Suddenly it was as if all the pain of the past had been lifted, the slate of my life wiped clean.

CRAZY GLENN started asking me questions about the script, as if it might actually get made. Was there any reason the Summertime Party couldn't take place in the Valley instead of up in the hills? Did I think David Arquette was right for the husband character? Could they go to the Bahamas for their honeymoon instead of Paris?

Was he for real? There wasn't even an ending, and I didn't know if I would ever be able to write one. But I smiled and nodded and said yes to everything, and I pretended I had it all under control.

ONE MORNING I got up early with Ben to watch him surf. He stuck his surfboard under his arm and we rode our bikes to the beach. Across the sand, in the early-morning sun, boys bobbed on the blue waves, searching the horizon. Ben kissed me and ran into the surf. His strong silhouette against the rising sun was so real and true and gorgeous, tears came to my eyes and my throat ached. It was like something out of a dream, or a movie. I thought of our lives here, of how I felt like I was on an eternal vacation, and I realized then that that was the allure of L.A.—it could make reality so lovely, so easy and slow and perfect, it didn't even feel real.

And I thought then of the studio lot where I worked in Hollywood, where more than once I'd walked across vast expanses of pavement on a balmy evening, tired from a long day, yawning absently, headed to my car, only to stumble into some dimly lit scene from another time—a Saigon café in the late sixties, a turn-of-the-century western shoot-out, a game of stickball on a Bronx street, circa 1955—and feel sure that I was dreaming. When the cameras rolled and the director yelled "Action!" it was so still and quiet that time stopped and the walls of the world fell away and there was only the scene playing out before us. It was the closest thing to time travel I could ever imagine.

In Hollywood it was our job to create a world that looked and sounded just like reality yet was not. We had meetings in which we discussed every detail of every scene: what color dress the star would wear, and whether the bar where she met her lover would be bustling or quiet, and what time of night it was, and how softly the rain would fall against the window, and what kind of flowers her lover might bring. And then all of the departments went out and did their part and bought their things, their props and their costumes and their rainmaking machines. But every time, without fail, when I saw the scene finally shoot, I forgot that it was all made up, that it was a reality we had conjured for ourselves. When the cameras rolled, I bought into it, all of it— believed that she was wearing the yellow dress because she knew he liked it best, that outside, the streets were deserted and damp, that a shadow fell across the doorway and then faded away because her lover had had a sudden change of heart. It was all magical, and for a few moments each day I understood with every bone in my body why people who worked in Hollywood wouldn't trade it for the world, why there was no business like show business, why the show must indeed go on.

BEN AND I rode our bikes to the beach almost every morning. Sometimes he surfed and I did yoga. Sometimes we just sat and talked. One day he asked me about my divorce, and I told him.

"It was the hardest thing I've ever been through," I said when I was done. "Someone once said to me, 'I imagine it's like death, only worse.' "

"And you think they were right?"

I thought about it. "I don't know. I've never had anyone I love die."

"My best friend died," Ben said.

"Oh God, I'm sorry. I hope that didn't sound insensitive."

He shook his head.

"How did he die?"

"It was four years ago. Neil and I were climbing in Nepal and it got really cold one night and we didn't have the right supplies and he got hypothermia. He died on the mountain. I had to leave him up there."

I was stunned.

"It took me a long time to get over it. I was angry at myself for years. I felt responsible. His family doesn't speak to me anymore, and he and I had grown up together."

"I'm sure they don't blame you."

"Oh, I'm sure they do," he said ruefully. "And maybe they should. Neil and I were both reckless. We thought it would never happen to us. I wasn't as good at taking care of people back then as I should have been."

"Taking care of people is a hard skill to learn," I said.

He took a long breath. "I wasn't good at taking care of my wife either. I was always running around the world doing my show, climbing mountains and surfing rough waters. It was too much for her to deal with, the separation, the risks, the feeling that I didn't put her first. Finally, after Neil died, she asked me to choose between the lifestyle and her, and I told her I couldn't give up the lifestyle, and so she left me."

"Wow," I said. "I'm sorry." I reached for his hand. "I know how painful divorce is, under any circumstances, and that couldn't have been easy."

He took a deep breath. "I guess I'm telling you this because I want you to know I'm not the same person I was then. We haven't known each other for very long, but I know you've been through a lot, and I want you to know that if you asked me to put you first, I would."

Eleanor would have been proud of me. I finally let it out and cried.

ONE OF MY DAD'S DEALS had gone through. He'd bought a bigger apartment in New York and a condo in the islands. The success had grounded him a bit. He'd been dating the same woman for six months now; she met all four of his requirements and then some; he was talking about the possibility of marriage. I didn't buy it, but I told him over the phone that I was excited to get back to New York to meet her, to resume our dinners, our theater trips. He interrupted me.

"Are you sure about this, Lacey?" he said.

I laughed. "Last time we went through this, you didn't want me to leave. Now you don't want me to come home."

"If you came back to New York, I'd be happier than you can imagine," he said.

"I'm coming," I said.

"I just want you to remember that this is your life, kiddo. I know I made you feel guilty about leaving me all those years ago, but that was a mistake. This is your life. You do what you want to do."

"I want to come home," I said.

"Well, then I can't wait," he said. "I'll throw a huge party at Carmine's to celebrate. We'll rent out a private room and drink champagne by the gallon."

MY MOTHER CALLED to say Palm Beach was having a heat wave and she needed to escape. "I have to say, I do like your weather out there," she said. "Richard and I were tossing around the idea of coming out for the summer, renting a place in Malibu. What do you think?"

"Well, that would be nice, Mom, but by then I'll be back in New York."

"Oh, you're leaving that quickly. Well, good for us, we'll have you back."

"Malibu sounds like a fun idea, though."

"Maybe we'll do it next summer," she said. "You'll be missing L.A. by then, I'm sure."

ONE MORNING after Ben slept over, when I walked him outside and kissed him good-bye, a blue SUV parked out front started its engine and then peeled away with a screech.

Ben didn't seem to notice, and I didn't say anything. But the driver had looked like a woman with long dark hair, like Ben's ex.

After that, I started having trouble sleeping whenever Ben spent the night. I would get up in the middle of the night and creep to the window in the darkness and search the street for a blue SUV. Once I thought I saw it, parked way at the end of the block, its fog lights glowing like eyes.

I thought about mentioning it to Ben, but then I didn't. There were only seventeen days left.

———

CATH AND HENRY and Misty and Nick and Ben and I drove to Vegas for the night on a whim, and I won a thousand dollars on a single spin of the roulette wheel. I wanted an excuse to throw one last big party, so I had one for my thirty-fourth-and-a-half birthday, and everyone I had ever known in L.A. came and drank and danced and wished me happy half-birthday all night long. Ben and I skipped work one day and biked all the way to Malibu, where we stopped for crabs and beer at Neptune's Net and then climbed down to the sea and the rocks and the crashing waves and fell asleep under the sun.

There were thirteen days left.

THERE WAS SOMETHING to this whole spring break thing, I could see that. I was acting out some life lesson, some Buddhist philosophy. I was truly living in the moment. And wasn't that the cliché of what makes a happy life? To live each day as though it might be your last?

But Glenn Steelman needed an ending. And time was running out. I knew I had to write one. Yet I couldn't, and Ben's ex was haunting me. I needed a session with Eleanor, but she was still in the hospital, under observation for her vocal chords. So I started sitting alone on my couch and pretending to talk to her. I knew her so well, I believed I could predict our conversation.

"So you can't write the ending because you're afraid of the future," Eleanor would say. "Can you think about the future?"

"No," I would say back.

"Can you imagine what you'll be doing next month?"

"No. I know I'll be in New York, but that's it. I can't get into specifics."

"How about next week? Can you imagine that?"

"No."

"How about tomorrow?"

"Well, I'm going for a bike ride with Ben. But beyond that, no."

"But why?" She seemed genuinely confused. "There's something you're not telling me."

She was right. I was holding back. The truth was, I was afraid to write the ending. I knew I had to do it, yet I also knew that doing so meant looking ahead, predicting how things would turn out for me. And if I did that, I truly believed that I'd be messing with things, with karma, with the future, with my own destiny. I had committed myself to living in the moment, and I felt I had to honor that. I could not look ahead; it would go against everything I'd started to believe in over the past few weeks, everything that had made my life seem like it was about to change for the good.

I opened my eyes. My time was up, my session over. I didn't know what Eleanor would say to all that. I wished I did. She would probably remind me that, yes, I had to honor my desire to be present in every moment, but karmic destiny aside, I also had to give Glenn an ending—no matter what.

And then I suddenly knew what I would do. I would write the ending at the *end*—on May 31. Not before. I would stay up all night if I had to and write it. And wherever I was with my life then—on that day, on May 31—that would be the ending.

ON MAY 24, Ben took me rock climbing out in the desert in Joshua Tree. He taught me how to walk up boulders. We started on a baby slope, but it was still pretty steep and I was scared. I had to walk upright; I wasn't allowed to squat or use my hands. Ben walked up it himself, showing me how, then waited for me at the top.

"Put your weight on your front foot," he said. "Commit to each step and you'll be able to take it. Commit, then come forward." He stood there, nodding, keeping his eyes on mine. I was hesitant. "You can do it," he said, reassuring, patient. "Just commit, then come forward. Commit, then come forward straight and true."

Come forward straight and true. Had there ever been a better sentence? I looked up at him, waiting for me at the top, holding his hands out to me as if I were a child learning to walk, and I repeated that line in my head like a mantra, as if that was all I needed to do in life. *Come forward straight and true. Straight and true. Straight and true. Straight and true.* I was scared, but finally I did it, I took one step and then the next, and then I committed, and suddenly I found I was walking up the side of a rock.

"Good job," Ben said, breaking out into a proud smile. When I made it to his outstretched arms, my heart beating out of my chest, he scooped me up in a hug and held on to me tightly. The relief of his strong arms around me made me feel like I was going to weep. I buried my head in his neck and held on. "You're okay, baby," he murmured into my ear, holding me tighter. "You're safe now."

ON MAY 26 I had a garage sale. I sold everything in my house, including my wedding china, and Ben and I took the nine hundred dollars I'd made and went down to Laguna Beach and rented a room at a little inn and sat on the beach all day with a picnic laid out on his surfboard.

"So Hollywood kicked your ass career-wise, and your husband kicked your ass emotionally, and now you're going to leave," Ben said as we lay under the sun.

"I think I've given it a pretty good shot," I said.

"Let me get this straight—you married your husband and you were both immature, and you thought you could grow up together and make it from scratch together, but then you kind of wanted to grow up and he didn't, and that made you angry."

"Was that even English?"

"Was I right?" he said.

"Maybe," I said crossly.

"I'm right."

"You know," I said, smiling, "just because you know how to do all these crazy sports, and you have this deep sense of integrity and all that, doesn't mean you know everything."

"I really don't want you to go," he said.

I was silent.

"Are you really going to leave?"

"Yes," I said.

"Fine," he said, and he looked out at the sea.

"Fine," I said, and I looked out at the sea, too.

SAM AND OLIVIA and Lee were still living in India. Olivia was expecting their second child, and Lee was going to nursery school. Sam had finished his studies and was focusing on his business of exporting fabrics from their village. We spoke on the phone about once every two weeks.

"There's this guy," I told my brother, "and I think I love him."

"He loves you, too?"

"Yeah," I said. And then I started to cry.

"Lacey?" he said. "Why are you crying?"

"I'm moving back to New York."

"Why?"

"Because that's home. When I get back there, and I get settled, will you come home, too?"

"No," he said.

"Are you ever coming home?" I said.

"No," he said. "Look, Lacey, you can love someone again. All you have to do is be happy. Right here, right now."

"But that's what I've been doing."

"Don't do," he said. "Just be."

After a silence, he said he loved me, and hung up.

I sat there with the dead phone in my hand. I knew my twin brother was right, that I was afraid to love someone again. But I didn't know how to change that.

ON MAY 29 I was packing boxes in my house, waiting for Ben to bike over so we could go to the beach, when the phone rang. It wasn't Ben, it was an emergency room nurse at Saint John's hospital in Santa Monica. He had been hit by a car while riding his bike. He was asking for me. "Can you come now?" she said.

"Is he okay?"

"I'm sorry, I don't have the details of his condition." She hung up.

I got there in fifteen minutes and burst into the waiting room, glancing wildly around, as if Ben might be sitting there, totally fine, sheepishly holding an Ace bandage around his arm, ready for me to take him home. He was not. I spoke to the nurse. I could not see him; he was being looked at by the doctor.

"But he's okay, right?" I said.

"I'm sorry, I don't know his condition yet," she said. "But someone will come and talk to you as soon as the doctor is finished."

I returned to the waiting room. I sat there for a while, crying a little. I called Cath and told her, and then I didn't know what to do. Should I call his family? I didn't have their numbers. I didn't have anyone's number; not even his friends'. How could this be? Because, I thought ruefully, he was supposed to be a one-night stand.

I approached the nurses' station again. "Have you called his mother?" I said. "She lives in . . . somewhere outside Boston, I think—"

"Framingham," said a voice behind me. "She lives in Framingham."

I turned, and there was an angry, pale-faced woman standing right up close to me, right in my face; she was wearing a baseball cap, and she looked around my age, with puffy red eyes. "I already called her, by the way," she said. "I'm his emergency contact, you know, so they called me, and I called her."

"Oh, great," I said. "That's great."

Just then a nurse came out.

"You're waiting for Ben Williams?" she said to me.

"Yes," I said.

"Is he okay?" asked the woman.

"You can see him," the nurse said to us both. "But one at a time."

I turned to the woman. "Excuse me," I said. "I'm his, um, girlfriend, so I'll be back in a minute and then you can go in."

"No, excuse *me*," she said angrily. "Do you know who I am?"

I looked at her. "I'm sorry," I said, surprised at her tone. "I don't know all of Ben's friends."

And then suddenly I realized who she was. And then I felt like the biggest idiot in the world. Of course I knew who she was. Everyone in the world knew who she was. With recognition, her quiet beauty sprang suddenly to life, like a flower waking.

"Oh," I said quietly, bowing my head, "I'm so sorry. I should have recognized you."

"Not *that*," she said impatiently. "Not *me*. I don't mean who I *am*. I mean do you know that I'm his wife?"

"Of course," I said. "He's told me about you. He's a big fan of yours." Oops. That sounded weird.

"Then you know that I should be the one to go in there," she said fiercely. "I mean, how long have you two even been dating?"

"Not long," I said quickly. "I don't mean anything to him, I promise. I'm just a one-night stand."

She looked relieved and appeased for a moment, but then quickly turned angry again. "Why are you saying that?" she snapped, as if I were trying to fool her. "I know it's not true."

She stared at me coldly for a moment, then burst into tears, her famous face collapsing. I felt like she was playing a scene with me, except she really did seem upset; she didn't seem to be acting.

Just then, a photographer barged into the waiting room and started clicking away at us. Ben's ex tried to shield herself. Horrified, I stared at her as she tried to hide her tear-stained face in her hands. I felt terrible.

"You go in," I whispered quickly, lightly touching her shoulder. "I'll wait out here."

She looked up, surprised. "Thank you," she said. Then she followed the nurse through a swinging door and disappeared.

I sat in the waiting room again; the photographer took some pictures of me, assuming I must be someone if I knew Ben's ex-wife, I supposed.

After about twenty minutes she came back out, and the photographer clicked away at her again. She didn't seem to notice him as she stopped in front of me.

"I'm sorry," she said after a moment. "I shouldn't have forced my way in like that."

"It's okay," I said.

"It's just, when we were married I was always prepared to hear that he had done some crazy thing and died, and for some reason when I heard it this time, I was convinced that this was it, and I pictured him dying without me saying what I needed to say to him, and I just . . . lost it."

"It's okay," I said, "you're his wife."

"*Ex*-wife," she said.

"Still," I said, "I totally understand," and I did.

I thought about Toby. If he were on his deathbed, would I go to him? Maybe I would. But why would I go to him then if I wouldn't now? So I could forgive him, I supposed. So I could forgive him and he could forgive me and we could say good-bye. But it would probably take the prospect of death to bring us together again. And soon even that wouldn't be enough. I was forgetting him, forgetting his face and his jokes and the years we had shared together. Soon enough, I knew, we would be strangers.

I turned back to Ben's ex-wife. She seemed to have calmed down.

"How is he?" I said.

"He's fine, of course," she said, rolling her eyes. "He's got some glass in his eyes, but it's not serious. Don't freak out when you see the bandages. They look dramatic, but they'll be coming off tomorrow." Then she turned and left, the photographer snapping as she went.

I went to Ben's room. He was sitting in bed with a white bandage around his eyes.

"Who is it?" he said.

"It's me, babe," I whispered.

He smiled. "Hi. I guess this is just my shameless way of trying to get you to stay."

"Are you okay?" I said.

"I'm fine," he said. "They're coming off tomorrow and I'll be surfing the day after, I promise."

Then it hit me: I was leaving him the day after tomorrow. Looking at his sweet, brave smile, his trusting face, I started to cry, but silently, not wanting him to know.

"Babe?" he said. "Are you still there?"

"I'm here," I lied, choking back sobs. "I'm right here."

AFTER I LEFT Ben's room, I suddenly realized that Eleanor was recuperating in the same hospital. I went to the desk, asked where she was, and found her room. I got a nurse to go in and ask if she would see me. She said she would, so I nervously went in. She was alone, reading, something about Buddhism, it looked like from the cover. She put the book aside as I entered.

"Hi," I said shyly.

"Hello," Eleanor said, smiling.

She looked a little bit weak, of course, lying in bed in her hospital gown, and suddenly I worried that this might have been a mistake—that it might be too strange and unnerving to see my therapist, the person who had taken care of me all this time, in such a helpless state—but after a moment it became clear that I needn't have worried. Eleanor was still in control; her calm strength emanated from her like a force. I was relieved.

I didn't have any flowers or a gift, but somehow the lack of things seemed appropriate: it managed to preempt all the unnecessary chatter and make clear the purpose of the moment. It was just about her and I saying good-bye.

I did not know how we would do that. Eleanor did, though, of course. She told me I was going to write the perfect ending, and that after it was done, when I went to New York, we could talk on the phone whenever I needed to. But, she said, she believed I was ready to cut her loose now and go out into the world on my own. When I told her I would miss her, my throat closed up and the tears finally came. She smiled and took my hand. "I'm not going anywhere," she said, as always.

BEN GOT OUT of the hospital the next day, the day before I was leaving. There was not much more for us to say. He knew that I had to go back to New York. I knew that he would not come with me; he belonged in California, with the waves and the sun. We were at an impasse. We decided not to dwell on that, not to say good-bye, but to remain in the moment, to live the last day we had together as we had the past month. My house was packed and ready for the movers, who would come after I was gone, but we sat and talked in my back-yard as we had the night we'd met. Then we biked to the beach and had a drink at the same ocean bar we'd gone to on our first date. In the late after-noon we went back to his house and lay in bed and held each other.

We were not going to spend the night together. I still had to write the end-ing for Glenn, and I'd wanted to spend my last night in L.A. alone anyway; this had been important to me. I did not want my ending to be about a boy.

Finally, under the still-light sky, he walked me outside. The ocean lay be-fore us in the soft evening. Ben pointed out to the water. He would be surfing at dawn the next day when my plane took off. I should look for him down on the beach, where he'd be looking up at me from a wave.

Then he pulled something from his pocket; it was a custom-made gold compass with tomorrow's date engraved on it. We stood there together, look-ing down at it, watching as the compass needle spun north and south, then fi-nally pointed west, toward the water.

We hugged for a long time, and we did not say good-bye, and then he went inside and I went to my bike and cried.

WHEN I GOT HOME I pulled out my laptop, but I felt too unsettled to write, so I decided to go for a drive up the coast for a bit, along the Pacific Coast High-way. I was planning to drink in the sea one more time, to watch the waves shimmering under the bright white moon, but when I got into my car and turned on the music, I knew where I needed to go. And so I turned away from the beach and headed east instead, toward Hollywood, toward the past.

I drove up Mulholland, where I looked out over the Valley on one side and then Hollywood on the other, and then I drove down twisty Laurel Canyon, past the late-night host's house where Toby and I had gone to the Summertime Party and met Charlotte and Jack, then past the red cottage Toby and I had shared before we got married, where we'd had all those lovely dinner parties, then down into the flats, where Cath had told me she was pregnant, and then into the heart of Hollywood, past the studio where I'd worked on RJ's show, and the club where Jimmy James and Toby and I had seen the famous actress, until I was only a few blocks away from the little apartment I'd shared with Toby when we were splitting up.

My chest tightened a little. Did I really want to drive past that place, where so much pain and loss had happened? Where Toby and I had thrown all those stupid limes at each other instead of saying what we needed to say, where I'd taken off my wedding rings, where he'd told me he didn't love me anymore? I wasn't sure I wanted to see the apartment again. But then I thought, well, why not? It was certainly part of the farewell tour. And it wasn't like Toby still lived there; he was living up in his dream house in the hills with his new wife and their perfect baby, after all.

Still, I felt anxious, guilty, stealthy, as if someone I knew might see where I was heading and call me on it. When I got to the block, I drove slowly, silently, and then I cut my lights and pulled the car over in the darkness. I looked up at the apartment, on the second floor. It was flooded with light, and its huge French windows were thrown open to the balmy night. I could see into all the rooms.

Oddly, I recognized the living room curtains instantly. They were the same curtains I had hung when Toby and I had lived there together three years earlier. They were raw silk, a deep raspberry color, and too long. I could picture their hems spilling onto the floor in a heap. How strange that they were still there—perhaps Toby had left them behind for the new people who'd moved in?

But then I recognized the curtains framing the bedroom windows, too—the dark blue silk ones with the tiny white pom-poms, the ones I'd bought because Toby hated the sun in the mornings, and then in the dining room I recognized the carved wooden chairs that we'd found at a yard sale, and the round mirror on the wall that had been a wedding gift from Toby's cousin, and the two blue chairs in the living room by the window that we used to sit in and smoke and talk.

Tears sprang to my eyes. After all this time, after all the struggle and change and growth that I had gone through, after finally living the life I had worked so hard to make for myself—to find that Toby was still living here, still living our old life, among our old things, and to see that old life preserved there, as if in a museum—well, I felt as though time had stopped, as though I could just walk up the outdoor stairs to the door of the apartment and knock on the door and Toby would answer it and I would come in and set down my purse and hug him and say, "Hi, Smooch, how was your day?" And it would be like none of this had ever happened, like our marriage had never imploded in less than a year, like I had never had to go through all that pain and loss and learning to get where I was today, like I had always been healthy, living a normal life. It was so surreal, I truly believed I was living a waking dream.

Just to test this feeling, just to see if this were a dream or reality, I opened my car door and stepped out, and I walked around the back of the building to the outdoor stairs, and I climbed them, and there outside the apartment door were the flip-flops that Toby wore every day and the woven beige doormat I had bought four years earlier. I knocked on the door. I heard the TV blaring, some action movie, pictured Toby looking up from it, heard him pause it, heard him walk across the wood floor to the door, and then he opened it.

The realness of him was shocking. I'd forgotten how he looked, but then, seeing him, I instantly remembered. Suddenly I knew his face and figure as well as I knew my own body. He looked the same, maybe a little thinner, maybe a little grayer.

"Hi, Smooch," I said without thinking.

He seemed surprised; it did seem to take him a minute to register me. Then: "Hi, Smooch," he said back.

I didn't say anything. I waited to see if he thought we were still married. But he just kept looking at me, and then he said, "Well, sorry, I mean, come in."

"Okay," I said, and I did, and he closed the door behind me and then we stood there inside the apartment. I made a movement toward him that was something like a hug, and he did the same. We embraced loosely.

I noticed a huge flat-screen TV anchored to the main wall. The screen was frozen on a scene from the second *Lord of the Rings,* one of his favorite movies. The TV was almost as big as a movie screen; it dominated the room. Had he gone out and bought it today while I was at work? Or had he done it at some point during the past three years while we were divorced and I was living in Venice?

"How was your day?" I said, just to see what would happen.

"Um, it was fine, Smooch," he said, looking at me curiously. Then: "Are you okay?"

"Sure," I said, and I think we both thought I might go on, but I didn't.

After a minute Toby said, "Well, it's good to see you. I mean, it's been a while."

"Yeah," I said, and then, just to be sure, I said, "So we're not married anymore."

"I know," he said, looking at me curiously again. "Are you sure you're okay?"

I took a deep breath and shook my head, trying to wake myself out of the dream. I attempted to ground myself in reality. Suddenly I felt worried for myself. What was I doing here? Had I gone crazy?

"I'm sorry to drop in on you like this," I said.

"It's fine." He laughed. "I'm not doing much." He nodded at the TV.

"It's just that I'm leaving L.A.," I blurted suddenly, as if that explained my showing up on his doorstep out of nowhere after three years, pretending we were still married. "I'm moving back to New York."

He nodded. "I wondered when you would," he said. "I never pegged you as a California girl."

My throat tightened and I knew his words had done something to me. I waited a moment to let my feelings settle down.

"I don't know," I said. "L.A.'s not so bad after all."

He looked at me with surprise. "Are you sure you want to leave?"

"Everyone keeps asking me that," I said. And I was going to go on, to try to explain why I needed to leave—but suddenly I realized I didn't have to. "How are you?" I said instead.

"I don't know," he said, looking around at the apartment. "Okay. The same I guess."

I looked around, too, and I realized he really was the same, and then through the haze of the past I saw the ghosts of the two of us before we got married, when times were still good, giggling on the couch in front of a TV, and in the dining room I saw our dinner parties, and the ghosts of our friends squeezed around the dining table making jokes and telling stories.

"We had some good times here," I said.

"Maybe more good than bad," Toby said.

I wanted to believe that, and so I did. It felt good.

"How come you never moved out of here?" I said. "All the memories in this place . . . don't they bother you?"

He shrugged and looked around. "I guess it just feels like home."

"I understand that."

"So when are you leaving?" he said.

"Tomorrow at dawn."

"Wow," he said.

"Anyway," I said, "I just wanted to come by and . . ." What? What had I wanted from this?

"Say good-bye?" he said.

"Yeah, and also, I guess, to tell you that I wish you the best."

"I know you do, Smooch," he said. "I wish that for you, too."

"Thanks," I said, and then after a moment: "I guess I should get going."

"Okay," he said. "I'll give you a call soon to see how you're doing in New York."

I thought about that and then shook my head. "No," I said. "I don't think so. I think this is it for us. I think this is really good-bye."

Toby considered that for a moment, then shook his head back at me. "Nah, we'll see each other again. I'm sure of it. We'll run into each other on the street in New York in like twenty years."

I laughed. "By then we'll be in our fifties."

"We'll be old and gray and we almost won't recognize each other."

"But we will," I said, with strange conviction.

He nodded. "We will. And we'll both be in a rush, we'll have places to go and responsibilities, but we'll blow them off and instead we'll duck into some dark old bar and have coffee for like three hours and talk about everything that's happened in our lives. Our kids and our spouses and our ups and downs. About how far we've come and how long ago all of this feels."

"It's a deal," I said, and we shook hands, and my throat closed up and I thought I might cry. But I didn't fight it, I just waited for the feeling to move through me, and it did.

I thought then about how far I had already come, and of how our divorce had been the catalyst for so much change in my life, and of how many people it had affected besides me—my family and my friends and the people I worked with and the boys I dated and the innocent bystanders who just happened to cross paths with me. I thought about how huge a circle of people that was— hundreds of people, even thousands, even the entire universe, if you believe in connected energy and that kind of thing—every one of whom had been impacted by our divorce.

And then I thought about how it had all started with the two of us, just the tiny little pair of us making a vow to each other in a green field in Vermont on a summer day, and how now, when it came down to it, to the very end of the end of it, it was still really just between us, between Toby and me. There was still no one else in the world who could understand what I had gone through the way he could, and there never would be.

I looked at him. "Do you think there was a point to it all?" I said then. "Some lesson we can carry with us?"

He was silent for a moment and I knew that he could feel what I was thinking, that he wanted an answer, too. He opened his mouth and almost said something, and then I opened my mouth and almost said something, but in the end neither of us did. We both knew we were going to have to wait. We stood there for a few minutes, and then I opened the door.

"See you on the other side," I said.

He nodded and smiled. "See you there."

I walked out of his apartment and down to the street, and the moon was high and full, and the night was so fresh and bright it felt like diving into a crisp white sheet. I got into my car and drove home to Venice, and I stayed up all night with my laptop under the California stars, thinking about the past and the present and the future, and writing my ending. It was filled with mystery and adventure, stability and love, and a life on both coasts. In the morning I sent it off to Glenn Steelman, and at dawn I missed my plane and rode my bike to the beach.

It was early, and the beach was vast and white and empty, and all along the coast the green tops of the palms blew hard and fast in the gusty wind. I searched for Ben against the horizon, and then finally I found him, far out in the water, alone. The waves that morning were higher than I'd ever seen them, towering and curved and glossy black-blue, crashing down on the earth again and again, but each time they came for him he rose with them, standing tall as a god, eyes to shore, riding the water right onto the sand. And when he was done I watched him as he came out of the ocean, the sun rising fast behind him, and then I rose too and waved, and he shaded his eyes and smiled, and I came forward toward the sea to meet him.

ACKNOWLEDGMENTS

Lisa Glatt and the talented writers in her Sunday workshop, especially Cheryl Alu, Vidya Madiraju, and Michelle Bitting Abrams, were Lacey's first fans. Their astute criticisms and much appreciated enthusiasm over several years gave me the confidence to keep writing. Huge thanks to them, to Leelila Strogov at *Swink* for first introducing Lacey to the world, and to Kate Deirdre Milliken, whose wise counsel and spot-on critiques have improved my work immeasurably.

The Millay Colony and the Kimmel Harding Nelson Center both gave me a room of my own in which to work, and *Folio* magazine at American University, *Swink,* and Sally Shore at the New Short Fiction Series helped bring the results into the light. Craig Kerrick at St. Mark's School encouraged me to start out on this path, and Mark Jay Mirsky has always treated me like a writer, even before I was one. Eric Overmyer saw this book before I did, Sloan Harris took a chance on me, and Elwood Reid helped make it all happen. Thank you, Elwood.

My agent, Katharine Cluverius, believed in me and in this book from the beginning. Her calm presence was almost as helpful as her fantastic notes, which helped shape the book into what it is today. She also found the absolute perfect home for the book with Laura Ford at Random House. Laura's enthusiasm for the book was infectious, her perceptive notes helped give the story more depth, and her attention to detail brought Lacey into sharper focus. Laura also patiently held my hand through the whirlwind of the publication process. I am incredibly lucky to have her as my editor. Enormous thanks are also due to everyone at Random House for their kind support of this book.

I could not have kept on keeping on without love and support from Daye Case, Lindsey Page, Allison Ryan, Perrin Keeler, Jessica Gray, Nonie Cameron, Ira and Cecilia Wolfson, Teal Paynter, Liz Tigelaar, Jovana Keyser, Shep Gallagher, Josh Reims, Kristy Mongiello, Jami O'Brien, Jane McFadden, Sara Anderson, and the Williams clan. Thank you all for being there. Special thanks to Rebecca and Nick Eaton, gifts in my life, who opened the champagne all along the way, even when I was afraid to; to Katherine Friedman Holland, talented writer, and Grant Holland, award winner, for being there every single day in every single way; and to Victoria Mihich, miracle worker, for her extraordinary wisdom and grace. Special love to Elizabeth Brokaw for inspiring me, to all the Gibsons for welcoming me with such affection, and to Wendy Donner, who fills my life with sunshine and then holds the umbrella when it rains.

Thank you to the best of all possible families, for everything: to my amazing and loving mother, Danné Munford, for being interested in the smallest moments of my life and helping me get through the biggest; my father, Crawford Shaw, for being a bright light and a powerful force of love; my brother, Crawford Shaw Jr., for standing by me and making me laugh at the most crucial times; Carol Bird for always being there; and my sister, Melissa Shaw Fleming, my brother(-in-law) Greg Fleming, and Andrea, Charlotte, and Rory Fleming for their huge love and support, which has made such a difference in my life.

Finally, much love and deep gratitude to my husband, Jay Gibson, for teaching me how to rock climb, surf, and stand on my head, among a thousand other magical things; for continuing to take me up that winding green road in Chiang Mai, every day; and most of all for making the journey worth it.

ABOUT THE AUTHOR

DEIRDRE SHAW has written for television in Hollywood, and her non-fiction has appeared in *The New York Times, The New York Observer,* and *The Philadelphia Inquirer.* Shaw's fiction was included in the New Short Fiction Series Emerging Voices Group Show in Los Angeles in 2005, and she was awarded a 2004 Hackney Literary Award for National Short Story. She has held fiction residences at the Millay Colony and the Kimmel Harding Nelson Center for the Arts. Shaw has a B.A. from Duke and a master's in journalism from Columbia. She lives in Los Angeles with her husband.

www.deirdreshaw.com

ABOUT THE TYPE

This book was set in Sabon, a typeface designed by the well-known German typographer Jan Tschichold (1902–74). Sabon's design is based upon the original letterforms of Claude Garamond and was created specifically to be used for three sources: foundry type for hand composition, Linotype, and Monotype. Tschichold named his typeface for the famous Frankfurt typefounder Jacques Sabon, who died in 1580.